"Dakota never disapp
—MaryJanice David

PRAISE FOR
ACCIDENTALLY CATTY

"This light, comedic paranormal romance delivers simple, unencumbered entertainment. A lively pace, the bonds of friendship, and bright humor aided by vampiric sarcasm make for a breezy read with charming characters and no shortage of drama. Cassidy's fans are sure to enjoy this, while newcomers will be reminded of MaryJanice Davidson's or Kimberly Frost's work."   *—Monsters and Critics*

"I have been a fan of Dakota's since *The Accidental Werewolf*, book one of this series. I loved all of the books in the series, but I think this book is my favorite . . . *Accidentally Catty* is very funny, cute, and sexy."
—Night Owl Romance

"A fun read with some meat to it that will have people looking at you wondering why you're laughing if you're out in public."   *—Fresh Fiction*

ACCIDENTALLY DEMONIC

"The Accidental series by Ms. Cassidy gets better and better with each book. The snark, the HAWT, the characters, it's all a winning combination."   *—Bitten by Books*

"An outstanding paranormal romance . . . Dakota Cassidy delivers snappy dialogue, hot sex scenes, and secondary characters that are just too funny . . . *Accidentally Demonic* is a hold-your-sides, laugh-out-loud book. With vampires, werewolves, and demons running around, paranormal romance will never be the same."
—The Romance Readers Connection

"Dakota Cassidy's books make me laugh and laugh. They are such great fun that I always look forward to the next one with gusto . . . I totally loved this book with a capital 'L.'"   *—Fresh Fiction*

continued . . .

THE ACCIDENTAL HUMAN

"I highly enjoyed every moment of Dakota Cassidy's *The Accidental Human* . . . A paranormal romance with a strong dose of humor."
—*Errant Dreams*

"A delightful, at times droll, contemporary tale starring a decidedly human heroine . . . Dakota Cassidy provides a fitting twisted ending to this amusingly warm urban romantic fantasy."   —*Genre Go Round Reviews*

"The final member of Cassidy's trio of decidedly offbeat friends faces her toughest challenge, but that doesn't mean there isn't humor to spare! With emotion, laughter, and some pathos, Cassidy serves up another winner!"   —*RT Book Reviews*

ACCIDENTALLY DEAD

"A laugh-out-loud follow-up to *The Accidental Werewolf*, and it's a winner . . . Ms. Cassidy is an up-and-comer in the world of paranormal romance."
—*Fresh Fiction*

"An enjoyable, humorous satire that takes a bite out of the vampire romance subgenre . . . Fans will appreciate the nonstop hilarity."
—*Genre Go Round Reviews*

THE ACCIDENTAL WEREWOLF

"Cassidy, a prolific author of erotica, has ventured into MaryJanice Davidson territory with a humorous, sexy tale."   —*Booklist*

"If Bridget Jones became a lycanthrope, she might be Marty. Fun and flirty humor is cleverly interspersed with dramatic mystery and action. It's hard to know which character to love best, though—Keegan or Muffin, the toy poodle that steals more than one scene."   —*The Eternal Night*

"A riot! Marty's internal dialogue will have you howling, and her antics will keep the laughs coming. If you love paranormal with a comedic twist, you'll love this book."   —*Romance Junkies*

"A lighthearted romp . . . [An] entertaining tale with an alpha twist."
—*Midwest Book Review*

MORE PRAISE FOR THE NOVELS OF DAKOTA CASSIDY

"The fictional equivalent of the little black dress—every reader should have one!"
—Michele Bardsley

"Serious, laugh-out-loud humor with heart, the kind of love story that leaves you rooting for the heroine, sighing for the hero, and looking for your own significant other at the same time."
—Kate Douglas

"Expect great things from Cassidy."
—*RT Book Reviews*

"Very fun, sexy. Five stars!"
—*Affaire de Coeur*

"Dakota Cassidy is going on my must-read list!"
—*Joyfully Reviewed*

"If you're looking for some steamy romance with something that will have you smiling, you have to read [Dakota Cassidy]."
—*The Best Reviews*

ACCIDENTALLY DEAD, AGAIN

DAKOTA CASSIDY

BERKLEY SENSATION, NEW YORK

THE BERKLEY PUBLISHING GROUP
Published by the Penguin Group
Penguin Group (USA) Inc.
375 Hudson Street, New York, New York 10014, USA
Penguin Group (Canada), 90 Eglinton Avenue East, Suite 700, Toronto, Ontario M4P 2Y3, Canada
(a division of Pearson Penguin Canada Inc.) • Penguin Books Ltd., 80 Strand, London WC2R 0RL,
England • Penguin Group Ireland, 25 St. Stephen's Green, Dublin 2, Ireland (a division of Penguin
Books Ltd.) • Penguin Group (Australia), 250 Camberwell Road, Camberwell, Victoria 3124, Australia
(a division of Pearson Australia Group Pty. Ltd.) • Penguin Books India Pvt. Ltd., 11 Community
Centre, Panchsheel Park, New Delhi—110 017, India • Penguin Group (NZ), 67 Apollo Drive,
Rosedale, Auckland 0632, New Zealand (a division of Pearson New Zealand Ltd.) • Penguin Books
(South Africa) (Pty.) Ltd., 24 Sturdee Avenue, Rosebank, Johannesburg 2196, South Africa

Penguin Books Ltd., Registered Offices: 80 Strand, London WC2R 0RL, England

This book is an original publication of The Berkley Publishing Group.

This is a work of fiction. Names, characters, places, and incidents either are the product of the author's imagination or are used fictitiously, and any resemblance to actual persons, living or dead, business establishments, events, or locales is entirely coincidental. The publisher does not have any control over and does not assume any responsibility for author or third-party websites or their content.

PUBLISHING HISTORY
Berkley Sensation trade paperback edition / June 2012

Library of Congress Cataloging-in-Publication Data

Accidentally dead, again / Dakota Cassidy.—Berkley Sensation trade paperback ed.
p. cm.
ISBN 978-0-425-24751-8 (pbk.)
1. Vampires—Fiction.   I. Title.
PS3603.A8685A663 2012
813'.6—dc23
2012003868

PRINTED IN THE UNITED STATES OF AMERICA

10 9 8 7 6 5 4 3 2 1

ACKNOWLEDGMENTS

Über-thanks to Saranna DeWylde—authoress and, probably by the time of this book's publication, a superstah in the literary romance world! After a totally random check-in email, you gave me the best ideas ever for this particular edition of the Accidentals. Much love, chica. You're a rock star!

My son Cameron, who's so brilliant it frightens me (He really is. Buy this book because he wants to go to an Ivy League school. Pleaaaase.), and who came up with such a terrific idea when talking this plot out with me. And my pal and beta reader Kaz who gave me a deeper insight to this particular plot.

To all my Facebook/Twitter fans and friends—I can't begin to express to you the rollicking good time I have with you every day in proper words. You hang out, you answer my questions of the day, we talk books, we snark *American Idol* auditions and *The Bachelor*, or we just talk life. Whatever we're doing, know how much you're appreciated and adored by me. And to Mark Boyer, the hilariously funny man I based Phoebe's best friend on and an active participant on my Facebook fan page who might be sorry he won that contest!

Also, to all of you soap opera fans out there: I loved soap operas and was a faithful watcher for many, many years. My shout-out to them (in my parody sort of way) is with the greatest love and the absolute deepest respect. ☺

And huge, huge thanks to the following shows, all of which had a hand in this book: *Castle*, *Glee*, *The X-Files*, *Fringe*, *Grey's Anatomy*, and *Psych!*

Most especially to Melissa Dwyer, whose emails not only make me smile, but remind me the human spirit is not just alive, but on fire! I love ya, honey——you're one helluva fighter!

And, as always, to my (in earlier Accidentals dedications) one-time boyfriend, now husband, Rob. I could never do this if I didn't have a safe harbor to park my whine in. That safe harbor is you. ☺

Dakota ☺

CHAPTER 1

"Will I sparkle in the sunlight? Because confession: I'm uncomfortable sparkling," Samuel McLean said.

"Oh, dude, if you go out in the sunlight, I can promise there'll be no sparkling. Now sparks? Hmmm. Could be. Definitely some fucking flames. For sure a whole lotta screaming, 'Oh, my God, it burns!' but no sparkles. Though, I gotta give it to you, dude. With what you're wearin', you give sparkly a whole new level of ugly."

He ignored the crude woman's crack about his dress. According to the lady in the thrift store, he'd gotten a good deal on it, and it was a hot color this season. So, yeah. "Another pressing thought?"

"Shoot."

"Do I have to pick a team? I don't want to screw with Edward or Jacob's self-esteem."

A cackle with a definite hint of devious pleasure threading through it followed Sam's question. The deep chuckle literally clanged in his ears to the point of painful, leaving him feeling like one full-bodied raw nerve. He shifted in his chair at the basement offices of OOPS, pulling uncomfortably at the front of his red sequined dress to create some much-needed airflow.

Christ, it was hot. Why was it so damn hot?

From behind him, the lingering presence of the woman who'd plowed into the office like he owed her money was downright imposing. When she leaned over his shoulder, Sam forced himself to forget he was wearing a *hot little number*. He mentally put his man-suit back on and asked, "*You* are, again?" with as much of an arrogant, I'm-still-in-charge-of-this-situation tilt to his penciled-in eyebrow as he could muster.

For which the imposing female wasn't at all fazed. "Nina. Nina Blackman-Statleon. *Vampire.* The non-sparkly kind."

The breathtaking brunette in jeans and a sweatshirt clamped a hand on his shoulder. She clenched it with fingers of steel that burned clear through his shifting shoulder pads and made his big hoop, clip-on earrings sway. "Man, as soon as I heard you were here, I skipped right over like I was on my way to the flippin' Ring-Ding factory VIP tour. So. Jazzed. Look."

She came to stand in front of him, holding out a basket before she unceremoniously plunked it in Sam's lap. "When Marty called me, I got so fucking excited you weren't a whiny female this time round, I threw this shit together. We've never had a legit dude accidentally bitten before. So call it my Vampire Welcome to the Clan gift."

She grinned, beautiful and maybe just a little too smug for his liking, quite obviously pleased with her generous contribution to this vampire thing.

Samuel's eyes trailed down to the wicker basket in his lap and pushed his skirt toward his knees in the effort to keep his man bits properly covered—still too dazed to respond. Though not so dazed he missed the packet labeled BLOOD in bold black letters. It glistened, red and delicious, taunting him from its plastic casing.

Hungry, Sammy?

He clenched his jaw again, grinding his teeth together——which wasn't easy, considering their recent growth spurt. Fuck. He was actually eyeing the blood like it was a filet. Apparently a delicacy, as part of Marty's Welcome to the Night Dwellers Club information packet, he'd never eat again.

"Oh, look," the aforementioned Marty remarked in dry tones, leaning against a chipped desk with her arms crossed over her chest. "Nina the Sensitive was kind enough to make you a vampire care package, Mr. McLean. Suppose you could've waited until he knew everything he was in for before you threw him into the dark overlord deep end of the pool, Nina?"

The brunette turned her middle finger up at the blonde with a smirk. "Blow me. He's a *man*, Marty. He'd better take it like one. Which means he needs to get used to the fact that if he goes out in the sunlight without that goddamned SPF two trillion, he'll burn like a Yule log. And he's got to feed or he'll shrivel up just like all of his useless organs have."

Sam fought hard to keep the *man* in his male equation intact and not flinch when Nina reminded her friend his organs were now persona non grata and his time-share in Aruba was going to be a future Craigslist ad.

He squared his shoulders. Not that it was easy to do in a sequined red dress and heels.

Project his manliness, that is.

How the hell did women keep these skimpy dresses in place? For that matter, how did they keep their legs closed, their nylons from ripping, their bra straps from digging a hole in their skin, apply false eyelashes with diamond studs on them and not end up with glue all over their faces, *and* walk in heels all at the same damn time?

Suffice it to say, Sam did not enjoy being a girl. He looked down at his chest in disgust, adjusting his half deflated gel bra with impatience when the third woman in the trio spoke.

"Did you say manly?" a chestnut-haired brunette remarked with a snort at Nina's comment. "You mean like the way you took it, Nina?

All manly?" she taunted with a raised eyebrow, her eyes gleaming with laughter.

Nina made a face, distorting her beauty, and plopped down in a chair behind a duplicate of the desk Marty stood in front of. "Shut the hell up, Wanda. I did not either cry."

Wanda. Yes. Sam remembered now. The elegantly dressed, gracious lady was Wanda Schwartz-Jefferson—the werevamp. At least that's what he recalled her saying when he'd woken up in their office to find himself being hurled into a chair with the declaration that he had the ugliest pumps ever. Though, they'd assured him, his color something or other was spot on.

That had been Marty's contribution to his condition.

Marty Flaherty . . . *the woman*. Who'd lifted all six-foot-five and two hundred and thirty pounds of him like he was nothing more than a curling iron. Marty the werewolf-woman, that is.

So. Much. Crazy.

Wanda clucked her tongue. "No. You didn't cry, badass. You pissed and moaned and carried on for days. That's what *you* did." She snapped her fingers together to shush Nina, who was quite obviously ready to react. With venom, if Sam was accurately reading her vibe. "Now, before things get out of control like they always do, *shut up*, Nina. Yes, you're the expert on vampires here. Yes, I'm sure you'll have plenty to add to Mr. McLean's misery because that's all part of the Nina genius. But you're not going to do it for the pathetic glee the shock value brings you. Not today, Elvira. I refuse to have one more accidentally turned client fill out that infernal comment form Casey insisted we put on our site with another negative review about your skills as a paranormal crisis intervention counselor. *Refuse*."

Nina brushed imaginary lint from her sweatshirt that had a thumbs-up sign and read, VAMPIRE SEX. 24 PEOPLE LIKE THIS. "Oh, please. We all know that dude was a total dick. Of course we weren't helpful or whatever the fuck he said. He wasn't really accidentally anything—except maybe a moron. He was no more accidentally turned into a dragon than I am the new Miss Fucking Universe. He had eczema—not scales. Bet he'd take that shit off the OOPS site if he knew his ass was in for a poundin' from me. Shoulda just killed him when I had the little douche in the trunk of the car."

Wanda took a deep breath, her hands gripping the edge of her desk. "The point being, he should have never been in the trunk of your car, Nina! For the love of—you can't just throw someone who makes you angry in the trunk of your car and threaten to make them a pair of cement Louboutins—even when they send us on a wild-goose chase! We are professionals. Now, false report or not, Chester wasn't the only one who left a comment that was less than favorable about you, Mistress of the Dark. So knock it off! This is someone's life—not a game where the poor, accidentally turned is the hunted and you're the hunter. So stay seated, quiet your ever-unhelpful mouth, and let us assist Mr. McLean."

Nina's lips formed a thin line, but upon Wanda's order, she leaned back in her chair, letting her ankle rest on her knee.

Watching their interaction, one that had a certain rhythm to it, Sam was capable of only one assessment. It was damn obvious these women were experienced in this sort of thing. So had it just been luck that he'd landed here? Or was it a calculated stop, drop, and roll on the doorstep of three women who just happened to claim they were supernatural? His usually sharp-as-a-tack mind couldn't process much further than the scenario before him.

Maybe he was being punked by his new poker buddies? How did he know these women were telling the truth about all these accidents they lay claim to? Seriously, who thinks a werewolf looks like a dog, and did vampires really have dental plans?

If you listened to Wanda and Marty and the tales they'd told him about their accidental events, apparently, they did.

How did he know they could really help him? Sure, they claimed they knew what was happening to him and that they could assist, but how did he know he had what they had?

How did he know they had anything to begin with? Maybe what they'd shown him had David Copperfield properties to it, and he'd fallen for it because, let's face it, he'd lost a day of his life—somewhere—somehow in a bizarre comatose-like state. He'd have called drunk for all the ensuing craziness, but the fuck of it was, he hadn't had a drop to drink the night this had all begun. He never drank on the job . . .

Maybe he was just tired, and all that snarling, shedding, and showing of the fangs they'd given him as *proof* was his eyes playing tricks on him.

Or . . .

Sam, Sam, Sam. Don't be an asshat. Did you not bear witness to what that Marty called the shift? *You'll be picking fur out of your teeth for days for all the openmouthed horror you displayed.*

Okay. There was no denying what he'd seen, whether he was recovering from a bender he couldn't remember having or not. This was real. Marty *had* turned into a werewolf right in front of him, and Wanda *had* lifted not one, but both desks with a mere two fingers from each hand.

He'd seen. Fuck. It had been like that crazy show his ex-girlfriend used to watch. Super-something with men she'd called lickable that were always fighting, not only with each other, but with Lucifer and his demons because they were vessels. Shit. Was he a vessel, too?

Damn. It would suck to be a vessel in a dress and these big hoopy earrings.

How could this all really be true?

"Mr. McLean? Are you still with us?" Wanda asked, her worried glance to the other two women making him reposition his slouching frame.

Be a man, Sam. All man. "Sam. Please, call me Sam." *Or Vampire. Mr. Vampire.*

Wanda perched on the edge of her desk, crossing her slender legs. Her black heels clacked together in an abomination of sound so sharply distinct, Sam gripped the arms of the office chair they'd given him to sit in upon his awakening. It was all he could do to keep from screaming at Wanda to shut up. Everything was so loud and abrasive. "Okay, so here we go, *Sam*. Obviously, you realize you've got a . . . problem."

As problems went—this probably would classify. He was in the office of women who declared they were paranormal crisis counselors and ran an organization titled OOPS. He had no idea how he'd gotten here. Add to that, he had on a dress, matching heels, nylons, fake eyelashes, and a blond wig. Definitely problematic.

Sam watched Wanda's pink-glossed lips nibble at the end of her pencil while she waited for him to answer. "Yes. I think these"—he lifted his upper lip, taking care not to poke himself with the Lee Press Ons still stuck to his fingertips, and revealed the fangs the women had shown him he was now the proud owner of when they'd made him run his fingers along his newly elongated teeth—"are a definite problem. There's also the small, but quite possibly deadly issue of my urge to eat anyone who has blood pumping through their veins—which I'll be honest enough to tell you, I'm really fighting. I'm guessing 'I'm a vampire' won't be a solid defense in a court of law where murder's concerned."

Insanity be thy name.

"I'd like to attribute this to the world's worst hangover, but as far back as the night this happened, I can't remember even having the chance to grab a beer."

Marty's hand shot up, her bracelet-covered wrist shiny under the brash ceiling light. "Hold on. You were rambling just a little when we dragged you in here. Let's hear what happened once more for posterity so Nina's filled in?"

Sam's mind raced back to two days ago when he'd been talked into going to his new friend Joel's Halloween costume party. Dumbest ass thing he'd done in a long damn time. But Joel had convinced him he needed to mingle more instead of burying himself in his work. "I think, to my best recollection, it happened at my friend Joel's costume party—"

"So you don't always dress like Marilyn Monroe OD'd on steroids?" Nina queried with a wave of her hand at his torn dress and cracked heels.

Sam pushed a blond curl from the wig he was still wearing out of his eyes. Eyes that had taken one look in that hand mirror these bunch of women had given him when they'd spouted their paranormal pitch, and had nearly fallen out of his head.

And it wasn't due to the fact that he didn't need his glasses to see his reflection clearly anymore, but more because he had absolutely *no* reflection, period. "Um, no. It was a *costume party*. You know, Halloween? I thought it would be funny if—"

Nina cut him off again with a flap upward of her hands. "No judgment here, dude. You can be whatever you want to be. If you dig dressing up like a chick and bein' swishy, you won't hear me point out that the dress you're wearing is a shitty color for your stupid color aura—or whatever. But I'm crushin' on your earrings."

"They were a total steal at some place in the mall called Claire's. And hold on," he protested. "Marty said it was a good color for me . . . and it *was* a costume party . . ." Hey now. He stopped short, clamping his piehole shut.

"Nina!" Wanda chastised, her frown disapproving. "I'm sorry, Sam, but if you choose to work with us, she's a part of the deal. Forget your color wheel and your dress and those ghastly heels and try to focus on the fact that Nina mostly knows what she's talking about. She is the vampire in our equation. Full vampire, as opposed to my only half."

Right. Wanda was halfsie, as she'd jokingly referred to herself on a snort Marty had mirrored. That he could remember any of this after waking from what felt like a coma continued to amaze him.

Wanda rustled on the desk, regaining Sam's attention. "Please, continue, Sam."

He scratched at his legs, ripping another hole in his pathetically shredded pantyhose. "Anyway, I went to this costume party where I met a woman dressed as a vampire and . . ." And she'd been hot as Hades. Maybe hotter.

They'd made sizzling eye contact over the apple-bobbing barrel and the rest was as clichéd as it got. He wasn't one for one-night stands as a rule, but this woman, mysterious, round in all the right places, and with a pair of eyes so oddly tinted violet, he couldn't help but pursue her.

But he wasn't going to share those thoughts with a roomful of females who'd made it clear they could take on an entire football team while they polished their nails.

"Oh, pick me! I know what happened next," Nina teased, maniacal amusement glinting in her coal black eyes. "Your man parts thought getting your wonk on with a complete fucking stranger at a costume party was a good idea. The two of you left the party, went to some skanky hotel, she gets ya all juiced, and bam, you wake up Dracula. And they say the male gender is the superior one."

"Hey," Sam scoffed, affronted. "It wasn't a skanky hotel." A weak defense but a defense nonetheless. It hadn't been a skanky hotel—it had been a perfectly fine Days Inn, even if the rest of what Nina had retold was mostly the truth. And he'd paid for the taxi.

"It wasn't a skanky hotel," Nina mimicked his protest with a laugh and a roll of her neck. "Is that the best ya got, Romeo?"

"Ohhhh, listen to the pot calling the kettle black, Nina Statleon!" Marty accused. "Sit down and still your trapdoor, girlie, before we have to remind you of your premarital 'Oh, look. An unsuspecting man who needs an ego shredding with his one-night stand' days."

Nina's eyes narrowed at Marty. "You wanna try vampire versus werewolf and see if I don't take you out?"

"You wanna lose those elephant tusks, Fang?" Marty countered, hands on her svelte hips.

Wanda was up in a shot, moving to the middle of the room,

glancing Sam's way with a look of apology, her jaw tight. "Do you see why I've put them in separate corners, Sam? I swear on all that's holy, it's like crack-induced kindergarten. Nina, Marty—do not make me! Never you mind about one-night stands and skanky hotels. That's Sam's business! Now shut it!"

Sam's teeth tried to grind together again while he fought to remember he was, first and foremost, a gentleman—rare one-night stands aside. "Yes. My cave-dweller instincts got the best of me. I hang my head in shame. I'm an utter and total pig. The moment I find some spare time, I'll make it my mission to put that on a billboard—all big and readable. But because I'm an in-the-moment kind of guy, I really think addressing my new teeth, my lack of lung function, the fact that I can not only hear but almost *see* noises, which means I can hear Marty's blood course through her veins from clear over here, presents a bigger problem than my cad status or even my red dress."

Nina leaned forward in her chair, smiling at him—the tension between the two women as though it had never been. "Hah. Dude's got a sense of humor. Good thing, too. You're gonna need it, living as a vampire."

Sam yanked off his wig, pushing his own matted hair back. "So let me be clear on this just one more time. There's no going back, right?" Marty had been, at his request, straight up about that much when they'd explained his current situation. He wanted to deny what was happening to him, but there was no denying he wasn't breathing, and the hand he'd placed on his fake gel-breasted chest where his heart should be wasn't feeling a steady rhythm.

Wanda hesitated momentarily, clearly measuring her words. "We wouldn't rule anything out at this point, Sam. Not anything. We've seen some pretty crazy things since this happened to us, but more than likely, you're a vampire for good. You'll eventually be able to fly, read minds, kick some serious butt without much effort. Almost everything you've ever heard, read, seen in a movie pretty much applies to you now."

"Except for the sparkling thing." Why he couldn't let that go seemed ludicrous, but of all the things he'd have to incur if what Wanda said was true, sparkling had to be the worst of all offenses.

"Yeah," Nina's response was dry. "Except for the sparkly stuff, Twilight. That's the least of the shit you have to worry about."

"So you remember absolutely nothing after that night in the hotel? Maybe this vampire lady's name?" Marty inquired.

If he wasn't a candidate for induction into the Shithead's Hall of Fame after admitting he'd copped to a one-night stand, he was well on his way for what he was about to confess now. *Own it, McLean. You were on a strictly don't-ask, don't-tell basis.* Straightening his back, Sam looked them each square in the eye. "We didn't exchange names." There. The lack-of-name-sharing bomb dropped.

Kaboom.

However, Wanda, whether purposefully or not, granted him a reprieve. "So we have no idea not only who accidentally turned you but who was responsible for dumping you on our doorstep like you were a newborn on the steps of St. Mary's."

Nina rolled her tongue in her cheek, her eyes narrowing to black slits. "We also have no idea if this woman Sammy wanted to slam was really a vampire. He can't remember shit after meeting her. How do we know what really happened to him from the time they went to the hotel until he woke up? And BTW, who says this was a fucking accident, Wanda? First, don't you think it's suspicious that he was dropped here? With us? And second, I gotta tell ya, most of us, the decent vamps anyway, would own biting someone by accident just like Greg did with me. This shit ain't sittin' right with me."

Both Wanda and Marty gasped in unified horror. Wanda was the first to speak. "You think someone did this purposely, Nina?"

Sam held up a hand to stop that idea in its tracks. "Wait. I do remember this much. I don't know where I was or when it happened during that night, but I remember the words, 'I'm sorry—I didn't mean it. It was an accident.'"

Yes. He remembered that much. The pleading tone to mystery woman's voice when she'd whispered those words.

Nina scowled. "We'd better hope the fuck so. Otherwise, it means we have some rogue vamp running around, biting innocents like pretty boy here."

Now Sam was astonished. In fact, he'd gasp—if he still could. "You mean you vampires really do this on purpose?" That wasn't what Marty and Wanda had said. Quite the contrary. After they'd told him about their no-humans-harmed policy, and that he needed blood in order to survive, he'd had visions of himself stalking the surrounding farms around his cabin upstate so he could suck the life out of some poor herd of sheep in the name of survival. But it didn't entail sinking his teeth into humans.

Jesus.

"No. Draining humans, even just drinking from them, is a big no-no in my vampire circle," Nina informed him. "That's rule number one in Vampire-landia. We buy blood from an approved donor. So all those crazy urges you're having while you watch Marty's pulse beat in her neck end now, bloodsucker. Or I'll kick the living shit out of you. You have to learn to keep that shit to yourself. And if anyone ever drains Marty dry, it damned well better be me for all the bullshit discount designer mall shopping she makes me do with her." She snickered.

Instantly, Sam's eyes fell to the hem of his dress in guilt. Yeah. The blonde's neck was looking better than any beer he'd ever had. "No people bloodsucking," he repeated, fighting a shudder of horror mingled with an unbidden sick delight at the thought. "Got it."

"Because I will stop you, but not before I yank your sacs off," Nina warned, growling at him. "With my teeth."

A wave of dizziness washed over him once more. The same wave he'd experienced shortly after he'd woken up at OOPS. He gripped the arms of the chair again to keep from wobbling.

Marty and Wanda were at his side in a blink. Marty tipped his head back, gazing into his face, the scent of her perfume assaulting Sam's nose. "He needs to feed, Nina, before he passes out."

Feed. Such an odd word.

Nina slapped her hands against her thighs, rising to come toward him. She picked up the basket from his lap and dug around in it, pulling out the packet labeled Blood. "Marty's right—you look like shit. That'll happen if you don't feed a lot in the beginning stages of your turn. So, seeing as you're all man, I guess we don't have to deal with a bunch of snot while we hand you a buttload of tissues and lie to you about how everything's gonna be all right. Let's move on to the next dealio at hand, Sammy. The rest of the minutia can wait till your head's clearer."

Becoming woozier by the second, Sam's head fell back on his shoulders with a boneless flop. He stared up at Nina, who took hold of his chin and shook it, knocking one of his bargain-basement hoop earrings to the floor. "Feed?" he managed.

Nina's eyebrow rose; her lips flirted with a mocking smile. "Yeah. Like drink blood. It does a vampire good. And by the looks of you, you're fading fast. So let's get you juiced before we do anything else."

Sam cringed, making a weak attempt at pulling from Nina's grasp. He fought to find clarity in his next words. "I think this might be where I have to get off the merry-go-round. I know I was all about taking this like a man, and you have to admit, I haven't shed a single tear, nor have I retreated to the corner and assumed the rocking position. But I gotta draw the line at blood." No blood. Whether his stomach was doing handstands filled with anticipation about it or not. No. Blood.

That couldn't be the answer to his sudden weakness.

Nina used her teeth to rip open the package. "Don't go pantywaist on me now, pal. You have to feed or risk the chance of being expunged. You don't want that, do you?"

His hand gripped Nina's wrist. "Who says I'll be ex . . . ex-whatever?" He slurred the last word, unable to make his tongue cooperate.

Nina squeezed harder, making his lips pucker like a goldfish. "Expunged, Sammy, and Nina the Vampire says so."

"You're *Nina*?" a voice from behind them said, warbled and distorted to Sam's ears, but clearly laced with astonishment.

Nina's head popped up, her eyes scanning the door just behind his chair with suspicion. "Maybe. Who are you?"

A woman rushed in, her scent sitting in Sam's nose when she stopped short in front of them. The heat of her body swirled around him, enveloping his every sense while his vision cleared enough for him to momentarily focus on the woman.

A redhead with creamy skin and full red lips, her eyes were gray blue, her bangs partially covering the thick fringe of dark lashes around them. She wore a white shawl, casually slung over her shoulders. Her rounded hips were encased in a sleek, gray skirt that fell to just above her knees, knees that were attached to shapely legs.

The click from the heels of her suede boots was brisk as she paced and asked, "So you're *really* Nina? *The Nina*. I can't believe it's really you."

Sam caught the hesitation in this woman's voice, heard a faint glimmer of worry, maybe even fear, but he was, at this point in his vampiric state, rendered immobile. All he could do was observe in a limp slump from his chair. For a man like him, it was infuriating.

Nina's fingers dropped from his mouth, leaving it slack and wide open. She cornered the woman in preylike fashion, looming over her by maybe an inch. "Yeah. I'm Nina. Now who the fuck are you, Flame-haired Barbie?"

The woman, though shorter than Nina, didn't cower when

growled at by the fierce vampire. There was only a slight tremble of her peach-glossed lower lip to indicate she was intimidated.

Instead, she sighed with a roll of her eyes. "Wow. You really are cranky, aren't you? Ah, well. I should have known better, but silly me and my impatience." She waved a gloved hand under Nina's nose, making her large hoop earrings sway. "Never mind. Listen, we really need to talk. Is there somewhere private we can go?"

Nina's eyes narrowed. Whoever this woman was, she either sucked at social cues, or she was a glutton for an ass whoopin', because Sam noted, she didn't back down. "Did I not speak in words small enough for you to understand, lady? Because I'm kinda busy here. Now who—the—fuck—are—you?" she repeated, intention-ally condescending and slow.

The woman's shoulders slumped just a little from Sam's vantage point, but she took a deep breath and straightened. "I really don't think you want to do this in front of your colleagues and . . . well . . . Mr. Fancy Pants." She waved a dismissive hand toward Sam and winced.

Hey. He was not fancy and he wasn't wearing pants.

Shut up, Sam. Red dress and heels. 'Nuff said.

Right. Shut up. Plus, he was too weak to even consider respond-ing, though not for lack of trying. When he attempted to move, he fell to the side of the chair in a heaping slump.

Marty and Wanda were instantly at Nina's side, tugging at her arms. "Nina!" Wanda admonished, her brow furrowed. "Back off!"

Nina gave them a hard shrug and growled. Like really growled into the new woman's face. "I'm not going anywhere with you until you tell me who the hell you are and how you know me."

Marty jumped between the women, placing a firm hand on Nina's shoulder. "Nina, back up! Let the poor thing breathe." She turned to face the redhead, a smile on her face Sam could tell was phony even from his blurred observation. "Now, what's your name and how can we help you, dear? Oh, and pretty hair. I want to accuse you of getting it from a bottle, but that would just be me sick with envy."

The redhead smiled, preening at Marty's compliment even with Nina's evil eye glued on her. "Thank you. I take great pains to keep it in tip-top shape." She stuck her hand out to Marty. "I'm Phoebe Reynolds. A pleasure."

"Well, that settles it," Nina crowed. "I don't know anyone named Phoebe. So conversation over."

Phoebe stepped around Marty and reached for Nina's arm, clasping it. "No. It's not over."

Noooo, don't do it, Phoebe. Vampire red alert! Sam wanted to warn, but couldn't manage.

Even in his growing stupor, he recognized Phoebe had just made an epic mistake, and he couldn't do anything to save the poor woman from the wrath that was the crabby Nina. Instead, his mouth fell open wider and his body began to slide from the chair to the floor like he was some kind of human slinky.

And his legs had spread open. No fine, upstanding lady would ever allow that to happen—even under such trying circumstances.

Nina looked down at Phoebe's hand like it belonged to Lucifer himself. "I know you didn't just put your hand on me, princess."

Phoebe's eyes glinted determination. "But I did, and if you'd please just listen—"

"I'm busy here. I don't have time to listen to whatever you're selling, lady." Nina swung back around with flashing eyes and a menacing stance. "Now take your hand off my arm. Or I'll chew it the shit off."

Damn. Phoebe was too cute to be eaten alive so young, Sam reflected when his spine became Jell-O and his legs crumbled beneath him. He slid completely to the floor, his mouth now impossible to close due to the size of his teeth—which, ironically, had grown in seconds.

Phoebe's eyes widened, then went soft as though she understood

Nina's outrageous reaction toward a complete stranger. She smiled again—this time with a definite appeasing hint to it. "You're exactly like my mother described, er, times ten maybe, but exactly. But it's okay. I knew we'd have some bumps in the road upon our first meeting. It's to be expected. I've caught you unaware. Still, I'm convinced we can make this work. So as soon as you're done here, let's go somewhere quiet, maybe have a latte and chat? On me, of course."

"Your mother?" Nina ground out her disbelief, her stance ominous from Sam's still semiconscious vantage point on the floor where, excuse him, no one seemed to remember he was ex . . . Expiring? Excommunicated? No. Nina'd said *expunging*. Yes. He was going to expunge in a roomful of angry, perfumed, supernatural females while Nina tore Phoebe limb from limb and he wore a dress. How inhumane.

"Yes," Phoebe answered in solemn tones. "My mother."

Nina appeared to Sam as though she'd been caught off guard. "That's it! Lay the fuck off the cat and mouse and tell me who the hell you are!" Nina roared, making Sam wince from the floor— where it was hard, and he was trying not to peek up Phoebe's skirt. But he couldn't move his head, no matter how hard he willed his body to work in his favor.

Phoebe wavered then. Not a lot, but just enough for Sam to see she was indecisive. Then her expression changed and the look of determination returned in full force. Squaring her shoulders, she tilted her chin upward in a defiance that rather resembled Nina's and said, "All right. But please remember, I did ask you for some privacy."

Nina poked her in the shoulder. "Spit it the fuck out, princess!"

"I'm your sister."

Wow. Silence really did have sound to it.

Nina's angry glare made the hair on Sam's arms rise. *Oh, Phoebe. From the very little I've borne witness to, I'd advise you to run long from the Nina experience, but my tongue's out of order.*

The sharp gasps from Wanda and Marty, followed by the eerily long silence one could only describe as the calm before the all-out tsunami, might have deafened him. Except, as described by Wanda, he now had bionic hearing and he could hear blood coursing and heartbeats pumping wildly.

When Nina finally replied, it was low and threatening. *"My what?"*

"I said. I'm your sister. S-I-S-T-E-R. You know, *sisters*. Like the kind that tell each other secrets, share clothes, and stay up all night talking about boys? Okay, I'm only your half sister if we want to be crazy technical, but we're family regardless. So I don't see why it would prevent us from talking about boys or all sorts of things, for that matter," Phoebe said with a breathless almost excited hitch to her words.

And then, at least from Sam's point of view, things got a little unnecessarily out of control. As a point of reference, should he decide these women were the best candidates to help him through this paranormal crisis, he'd make damn good and sure he remembered Nina was like a snake, easily riled, always coiled and waiting to go in for the venomous kill.

Now there was the rush of footsteps as Marty and Wanda came to someone's aid, hopefully poor innocent Phoebe's, because it was clear they understood their friend Nina's short fuse. Phoebe, as brave as she'd like to appear on the outside, was no match for Nina the Hun.

Next, someone stepped on his index finger in a tangle of rutting feet—which was okay due to the fact that he couldn't feel it anyway. Observing it, knowing he should react to it was rather like an out-of-body experience.

And there was the cursing. Creative and punctuated by more than one cautionary, "Nina, remember your strength!" and "If you harm one hair on her head, we'll be forced to put you in the duct-taped time out!"

Sam thought what ensued next could be described by some—okay, him—as euphoric and others as catastrophic. It just depended on whether you were a glass half-empty or half-full personality.

Nina, as Nina was clearly wont to do, went in for the kill. Or maybe kill was too harsh a word, but when she stalked toward Phoebe, covering the inches between them in seconds, she, in her defense, probably hadn't planned on Phoebe actually backing down.

Though, Sam didn't blame her one iota for doing so. The mask of death Nina wore would make even those with the ability to cold-bloodedly kill cower in fear.

The trouble with that, Sam realized while he lay motionless and numb from head to toe, was Phoebe had picked the worst time ever to not just back down from her warrior sister, but back away from her, too.

As Nina took those threatening steps toward her newly found relation, Phoebe, her bravado gone, stumbled on Sam's—dubbed *ghastly* by Wanda—high heels, tripped, and fell backward to land on his chest. Thus jamming her cute butt right up against his slack mouth.

He heard her scream of shock, and assumed it was probably mixed with some pain.

The pain having to do with his overgrown fang imbedded in her bottom to at least a quarter of an inch deep.

Which covered the euphoria part for him.

Huh. Nina was right. This feeding thing definitely made him feel better. How unexpected and maybe even a little gory all at the same time.

The catastrophic part, well, he figured that was on Phoebe.

Surely she'd find it catastrophic that, if the chain of vampirism was as he'd been told, because his teeth had pierced Phoebe's flesh and he'd tasted her blood, she was now a vampire, too.

And he'd done it all while in drag. Nice.

Though, somehow, Sam had the distinct impression Phoebe, in all her obvious good taste in clothing and makeup, wouldn't mind at all if she ended up sparkling in the sunlight.

CHAPTER 2

Phoebe woke with a start and a rush of white-hot heat coursing through her veins. It stung sharply, making her spring upright with a jolt so hard she nearly flung herself from the unfamiliar couch she was propped up on.

Her fingers squeezed the fabric beneath her hand to keep her body firmly planted on the furniture. What she assumed to her practiced hands was leather, crunched, then began to split, making her fingers almost sink deep into the foam. Phoebe yanked her hand away in guilty horror at the mess she'd made, placing her clenched fist in her lap.

Hey, couch killah, where the hell are we?

Her first thought was, this was a lot like the time Marvella Constantine from one of her all-time favorite soap operas *Connections* woke up in a strange place. That place happened to be Kazakhstan where Marvella's evil, jealous niece by marriage, Drucilla, had her dumped after a gang of traveling gypsies kidnapped her to keep her from marrying Enrique—the mayor of Maple Dell. Or something like that.

Not that she'd ever be so lucky to have something so exotic happen to her. She was probably going to open her eyes in some trailer park in Idaho. So she opted to keep them closed and imagine a far-off place like Istanbul.

"So, how's it going?" a deep, resonant voice rumbled with just a hint of a Southern twang.

Phoebe forced an eye open at the gravelly silken tones of a man's voice. But just one, because she had a headache throbbing with such intensity between her eyes she should be blind from it. As her vision came into focus, she sighed.

Or gakked, depending on how one looked at it.

Wait. Where was that release of air that typically followed an exhalation of audible discontent? Where was the relief she so needed to ease the tension in her chest? Phoebe tried once more to sigh, only to make a dry-heaving noise that sounded much like her cat, Optimus, when he was hacking up a hairball.

Huh.

"Are you all right?"

Her right eyeball strayed to her left.

Oh, look. RuPaul. Or aka the man whose mouth her backside had been in. "What happened to me?"

He shifted on the couch beside her and shrugged his broad, red-sequined shoulders. "Some stuff," was the solemn yet evasive reply.

His vague answer made Phoebe open her other eye and fully take him in. The dark stubble caressing his cheeks and hard jaw revealed the hint of a handsome man hidden beneath his too-red lipstick and the frosted blue eye shadow he'd so mistakenly chosen to highlight his deep chocolate brown eyes with.

Her nose twitched when she took another sidelong glance at the color of his lipstick. Literally, she could *smell* the scent of it. She knew it well. Pack Cosmetics had a scent and a flavor for every hue in their new lipstick line. Marketing genius as far as Phoebe was concerned. The aroma she detected had a splash of cinnamon in it. Rip-Roaring Red. That was it.

Curious.

But her momentary bionic ability to smell lipstick was forgotten. Shifting positions on the couch, Phoebe turned to face this man and made herself focus on his mouth to keep from laughing out loud at his unevenly penciled eyebrows and the stray false eyelash stuck to the bridge of his nose. "I'm sorry. Where were we? Oh, right. Stuff," she offered. He'd said stuff had happened.

"Oh, yeah. Lots of stuff."

"Care to explain *stuff*?"

"I'm Samuel McLean. Or just Sam."

"That's not an explanation, that's an introduction. I need more in order for us to have a fulfilling beginning to our relationship. And I'm Phoebe Reynolds."

He nodded and fluffed the platinum blond wig in his hands before letting it fall to his lap. "Yeah. I heard. You know, from my place on the floor. Anyway, I'm not sure I'm mentally ready to say the words to explain what the *stuff* is out loud yet. I'm in what those three"—he nodded his head in the direction of her newfound sister, who stood by an enormous fireplace with the other two women who'd kept Nina from killing Phoebe—"call the third stage of denial. Grief. I think. I don't know. I can't remember the number of the stage. I just know I've exceeded most who encounter this strange new way of life, and thus far, they claim I'm their star pupil at OOPS."

When Phoebe had begun the search for her only living relative and she'd found out that Nina was part of an organization titled OOPS, she hadn't known the meaning of the acronym. Nor had she spent a lot of time researching it due to her excitement over finally finding the address where her half sister worked.

So, OOPS plus the stages of grief plus Sam had to equal out of the cross-dressing closet—like out big in Sam's case. What the letters *p* and *s* could possibly stand for escaped her.

The last information she'd found on Nina had her employed as a dental hygienist. How you went from cleaning tartar and fluoride treatments to counseling men who liked to dress in women's clothing was a leap she hoped to be able to sit and talk about with Nina someday.

Well, when she wasn't so hostile and violent, that was.

But that didn't explain what Sam's *stuff* and the stages of grief had to do with her.

Right now, it hurt to think. So she didn't. Instead Phoebe said, "So what does your lifestyle and denial thereof have to do with the *stuff* that happened to me? I mean, I love makeup, obviously, and heels and shiny dresses, too, but I'm not conflicted about it. Not even a little."

His expression went from attentive to confused, his dark brows knitting together. "I'm not conflicted about it, either."

She patted him on the knee, avoiding the bare spot where his shredded nylons revealed thatches of springy dark hair on his thighs. "Good. That's so healthy to feel free enough to be you, even if you need a lesson or two in makeup application. You'll get it with more practice. It's all about the blending. I'm a personal stylist by trade, so when I locate my purse, I'd be happy to give you my card and maybe you can make an appointment and we can discuss . . . er, *this*." She waved her hand in a sweeping up-and-down motion at his choice of outfit.

Sam cocked his head, his garish red mouth a perfect O.

And yet another crazy thought struck her. "You know what this reminds me of?"

His glance was wary. "That it reminds you of anything ever gives me great pause, but I'll bite. What does this remind you of?"

"This conversation we're having right now reminds me of the time when Alejandro Delacortez had to come to terms with his . . . um, preferences and out himself to his very strict, Catholic family. Sweet purgatory, his mother, Lucinda, behaved like he'd just told her he'd murdered his secret twin brothers, Frank and Giuseppe, who, by the way, were the result of a torrid night with a possessed-by-the-devil Father Duncan. But it's not exactly like that because, of course, you're not a swarthy Puerto Rican, and I would never judge you the way Alejandro's mother judged him. Of that you can be sure."

Sam nodded his head in serious confirmation, but his beautiful eyes glimmered. "Oh, yes. I can see where this is almost *exactly* like that."

Phoebe smiled at him, sensing he understood that she had a zero tolerance for bigotry of any kind. "So we're on the same page? And I hope, after I figure out why I can't remember getting from point A to point B, B being this unbelievably gorgeous house, we can sit and swap makeup tips. But for right now, I just want to know where I am and how I got here."

Sam's deep brown eyes clouded with bewilderment and then obvious concern. He braced his arm on the back of the couch and leaned in to examine her.

Despite his melting makeup and smeared lipstick, he had a presence. One that demanded female attention in the way of hard muscles and sculpted upper arms that rippled when he shifted positions on the couch. He pried one of her eyes open wide and peered into it as though he were inspecting something, then let go with an abrupt removal of his finger. "You really don't remember . . . ?" Sam shook his head. "Forget it. How do *you* feel, Phoebe?"

What a gentleman. She'd all but punctured his lung by landing ass first on him, and he'd just come out of the proverbial closet—which had to be freeing and frightening all at the same time. Yet, here he was asking how *she* had fared.

So decent and maybe even a little bizarre, if she were to judge the intensity of his eyes when he asked the question . . .

But what about this day hadn't been bizarre? It had been filled with bizarre. This man in the shiny dress, lying on the floor in a heap of women's shoes, for instance. Or the two women who'd rushed to her defense and shouted words at her half sister like *superhuman* and the phrase, *Remember you can take out a Sherman tank singlehandedly!* just before Nina had made her trip and fall. Or Nina herself, who gave the title *antagonistic bitch* a shiny new meaning.

Phoebe had expected upon meeting and introducing herself to

Nina that there would be some anger and resentment involved. Who wouldn't be angry to find they weren't the only apple of their beloved father's eye? Before her death, her mother had forewarned her about Nina's temper and infamous mouth. According to her mother, their father, Joe, had fretted over Nina often just before he'd died. So she'd been mentally prepared for some irate swearing.

However, she certainly hadn't anticipated that anger would involve intimidation and flying fists. Without a doubt, she hadn't planned their conversation to end up with her ass in some stray drag queen's mouth.

But there it was. So there was only one thing to do and that was onward and upward. She'd asked Nina for some privacy in order to reveal her secret. The last thing she'd wanted to do was blindside one of the only living relatives she had in the world—or worse, alienate her.

Phoebe had definitive proof that Nina was her half sister. But she'd wanted to share that with her in a sensitive manner, not in some screaming match. Phoebe wasn't so uncaring that she didn't realize she'd also be met with a certain amount of disbelief and betrayal, and she'd prepared herself to deal with that, too.

In fact, in the year she'd spent looking for Nina, she'd run a million scenarios of their eventual meeting over and over in her mind.

But Nina's refusal to at least grant her some alone time and her almost dare for Phoebe to spit out the reason for her appearance at OOPS had gotten the better of her.

Sometimes you get what you wish for.

In most cases, Phoebe had learned to keep her temper and her competitive spirit in check. But a dare was a dare. And now she was here, wherever here was. She didn't remember much other than the ground falling away from her and landing on Sam. She hated to admit it, but she must have hit her head and passed out after that.

How weak she probably looked to these people. Weak was something a Reynolds just didn't do well.

"Phoebe?" Sam's voice filtered through her reverie when he placed a cool hand on her arm. "How do you feel?"

Feel? She felt like an utter moron. That's how she felt. And her ass hurt as though a pin had punctured it. "I feel like an explanation is in order. Did I pass out when I fell, and where are we?" She craned her neck to take in the beauty of the enormous home she was in.

Sam rolled his tongue in his cheek, a look of disbelief passing over his expression. "We're at Nina's castle, er, house . . . no, castle. Yes. It's definitely a castle with a moat and everything. In Long Island."

Her head began to throb, and her lack of anything in the way of sustenance other than some fruit and cottage cheese for lunch hours ago left her with a gnawing hunger. "And we got here *how*?"

Sam held up a finger with one red nail still precariously attached to it and paused as though to gather his words. When he finally spoke, it was low and husky. "Again, I'm still not sure I can properly articulate the form of transportation that brought us here. It's mind-bending. Which leads me to believe these women have pegged my emotional state all wrong. I think I have more work to do on these stages of grief than they think, because I'm just one bullet shy from a loaded Glock."

Commotion from the area of the enormous fireplace thwarted further investigation, making Phoebe shush Sam with a finger to his mouth so she could eavesdrop.

The woman who wore a pencil-slim skirt and a silk blouse like she was the Queen of England crossed her arms over her chest and addressed Nina. "So do you think this could be true, Nina? Is it possible that she's your sister?"

The blond Phoebe vaguely remembered complimenting her on her hair color gave Nina a squinty-eyed gaze. "Who, for the love of all things chosen, would declare *Nina*, of all the sisters in the world to choose, hers if this woman wasn't telling the truth, Wanda? I mean, honestly. Ask yourself, would you tell anyone—*an-ee-one*—Nina was blood unless she was someone famous like, I don't know, Lady Gaga? Oprah, maybe? You know, someone who at least had some fame as a redeeming quality to make up for the fact that they're the single most difficult person in the world to get along with? Why couldn't you have at least given her a chance to explain so we knew her story before you snarled and raged, Nina? Because guess what, Houston, we have a problem. Twice the problem we had before you got involved, night dweller."

Nina flicked the woman's hair with a long finger. "Blow me, Marty. I never touched her. She tripped."

"She tripped because you intimidated her with your boot camp Marine Corps tactics. Nice job, you reincarnated Neanderthal. You've so done it now," Marty snipped, shaking a finger in her face, her band of bracelets clanging together. "If just once you'd not react like a raving lunatic, none of this would have happened. I can't wait until you have to explain this to Greg."

Nina's chin tilted in defiance, its sharp edge glinting in the orange-hued light coming from the flames dancing in the fireplace.

She used her height to hover over the petite blonde much in the same way she had Phoebe. "Fuck you, Marty. You did hear what she said, didn't you? She said she's my fucking sister. That's some serious shit. Shit I don't need. I don't have a sister. I have Lou. End of."

"And that meant you had to rush her like you were the shopper and she was the Filene's Basement sale?" the chestnut-haired woman named Wanda asked, her lips thinning in disapproval. "Nina, your temper is foul. You know it. I know it. I've warned you time and again, and you've created more than one problem for yourself because you go from zero to a hundred and ten in a half second flat. But this? Oh, this is beautiful. Just so much fabulous. Now we don't have just poor Sam to deal with, but this innocent woman, too? So what if she said she was your sister? Now, it doesn't matter if she's related to you or not because this is your fault and we absolutely must—nay, *will*—make this right. You can't threaten to clock every crackpot simply because they're a crackpot, Nina. Because guess what, vampire? It ends up like this!" Her hand made a sweeping gesture in Phoebe's general direction. "And now you might not just have a sister, you might have a vampire sister!"

Phoebe chose to dismiss the word *vampire*—a strange mystical word when attributed to Nina indeed—and she dismissed the fact that she was in a strange house with, for the most part, strangers.

She also dismissed the notion that in getting from that dank basement office where she last remembered being to this incredibly tasteful great room with its crystal chandeliers, winding staircase, and big, overstuffed furniture, someone would have had to physically bring her here and she'd missed it all due to her unconscious state.

Those were things to ponder for later.

For now, Phoebe popped off the couch upon the use of the word *crackpot* with reference to her. She was on her feet, thwarted only by a slight dizzy spell that made her sway momentarily, fighting the strange croak in her voice and the thickness of her tongue in order to speak. But speak she did—even with Sam at her side attempting to prevent her from doing so. "I have proof Nina's my sister, and I resent the word *crackpot*. I'm not a crackpot."

Three heads in varying degrees of color shot up, their eyes landing on Phoebe, who was running a hand over her wrinkled skirt. "Yeah?" Nina crowed, pushing the other two women away. "Well, I resent the word *sister*."

Phoebe's eyebrow rose with a condescending tip upward. Boohoo. "Then isn't that just too bad for you?"

Nina growled. *Growled.*

There was a grunt, which Phoebe determined was a warning from Sam the Drag Queen. He waved a limp hand at her and shook his head in the negative—with vigor. "Don't do it," he mouthed, his eyes wide and wary when he set her almost behind his big, sparkly body.

Like a warning from some silly man in a dress and heels was going to keep her from defending an absolutely unwarranted label like crackpot.

The hell.

Nina parted the women with her hands and narrowed eyes before stomping toward Phoebe in a clunk of worn work boots and heavy footsteps. God, how had she ended up with such an in-your-face fashion nightmare like Nina for a sister? "You wanna repeat that shit to my face?"

She fought the urge to blink her eyes when she realized she could see every pore in Nina's strangely pale face with the kind of clarity only the best cosmetic magnifying mirror allowed. Instead, she poked her head around Sam's body and shot back, "Did I stutter?"

There was a snort of muffled laughter and an exclamation of "Hoo-boy" that followed from behind Nina's back before a hasty shuffle of feet as the other two women came to stand beside Nina, their stances indicating they were preparing to hold her back.

"I don't know about you, Marty, but I see a family resemblance right in the area of Phoebe's *big, antagonistic mouth*. You?" Wanda asked over top of Nina's head.

"Yeah," Marty agreed, thoughtful. "Definitely. That and her eyes. Same shape as our fair Nina's, just a different color. Beautiful, don't you agree, Wanda?"

Nina's lips smacked and her dark eyes narrowed. With clenched fists, she gave her friends the eye. "Quit sleeping with the enemy, you two. And as for you, buttercup, nope. You didn't stutter, but you can bet your designer ass when I'm done breaking your Barbie jaw you'll stutter. While you scoop your teeth off the floor, that is."

A spike of anger shot along Phoebe's spine. Oh, really? She put her hands together and cracked her knuckles. It was always better to loosen up before an impending fistfight. Especially if another girl was involved. Their jaws were usually much less fleshy than a man's and could possibly cause damage to the fine bones in her hand.

Not a risk she was willing to take. Being a personal stylist new to the scene meant you carried a lot of bags to your clients.

Knowing her next question would garner an unfavorable, possibly violent response from Nina, Phoebe didn't think twice when she asked, "Are you threatening me, *sister?*"

There was a glimmer of surprise in Nina's eyes before she lunged at Phoebe with a snarling growl. A lunge not only did Sam react too late for but one Phoebe sidestepped much more quickly than she'd ever considered herself capable of. And in three-inch-heel boots, too.

Looking down at Nina as she tripped and stumbled before righting herself, Phoebe thought, *Ya still got it, Reynolds.*

"Nina!" the two women yelped, rushing Nina and latching on to her arms with white-knuckled grips while she all but foamed at the mouth.

Phoebe sauntered toward her, ignoring the crazy buzz in her head and the painfully sharp noise the scrape of her boot heels to the floor made in her ears. And she ignored Sam, who clutched her arm and hissed in her ear, "Danger, Will Robinson, danger!"

She rolled her head on her neck, placing her face inches from Nina's. Their eyes met. Nina's glazed with ire. Phoebe's dripping with a challenge. "Wow. Are you ever a tight ass. You'll take years off your life that way. Not to mention the wrinkles you'll accumulate from frowning so much."

Marty's nod was of vigorous agreement, the shimmery highlights of her blond hair glinting in the dimly lit room. "You know, Phoebe, I tell her that all the time. But does she listen? Noooo. She's all venom and fury. I'm Marty Flaherty, in case you missed it the first time. We met earlier before you . . . well, before . . ." She smiled, then frowned when the elegantly dressed woman chastised her with just one searing glance.

Between clenched teeth, the woman who wore a slim chocolate brown skirt and silk blouse said, "Marty? Shut it." Yanking at Nina's arm, she gave it a jerk. "Nina? Stand down or I'll take you down. This is a new blouse and I won't have it ruined because you behave like a two-year-old. I'm Wanda Jefferson, Phoebe. One of the easily riled Nina's BFFs. And don't look so shocked. I'd bet even Hannibal Lecter had a best friend. A vegetarian, no doubt."

Wanda gave Nina a hard shove toward a dining area where there were chairs around a long rectangular table. "Now, we're all going to sit like ladies and gentleman and figure this out. *This* being the thing that wouldn't have happened if you weren't such a bully, Nina Blackman-Statleon."

Phoebe was taken aback by Nina's last name. Statleon? "You're married?" *To what?*

Wanda clamped her hands on Phoebe's shoulders with a solid grip and ushered her to a chair at the opposite end of the table from Nina. "She is. And when her husband Greg gets back from Boca and finds out what's happened, hell will surely rain down upon us all. We were already skating on thin ice with our men and this OOPS thing. Your predicament will only make things worse."

Nina dropped her fist on the table, making the beautiful copper candelabra in the center shake. "The hell I'll take the flack for this, Wanda. She started this bullshit when she declared herself kin. No kin of mine dresses like that," she snapped with a wave at Phoebe's white shawl, now askew on her shoulders.

Phoebe slid into a chair and clucked her tongue, refusing to give in to the wobble of her knees and the almost desperate growling of her stomach. "No. I don't suspect they would dress in anything other than pelts in Neanderthal-topia, would they?"

Marty was up and holding Nina down before Phoebe's brain could process her movement. She leaned over the back of the chair and whispered, "Stay loose, pal—or we're going to have a head-to-head. I just had my hair done, and much like Wanda, I'm not up for wrecking a perfectly good hair day. Now down, Nina-nator." She gave her a final pat on the shoulder, then turned to Sam and waved him over with a smile. "Sam? Join us, would you?"

With a weak grunt, Sam kicked off his cracked high heels and went to a chair next to Phoebe's, tugging hard at his dress so it would fall to the tops of his thighs.

Phoebe couldn't help but notice his stride was anything but feminine despite his dress and garish makeup. In fact, his build was downright manly. He was clearly still in the awkward, I-want-to-dress-like-a-woman-but-I-have-no-idea-how-not-to-let-my-knuckles-drag-on-the-floor phase of his cross-dressing.

Wanda stood at the head of the table and clapped her hands. The sound pinged in Phoebe's head, making her wince and run her fingers over her temple. Every sound and smell was so magnified it almost hurt.

"People, we have a lot of ground to cover, and time is of the essence. We clearly have a situation. So, in the vein of waste not, want not, and in light of the fact that Phoebe's proven to be quite the spitfire, I'm going to go with my gut and take it for granted that she'll handle her current state with the same set of jingle bells she confronted Nina with."

Phoebe frowned. Hold the phone. What was her current state? And why did she need jingle bells to handle it? Oh, she had nads all right. Nads she wasn't afraid to let drop from her frilly underclothes when the situation presented itself. But why would she need them other than to deal with her sister, who was quite obviously not taking the information that she had a sibling well? Phoebe shuddered at the very thought that she hadn't even had time to tell Nina everything . . .

As the fragmented pieces of not just her unfamiliar surroundings but the snippets of conversation she'd heard before she'd burst through OOPS's door sank in, she began to experience a rise of slow panic. Though she wasn't necessarily afraid of these women and the pretty boy, she wasn't unafraid, either. Phoebe cast a dubious glance at Wanda and raised her hand.

Wanda generously gave her the floor with the sweep of her hand.

The fear her confusion stirred began to rear its ugly head, and it was an effort to keep a calm facade. "Can you explain the bit about my *current state*? I'm a little unclear about what that means. And for that matter, how did I get here, and what happened to me that I can't remember leaving your offices?"

Nina snorted from her end of the table and cracked her knuckles. "You got here because I *flew* you here."

Phoebe eyed Nina, making her irritation clear. "Aren't you the Jeff Foxworthy of Unevolved Village?"

A hand snaked around her neck and clamped over her mouth. Pulling her toward him, Sam whispered in her ear, sending an unexpected thrill of goose bumps over her skin. The hard shelter of his chest had certain rugged properties to it she found incredibly inviting. "For the last time, some advice. Shut your pretty mouth. I beg of you. Listen closely. Or you will pay. I have *seen*. This is your final courtesy warning."

Phoebe placed her hands on his forearm, a strong, muscled forearm indeed, and yanked with more force than she intended. "Put your hand on my mouth again, and we'll see who pays, America's Next Drag Queen. Now, where were we? Oh, right. I was waiting on the answer to why I'm here and how I got here. The real answer." She shot a glare at Nina filled with irate disapproval.

Nina leaned back in her chair and threw her feet up on the table with a bored look. "I say we just have at her, Wanda. You know, seeing as her love eggs are all scraping the ground."

Wanda sighed and paused as though she was taking care in her next words. And then she spoke, her gaze meeting Nina's. "I don't say it often, but I say you're right. Let's do this."

"Oh. Jesus," Sam muttered, running a hand over his matted black hair.

Wanda's words sounded like a challenge. Never one to back down from a challenge, even when she didn't exactly know what the challenge was, Phoebe threw down the gauntlet, ignoring Sam's clear hesitations. "Fine. Let's do this."

NOTE to self. From this day forward, be far more careful when hurling metaphoric gauntlets around so carelessly. Damn her and her competitive streak.

Phoebe fought the urge to run screaming from Nina's house, er, castle. Not that having the adjective of her location made what she'd just seen any easier to swallow.

Forcing herself to sit upright in the chair, Phoebe made herself look these women in the eye—these crazy, crazy, mentally unstable, in desperate need of a psyche ward women. "So let me get this straight. When I fell on Tyra Banks—"

"Hey!" Sam tapped her shoulder from behind, his voice a gravelly sin upon her ears. "I'm really coming to resent that. I'm not fancy, and I'm not a drag queen. I went to a costume party dressed like this, okay? And I think wearing a dress says a little something about how secure I am in my manhood. So lay off, lady. I'm just as bent about this as you are. You're not the only noob vampire in the room. This isn't just about *you*, sweetheart, and it doesn't help when you call names. Now knock it off."

Phoebe waved him away, suddenly incredibly hot and irritable. "Fine. When I fell on the manliest man I've ever fallen on in my entire thirty-three years, or should I say, when I was so rudely backed into a corner and fell on him, because his tooth pierced my skin—"

"Your ass, cookie. He bit that big booty-Judy you got." Nina cackled, cracking her knuckles.

Phoebe tried to clench her jaw but ran amok when her new fangs clashed together. As much as she'd like to prove to Nina she could take whatever she doled out, right now, she had some pretty pressing issues. Like no more coconut macaroons or blueberry cheesecake. Ever. It was cause for deep sorrow. "So that meant I automatically became a vampire, too?"

Wanda straightened the bow on her collar. It needed straightening after that crazy circus sideshow of superhuman strength and inhuman twist of tendons. "You did."

"And he's a vampire, too?" She wiggled a finger over her shoulder at Sam, quelling the squeak in her voice by clearing her throat.

"As is your alleged sister," Marty said, rolling her head on her shoulders to work out the obvious kinks one would surely encounter when their bones crunched so they could change shape and take on their *werewolf* forms. "I'm the only full werewolf. Like we explained, Casey, who's not here tonight but will join us as soon as she can, is a demon, and Wanda's what we lovingly call a halfsie."

"Half vampire, half werewolf, BTW," Sam offered in a smugly in-the-know way. "I'm learning the lingo. You know, so I'll fit in with the clan."

Suck-ass.

Phoebe tried to focus on all the information she'd been given after they'd each shown her their unique, paranormal abilities. The contents of which included all the gory deets on each woman's accidental turn into a paranormal species, and their quest with OOPS to help others like them who had nowhere else to go when a crisis of this magnitude occurred.

She still wasn't quite sure she understood the entirety of their situations or how they'd fallen in love with the men who'd created their personal paranormal dramas, but she did get that it was real. She'd seen the reality of it. She wouldn't waste time denying what they'd shown her or even believing that her eyes were playing tricks on her.

That was all well and good.

But if it was real for *her* remained to be seen. There was no proof other than their word she'd soon be drinking blood and mind reading. "So let me be clear. You help people at this place called OOPS who've suffered a paranormal crisis, and all of you were accidents, including me and Sam?" Which left Sam where? In the cross-dressing paranormal slot?

Wanda slid into the chair near Phoebe and placed a reassuring hand on her arm. "We know firsthand what you're going through. As to Sam, he's suspect right now. It's clear he's vampire, but we have little information on how or why he got this way. We don't know what exactly happened to him, Phoebe. Sam's memories of what happened before he woke up with us are fleeting at this point. Like we told you, he was just dumped on our doorstep and he was unconscious. But we're all in for helping him figure it out. And naturally, we'll help you, too."

How shiny. Phoebe's head swiveled on her neck when she turned to face Nina. "Wait a minute. It's because of you and your outrageous reaction to my claim that I can't ever go out in daylight again?" Or dine at Bergdorf Goodman's or wear a cute bikini on the boardwalk at the Jersey Shore, or breathe, or feel her heartbeat quicken when she found the perfect outfit for a client.

Ah, but there was compensation. Soon she'd be able to read minds and fly.

Mucho badassery.

"Technically, it's because of me and my incisors," Sam offered, grinning a grin so delicious it actually made Phoebe shiver—sort of. "But I'm okay with you laying blame squarely on Nina. At this fragile point, I feel she can probably better handle your wrath than I can right now."

Nina rolled her beautiful eyes. "Oh, lay off the drama-queen bullshit. You can too go out. You just have to wear SPF gotrillion and two. But you'll probably be too tired to go out in daylight anyway. Vampires sleep during the day. All day, and we don't get out of our coffins till sunset. So I hope you're down with a good *Hoarders* marathon on late-night TV."

Phoebe blanched while her fingers tightened into a tension-filled fist. "You sleep in a coffin?"

Nina's smile was sly. She was clearly enjoying toying with her, and Phoebe'd stepped right into her trap. "And before you ask, because you look like the kind of chick who'd be thrilled right down to her stupid-ass pedicure about it. No. You won't sparkle in the sunlight."

"Oh, damn," Phoebe mocked. "And here I was all set to throw away my metallic body glitter and run off to join Team Edward."

Instead of taking Nina down a peg, Phoebe's smart remark appeared to only fuel her fire. "Well, it's like I told Fancy Sam here. You won't sparkle, but you will fucking fry."

Her slight panic began to take a dangerous turn toward full-on freak-out. "Fry?"

"Snap, crackle, pop," Sam quipped on a grin, planting his hands on his incredibly muscular thighs.

For the first time, Phoebe visibly cringed.

But Nina was paying little mind to anything but getting rid of her. "So I guess you need some time to absorb this, huh, *Phoebes*? Why don't you go do that shit in your own crib? You can give us a little jing-a-ling when you're all settled and past the oh-fuck-I-can't-see-my-reflection-anymore stage."

She couldn't see her reflection anymore? That wasn't just some ridiculous made-up Hollywood movie ploy?

Wanda jumped up and swatted Nina's shoulder, shooting her a sour look of disapproval. "She'll do no such thing. You know what the turn and subsequent adjustment to it is like. She needs round-the-clock support, as does our Sam."

Sam leaned into Phoebe again with a conspiratorial wink. "Nina cried when she found out she was a vampire. I heard Wanda say so. If *she* cried, I think you should rethink your pending departure."

Nina gave Sam a hard nudge to his shoulder. "For the last time, there was no fucking crying, but I'll make you cry if you make one more crack."

Sam's hands flew up in white-flag fashion. "You da man."

Wanda shot a stern finger in Nina's direction and pointed at a chair for her to sit in. "Okay, so here's where we're at. Clearly, you're both tougher than any of us. You've skipped several of the stages involved in accepting your new fate. I guess that means we move right along to teaching you both how to cope with the way of the vampire, and unfortunately, that means Nina's your most knowledge-able guide. But I promise we won't leave you alone with her."

Phoebe looked down at her wristwatch and shook her head in the negative while she rose to leave. "Do you have some kind of paperwork we can read? Maybe a brochure or a book of vampire etiquette? Because I have an early-morning meeting with a client I can't miss. Which means I need to go home and get a couple of hours sleep. I don't have time to attend the Vampire Academy for Noobs tonight."

"Fuck," Nina muttered, letting her head fall to her folded arms on the table in purposely evident disgust.

Phoebe's eyes flashed. "Fuck what?"

Wanda came to stand beside her, placing her arm around Phoebe's shoulder, the smile on her face warm and sympathetic. "I think what our most outspoken OOPS member means is, you're not exactly in the place we thought you were. This lifestyle you'll be forced to embrace isn't like adjusting to a new pair of shoes, Phoebe. It's so much more than that."

Nina shoved away from the table, letting her chair rock on two legs. "And cue the whine. Damn it, Wanda. I was so down with Sammy. He took this shit like some kinda champ. Now we'll be here all night while she pisses and moans until she passes out. We should have just left well enough the fuck alone."

Marty planted her hands on her hips and glared at Nina. "No truer words, Gladiator. But you created at least half of this problem, and the hell you're not going to help solve it. Whether she's really your relation or not. What would you have done if Greg had just left you to your own devices, nitwit? You'd be ashes. That's what. Now not another word out of you. You'll see this through to the end like a good vampire or I'll see your end."

Phoebe stared at Wanda head-on, her senses suddenly and inexplicably on fire. The struggle to maintain not just her cool but her ability to think of anything else but going home became a force to contend with.

She needed out and she needed out now. "I understand exactly what you're saying. I heard everything you said. I'm a vampire. I can't eat food anymore. I have to drink blood. I have no organs. I'm dead on the inside. But if I'm super-duper lucky, I'll fly just like my big sister, Nina, someday. I get it, and now I have to go home." Rather abruptly, she was overwhelmed, and when that occurred, she needed space.

Wanda's pink dappled cheeks puffed outward then deflated. "We've got trouble, ladies."

Nina was the first to rise, blocking Phoebe's path to the wide double doors with reluctant feet. "You can't go home, Phoebe."

Phoebe cocked her head, crossing her arms over her chest. "Look. I'm not sure if you've noticed, but I'm you only more cutting-edge fashion, less ghetto back-alley goth. Oh, and far less likely to use the word *fuck*. I'm not afraid of you like Sam over here. So if you thought you could stop me from leaving, rethink. Now move. Please. Or things could become very chaotic for you."

Sam's indignant grunt floated to her ears. The scrape of his shredded nylons rasping as he crossed his legs make Phoebe shudder. His expression was affronted. "I'm not afraid of her. I'm leery. There's a difference. A big one, thank you very much."

Nina cracked her jaw, and to any bystander, it was clear she was fighting to keep her rage in check, but it was clearest to Phoebe, who understood the struggle to maintain her quick temper and sharp tongue on a daily basis. That Nina had the nerve to claim they weren't related was like declaring Prada made hot dogs. But the proof of her legitimacy would have to wait for another day.

Like one where she didn't feel like she was on fire.

Nina's eyes flashed an emotion Phoebe recognized as sympathy, but she quickly let her thick eyelashes flutter to her cheeks in order to hide it. "Seriously, our differences and your crazy claim aside, cupcake, you can't go home—not without us. Shit's about to go down that you don't know how to deal with, and you'll need help. Our help. *My* help."

Phoebe's eyebrow rose to a new height of condescending even as her stomach revolted and her legs shook. "I said I'm going home."

Nina scrunched up her face, blocking her path. "Yeah. And I said you're not."

Sam rose to his feet now, too, putting a hand on Phoebe's shoulder to keep her from moving. A hand that created a multitude of reactions. Irritation, a strange sexy slither of pleasure, and more irritation. "It's in your best interest to listen to Nina. I know you don't like it, but you don't seem to be getting the big picture here. Now stay put until you do."

Whether it was Sam's demand that she remain or Nina's glare, she couldn't have said. The only thing Phoebe was capable of thinking about was how much she wanted to slug first Sam, then Nina and the word *home*.

Home. Home. Home.

And like the saying goes, sometimes you get what you wish for.

Because when she opened her eyes to unleash her fury on Sam for having the gall to order her to do anything, he wasn't there at all.

And neither was her gangster sister or her gangster sister's friends or the beautiful fireplace she'd so admired when she'd first opened her eyes at Nina's.

When she opened her eyes, she was standing in one of the rare kitchens in Manhattan that was bigger than a shoebox and affordable.

The kitchen she'd searched high and low for months in order to find.

The one where, if she listened to the Three Paranormal Musketeers, she'd no longer have any use for.

And that kitchen was hers.

CHAPTER 3

Mark, her roommate, business partner, and her best friend since grade seven when she'd punched Ernie Horowitz for calling him a queer, screamed a piercing squeal that continued to ring in her head long after it was over. "Jesus Christ in a pair of Choos, Phoebe! Warning, please, huh? I didn't even hear you come in. Are you trying to scare the wrinkles into me? Don't sneak up on me like that—especially when I'm in the middle of steaming my pores."

As Phoebe's eyes focused, she caught the tendrils of steam rising from the pot Mark hovered over on the stove. The scent of eucalyptus, normally pleasant to her nose, made her gag. Or dry heave. However you wanted to look at it.

The towel Mark had tented over his head fell to the floor when his gaze fell on her with openmouthed horror. He gasped. "What . . ."

Phoebe frowned, gripping the edge of the Formica countertop to keep from falling over. What now? Was there more after teleporting here like some other-dimensional space traveler? "What-what?" she asked, commending herself for keeping her voice steady.

He held his arm out straight; at the end of it was his hand mirror. The one he used to pluck his nostril hairs. He shoved it at her. His eyes were accusatory. They said she should know what. "That's what-what." Mark tapped the mirror for emphasis, his lips pursing.

Phoebe's eyes flew open wide and her hand went to her face with a whimpered mewl. Fangs. She had fangs. Big, gleaming white incisors that had just begun to make an appearance over her lower lip.

They were exactly like the fangs Nina had so blatantly flashed in her face when they'd given her the Cirque du Paranormal experience back at the castle. How did you explain fangs? Did you even try? And hadn't Nina said she'd never see her reflection again? After seeing her teeth, maybe that wasn't the boil on her ass she'd originally thought it would be. Her mind raced to put together an explanation, but Mark saved her from having to say anything.

Mark set the mirror down and gave her a look of admonishment. "Halloween's over, honey. And lay off the highlighter. You've gone overboard with your youthful glow and jumped into the *Bride of Chucky* ocean. It's creepy. And where have you been? It's almost midnight. You missed a perfectly fabulous tuna tartar with pumpkin risotto and steamed asparagus. You could have at least called, you dirty stay out," he chastised on a snicker, shooing her away from the counter with a flap of his hand to turn the stove off. "So was it a date with that guy Joey from the bodega? He's sweet on you, sunshine. I've got the extra half pound of pastrami to prove it. All I have to do is utter your name and he's all assholes and elbows at the meat slicer, shards of pig flying in the hopes I'll give him your number."

Phoebe slid her boots off, still stunned, but forcing herself to form words. "No. No Joey." She ran a hand over the kitchen wall just to be sure it was real. That she was really in her kitchen in lower Manhattan with the tiny balcony off their living room and the ridiculous painting of Cher hanging between the pictures of her and her mother.

"Wait," Mark said with hesitance, alarm in his voice, his sweet round face wary. "You didn't forget to come home, did you, honey?"

Most people would think that a strange question, but not her. Not since . . . "No," she replied, the word hushed but meant to reassure. "I didn't forget. I just got caught up."

Standing behind her, Mark rested his rounded chin on her shoulder. "Darling?"

His voice, in her ear, normally pleasant and nurturing, was maddeningly abrasive, leaving a residual ringing in its wake. "Yeah?" She wanted to scream the word, but managed to only whisper.

"Did the earth move for you or something tonight? Because you're behaving like I did after that delicious night I had with Raul in Meheeco," he mimicked a poor Spanish accent. "Sort of dazed and confused with just a hint of sinfully satiated." Mark clucked his tongue. The smile the memory wrought from him reflected fondness. "Remember that trip? Soft sand between our toes, mojitos in hand, festive, colorful beach wraps, waves lapping at our feet. Heeeaven," he sang. "We should go back—soon by the looks of you. Oh, and Penny called tonight. I told her you'd call her back." He dropped a kiss on her forehead and scooped up her boots, taking them to the small closet in the hall.

No sooner was she paying homage to the universe for keeping her from having to explain to Mark what was going on with her teeth and her complexion than her doorbell rang.

Phoebe had to jam a fist into her mouth to keep from screaming out loud the earsplitting pain that jangled her eardrums. Every nerve in her body was raw—raw like someone had used sandpaper on them.

"Who could that be so late? You don't think Helen fell again?" Mark ran for the door, worry creasing his round face. Helen was their elderly downstairs neighbor who refused to use a walker as per doctor's orders. Ornery and stubborn, she'd slipped and fallen last year, breaking her hip. Helen's husband, Otis, had run into them in the elevator, panicked and worried, and they'd offered to sit with the couple until the ambulance arrived.

Since then, they'd spent almost every Sunday dinner downstairs in the Gaglianos' apartment with the scent of mothballs and tantalizing homemade ziti surrounding them.

Phoebe managed to make her way to the end of the kitchen on ever-weakening legs when Mark stuck his head around the corner, grinning. "Eminem and the Unabomber's bride to see you," Mark said on a snicker, clearly referring to Nina's black hoodie and Sam, who must still be in drag. But she'd already known it was Nina and Sam. She'd smelled them the moment Mark had opened the door, and Wanda wasn't far behind, if her nose was correct.

That stopped her in her tracks. Sweet Jesus in Manolos. She was applying scents to people who were more than two hundred feet from her. Her terror ratcheted up yet another jolting notch.

Phoebe fought the swirl of colors before her eyes, pinching Mark's arm when she clung to it to keep him from going back to the front door. "That's *her*," she whispered to him. Mark had helped her when she'd decided to find Nina. He'd logged just as many frustrating hours at the computer as she had.

The look of horror on his face would have made her giggle if not for the fact that she was having trouble holding herself up. "Her-*her*? Your long-lost sister her?" He put a hand over his mouth and whispered from behind it, "Shut the front door."

"You know what this reminds me of?"

Mark nodded with vigor. He knew the soap opera reference she was referring to. "I'm right there with you. It's just like the time when Fabiana Jones found out she had not one but two sisters separated from her at birth. Oh, Holy mother of all things melodramatic.

Really, who could believe that guttersnipe Tanya from the planet Ghetto was the ultra-swank Fabiana's sister?"

Phoebe shushed him. "It's inconceivable, right? We're so different."

"Well, you're not the Doublemint Twins, count on that. So who's the dish? Never mind. I just want to know how you two can genetically be related. Oh, dear God in heaven. How . . ." he sputtered in wonder, his blue eyes wide.

"I know, I know. We're poles apart. She's like Dreary Barbie dressed for the fashion apocalypse. Genetics are LOL, huh?"

"Yeah, totally ROFLMAO those genetics. Funny, funny, funny," Nina said on a grunt, pushing her way past Phoebe and picking Mark up only to set him down by their small kitchen table.

She rounded on Phoebe, cornering her against the pantry door. "You need to feed. You look like shit. Sit. I brought something that will make you feel better. We'll talk about what the hell that was back at my house after you feed."

Mark tapped Nina's shoulder, making her turn to face him. No matter what, Mark always had her back. "Feed? Is that what thugs call it these days? Where I come from we *dine*."

Nina's nostrils flared, alerting Phoebe to the potential disaster Mark was headed for. She wrapped a finger around the collar of his polo shirt, stretching the dark blue material as she did, and lifted him up as though he were lighter than the proverbial feather. "Where I come from, we *dine* on worms like you." She waved a dismissive hand under Mark's nose. "Now go take a bubble bath and listen to some Liza or something, and leave us the hell alone. We have shit to do."

Mark crossed his arms over his chest in defiance, even with his slippered feet dangling. If Mark was nothing else, he was no coward. Phoebe knew he was more than likely petrified that a woman had scooped him up off the ground like he was nothing more than a stray sock, but she also knew he'd never let anyone see him sweat.

Eye to eye with Nina, he let his eyebrows rise in full-blown diva arrogance and his voice only held a hint of a quiver. "The hell I will. You're in my home, accosting my BFF. Not on my watch, pale-face."

Sam grumbled his disapproval from behind. "Nina. Put him down." Sam poked his head around her shoulder and gave her a hopeful grin. "Please," he tacked on.

Nina dropped Mark with a thud, the slap of his slippers echoing in the silence.

Sam shot Nina a grateful, approving smile. "Now, uh, Mark, is it?"

"Single, is it?" Mark cooed with a flirty wink.

Sam dragged a hand through his hair, *fed up* written all over his chiseled, smeared made-up face. Yet, his words were patient and served up with a kind tone. "Look. Could we maybe go sit down in the living room and let Phoebe and her sister talk? I promise you I won't let anything happen to her."

Mark walked his fingers up Sam's muscled forearm. "Only if you tell me where you bought that dress. It's cute, yet sexy and fun all at once, handsome. I can think of three of our clients off the top of my head who could wear that."

Sam's teeth, now back to their normal state, visibly clenched, and the muscles in his jaw twitched. "Please." He waved a hand in the direction of the living room to encourage Mark to exit.

Mark paused and reached for Phoebe's hand, searching her face. "You okay, kitten?"

She gave his hand a squeeze. "Fine. Go. Peruse the fresh meat," she teased, making herself smile at him.

"Now *that* I can do. And take those things out of your mouth. They look strangely real and it's freaking me out." He blew her a kiss and skipped off behind Sam.

Phoebe plastered her body to the pantry door, praying it was enough to hold her up, and confronted Nina. "What. The. Hell. Was. That? One minute I was in Castle Dracula, the next I was here in my kitchen. I want explanations and I want them now. What did you do to me?"

Phoebe's ears noted the front door opening again and then Wanda was suddenly in her line of vision, blurry, but as elegant as ever. She clamped a hand on Nina's shoulder and gave her a yank backward. "This conversation will wait until you feed, and, yes, by feed I mean drink blood. You know, that beverage you so flippantly chose to ignore back at Nina's? It's your beverage of choice from now on, kiddo. And if you give me a hard time about it, I won't just make you feed, I'll pry your mouth open with my toes like the Jaws of Life and dump it down your throat. So no arguments, because Auntie Wanda's had it. One of you was enough. Two of you is like loony day camp. *Now. Feed.*" She handed Phoebe a bag that looked like one of those sippy drinks she saw dangling from children's mouths at the park.

But it wasn't the orange sunburst party-in-a-cardboard-carton juice box she was used to seeing. It was blood. *Blood.* Just the scent of it drove her mad. There was a distinct moment when she literally tasted the coppery tang of it on her tongue—salivated at the very thought of it trickling down her throat.

And then she blanched. Blood. It was abhorrent and enticing rolled together in one sick, vile, disgustingly appealing package.

Then why, why, why did it sing to her a siren's song of bliss, which under normal circumstances, only a slice of New York blueberry cheesecake could evoke? She tried to gulp back the distaste the image of her favorite dessert wrought and found she wasn't capable. Of gulping.

OMG.

Nina's eyes flashed amusement from over Wanda's shoulder while she watched the play of emotions skitter across Phoebe's face. Almost as though she was waiting for the opportunity to call Phoebe a chicken.

Chicken this. She'd gone to college. Nobody, not even to this day, did boilermakers like she did. She was legend at NYU.

Chugalug, baby.

Grabbing the packet from Wanda with trembling hands, Phoebe yanked the straw out, held it to her mouth, and squeezed every last drop from the tiny hole until she'd wrung it dry. Then she threw it on the floor like a discarded dirty whore, stomping her foot on it in territorial ownership.

A surge of power so revitalizing, so invigorating, slithered along her raw nerves, soothing them and leaving her blissfully sated.

And then everything was clear again. Nina's beautiful face came into focus, her lips in the form of a sneer sharp and crisp, her eyes so black they were like pieces of coal. Wanda, who brought to mind words like *stately* and *collected*, smiled her approval, each laugh line on either side of her mouth jumping out at Phoebe's now perfect vision. She rubbed Phoebe's arm. "Better, right?"

"Better," Phoebe mumbled with reluctance. Weirdly so, but definitely better.

Wanda's smile was warm and approving. She reminded Phoebe so much of her mother, not only in the way she nurtured you one moment and scolded you when necessary the next, but in the way she took such great care in her appearance. Her mother had always been meticulous about her appearance. She'd dressed like she was going out, even when she wasn't.

Phoebe remembered her words of advice well: "You just never know what might come up, Phoebes. So in order to be prepared, you should always look your best." What Phoebe later realized was her mother always wanted to be ready for her father Joe. He came into town more often than not without warning, and her mother prettied up on the off chance he'd call and take them out to the diner for dinner or ice cream.

Wanda took her by the hand and led her to a chair at the kitchen table. "And now we need to decide where to go from here, Phoebe. So please, sit and let's talk. We genuinely only want to help you. Despite Nina's brash behavior, the last thing we want to do is frighten you."

Stinging pierced Phoebe's eyes with the familiar onset of tears. Tears that refused to flow, for which she was grateful with Nina staring her down, just daring her to curl up into a little ball of snot-dripping, whining baby. "How did you find me?"

"I went through your purse like all good thugs do. You left it at my house when you tripped the light fantastic," Nina said, sarcasm in her every word as she hoisted herself up on Phoebe's small countertop and wiggled her fingers at Phoebe's silver cat, Optimus, who'd finally made an appearance. He hopped up into Nina's lap and began to twirl his traitorous tail around her stroking fingers with a humming purr.

"What is happening?" Phoebe implored, the quiver in her voice making her angry with herself for showing her fear, especially in front of her tougher-than-shoe-leather sister.

Wanda shook her head, rolling one of the fresh lemons Phoebe had put in a decorative bowl just this morning under her palm. "If what you mean by that is teleporting yourself, I don't know exactly, Phoebe. Nina can't teleport herself anywhere. Like we said, this is the list. She can fly. She can read minds. She's stronger than the NFL as a whole. She can be so much stubborn, difficult bitch you want to choke her, but she can't do what you did. Which means investigation is in order."

"And how do we go about investigating something like this?" Did you make an appointment with the Center for Paranormal Diseases? Was there a specialist in teleportation?

Wanda's glance at her was wary. "First and foremost, we keep a low profile, Phoebe. You'll soon find this isn't like the movies where ET gets to phone home and everyone skips a happy circle at discovering *Close Encounters of the Third Kind*. There is no definitive happy ending to this lifestyle. Just a happy medium where we make our way in the human world much the way we did before, but with a great deal of caution. No one takes our shapeshifting seriously because no one believes it really exists. That's why we can get away with OOPS. We get a lot of crank calls. More often than not, people think we're a cult who just calls themselves shapeshifters and live wannabe paranormal lives. No one really believes Nina has to drink blood in order to stay erect. If the population at large really knew the truth—if they saw—we'd be lab rats in no time flat. So living this way sometimes involves fibbing."

"No, Wanda. We don't fib, we tell bald-faced lies," Nina corrected with devilish glee while she cuddled Optimus. "You know, like you lie to that crazy bitch you and Marty both go to for a leg waxing every other flippin' day. Tell her what you told that poor, confused, non-English-speaking cosmetician, Wanda. You told her both you and Marty have some rare disease that accelerates the hair growth on your legs. You even told her you met in a clinical trial for a hair-removal hormone. You don't fib. You fucking lie. Big-big lies, baby. All day long. All day strong."

Wanda sucked in her cheeks, letting her chin drop to her chest. "Yes, Nina. Thank you. This lifestyle does mean you sometimes have to be creative. And you have to keep track of your creativity. There's also the bit about keeping your abilities to yourself. Which means we can't have you teleporting out in a crowd. And it also means we need to understand how you can control it and help you learn how to manage it."

"And we do that how?" Phoebe asked.

Wanda's lips thinned. "We find the source, aka the biter."

Phoebe looked out the small window of her fourth-floor apartment, wincing as the glare of traffic lights passed by. "The source . . ."

"Yes. The woman who we think is responsible for biting Sam is the source," Wanda said. "Whatever abilities she has she gave to Sam, and by proxy, now you have them, too."

Phoebe was astonished, and she didn't bother to hide it. "A *woman* bit Sam?"

"Yeah. The one-night stand woman."

"Nina! Hush," Wanda reprimanded. "That's no one's business but Sam's. Client profiles should be confidential, mouth."

Phoebe was taken aback. "So Sam's not a cross-dressing gay man?"

"I think the one-night stand with a woman implies he likes chicks, but he might wish he'd switched to the other team after this shit. He was wearing the girlie crap because he went to a Halloween party. That's where he was bitten," Nina informed her.

As thoughts started to formulate in her clearing brain, so did the questions. "So," Phoebe began, casting her gaze upon Nina, "you can't transport yourself, but you have other um, abilities? What does this mean? Why, if I'm a vampire just like you, do I have different abilities? Are there different breeds of you people running around?"

Nina stirred on the counter, shrugging her shoulders. "Fuck if I know. I don't know a single vampire in our clan who can do what you did. Doesn't teleportation require you to use your noggin? What was going on in all that air between your ears when it happened?"

"I was thinking I wanted to get the hell away from you and go home," Phoebe said from the side of her mouth.

Nina gripped the edge of the countertop with her fingers as a blatantly obvious call for patience. "So all you did was think about home and you ended up here?"

Phoebe nodded, pushing her mussed hair behind her ear. "I just thought the word *home* and boom."

Wanda shook her head in awe. "Amazing," she whispered, placing a hand over her mouth.

Phoebe fought the fear this added to her already precarious situation. The situation that had finally forced her hand in looking for Nina in the first place. "So what do I do, paranormal counselors? How can you possibly hope to help me, if you don't have someone who can show me how to use it? How to control it? What if I think up Bora Bora or some other crazy place I can't get back from?"

And what if she wished up the wrong destination at the wrong

time and couldn't find her way back? She'd had an episode or two
in the not too distant past where she'd ended up somewhere unfamiliar, frightened and alone. But now that she could possibly transport herself anywhere, who knew what could happen. She had to
tell them the whole of the reason she'd sought Nina out.

But doing that meant she'd have to bear witness to eyes round
with pity and sympathetic words. At this stage of the game, and with
Nina so reluctant to acknowledge her familial tie to her, Phoebe
couldn't bear it. More than likely, Nina would think it a ploy to
worm her way into her life through sympathy anyway.

Nina scoffed, crossing her long legs at the ankles and giving Optimus a scratch under his chin. "I get the impression you don't think
about much but clothes and shit to decorate your face. So if we lose
you, we'll get right on that shiz and send out the rescue dogs in the
direction of a Macy's white sale—or maybe the mall."

Phoebe's eyebrow rose. "In that case, we should be glad it's not
you who can teleport. I imagine picking through a Jersey dump to
find your skinny butt would prove unpleasant."

"Oh!" Wanda exclaimed on a laugh, clapping her hand against
her thigh. "Touché. Now enough, girls. We have things to do. The
first of which is getting a list of the names of people who attended
that party Sam went to. Whoever it was that turned Sam must have
this ability—and if we can find her, maybe we can get some answers."

"She dumped the dude at our door, Wanda. Do you really think
she still has her engraved invitation from the ball in her pumpkin
turned coach? You know, right next to her glass slippers and
mouse driven coach? Jesus. Don't be a moron. This shit ain't sittin'
right with me at all. First of all, I don't think this was the accident
Sam said it was. Or thinks he heard her say it was. And second, not
even Darnell knows anyone who can do what Frou-Frou Barbie
does." Nina held up her BlackBerry to show a text from someone
named Darnell. A text Phoebe saw as clearly as she did the hand that
clenched into that tight fist of stress in her lap.

Wanda patted Phoebe's arm, giving it a light squeeze. "First, we don't know how Sam got on our doorstep. We don't have any proof it was the woman from the party. Now, Phoebe, don't fret. We've dealt with the unknown before. Just recently, the unknown being a veterinarian turned cougar. We'll figure this out, Phoebe. Somehow. Until then, you need to stay close to us. So I hope you have a spare dark hovel for Nina to roost in."

"The. Hell. I'm staying here with Barbie and Skipper, Wanda. I can keep an eye on her from home."

Phoebe bristled, pulling her arm from Wanda's reach. "I don't need a babysitter. Especially not one who looks like she's fresh out of *The Shining*."

Nina narrowed her eyes and clenched her jaw. Yet, she said nothing.

Wanda rose from her chair and stretched. "The hell you won't, Nina. Phoebe and Sam both need twenty-four-seven at this point. That's what all our clients get from OOPS."

"But I didn't hire you," Phoebe stated, unsure if it was a good idea for she and Nina to be in such close quarters.

Wanda cocked her head with a smile. "In order to hire us, you'd have to pay us. We're nonprofit. That aside, you claim to be Nina's *sister*. No way we let family go it alone. Especially when alone means having no idea where you'll scamper off to if we're not keeping a close eye on you. Add into the mix Sam and whether or not he can teleport, too, and we have one big paranormal launch pad just waiting to shoot off a spaceship. So we stay. Adjust. Deal. Oh, and learn to love your Auntie Wanda." She winked on a giggle.

"We don't have any proof she's my sister, Wanda. So clam up," Nina growled.

A rustle of paper caught everyone's attention when Mark breezed in. He held up the DNA test Phoebe had paid a fortune for in front of Nina's face, giving it a sharp snap. "Au contraire, Crabby Patty. We do have proof Phoebe's Joe Blackman's daughter. So unless you're claiming Joe wasn't your father, guess what? Surprise! You have a sister. Though, I struggle to comprehend why she'd want anyone to know the worst thing since Manson was related to her. Either way, she doesn't just have a DNA test. She has pictures of her with her father and all sorts of things to give to you so you'd know she was telling the truth! So why don't *you* clam up? And while you're at it, lay off Phoebe or it'll be me and you and a vat of green Jell-O with boxing gloves. Phoebe's had a really rough time of it lately, and she's not wel—"

"Phoebe's fine!" Phoebe cried, rushing to Mark's side. She gave his arm a squeeze, prying the paper from his hands and folding it into the neat square she'd left it in on her dresser. "I'm fine, Mark. Swear it. Please. Go back into the living room. Finish accosting poor Sam with your charm," she teased, hoping to divert his attention away from Nina and back to the prime piece of hunk.

Mark rolled his eyes, planting a hand on his hip. "Please. Barked up that tree only to find out it was a sturdy oak, not the cherry blossom I'd hoped for. He's so straight he's like a flat iron. We had a total moment of man-candor. So forget it. Though, he's a sparkling conversationalist. Unlike the grunter over here." Mark shot a finger in Nina's direction and she promptly snapped her teeth at him. "Did you know he works for O-Tech? He's a scientist. With a job. I don't think I need to say any more. Now that he's up for grabs, I suggest you don't spend any time lollygagging in here with your evil twin and go get you some manly man."

Sam's head poked around the corner of the kitchen, dark, mussed, uncomfortably delicious. "You rang?" he said with a teasing grin. He'd pulled off his eyelashes and nails and washed his face free of his makeup.

And it would have taken Phoebe's breath away if not for the fact that her breathing was on the fritz.

Sam's face.

It was lean and sharply angled along his jaw where stubble dark-ened it. He had clear eyes the color of melting chocolate that zeroed in on hers with a twinkle. The lashes framing them were thick and dark, making Phoebe green with envy. His mouth was a sensuous line of delicious with a deep dimple in his chin directly beneath it.

And it caught her off guard. She'd been so convinced he was gay, she hadn't spent much time dwelling on how ruggedly handsome he truly was.

"So, are we good in here, ladies?" he inquired. "Because these heels are killing me. I don't know if I have it in me to break you two up in heels."

Nina hopped off the counter, tucking Optimus under her arm and flicking Mark in the shoulder before turning her back on him to face Sam. "Oh, we're golden, homeslice." She held two, undoubt-edly sarcastic, thumbs up.

"Good to hear. So what's next?" he asked, bracing himself against the doorframe.

Mark cocked his dark shortly cropped head in question and planted his hands on his hips. "Next? And for the record, what exactly is rock-hard man doing with you ladies? In fact, as I recall, pale-face said something about feeding, but I see no napkins and plates. Not that this surprises me. She *is* a heathen, but I don't think I have all the pieces of the puzzle here. Something's just not adding up." He crossed one arm over his chest, balancing his other elbow on top of it. From behind the fingers of his hand, he said, "So why are you all here so late, and why do you have a man dressed in drag with you?"

"I call we show Mark why we're here, Wanda." Nina slapped Mark on the back, making him jolt forward and cough.

Sam held up a hand to thwart Nina. He captured her in what would appear to anyone else to be a fond embrace. "I say we don't do anything *rash*, Nina."

Nina gazed up at him, her eyes peering out from her hoodie. "Are you telling me what to do, Gigantor?" She clucked her tongue, waiting.

Sam leaned down toward Nina, making Phoebe shiver as though she were the one he was so near. Even in his red dress, with his gel bra peeking over the top, since he'd gotten past the initial shock of this vampire thing, his presence had become commanding. "Never. I'm simply making a suggestion out of love and the idea that Mark probably likes the term *sane* when referencing his mental state."

Wanda pushed her way between the two, placing a hand on Sam's shoulder. A hand Phoebe found herself wishing was hers. "He's Phoebe's roommate, Sam. Under normal circumstances, we have a pretty strict code about this kind of thing in that we hope people won't ask, and we won't have to tell. But there are several exceptions. Mark's going to have to be one of them. Of course, it's totally up to Phoebe's discretion."

Phoebe winced. She couldn't even get Mark to keep his eyes open during an episode of *Fringe*. How would he react to *The Exorcist* and grown-up *Twilight* all rolled into one? "Maybe we shouldn't. I . . . He's . . . Mark's . . ."

Mark jammed his face in hers, rolling his head on his neck, clearly sensing her misgivings. "Mark's what, girlfriend? And what is Princess Di talking about? What do you hope people won't ask?" His voice began to rise, much like it had when they were kids and he thought she was keeping a secret from him. Mark loved a good secret. More than he loved *What Not to Wear* or even the Jonas Brothers.

"Mark," Phoebe croaked. "I need you to sit. On a chair. And listen to me. Like really listen without interruption." She planted a hand on his shoulder and walked him backward to the chair Wanda had abandoned. He plunked down with a confused look, his blue eyes concerned.

Taking his hand, she placed it over her heart. The plan being to show him her organs no longer worked.

But a loud crash against their apartment door prevented her from giving him an explanation. Dropping Mark's hand, she lunged for the door; her feet moved so quickly she stumbled to keep them under her.

She skidded for the door, peeking through the peephole to see nothing but the top of what appeared to be a woman's head, slumped against the wall. Flipping open the multiple locks Mark had insisted they have, she stepped back into Sam's hard chest when she made room to let the door swing wide.

A heavy thud followed the swish of the opening door and then Sam was kneeling at her feet, muttering under his breath. Words Phoebe clearly heard but didn't understand the relevance of.

Nina came up from the rear, stopping short behind Sam, who hovered over an unconscious woman's body. He rolled her over and hissed when her fangs were revealed.

Nina let her cheeks puff outward. "For the love of fuck—another one? Jesus Christ in Grand Central Station. How many of them are there? It's like raining goddamn vampires."

Phoebe's eyes were wide. Yeah. How many of them were there? Surely there were only so many sets of fangs loose in New York City?

"Vampires?" Mark squeaked, latching on to Wanda's arm.

But no one paid any attention to him for the commotion the woman had created.

Sam scooped her up and carried her to the couch, draping her on it with a gentleness Phoebe couldn't help but note. The Victorian-era dress she wore was filthy and shredded, covered in streaks of something greasy and black. The lacing on her bodice hung open in gaps, revealing the curve of her generous breasts.

Her hair, the color of midnight, tangled and matted, splayed across the creamy beige of Phoebe's couch. Her face was so pale the blue tint of her veins was visible beneath her milky skin. Her cheekbones were gaunt and deeply sunken, making Phoebe wonder if she'd eaten in the last ten years or so. Her lips, ashen and dry, were cracked, and her fangs protruded from her lower lip, pinching the fullness of them.

Sam lifted her hand, concern on his handsome face. The mystery woman's exposed flesh was covered in some sort of angry red rash. "What the hell?"

At the sound of Sam's voice, her eyes fluttered open. Glassy and so beautifully violet even Nina grunted her apparent appreciation. "You . . ." she whispered hoarse and gravelly.

Sam ran his large hand over her forehead with tender fingers. "*How* did you find me?"

Her eyes began drifting downward, but not before she whispered, "Smelled. I smelled . . . had to find you before . . ."

Nina knelt down by the side of the couch and stared at the strange woman for a long, painfully silent moment. Pressing the back of her hand against the woman's forehead, she shook her head. "Fuck, she's on fire, and I can't get anything from inside her head. She just keeps repeating your name over and over in her mind. She knows your name! Who *is* she, Sammy?"

Sam paused, the lines of worry on his forehead creasing. "The woman I met at the party."

Wanda emitted a small gasp, pulling Mark closer to her protective embrace. Pale and somber, Mark trembled against Wanda. Phoebe might have laughed at the image the pair projected if not for the severity of their situation. Mark, at least a good seven inches taller than Wanda, plastered to her side like she was the raft of life. Wanda, sturdy as any oak, held Mark up.

Again, the woman's eyes fluttered open, riveting Phoebe's stunned gaze back on her. Her stare was a direct connection to Sam's. "Party. I'm sorry . . . So sorry. Mistake. Accident . . . swear . . ."

Sam leaned in close to her, letting his ear rest in the vicinity of her mouth. She reached out to him, grabbing fistfuls of the front of his dress, her lips moving without any sound coming from them.

The knuckles on her hand strained, pushing against her skin until Phoebe thought they'd burst from her flesh.

"Who are you?" Sam rasped, the muscles in his neck straining as the effort he made to keep from shaking the information out of her became clear. His free fist clenched into a tight ball. "*Why* did you do this to me?"

Her head began to thrash against the couch while she struggled against Sam, her face a wreath of pain, her violet eyes filled with some unseen fear. "I . . . listen. *Please*. To me. Help. I want to . . ." She moved her head back and forth, frowning as though she couldn't get the words right. "O-Tech . . . Not long now . . ." As suddenly as she'd begun to flay about, it was over, and she slipped back to wherever she kept retreating, slumping against the couch with a hard jolt.

Sam's hands cupped her face, brushing the hair from her eyes, he lifted her prone upper body. "Not long until what?" he asked, the urgent rise of his voice sending a tremor of more fear skittering up Phoebe's spine.

And then there was silence from the woman. So chilling, so still, it left an acrid aftertaste in Phoebe's mouth. She ran her tongue over her lips in nervous contemplation.

What the hell was going on? Demons and werewolves, mind reading and teleportation. Vampiric one-night stands gone horribly wrong, and blood drinking and a mystery woman with a rash. All of it began to crash down around her. Phoebe fought to hang on to the here and now, clenching her teeth and willing herself to stay conscious.

No one moved. Not even Nina, who watched the woman with concerned eyes while she ran soothing circles over her skin. Mark's labored breathing became the only sound in the room, a harsh but rhythmic rise and fall of his chest.

Sam's eyes flashed worry. He leaned back in toward her again, his next words filled with the frustration she knew he was experiencing. "Not long until what? I don't know what you mean!"

Like a shooting iron ball from a cannon, the woman bolted upright. "Until you diiieeee!" she screamed in an agonizing wail before collapsing.

Yet, this time when she fell back to the couch, she didn't lay still. She writhed in an excruciating dance of horrified screams, slapping at her flesh as though her skin had suddenly become an insufferable suit of armor she had to rid herself of.

Her arms flailed, clapping against Sam's skin when he attempted to hold her still. She tore at him, rearing up and bucking against his chest. Red welts began to appear on Sam's ruddy cheeks where she scratched at him like a wild animal.

But Sam held her firm, refusing to let go, forgetting his own pain in favor of this stranger's safety.

Nina came around the arm of the couch in a flash of color, placing her hands on either side of the woman's head, hovering near her, whispering soothing words. Her eyes sought Wanda's from over the top of Sam's head, and they held a frantic question.

But Mark voiced it when he yelled with a terrified, trembling squeal, "What. The. Hell?"

"I don't know how much longer we can hold her, Wanda!" Nina howled. "What the fuck is going on?"

Wanda shoved Mark behind her with so much force he toppled backward, crashing into their small antique buffet and slamming against the wall. "Stay back!" Wanda ordered over her shoulder at him.

But all eyes fell to the woman when she roared, her mouth falling open with the force of the howl's ejection from her throat. It was so much like *The Exorcist*, Phoebe, even in her heightened state of terror, wondered if Mark wouldn't pass out from the fear. She rushed to his side, scooping him up like he was nothing more than a dirty sock left lying on the floor. She propped him up against the wall, then flew across the room to aid Nina and Sam.

Her eyes met Nina's over the woman's screams, and in that moment, she saw the tiniest hint of admiration for her. Phoebe wrapped her arms around the woman's legs, throwing her torso on her to keep her from crashing to the floor.

Yet keeping her from harm turned out to be the least of their worries.

She spewed one final scream of agony, long and eerily high, and then there was a crack, brittle and harsh, punctuating the room in an exclamation point, followed by an ear-splitting tear.

Of flesh.

And bone.

Like some weird time-lapse photography you might see on the Discovery Channel, the woman's hair went from stunningly blue black to gray. The strands became wispy and drifted from her head like cobwebs, floating off and disappearing.

Horror washed over Phoebe when her flesh began to fall away from her snapping bones, turning to ash, crumbling as though she were made of stone.

She was withering, Phoebe's brain screamed, aging and decomposing right before their eyes.

Mark's high-pitched scream of fear was the last thing Phoebe heard before the woman turned to dust.

Phoebe fought the dizzy rushes of panic and sank back on the couch, catching sight of the pile of ashes on her couch.

Now that would definitely leave a stain.

"Sam?"

"Phoebe."

"Let me clean those scratches," Phoebe offered from behind him, pushing her eyes downward to the floor to avoid the strange lust his broad back stirred in her. This was without a doubt the most inappropriate of times to find she was physically attracted to a man. "She really got you good."

He lifted his dark head from his position over the sink and looked into the mirror; his left eyebrow rose in response to his lack of reflection. "I think that's taken care of," he remarked, dry and tired. "At least it feels like it is. I can't tell for sure because I can't see myself."

Phoebe's head shot up, her eyes straying over Sam's shoulder to glimpse his jaw. He had no reflection, but she did. Wow. Sam also had no scratches. Her jaw unhinged much the way it would at a half-off MAC makeup sale.

"Yay, vampire," he drawled.

The left side of her mouth lifted in a smirk in response. "Yeah. Booyah. I'd get my pom-poms and make up a cheer or something, but my thinking cap's in the shop right now."

Sam rubbed a knuckle over his forehead. "I want to be freaked out. I should be freaked out. Yet I find myself not only horrified but amazed that I just self-healed." He shook his head in bewilderment, turning it from side to side with short jerks.

Phoebe reached out to run a finger over the place where a deep scratch had cut across his sharp cheekbone in an angry slash just twenty minutes ago.

It was gone and in its place, the clear, pale reminder of their new state. She snatched her hand back, tucking it under her arm with a stern mental reminder to her fingers to quit straying where they didn't belong. "Mark mentioned what you do for a living. That you're more amazed by something so astounding, so unbelievable rather than drooling and rocking in a corner ranks you high on the Trekkie list of all-time sci-fi geeks. I imagine you'll be given your own *Enterprise* as a reward for stoicism."

Sam chuckled, deep and resonant in her small, mint green and white bathroom with the mosaic tiled floor and claw-foot antique tub. "I think my own spaceship isn't as out of the realm of my possibilities after what's happened tonight."

The easy moment between them passed and reality settled back into the pit of her stomach. "I think you're right. So why do you suppose I can see my reflection but you can't see yours?"

"The Great and Powerful Vampire Oz decided it was more likely you'd miss seeing yourself in the mirror than I would?"

"Follow the yellow brick road," she murmured.

Sam ran his wide hand over his hair and turned to face her. "Is Mark all right?"

Phoebe had changed into a pair of jeans and a long camel-colored pullover sweater. She plucked at the front of it, guilt for exposing Mark to this without even a little warning at a premium. "Define *all right.* If you mean does he still know who he is and what year we're in, then, yes. He's all right. Was picking that information out of all the other babbling he's doing easy? Then, no. He's not all right."

Sam grimaced, his concern for others warming her from the inside. "Will he be?"

She managed to smile up at him. "Mark's not as weak as he appears right now. It takes him about a week to get over even a horror film that's just a little scary. When we saw *A Nightmare on Elm Street* for the first time, I thought he'd never sleep again. But he did—it took the lights on and some Prozac, I think, but he did. So I'm guessing with this being a reality, it might take some time for it to sink in."

"So at least *two* weeks' recuperation?" Sam teased.

"And a few hours at a good day spa with an extra-long massage."

Sam gazed down at her, his chocolaty eyes intense, his scent warm and inviting. "I'm sorry, Phoebe. None of this would have happened if not for me."

Phoebe's lips pursed. "I'm trying to be the bigger person and not blame. But if forced to call names, none of this would have happened if not for Raging Bull."

"Oh, stop trying to butter me the fuck up by calling me nice things behind my back and get out in the living room," Nina cackled in her ear, making her jump. Nina stopped short when her gaze went to the mirror. "Holy shit. Wouldn't it just figure that out of the two of you, Glamour Puss Barbie can still see her reflection? This is officially most-us fucked-upp-ed-us. Somethin' just ain't sittin' right. You two are like outsider vampire."

Sam barked a laugh—one Phoebe didn't share. "You're so inclusive, Nina. It makes me squishy on the inside."

"Yeah? Well, save that shit for later. Right now, Phoebe's BFF found a piece of paper with information on it or some shit when he was sweeping up the dead chick. He's pretty productive in his heightened state of freak. I should bring him back to the castle and let him dust the shit out of my torture rack. All those damned little nails are a bitch to clean around."

Phoebe's eyes narrowed in disgust at how cavalier she was being, but she pushed her way past Nina who stomped off to help Wanda in the kitchen and headed toward the living room, where Mark had indeed donned his apron, feather duster, and Swiffer. "Mark?"

He held up a hand for dramatic pause, hitching his jaw. "Do. Not. I'm just not ready." He ran the Swiffer along the underside of the chest they used as a coffee table with a frantic swipe.

"We have to talk sometime," she coaxed, smiling sweetly at him.

Mark threw up his middle finger at her. "Like. Hell. We don't ever have to talk about vampires and blood and fangs and women who cremate on command on my Jennifer Convertible!"

Phoebe winced, deciding on another tack. "You know what this is like?"

"A Wes Craven movie?" he squeaked.

"It's like an adventure, Mark. Remember how just the other day we were sitting around over chocolatinis all wishing for something to jump-start the humdrum rut we're in?"

Mark planted his hands on his Dockers-clad hips, his eyes wide. "*Jump-start?* This was more like being attached to a live electrical wire and jumping into the pool at the Y. When I said we needed a break from our routine, I was thinking more along the lines of, I dunno . . . spelunking or ceramic classes, Phoebe. Not a dead woman and Emo-licious in there!"

"You know what else this is like?"

His finger shot up to stab at the air between them. "*Do not* give me one of your crazy soap opera references. This isn't like anything on *Chances* or *Connections* or even the thank-God-someone-put-it-out-of-its-long-overdue-misery *Edge of Eternity*."

He was right. Even the *Edge of Eternity* couldn't top this. "Did Wanda and Nina have the chance to explain this to you?"

His head bobbed vigorously. "Oh, they explained. Yes, they did.

I heard all about their accidents and puppy dogs, dentists, exotic cats, and trips to hell. I learned cute new catchphrases I'm sure would be trending topics for crazy on Twitter given an opportunity. I heard, miss. Oh, yes, I did!"

She shot him a mournful glance, clasping her hands together in front of her. "So you get that I'm a vampire now? That, among other things, I'll never eat tuna tartar again?"

"Don't be such a silly. You'll be too busy drinking blood and reading minds to partake in my insignificant tuna tartar." Mark swatted at her with the feather duster, his words squeaky and watery.

Overwhelmed, Phoebe threw herself at him, wrapping her arms around his waist and squeezing his soft middle tight. She pressed her ear to his heartbeat, steady and sure. "I'm sorry. I didn't mean for this to happen or to get you involved. I'm still not even sure *how* it happened. I'll make the trauma up to you somehow. Maybe a facial or a massage? Wait. I know. I'll take bathroom duty for the next year."

Mark sighed against the top of her head. "How about a good brain bleach? You know, to wipe the god-awful images from my head?"

There was no making up for the kind of trauma she'd inflicted on him—even if she had no way of knowing it was going to happen to begin with. "I'll think of something. Promise. But until then, I really need you to stick by me this time. Now more than ever."

His grating sigh penetrated her eardrum, but he dropped a kiss on the top of her head. "Don't be ridiculous. Where else would I stick if not to you?" Mark patted her on the back and deliberately set her aside. "Now get off of me and look at this piece of paper I found over by the door where Vampirella was. She must have had it on her. It has O-Tech's letterhead on it." He pulled out a wrinkled dirty note from the pocket of his pants, palming it to her. "Go decipher it with that hunk of a man and let me process. And by *process* I mean someone's going to have their eye shadows alphabetized when all's said and done tonight."

Phoebe let her shoulders relax for a moment, relieved. Mark was organizing. A sure sign he was officially on the road to recovery.

"And take this." He handed her one of Optimus's empty cans of cat food with a pink Tupperware top. "It's the woman's remains. She deserves a decent burial. Whoever—*whatever* she is—was. Oh, dear God," he whimpered, promptly returning to his cleaning spree.

"I'll take that," Sam said from behind her, making heated chills climb her spine just by the sound of his voice. "It should be up to me to spread her ashes. Whatever her reasons, she came to find me, and I can't help but think she knew what her fate was. She was warning us."

She handed him the can, avoiding his fingers because they were probably sources of yet more tingles of awareness. "You're very honorable." And hot. Sexual napalm hot.

"She was trying to help us, I think. It's the least I can do."

"And she was our only connection to what happened with this new unexplored vampire power I seem to have acquired. A power we don't know whether you have or not, unless you're feeling adventurous and want to give teleportation a whirl."

Sam frowned, running his fingers over the dark stubble on his chin. His long, lean, well-manicured fingers. "It looks that way."

"Which means I should never think about a psyche ward again," she joked. She had to or she'd cry. Or dry heave. Whatever.

Taking her by the shoulders, Sam held her eyes with his. His gaze was serious and troubled. But that wasn't what garnered most of her attention. His touch was, and it left her unnerved. Just as she'd suspected it would. "Phoebe, look. I promise you, I'll figure this out. This mess is my fault, and I'll clean it up."

"Will you change before you do? I imagine that dress could be uncomfortable to clean anything in. Especially a mess as big as the one we're in."

His response was a chuckle, deep and rich, leaving a warm, resonant ring in her ears. "I promise to find some man-pants soon."

"I really thought you were a cross-dresser," she responded by way of an apology for labeling him.

Sam smirked, the dimple in his chin lickable. "In hindsight, I almost wish that was the case. But alas, I'm just a secure guy who isn't afraid to go for the laugh. This all happened at a Halloween party."

"I heard. That woman was your date."

"One I can't remember much about other than the way she looked."

"One-night stands are like that. Nameless. But I imagine it wasn't her name that attracted you to her." A stab of unwarranted, totally unexplained jealousy pinged her gut. It deserved absolutely no attention for its pettiness.

Sam averted his gaze and focused on a spot just above her shoulder. "So you know about that night, then?"

Phoebe flapped her hands dismissively, then clasped her ponytail, dragging her fingers through it. "No details. And no judgments. We all get lonely."

Sam paused for a moment, his eyes scanning her face. "Lonely is clearly a dangerous thing these days."

"It's not just the clap the singles of the world have to contend with anymore," Phoebe agreed wryly, then handed him the slip of paper, forcing her focus to remain on answers, not Sam's bedroom bunny. "Mark found this when he was stress cleaning. She must have dropped it on her way in when she collapsed. It's from O-Tech."

Sam held it up to the light and read it with a frown, the lines on his wide forehead deepening.

Fear came back in a jolt to her gut. "What does it say?"

"The letters *TDB*. It's my letterhead. It has my name on it, but it's not my handwriting." Sam held it up for her to see.

"What do you think *TDB* stands for?"

Sam scratched his head with lean fingers. "I have no clue."

Phoebe noted the scrawl of the mysterious initials was large and flowery, maybe even feminine. "What do you do at O-Tech?"

He gazed right into her eyes so intently Phoebe blinked. "I'm one of a team of scientists there. I'm an entomologist in research and development. O-Tech deals in pest control—among other things."

"Bugs?"

"Many winged things. Yes."

"You really are a nerd."

"Nerds are hot. Just ask Chuck."

Her grin was impish and easy. Too easy. She straightened, giving him an arrogant lift of her chin. "Are you flirting by way of extolling your virtues?"

Sam pursed his lips comically and winked. "I'm not sure. Clearly, if that woman was any indication, I'm not much for the foreplay of flirting. I prefer to tap right into the hot and sweaty."

Phoebe let her eyes fall to the floor, shifting on her feet to avoid the discomfort the woman's memory brought. "Well, that hasty, life-altering decision aside, we have trouble. So we need to figure this out, because I don't ever want to do what I did at Nina's again without maybe some warning—or classes on how to, at the very least, land in the middle of Bergdorf Goodman's. I know my way around there."

Sam grinned, devilish and amused. "Could save a bundle on air-fare."

She snorted, twisting her hair between her fingers. "Is that your shot at optimism?"

"I try to keep my glass half full."

Phoebe fought to keep herself from drowning in the deep color of his eyes and stay focused. "So the woman . . ."

"Yeah. Wow."

"You didn't know her?"

"Never saw her before in my life." His eyes shifted away from hers.

She noted his flicker of embarrassment in the way he looked up and away from her. "Was it a work-related party? Do entomologists party? I'm having trouble with that image."

"Obviously, we should stick to bugs, because when you let us loose, we party—big. And it's not something I do often."

"Party?" Phoebe hedged.

"That or indulge in one-night stands. Which technically, I don't think actually occurred, but it's all really hazy."

Crossing her arms over her chest, Phoebe couldn't help but smile. "I'm so relieved."

He wiggled his eyebrows. "That it wasn't a one-night stand?"

"No. That you don't party much. Late nights and booze are bad for your skin. You have nice skin." She paused, mortified she'd given him her assessment on his skin out loud. God. "So the woman . . ."

"The woman. Right. Yes, the party was work related, we had it right inside O-Tech's cafeteria, and there were a lot of people that I work with there. We bug dudes tend to run in stimulating packs of boring bug intellect."

"So she could have been from O-Tech?"

"O-Tech's a big company. She could have been anyone from the mailroom on up. Or not."

"Whose party was it?"

"My friend Joel organized it."

"Another bug guy?"

"No. He's from Human Resources at O-Tech. And before you ask, I texted him about the guest list. No guest list. It was sort of a last-minute thrown-together thing, according to Joel. And no one saw me leave with mystery woman, either. Or even remembers seeing a woman matching that description."

"So she just popped up out of thin air? Wait. Forget I said that. She probably did. Oh, Jesus." The reality of their situation sank back in.

"So that brings us back to what she said," Sam offered, though his reminder was steeped in hesitation.

Phoebe flapped a hand, pushing herself to stick to the facts and not speculate too much or she'd lose her mind. "Right. The dying thing. She said it wouldn't be long before we died. I don't know about you, but I really don't want to end up lunch for a whirring Dyson. That was brutal. No disrespect intended."

Sam shook his head. "Yeah. I don't get it. She vanished right before our eyes. If what Wanda and Nina told us, and the mythology of vampires is almost all true like they said, I was under the impression that vampires live forever unless they're staked through the heart with wood or their heads are chopped off."

"Yeah. They do," Nina stated, breezing in from the kitchen where she and Wanda had been contacting their vampire connections. "Vampires also turn to dust after five hundred years unless they mate for life. Good times, right?"

Phoebe grimaced, wrinkling her nose. "Golden. I have a little less than five hundred years to find the man of my dreams. That should be plenty of time to get things in order for my dream nuptials." And find the right man. The kind who wouldn't walk out on her at the first sign of trouble. Especially if the trouble was big.

Sam's look was of surprise. "Wait. Aren't you married, Nina?"

Nina nodded, her normally scowling face turned warm with a grin. "Yep."

"So you're mated for *life*?" Sam asked.

"For-ev-ah, yo. That's like rule number nine hundred in *Vampires for Dummies*. There's no divorce in Vampire-landia, kiddies. So when you get to pickin' a life partner—pick wisely, my friend, and don't wait until you're four hundred and ninety-nine and three-quarters to do it."

"You speak from experience?" Sam inquired, his eyes wide.

"Oh, you bet she does," Wanda called from the kitchen with a laugh.

Phoebe's brow furrowed. "So wait. Then maybe Sam's girlfriend turned to dust because she was five hundred and had no mate? That makes sense, right? Maybe she meant we'd die if we didn't find mates? Or maybe she bit Sam as an eleventh-hour kind of damn-I'd-better-get-to-gettin'-on-this-mate thing? You know, like an act of desperation?"

Nina shook her head, jamming her hands into the front pocket of her hoodie. "If that was the case, she kind of jumped the fucking warning gun, don't you think? You guys have four hundred and ninety-nine years to go. And she apologized for biting Sam. She said it was an accident and she said she wanted to *help*. I didn't read any malice in that head of hers. Just panic and fear. Not to mention, what happened on that couch isn't your typical vampire death. I've heard about the turning to dust thing, and it isn't like that shit we saw tonight. The five hundred gig isn't pretty, but it's not like what just went down with all that flesh-eating crap. That was some kind of heinous."

Everyone grew somber again at the memory of the woman's screams.

"She also mentioned O-Tech," Wanda said, weaving her way past Nina, cell phone in hand. "And she had that O-Tech memo with Sam's name on it. So if she didn't work there, and we have no way of identifying her to see if she did, my next thought is, what does a vampire have to do with a pest-control manufacturer and how did she get her hands on Sam's personal notepad? Did you have it with you at the party? In your purse, maybe? That dress you've got on doesn't look like it leaves much room for a Thin Mint let alone a whole piece of paper."

"Sarcasm. More, please," Sam responded dryly, cocking his eyebrow.

Wanda smiled in return. "Curtsy. So I'm guessing you don't carry around your memo pad with you?"

Sam's face went hard. "Nope. It never leaves my desk because I don't really use it. I use my phone to keep memos, reminders, et cetera. I can't read my own handwriting and I have no clue what the letters *TDB* mean. But I didn't write that."

"Yay," Wanda retorted with sarcasm, clapping her hands together. "Square one it is, then."

Nina's expression took a surprising turn when she gave them all a somber gaze, jamming her hands into the pockets of her jeans. "Well, we'd better figure out square two, because if what that broad said was true, Sammy and Fashion Spree Barbie are gonna bite it. *Soon.*"

Phoebe paid no mind to Nina's snarky reference to her. Instead, she found herself focusing on how she'd jumped from the frying pan smack into the fire. A couple of days ago, her life hadn't exactly been coming up roses, but it hadn't entailed a violent death the likes of which she'd seen on her sofa. Not one she'd remember anyway.

Everyone grew silent again, finding places to seat themselves other than the couch. Phoebe perched on the edge of an end table, listening to the hum of the vacuum Mark had broken out while she rethought her wish to be cremated.

When her cell phone rang to the tune of "Forget You," a ringtone she'd specifically purchased to signal an unwanted caller, Phoebe froze. Because it signaled the one and only unwanted caller she had.

A glance at the clock said it was almost two in the morning. What could *he* possibly want at this hour?

She made a dash for her purse in the kitchen where Nina had dropped it, a dash that left her body trying to catch up with the rest of her. She crashed into the chairs surrounding their kitchen dinette like a bowling ball and just managed to catch herself before knocking the entire table over.

Dumping the contents of her purse on the table, Phoebe fumbled for her phone and clicked on "answer." "I thought our booty calls were officially over, Randall? So what inspires a phone call so late?"

Randall cleared his throat, shifting on what Phoebe suspected was his bed with the checkered comforter. "I thought you'd be long in bed with your phone on vibrate. I was going to leave a voice mail."

Phoebe made a face into the phone, pacing the small space between her table and fridge. "Meaning you're no less of a sissy than you were last week when you broke up with me?" *So petty, Phoebes. So.*

There was a pause and then a long drawn-out sigh. "Please don't be like this, Phoebe."

"You have some nerve, Randall," she drawled, scooping up a fallen chair and righting it. "So what do you want? Did you forget to collect one of the knives you left in my back?"

Randall's response crackled over the phone, as empty and meaningless as he was. "That hurts, Phoebe."

"Really? Have you seen the knife wound in my back? That's hurt, pal."

"I didn't stab you in the back. I was just being honest with you. Wouldn't you rather I was decent enough to tell you the truth instead of misleading you? Your condition is a lot to ask of someone you've only been dating for a couple of months."

Condition. Hah. Phoebe almost laughed when she considered her newest condition and how Randall would have handled fangs and blood-tasting parties. Instead, she stuck to the disgust he'd evoked in her the moment he'd told her their relationship was over. "You have no idea how grateful I am that you felt honest enough to tell me you're a spineless coward who couldn't handle my condition in a *text message.*"

"I won't deny that after I made the decision to break it off, the idea of seeing you in person became too awkward for me. But it doesn't mean I'm not worried for your safety. You have had some scary moments in the last weeks."

Well, tonight, she'd tipped the scary-o-meter. Not even last week's events topped tonight. "Well, I'm plenty safe, and you've officially been crossed off my list of Prince Charming candidates. So consider your guilt assuaged and we can call this a wrap."

"I don't want it to be this way, Phoebe. I really don't. I'd like to be there for you as a friend, if you'll let me. Maybe I could take you to that clinical trial your doctor told you about? Or we could have coffee afterward? I dunno, Phoebe. I'm just trying to be supportive for you in some way."

"So you can feel better about your charity work?" she sniped at him, then instantly regretted it the moment the words flew from her lips. In all honesty, Randall wasn't a bad person. In fact, he was a decent guy who just didn't want to step into a land mine of a relationship with a woman whose future didn't exactly need shades.

It hadn't broken her that Randall wanted out of their loosely committed relationship. They'd enjoyed a nice enough fling, and he was good company, decent enough in bed, but there'd been no browsing *Modern Bride* for her. What had hurt was the reason he'd broken up with her.

Because she was damaged and would become more damaged as time went by.

The mournful sigh from the other end of the phone deepened her regret for reacting in such a petty way. Phoebe ran her hand over her eyes, swiping at the brown smudge of day-old eyeliner she gathered on her fingertips. "I'm sorry, Randall. It's not your fault. You were honest, and for that you deserve my respect."

"So have you decided if you'll do the clinical trial yet? It did sound pretty promising."

Her eyes strayed to the stack of papers hidden behind a kitchen cabinet. "I haven't decided anything. To say it's been a crazy eight hours or so is underestimating crazy."

"I could go with you," he offered again, in typical gentlemanly Randall fashion.

A rush of emotion clogged her throat and tears she'd never shed again because she was a vampire burned her grainy eyes. "I appreciate that, Randall, but I'm betting you don't want to hang around with me while I fill out the eight hundred or so forms they make patients in clinical trials fill out. It's long and tedious."

There was a long pause, as there usually was when Randall was calculating his words, and then he asked, "Is there any hope in this clinical trial? Any hope at all?"

Hope. How funny that word was. When she was a kid, she'd hoped to become a personal stylist for the stars. Sort of like today's Rachel Zoe. Nowadays she just hoped she'd remember the names of all the stars she'd once hoped to dress. "I don't know if there's any hope for early-onset Alzheimer's, Randall. It's pretty rare, especially at my age, but I'm willing to give it a shot because, really, what do I have to lose?"

Except her mind.

CHAPTER 5

Sam's voice just behind her made Phoebe jump. "Phoebe?"

Shit. Shit. Shit. "I have to go, Randall. But thanks for calling and for your support. You take care." She slid her phone to the off position and scrunched her eyes shut, cringing.

Sam put a heavy hand on her shoulder, cool and comforting. It took all she had in her not to lean back against his hard chest, and she had to chalk that up to the crazy bag of emotions this night had wrought. It was a love-the-one-you're-with mentality, and Sam was the one she was with.

Her instant attraction to Sam the moment she'd found out he wasn't gay was more than just a little shallow. So he was good-looking and he had a great set of thighs. Chickens had nice thighs, too.

"Boyfriend trouble?" he rumbled, deep and shivery.

"Not anymore. I thought it best we call it quits, considering my new supernatural status. I didn't want to have to show him who's really the man at our weekly mud wrestling dates. Now that I have superhuman strength, it's just not a fair fight."

But Sam didn't laugh. Instead, he gave her a sympathetic apology. "I'm sorry."

Her eyes popped open when she waved a hand dismissively. "Don't be. We broke up last week. He was just doing the guilt call to be sure I wasn't lost in ice cream and potato-chip grief."

But Sam clearly wasn't buying her story. "Seriously, is everything okay?"

She moved away from his grip, shaken by the sound of his voice and desperately afraid he'd heard what she'd said to Randall with his super hearing. Putting a smile on her face, she joked, "As noob vampires go, everything's golden. A pasty white, fanged kind of golden. So what's up? Did we figure something out? Did you discover you can ice people with your laser beam eyes or maybe move objects with your ninja mind?"

He shook his head with a grin, taking another step toward her. "Nope. But according to Nina, the night is young, and after your teleportation, who knows what else could happen? Also, Nina made mention of her gut and a bad feeling, and all sorts of scenarios that would make your head spin exorcism style. So she wants us all to stay close to her. No one's left alone without a paranormal Big Sister."

Grand. Maybe they could bond over mugs of warm blood and fang floss. "I can't think of anything I'd like to do more than stay close to Nina. She inspires warm and squishy."

He grinned—wide and sexy. "Good to know, because we're going over to my place so I can get out of this bra. I don't know how you women do it, but I need to reassert my manhood by putting on a pair of jeans and my Stetson."

"You wear a cowboy hat?"

"Yes, ma'am. You can take the boy to the city, but you can't take the country out of the boy," he answered, thickening his once slight Southern drawl.

"Where are you from?"

"Wyoming. Jackson Hole."

Phoebe shrugged her shoulders and gave him a look of indifference. "I'd really rather stay here." Because even in all this chaos, all she could think about was what his butt would look like in those jeans. Their lives were on the line. Someone needed to reassess their priorities.

"Well, first, let me be really clear on something. I did this to you. I know you blame Nina for cornering you, but it was my fang that ended up in your . . . well, you know where. So I consider you my responsibility until we have this all figured out. Until I know you're safe, we stick together. And even if you don't like it, pretend you do or you'll hurt my feelings. Second, the head vampire demands it. I don't know about you, but I'd bet my false eyelashes you shouldn't cross her. Just a feeling. Wanda and Marty offered to stay with Mark on the off chance someone else shows up here."

Hackles rose on the back of her neck. She had to know Mark was safe. "Why would someone else show up here? Was there more than one person at your one-night stand, Mr. McLean, and you're just a modest stud? Did you have a vampire ménage?"

Sam let his head fall back on his shoulders when he laughed, hearty and rich, the thick muscles in his neck standing out. "You're funny. Just like your sister. Though, I'm not as impressed with your arsenal of crude. She's a much better cusser than you."

Phoebe's cheeks dimpled in a grin. "She has a way, doesn't she?"

"A way. A mouth. An attitude, but she does know what it is to live as a vampire. She deserves credit for at least trying to help us— even if it is with a chip the size of Gibraltar on her shoulder. Plus, I really think her bark is much worse than her bite."

She took a step back from him, creating some much-needed space. "You've known her for all of, what—twenty minutes—and you've already evaluated her marshmallowy center?"

"It's been probably more like five or six hours. Long, long, loud, chaotic, violent hours," he reflected on a wry grin. "But again, what do we know about being vampires? What if something else as unexpected as your teleportation happens? Nina'd be our best shot at survival, and Mark needs someone to stay with him. Would poor Mark want that someone to be Nina?"

"Point."

Sam smiled. He held out his hand to her. So noble. So filled with sincerity. So sexy. "Good. So we're in this together?"

Phoebe's reluctant brain wasn't as quick as her needy hand when she found her fingers straying toward his. "Oh, I'm all for finding out why we're going to die as a team. I wouldn't have it any other way."

Sam swept his arm comically in front of him. "Then after you, milady."

She held up a finger. "Wait. Promise me something."

"Name it."

"Duck if you hear the words *Barbie* and my name in a sentence come out of Nina's mouth. I wouldn't want to damage those nice cheekbones if you get in my way when I clock her in the chops."

He mock-preened. "You like my cheekbones?"

"I'd kill small children for them."

"You don't like kids?"

Kids. There'd be none of those for her. Not with a prognosis as grim as the one she'd been dealt. Rather than dwell, she shot him a flippant answer. "Not as much as I like your cheekbones."

He chuckled on his way out of the kitchen with a hesitant Phoebe lagging behind him.

SAM let his forehead rest against the door of his apartment, still disoriented by the idea that they'd *run* from Phoebe's place almost across town to his warehouse apartment in just under five minutes flat. The scientific half of his brain wanted to explore this incredible anomaly. The other half of it just wanted to find a quiet corner in which to mourn the passing of an ice-cold Corona and chimichangas.

But there was work to do . . .

Phoebe stood behind him, still rather dazed. "We just ran . . ."

Sam nodded. "I know, right?"

She looked down at her feet and back up at him, her eyes adorably wide, her lips sweetly plump. "I'm considering a spot on the track team at the Olympics. You know, as a fallback on the off chance I have no clients left when this is all said and done."

"I think you'd look really cute in one of those leotards and running shoes." He instantly nixed the visual of her naked and in running shoes. *Bad, Sam. No biscuit.*

But . . .

No buts. You know better. No naked in running shoes or otherwise. Nip it, pal.

"Her ass is too big for one of those leotards. It's definitely way too big to fit on a Wheaties box," Nina taunted, giving Phoebe a playful punch in the shoulder before stretching her arms above her head.

"You know what, Nina?"

"What, Barbie?"

"I'm not going to respond to that."

"That's because you're too slow."

"No. It's because I'm still too astounded you actually knew what the word *Olympics* meant," Phoebe shot back, sticking her face in Nina's and smiling.

Sam planted a hand on each woman's shoulder before Nina could get to Phoebe. "Girls? Where is the love, I ask you? Play nice or I'll be forced to separate you." He winked, then reached for his doorknob and remembered something vital. "Damn. My purse. The keys are in my purse."

Of all the things to lose. His thrift-store bargain purse. Thankfully, he'd only had a small amount of cash in it and his license. Nothing he couldn't live without or replace. Right now, all he wanted was to get the hell out of this ridiculous outfit and have a moment to think.

"Move," Nina ordered, shoving Sam out of her way and wrapping her hand around the doorknob to give it a good twist. The handle was mutilated, but the door was open. "It's good to be a vampire, huh, Sammy?" She clapped him on his broad back with a chuckle.

Phoebe's eyes connected with his for a moment, wide and filled with the kind of wonder/terror he'd expressed himself at least half a dozen times or so since this had started. But then she straightened her spine and squared her shoulders; Sam found himself admiring her determination to show Nina she was no slacker in the suck-it-up, you're-a-vampire department.

He found himself admiring many things about her. Aside from her physical attributes, which were aplenty, he mostly admired the fact that she hadn't completely given in to the side of her that wanted to turn tail and run screaming. Instead, she plowed ahead right behind her fearless sister in a silent battle of who was the badder ass.

Nina gave him a shove. "Let's do this, Gigantor. We need to hurry it up if we're going to be back to our coffins in time for daylight. You know, so we don't fucking burn to death?"

Phoebe's grunt of displeasure inspired Sam to move. "Right. Snap, crackle, pop. I'll make it fast."

Upon entering his apartment, everything was pitch black; yet, he could see every single detail as though it were brightly lit.

Every messy detail of it.

"Are all bug lovers so messy?" Phoebe asked, stepping on a pile of clothes in the corner of the living room and stumbling over a stack of old *National Geographic*s.

"Aw, hell," Sam muttered, reaching for the light switch and hissing along with Phoebe and Nina when the glare of the track lighting stung their eyes.

But the light brought with it clarity.

Nina's tongue clucked. "Goddamn it. Didn't I say some shit just wasn't right about what went down with you, Sammy?" she snarled, perusing Sam's overturned end tables and armchair. "You've been jacked, dude." She bent at the waist, lifting his mountain bike up with one finger and setting it upright. "The motherfuckers."

Stooping, Sam cleared a path through torn throw pillows and broken glass to make his way across the long length of his living room. The pictures that had adorned the deep barn red of the walls were ripped off, the frames shattered in black enamel pieces scattered over the barn wood flooring. His chest of drawers that he used to keep his live specimen containers and various other tools of the entomology trade had been tipped over, the drawers yanked free of the wood.

"Oh, Sam. I'm sorry," Phoebe whispered from her corner of his living room, stooping to pick up a fallen planter that once held the clippings of a Christmas cactus his mother had given him years ago so he'd always think of her. He took it with him wherever he went.

Sam's eyes scanned the room to assess the damage and noted how odd it was that the fifty-two-inch flat screen and sound system were still intact. "I'm beginning to think you're right. But what is it that I have, and *who* the hell wants it?" He kept his face expressionless, but his thoughts were moving a mile a minute.

"Shouldn't we call the police?" Phoebe asked, the tremor of fear in her voice easy to detect with his newly defined hearing.

Nina hunched her shoulders forward and scoffed. "And tell them what, princess? That we think some *vampires* trashed Sam's apartment? Do you want to end up in the nearest House of Crazy? We can't have cops here asking a bunch of questions we'll only have to lie about the answers to anyway. Remember the lay-low rule? That applies to everything from now on—which means this is clan business."

"Then maybe you should get to dialing clan nine-one-one—because I think Sam's been robbed, Bat Girl," Phoebe drawled, shooting Nina an arrogant raise of her eyebrow.

Sam clenched his fists and searched for the patience to deal with two women so at odds. "Nina's right. Until further inspection, I can't see that they did anything more than toss the place. My bike's still here. The TV and surround sound. I don't keep money lying around. I don't get it."

And then his eyes strayed to his desk, the desk that had been his since he was a kid in college. Something else that went with him wherever he went. The one that still held his O-Tech laptop and personal desktop computer.

Nina caught Sam's gaze of disbelief and said, "What kind of ass-clown thieves leave behind two computers and a flat screen? The ones trained at the blind division in the CIA?" Her nostrils flared and her nose wrinkled in distaste. She held a hand up in clear warning. "I smell vamp, dudes. You two smell that? It's nasty-ass vamp. Like no other kind of vampire I've ever smelled before. Take a deep whiff, kiddies, and memorize that stank, because whoever trashed your place is a vampire, but definitely isn't part of our clan."

"This sniffing out clan members?" Phoebe interjected, her eyes skeptical. "Is it like when dogs sniff each other's butts? Is that how we recognize each other?"

Nina crossed her arms over her chest. "Yeah, smart ass. So from now on, ask everyone you meet to bend over."

"Nina," Sam warned, flipping open the laptop to find that it was on.

"Look, your sense of smell's going to take on a whole new meaning, Strawberry Shortcake. You'll be able to smell others like you and others not like you. It's in your best interest to fucking learn the difference, because sometimes the others not like you are the bad guys. So pay attention."

Phoebe took an exaggerated sniff of the room, a gesture clearly meant to taunt Nina, but then her head cocked to the right. "Huh. I *do* smell it. Do you smell that, Sam?"

But Sam was too busy staring at his computer screen and the scattered DVDs to address it—a computer screen that was just like he'd left it before he'd gone to the party. A computer he'd turned off that was now on. "Well, whatever this vampire was looking for, they thought it was on my laptop, but it looks like everything's the same as it was when I left. But do note, I shut down before I left for the party the other night. This was on."

Nina was at his side in an instant, leaning over his shoulder to gaze at the screen. "So what's on it besides porn and a website for the rules on how to hook up with a vampire at a Halloween party?"

Sam scratched his head in feigned thought, planting a hand on the desk to brace himself, keeping his face blank. "Nothing important. It's my work computer. I bring it home a lot in order to work on pest-control formulas. All sorts of boring bug-related stuff you wouldn't understand. But it wasn't the sort of stuff breakthroughs are made of. It was just a bunch of research data, mostly old, mostly already marketed and sold. I keep copies of everything I had a hand in helping create."

Nina flicked the laptop with her finger. "So whoever the hell this was thinks you have something important from O-Tech—which means it isn't safe for you to go to work, Sam. Not until we know what the frig this is about."

Just when you thought you'd pinnacled the crazy meter . . . "So what do I do, call in vampire?"

Nina's eyebrow rose. "Got any sick days? Vacation days?"

Sam avoided her eyes, pretending to look down at the computer. "Yeah."

"Use them. Make some family bullshit up or whatever," Nina ordered, picking up a stack of computer paper and putting it neatly back on his printer. "And while you take that shower and change into your man garb, think. Think about anyone in the recent past that seemed suspicious at O-Tech. Any fucking little thing is worth mentioning. Go take a shower. We'll get this." She waved a hand at the overturned furniture.

Sam hesitated when Phoebe shot him a look of cornered animal from across the room. "If I leave the two of you alone, do you promise to play nice with Phoebe, Nina?" he asked, keeping his tone jovial and light.

Nina snorted, giving Sam a sly grin. "Don't you worry your cross-dressing, gel-bra-wearing head. Me and Barbie here are gonna straighten up the Dream House. You got so much shit all over the place I won't have time to beat the fuck out of her with a rope of garlic. Promise. But hurry it up, because I'm tempted."

Phoebe mouthed the words *thanks a lot* to him via her plump, full lips, then followed up with an upward jut of her middle finger.

He chuckled on the way into his bathroom, one room that was oddly intact but for the vanity, where an empty drawer was open. Grabbing a towel, he stopped at the mirror above his sink and wondered how he'd shave without tearing himself up if he couldn't see what he was doing.

Not that it mattered. He did have the ability to self heal.

And run like he was the millennium's latest answer to the bionic man.

And maybe, if he was anything like Nina, read minds.

Which meant he could find out if Phoebe thought he was as hot as Sam thought she was.

Flipping the tap on, he grinned at the notion, then chastised himself for wondering if she wanted to see him naked as much as he wanted to see her sans clothes.

Bad, bad Sam.

He had other things to worry about, and none of them included becoming involved with Phoebe. However, it was the *other* things that were going to keep him glued to her side whether he wanted to be or not.

Because at all costs, he was going to ensure her safety.

Duty called.

"I'M almost afraid to ask what this is," Phoebe pondered more to herself than Nina as she picked up a Tupperware container with the biggest beetle she'd ever seen. She dropped it on top of the dresser where Sam kept his specimens.

They'd been straightening up toppled furniture and bug specimens in relative silence while Sam showered and changed, giving her far too much time to think. How could she possibly keep her small business afloat if she couldn't go out in the daylight hours? Last she'd checked, Tiffany's wasn't open at midnight.

Mark could only handle so much without her input. They were already on client overload as it was, and next week was one of their biggest, most important client shoots. Scheduled for six A.M. so they could get the best lighting, so sayeth rapper Dawg and his crew of grill-wearing, drooping-trousered boyz.

Pressing a thumb to her forehead, Phoebe paused and wished she were still able to take a deep, cleansing breath.

"You all right over there, *princess*?"

Her spine straightened and cracked, she shot upright so quickly. Okay. Enough with the snide nicknames and openly rude remarks about her person. The Phoebe of just twenty-four hours ago would never have stood by and allowed anyone to take potshots at her while she bit her lip to keep from creating drama.

Nay.

The Phoebe of twenty-four hours ago would have confronted her attacker, whether she was her sister or not. Out of respect for their new situation, she'd fought the impulse to continually fire back, but really. She'd had it up to her eyeballs with the wisecracks.

She lobbed a colorful pillow she'd planned to fluff at Nina, marveling at the speed it sailed across the room with. "Lay off the stupid pet names, Nina. You do not want to tangle with this Barbie."

Nina's hand was in the air in a blur of lean fingers, deftly catching the pillow and dropping it to the floor. "Back at'cha, *princess*." Her pale face offered up a challenge from the confines of her hoodie.

Anger, red and hot, flushed Phoebe's gut. Anger she fought hard to maintain control of despite the surge of spiky heat along her scalp. "I said *knock it off*."

"Or what?" Nina spread her arms wide and rolled her neck. "You'll pull my pigtails? Please. Look, lemme lay this shit out for you, so I'm crystal fucking clear about where I stand on this bogus bullshit. So we're half sisters. Or whatever-the-fuck. You have proof. Big deal. Just because a piece of paper says I'm your blood doesn't mean we're gonna do each other's hair and play Mystery Date. I don't want a sister. I don't need a sister. I'm only in this to make sure you're all right because, in truth, I cornered you and made you trip over Sam. I own what I did. My bad. You need to own that you just weren't quick enough for the likes of me. Your bad. And now, I'm doing my part in this flippin' accident, but it doesn't mean I want to have Sunday blood brunches with you."

"Well, thank God for small favors. I'll consider myself lucky, then, because I'd bet you chew your food with your mouth open!" Phoebe spat, Nina's childish behavior finally getting the best of her.

Nina smiled her agreement. "Yeah. But I beat the shit out of people with my fist *closed*."

Phoebe's finger shot up in the air to punctuate a forthcoming thought. "You forget, *sister*. I'm just like you now. Just as strong. Just as scary. I also have that not-afraid-of-a-whole-lot gene you possess, and I had it before you did this to me, you poster child for anger management! So while we look and dress like we're poles apart, be warned. I'm the socially acceptable, better-grasp-on-the-English-language version of *you*."

Nina's hands clenched at her sides, the thin blue veins in her neck straining against her creamy white skin. "What the fuck is it that you expected from me when you showed up? Did you think I was gonna grab your hand and skip through fields of buttercups with you while we fucking picnicked and sang folk songs in the sunshine?"

Well, it hadn't exactly been like that. There were no buttercups.

Okay, so maybe there'd been a picnic . . . on a checkered blanket . . . in Central Park. So?

The dream had been more about them maybe having dinner together once in a while. Calling each other occasionally—like Christmas and birthdays. Nina being a supportive shoulder to lean on when her boyfriend dumped her because she was defective. Reaching out to someone before she wasn't able to reach out at all . . .

It had been about feeding her curiosity and checking off the no-regrets box before she literally lost her wits. It had been about ensuring the future of . . . She shook her head to ward off the one last piece of information she'd kept from Nina and the others. After Nina's reaction, there was no need to disclose anything else.

For all the warnings her mother had given her about Nina and her sour disposition before she'd died, Phoebe couldn't have possibly imagined the reality. She just hadn't expected the height of Nina's wall to be so impenetrable. "I expected next to nothing and got less. More's the pity. But my mother warned me about you. So I was semi-prepared."

Phoebe watched the play of emotions on Nina's hard face, the surprise that her mother knew anything about her wash over her. She also watched as Nina grappled with her own brand of curiosity. "And what the fuck does your mother know about me? I don't know your mother, and she sure as shit didn't know me."

Knowing she was stepping onto a virtual land mine, Phoebe chose to step anyway. Call it overwhelmed, fed up, whatever, but she wanted to rile Nina—to poke at her for being such a mean girl. "Ah, but our *father* knew all about you and he shared a great deal of it with my mother just before he died."

"Like?"

"Like that you were angry about losing your mother and that led to all sorts of trouble when you were a teenager. Obviously, your mommy issues have taken you right into adulthood."

Nina was across the room in a shot, her hand around Phoebe's neck. In a split second, she had her pressed to the wall, her dark eyes on fire. The menace, the hot angry film that glazed them, might have made Phoebe shiver if not for the fact that she'd purposely gone for the jugular, and she'd done it to wipe that smug look off Nina's face. "Never, *ever* mention my mother, Phoebe. You don't know jack shit about her or me and my life."

Phoebe lifted her chin, her mouth a thin line, her hands clenching and unclenching. "Let. Me. Go."

"When I'm ready," Nina squawked, jamming her face into Phoebe's.

"Get ready," Phoebe squawked back.

Nina's eyes became narrowed slits in her head. "I can kill you. You get that shit, right?"

Oh, she got it, and she was tired of the threat. Phoebe opened her mouth wide and pretended to yawn in Nina's face. "You bore me. You get that shit, *right*?"

"Now, girls," Sam said, poking his head between the two women. His gorgeous eyes amused, the fresh scent of his aftershave tickling Phoebe's nostrils even while she was pinned to a wall. "Has it come to this in just the amount of time it takes for me to grab a shower?" He propped a disapproving raven eyebrow upward. Wrapping his fingers around Nina's, he tried to pry them loose from Phoebe's neck with little success. "Nina? Let go. Please. If you kill Phoebe, I'll be all alone at Vampire Academy. There'll be no one to study my awesome mind-reading skills with. Now let go."

But Nina didn't budge.

He nudged Nina's shoulder and gave her a cajoling smile. "C'mon, vampire sensei. Let her go. We have more important things to do than kill Phoebe. We have to find the bad guy who trashed my place. We can't do that if we're too busy cleaning up Phoebe's scattered remains, now can we?"

Phoebe lifted her chin, and though she didn't reach to attempt to pull Nina's hands from her neck, she certainly wasn't going to back down. "Let go of me."

"Or?" Nina taunted, smiling sweetly at Sam before snarling in Phoebe's face.

Or she'd knock Nina into next Sunday, taking Sam with her?

THE burst of explosive anger that had sent Nina flying across the room with Sam behind her had Phoebe in a state of panic. Not just because she had no control over the force with which she'd shoved Nina, but due to what had happened to Sam who'd been caught in Phoebe's cross fire as a result.

Just as Nina was about to rush her in bull-like fashion, her eyes caught Sam's body, making her skid to an astonished halt.

Sam was stuck in the wall between his living room and what Phoebe guessed was his bedroom.

He wasn't the kind of stuck that entailed crumbling Sheetrock and cracked paint. Sam was literally wedged inside the wall.

In. The. Wall.

Well, that was that. Her crazy account was officially overdrawn.

For a stunned moment, all she could do was stare at him. His long legs, encased in well-worn denim, were sprawled outward at an odd angle, hovering *above* the deep wood grain of the floor. The black cowboy boots he wore peeked out from beneath his pant legs, floating in front of him. Her eyes followed the long line of his enormous body to his waist, where he disappeared inside the Sheetrock.

"Sam!" Phoebe yelled, scurrying across the floor to poke her head around the corner of his bedroom. His upper torso floated and twisted *Matrix*-ish above the deep brown carpeting, his handsome face disbelieving.

Nina was behind her in a flash, her eyes wide in shock. She slapped her hand against the doorframe in disgust. "For the love of Jesus and all twelve . . ."

"It's all fun and games until someone ends up inside a wall, eh, ladies?" Sam regarded them with a crooked smile. "So what to do, what to do?"

Phoebe was kneeling beside him in an instant, her eyes roving his body, her hands hesitantly suspended over him, afraid to touch him for fear she'd hurt him. "Does it hurt?"

Sam shook his head. "Nope. It's sort of like . . . like floating. That's the best description I can give it. Like I'm weightless."

"Should we try to move him?" Phoebe asked Nina.

Nina ran her fingers through her long, wavy dark hair. "Fuck if I know. Can you move on your own, dude?"

Sam wiggled his fingers and nodded. "Nothing hurts, I just can't seem to get any leverage to pull myself out."

Nina moved around Phoebe to stand behind Sam's head, bending at the waist. "Gimme your hands and I'll pull you."

Sam reached upward, the strong muscles of his forearms flexing when he latched on to Nina's hands, gripping them.

"Gimme a holla if it hurts, okay?"

"Fire when ready," Sam instructed.

Nina gave him a hard yank, but it wasn't necessary. Sam slithered through the wall like a knife through soft butter. Nina pulled him to his feet with ease and clapped him on the back with an awestruck expression. "What the fuck is next with you two? Invisibility? I don't get it. You can jam your ass in a wall, dude. She can teleport and see her reflection. Swear to Christ, if you two can eat, even one bite, I'll stake you myself. I haven't been a vampire very long, but I ain't never seen shit like this. We need answers, man. I can't help you if we don't get some. Soon." Her cell rang just then, and she looked at the number with a frown, prowling off to a corner of Sam's bedroom to answer it.

Phoebe's eyes, filled with remorse, found Sam's. "And the crazy just keeps on coming, huh?"

He shrugged his wide shoulders and smiled, running his broad hand over the unmarred wall with a tentative finger to find it swallowed his hand whole. "It's a little cool, if you ask me. How many people do you know who can get stuck inside a wall without breaking a sweat?"

Clasping his arm, Phoebe winced. "I'm sorry you got in the middle of the two of us."

He cupped her chin, trailing a finger over her bottom lip. "If we're going to get through this, you two are going to have to work this out. We clearly need our wits about us, and the both of you at each other's throats is nothing but a distraction we can't afford. Wanna tell me what that was about?"

Phoebe fought the urge to nestle against his hand. "I brought up her mother, a very touchy subject. I get that she's feeling insecure and betrayed because there was this whole world that existed for her father that she had no clue about. I'd be angry if she knew about me, but I didn't know about her, too. I was prepared for that. I wasn't prepared to have her call me names and snarl at me every time I move. I also wasn't prepared to become a vampire. *C'est la vie*. But you're right. I let myself be goaded. It won't happen again."

"That was some shove you gave her."

Phoebe looked at her hands as though they belonged to a stranger. "No kidding. I'm no candy-ass. I mean, I Zumba and I kickbox. I'm in good physical shape, but that surge of power was two things. Scary and damn heady." She didn't have time to reflect on her incredible strength further because Nina was plowing between the two of them and holding up her phone with a pleased look.

"So good news, Supernatural Barbie and Ken. Help's on the way."

"You've located the wall whisperer?" Sam quipped.

"Always with the funny, huh, Sammy? No. But it's someone who knows everything there is to know about vampires. He's been around forever." The doorbell rang just then, and Nina left to go answer it.

Phoebe took a step backward into Sam's bedroom, feeling

trapped. She clung to the doorframe, pressing her forehead to it. "I've decided I don't know if I'm up to another magical mystery tour tonight," she hedged. "I need to catch my breath."

"You don't breathe anymore," Sam reminded her, brushing a strand of her hair from her cheek.

"Or eat. Or go to the beach. Or—" Her anxieties were catching up with her.

"Hey. We're in this together, remember? I can't do any of those things anymore, either." Sam took her hand, cool and dry, and caressed her thumb with his in soothing circles. "But we won't be in anything but ashes if we don't find out what's going on and why we're different than all the other vampires."

"Very Rudolph."

"If only a shiny red nose were the only problem," Sam replied, his gaze grim.

Her worst fear rose to the surface, bubbling from her lips like the head of a beer. "What if we find out that there is no hope for us, Sam? What if we end up like that woman?" She needed a time frame—something to go on so she could prepare Mark and . . .

Sam's jaw tightened momentarily before his eyes warmed to deep chocolate pools, and his hand closed around hers. "Then we find out together."

A small measure of relief flooded her stomach, loosening the tight coil of fear in her belly.

However little hope those words gave them, suddenly, because Sam was holding her hand, everything seemed okay.

CHAPTER 6

The word *okay* had officially been cruelly ripped from Phoebe's vocabulary and replaced by not one but two words. *Never* and *again*.

Who was anybody kidding here? Nothing was ever going to be okay again. Nothing. Never. Sitting on Sam's couch as the clock struck four A.M., they'd listened to Archibald, Wanda's husband Heath's manservant (who was once a vampire but was now a human again in some bizarre twist of fate involving sires and words Phoebe didn't even know existed anymore), and his friend Dmitri the Vampire explain their theories on what they thought had happened to Sam and Phoebe.

And there were but three utterly redonckculous thoughts Phoebe couldn't shake during the entire conversation—none of which had anything to do with her almost certainly deadly fate.

They were actually rather meaningless.

First meaningless thought? Who still had a manservant? No matter how endearing or adorably British?

Second meaningless thought? Wasn't every vampire since vampire romances had been invented named Dmitri? Or was it Declan? Wait. Maybe Hunter? Wasn't that just a little too vampire cliché?

Not that Dmitri was just any vampire. No. In fact, he was one of the oldest surviving vampires in the history of vampires, who'd found Archibald in, of all places, a botany club. They'd reunited after all these centuries over rare species of roses and lilies, and it felt so good.

Third, didn't all vampires named Dmitri look like they'd just stepped off the cover of some gothic horror novel, complete with swirling black cape, menacing eyebrows, and imposing stances? If some of those romance novelists could see *this* Dmitri, they'd have to reconsider the visual legend the name was supposed to bring to mind.

Because this Dmitri was anything but gothic or imposing. He was the kind of vampire who'd clearly decided the seventies was a decade that should be celebrated for eternity, if one were to judge him by his long, graying hair and rainbow headband. The only thing missing from his bell-bottom jean-clad body and his printed disco-shirt-wearing rail-thin chest was a big, big bong.

Hearing what they had to say made Phoebe wonder if tokin' on a big, big bong wouldn't be the solution to this mess. Who cared if you ended up a pile of ashes when you were stoned?

"So I want to be clear here," Sam's luscious voice invaded her rambling, out-of-focus thoughts. "You think we have some kind of vampire virus?"

Dmitri nodded, leaning his elbows on his knobby knees and rolling an old toothpick between his lips. "Yeah, man. I've seen it once. Way back in the seventeen hundreds. Can't remember the exact date, but it was bad. Righteous bad. Haven't seen nothin' like it since."

Archibald gave a distinguished nod of agreement, his lined face riddled with unpleasant memories clearly best left buried. "Oh, indeed, sir. It was dreadful. Just horrid. Vampires running amok, biting not just the innocent, but one another, too. This led to an outbreak of epic proportions."

Sam shifted positions on the couch, his thigh grazing Phoebe's in the process. The strong line of his jaw was tight and sharp with tension. "Do you know exactly what created the outbreak?"

Archibald cleared his throat, brushing the wrinkles from the arm of his checkered bathrobe to settle back in Sam's overstuffed arm-chair. "As was and still is the way, Master Samuel, fear of anyone or anything different was widespread, most certainly that was the case back then. It was neither hip nor tragically cool to be a vampire. If a vampire was somehow captured, he was served up the typical death, burned at dawn, or by wooden stake through the heart. How-ever, not everyone's views on such matters were so black-and-white. One man in particular, a scientist of sorts, though mad, no doubt, thought a vampire was a thing to be studied, prodded, tested, and thus discarded when the researcher had no more use for what people called Lucifer's children."

Phoebe's eyes closed in horror. If her intestines really were out of order forever, you couldn't tell by the fear that clenched her gut at Archibald's words.

Dmitri shook his head in rapid agreement, his gnarled finger poking at the air. "Damn crazy was what that was! Fool scientist took a human waiting for the guillotine and did all sorts of things to him. Thought he could turn a human into a vampire with some kind of nonsense he'd hatched in his lab. Leastways I hear that was the goal."

"So in essence, he was developing something that would create a synthetic, albeit crudely bioengineered vampire," Sam muttered, dragging a hand over his chin.

Dmitri's eyes grew dark, the lines of age around them deepening. "Uh, yup. So anyways, he used this fella like some guinea pig, but instead of turning him into a vampire like you and me, he turned him into a monster. Somehow, this vampire escaped Dr. Nutball and went on a biting spree, turning a bunch of humans rabid and vicious. Vampires were turning to ashes everywhere—if they lasted long enough to escape us, anyway. It was an ugly, ugly time. No one bitten survived that."

"So you don't think this is the work of some crazy centuries-old vampire who's still running around loose, do you?" Nina asked.

"Bah!" Dmitri balked, toying with the peace-sign necklace he wore around his neck. "Even if the doc was stupid enough to test it on himself, he sure couldn't have survived it—and definitely not for this many centuries. No way, sister."

"Okay, so anyone infected lost their minds first before they turned to ashes, Arch?" Nina asked from her perch on the edge of Sam's desk, her tone carrying a distinct tremor.

"I'm afraid so, Miss Nina. Those who didn't were . . ." He let his balding head fall to his stately suit-covered chest.

"Were what?" Phoebe prodded, certain the answer would be as terrifying as everything else they'd retold, but not knowing had to be a worse fate.

Archibald reached out a weathered hand for hers and gave it a squeeze. "Slain, miss. Expunged for fear there would be no end to the spread of the disease. If the infected night dwellers weren't killed by the humans, vampires themselves took on the dreadful task."

"Did they display the kinds of symptoms Phoebe and I are displaying?"

Archibald's bushy eyebrows rose. "No, Master Samuel. I don't recall them having the specific gifts that have been bestowed upon the both of you, but the description of the death that young woman suffered . . ." He paused, composing himself. "That does fit the bill. However, vampires have evolved over the years. With a little help from technology, who knows what monkey business could occur in this great day and age? Who knows what some madman in a laboratory with today's advances could create? Who's to say teleportation and walking through walls aren't a viable option with a petri dish and the single desire for eternal life? I only know that vampires—even the oldest, most powerfully endowed, the most feared of the lot *do not* walk through walls, sir. Ever."

Phoebe's brow furrowed. She tucked her legs beneath her, letting her chin rest on her knees, fighting the continual rise of panic in order to sort through this rationally. "So you think this is a result of modern-day technology? That someone's literally creating vampires—testing whatever this is out on humans and clearly failing?"

"It damn well smacks of it, darlin'," Dmitri said, his voice somber, his green eyes capturing hers with his sympathy. "Where they're gettin' the humans and what they're doing to 'em is anybody's guess."

"So our deaths are inevitable," Phoebe forced herself to say. "But not before we let loose on whomever we can get our fangs into because we've gone vampire AWOL." God. That she could spread this whatever it was to someone unsuspecting without even knowing made her want to chain herself to the top of the Andes mountains until she French fried at daybreak.

Archibald clucked his tongue, his eyes steely with determination. "Now, miss, this looks grim, I'll admit. However, we've been in many a pickle and found our way to the other side with minimal harm to our persons. Haven't we, Miss Nina?"

Nina's hoodie had fallen off in their scuffle, and Phoebe wondered if she didn't always keep it on her head as a way to mask her emotions. Because her face said it all—even if the next words she spoke were to the contrary.

"You bet'cha, Arch. This wouldn't be the first time our backs have been against a wall. No one's dying on my watch." She hopped off Sam's desk and cupped Archibald's chin with affection in her dark eyes, an emotion Phoebe didn't know she was capable of. It even stung a little. Somehow, as cantankerous as she was, Nina had managed to surround herself with all these people who clearly loved her.

She settled herself on the arm of the chair. Archibald patted her hand and smiled like he actually liked her. "So what next, Miss Nina?"

This time, the grim look on Nina's face was apparent. "I dunno, Arch, but my gut tells me this has to do with O-Tech—especially after Sam's place was trashed and his work comp was on. Maybe whatever was on that computer didn't seem important to Sam, but somebody thinks it is. Now, O-Tech would have the kind of resources to facilitate something like this, wouldn't they, Sammy? You know, labs and all those crazy Bunsen things you herd of nerds play with?"

Sam's lips thinned. "But where, Nina? I've been in every lab in the place at one time or another, and I can't say I recall seeing anyone walking through walls. I think I'd know if they were testing humans."

Nina brushed her hands together. "Then you know what I say, Sammy?"

"What don't you say?" Phoebe couldn't help but quip to the tune of Archibald's delighted laughter.

She ignored Phoebe but gave Sam a sly smile. "I say we poke around inside O-Tech."

Phoebe detected a hint of discomfort in Sam's shift of position on the couch. It was subtle, but his vibe had clearly changed to one of uneasiness.

Huh.

"And we do that how? I thought we'd burn to a crisp if we go out during daylight hours."

"Oh, we're not gonna do it during daylight hours, Sammy. We're goin' in ninja style," Nina cackled, mocking a karate chop.

Sam's jaw tightened. "Despite the mostly harmless goings-on at O-Tech, we do still deal in dangerous chemicals, Nina. Which means they have armed guards. So how do we get past the security guards?"

She shrugged her shoulders like she'd stormed plenty of castles in her time. "You're the wall whisperer. She can teleport. Figure it out, brainiac."

Oh, dear God. Not only was she a vampire, but she was going to be a teleporting felonious vampire now, too?

"So you want me to just walk through a wall at O-Tech? I don't know if you saw what just happened only moments ago, Nina, but I wasn't exactly Mr. Miyagi at wall walking."

Nina glanced at her wristwatch. "Then you two better get to crack-a-lackin' and practice. You've got twenty-four hours. Eight of which will be spent passed out cold in vampire sleep not too far in your immediate future, Gigantor."

"Do you have any idea what could happen if we get caught?" Sam demanded, his voice, usually so easygoing and light, riddled with concern Phoebe distinctly heard.

Nina rose, pulling Archibald up with her. "Nope. But you do have an idea of what could happen if we don't figure this shit out. I don't know about you, but I bet that Mark would pass out cold if he had to sweep his Phoebes up off the floor. I bet all those nice pictures of your family you had all over the place are a sure sign they'd be pretty upset if you just didn't exist anymore, too. We got trouble, kemosabe. Big trouble. If I were you, I'd want answers."

Yeah. Answers. Phoebe internally rallied for answers while she pondered Sam's hesitance. Maybe he was just one of those rule followers who never balked at authority? But who could afford to follow the rules when they were destined for death? Wouldn't that light a big fire under your ass?

If your two choices were break some rules or die—she was choosing rule breaking. Whether Sam was in or not.

She sat silently, watching the play of emotions on Sam's face and waiting. But the moment had passed and his face lightened. "You're right. I'm just not a fan of breaking and entering. I have to go back to work sometime. Can't do that if I'm in jail."

Nina wrapped her arm around Sam's shoulder. "Sam, here's the word. You ain't ever goin' back to a day job because there isn't a sunscreen on the planet that can protect you from frying like so much egg come high noon if you're out in the sun too long. A full day of work just won't cut it until you build up a tolerance, and that takes time. You'd have to walk around covered from head to toe in clothing, and even then, it stings like shit. It can be done. I've done it. But it ain't no walk in the park and it takes time to build up a tolerance to it for longer than an hour or so. Get used to the fact that gray and overcast are your new BFFs."

Jesus. Phoebe grimaced. Always with the death threats. If one thing didn't kill them, something else surely would be happy to take a stab at it.

While Dmitri, Nina, and Sam hatched a plan, Archibald extended a hand to her, tugging her upward from her place on the couch. "So, miss, I hear a welcome to the fold is in order?" His pleasant smile and soft words made the hole where her dead heart lay ache.

"I think there's no room left in the fold," she said, keeping her tone light.

He clasped her hand between his, his eyes full of a twinkling amusement. "There's always room in the fold, miss. Sometimes the fold just needs a swift kick in the pants."

Phoebe laughed for the first time in what felt like eons. "I'd be happy to oblige."

Archibald's smile was warm, his rounded cheeks cheerfully dusted with color. "Ah, miss. Our Nina is as you young people say, a badass. But underneath all that bluster lies a heart, and while it no longer beats, it surely exists. She grumbles. She oftentimes yells. Indeed, her language is an abomination to one's ears. However, I've borne witness to countless selfless acts on her part. I do hope you'll stick around to see some of them."

This wasn't the first time she'd heard those words where Nina was concerned. Sam held the same sentiment to a degree. On impulse, Phoebe gave him a hug. "Thank you, and thank you for coming out so late to help us."

"I daresay it isn't pleasant news, but I have every faith we shall find an answer. As for now, you must rest. All good vampires need a minimum of eight hours or they turn into our fair Nina."

Phoebe smiled at him and giggled softly. "Then maybe I should shoot for ten—you know, padding my chances?"

He laughed before holding out his arm to her in a gallant gesture. "Come. You must drink in order to keep you strong during the final stages of the change. I shall prepare your evening feeding, and we'll get to know one another while your Sam finishes up."

"Oh, he's not my Sam," she made a point of saying, looping her arm through his and allowing him to lead her to the kitchen. "We just met a few hours ago."

Archibald's bushy eyebrow rose. "Chemistry is a funny thing, miss. Sometimes those who are experiencing it aren't always aware they are."

Oh, she was aware, she thought as she slid onto one of Sam's steel kitchen stools and watched Archibald produce more of the packets of the blood Wanda had given her back at her place.

She was more than aware of Sam McLean. She was aware of how his jeans hugged the tops of his strong thighs, and the tight abdomen under his shirt. She was sickly aware of his deep brown eyes with lashes for days and his long, lean fingers when they held hers. She was aware of the sexy Stetson he wore that shadowed his lean face.

The trouble was, she wouldn't always be aware.

And that was a problem.

"ARE they asleep?" Wanda asked, entering Sam's apartment via Nina and sliding off her shoes to set them in the hall closet.

Nina stretched, clasping her fingers together over her head and twisting her body from side to side. "Yeah. Finally. Who's got Marky-Mark covered?"

Wanda draped her jacket over Sam's couch and sighed. "I left him with Marty and *Say Yes to the Dress*. Good gravy, they're like a sister and brother from another mother, Nina. They were bonding over tulle and Swarovski crystals when I left. He'll be fine. Though, he was sick with worry over Phoebe. They've been friends since childhood."

"Good for them." Nina grunted, plopping down on the couch and dragging one of Sam's pillows to her lap. She patted a space next to her for Wanda to sit. "Now I just want some quiet without Barbie Fabulous yakking in my head. I'm an hour overdue for vampire sleep—which makes me Bitchy Vampire. Vampire Barbie's evil twin."

Wanda dropped down next to her best friend and patted her hand with a light chuckle. "It's been a busy few hours. We've got a lot on our plates. I'm worried, friend."

"Me, too, Wanda. Me fucking, too." Nina's words held a defeat Wanda knew she wouldn't have shared with Phoebe and Sam.

"Do you really think you'll find something at O-Tech?"

Nina burrowed into the couch, letting her head fall back on the arm. "The fucking idea that someone's creating vampires scares the shit out of me, Wanda, but it's as good a place to start as any. It's not like we have much else to go on but that memo pad from O-Tech the chick dropped. Like I told you on the phone, Arch and his stoner dude think this is some kind of research gone seriously south. Where better than a place like O-Tech to experiment with shit like that? No doubt, they have the resources."

"But with people? *Humans*, Nina? Sweet Jesus. It's horrifying. I feel so helpless. At least with the others we've been able to help in that we had something in common. We didn't know anything about cougars, but we did understand Katie and Shaw's need to shift. We had a semblance of understanding for their predicaments. But if this is some experiment gone awry, and they're manufacturing vampires, we can't even begin to anticipate what else could go wrong."

Nina grunted, her eyes fighting to stay open. "How are Doc Katie and those little beasts, anyway?"

Wanda held up her phone and scrolled through her pictures. "Katie sent me this today. Look at the twins—are they not just to die for?" she cooed.

Nina's return grin was filled with affection. "Yeah. Love those little buggers. Aunt Teeny, too. I'm glad she gave those old broads shit and started her own knitting circle."

They each fell silent with the memory of Katie, a veterinarian accidentally turned into a cougar, and the strange, fact-finding journey that had led their friend not just to a successful paranormal existence, but love with a man named Shaw, marriage, and subsequent twins boys.

Wanda let her head fall back on the couch. She poked her friend's leg. "Hey, Nina?"

"Now what, Wanda?"

"Talk to me," she demanded. "We've been so caught up in the chaos of this O-Tech thing and Phoebe and Sam, I haven't had the chance to really talk to you."

"About?"

"How you feel about all this. Tell me how you feel about Phoebe being your sister."

She shrugged, the roll of her hoodie rippling on her shoulders. "I don't feel anything."

Wanda scoffed. "Nina. C'mon. Some woman shows up and has valid proof she's your sister. That means your father had a long-term affair you knew nothing about, honey. Tell me how that makes you feel and what I can do to help you deal with it. And don't try to hoodwink me. It's just you and me all in the circle of safe."

Nina's eyes had begun to slide closed, but they popped open at Wanda's words. "First, get this shit straight. My dad didn't have an affair. He didn't cheat on my mother. She was dead by the time he hooked up with Princess Barbie's mother. My mom died when I was just a baby of a drug overdose, and I'm four years older than Couture Girl, if that birth certificate frilly boy slapped up in my face is right.

Second, I could only *feel* something if I gave a shit—which I don't. Just because some DNA test says she's my blood means squat. I don't know her. I don't want to know her, and when we're through with this bullshit assignment and she's done all that adjusting we have to teach her, I'm fucking out."

Wanda leaned forward, brushing the hair from her dearest friend's eyes. "Nina. Don't shut the door on this relationship before you've peeked inside to see what the room holds. Lou's getting older. We both know she's not going to live forever like us. But Phoebe will, if we can turn this mess around. Why not try to establish some kind of connection to her? She's family, Nina Statleon, and Lou has a right to know she has two granddaughters."

Nina shrugged Wanda's hands away. "You and Marty and your dumb-ass sister are my family, Wanda. Greg and Arch and Darnell, too. You really think I need more than the three of you loons mucking up my shit? And FYI, one chick that digs designer clothes and all that crap you slather on your faces in this group is enough. Doesn't it just figure that a sister of mine would end up being so much like Gucci-loving Marty? What the fuck was the universe thinking?"

Wanda rubbed her best friend's arm and smiled. "It was thinking if you can love Marty in all her girl-i-tude, you can love Phoebe."

Nina's chin jutted forward, the sharp line stubborn. "I don't love Marty. I tolerate her."

"You've tolerated her for four years, Nina. In fact, you've tolerated us all, despite your loud, sometimes rude protests otherwise. You're still here. You still come to OOPS every day. We're why you come back, because all your bitching aside, we're *framily*, as Casey calls us. You know, your friends who're like family? So why can't Phoebe be a part of that, too? She has no one but Mark, and it certainly isn't her fault your father had an affair with her mother, now is it? She reached out, Nina. She reached out because she's alone. Now, I know you're not very good at connecting unless it's your fist against someone's face, but reach back. Just a little." Wanda held up her index and thumb and grinned.

"The only thing I wanna reach is her neck—so I can wring the fuck out of it. And I have to tell Lou. Before Phoebe gets to her. We all know how subtle she is when it comes to surprises." Nina grunted.

"Uh-uh-uh, Nina." Wanda admonished, shaking her finger. "Let's call it like it was. She tried to get you to go somewhere private with her, but you did what you always do. Go on the defensive. If you'd have just listened to her instead of reacting, things wouldn't have gotten so heated between you, and she wouldn't have fallen on poor Sam. But clearly, she has the Nina gene. She's no coward, that's for sure."

Nina nodded her consent. The brief look of admiration for Phoebe came and went, though. "Whatever. Lou still deserves to know, I guess."

Wanda gave her a quick hug, making Nina squirm. "Now that's the Nina I know and alternately despise and love. The one with the hard outer shell but the big, gooey center. And don't fret about Lou. I'll help. We'll do it on pot roast night. She's always happy when she can cook food you can't eat and to this day doesn't realize you don't eat. You shove your face full of that glutinous mess she lovingly prepares all day, then spit it into a napkin while you tell her, and I promise to eat your portion when she's not looking. How's that?"

Nina gave her a sleepy snicker. "You'd eat Lou's pot roast for me?"

"Because we're framily. You know, I love you, you love me? Like Barney only with bad language," Wanda reminded her.

"I'm not fucking painting your toenails if some long-lost brother of yours shows up, Wanda. No can do, *framily*."

"Damn. I had the color picked out and everything."

"Fuck you, Wanda."

Wanda laughed, pinching Nina's cheeks and rising to drop a kiss on her forehead. "I love you, too, sugarplum. Now sleep, vampire. We have a busy day tomorrow."

Wanda slipped off into the kitchen, leaving Nina to seek a quiet moment to gather her thoughts before she sought solace in a dreamless sleep, too.

As Wanda's eyes scanned Sam's steel kitchen countertops and his painted black oak cabinets, she slid to a breakfast barstool and closed her eyes, her fear finally catching up with her after the adrenaline of the day.

For all her soothing words, for all her reassuring glances, for all the confidence she displayed in front of everyone else, she was terrified. Terrified they wouldn't be able to figure out how to keep Sam and Phoebe from ending up like that woman had. In these past years since she'd been turned, she'd seen things that would leave most in need of lifetime therapy. Yet, she'd summoned the courage and the strength to survive.

But this. The possibility that someone was using humans for sport until they got the experiment right? It was unspeakable.

The well of tears that threatened, yet never fell, blurred her vision. She let her head fall to her folded arms on the counter and allowed the silence of Sam's apartment to seep into her pores while she sent out a prayer to the universe.

Jesus.

Dear, sweet baby Jesus.

This time, OOPS just might have bitten off more than they could chew.

CHAPTER
7

"So like we practiced, right, Sammy?" Nina asked, the harsh, early November wind blowing the last of the fallen leaves around their feet.

Sam gazed up at the glass and black steel of O-Tech's building. They'd huddled at the south corner where Sam claimed a cafeteria lay on the other side with no security guards to interfere. It was the safest place for him to make his wall-walking debut. "Which time is that, Nina? Do you mean the time I couldn't get my *entire* head through the wall? Or the time I actually managed to make it through the wall and tripped on my own feet, fell, and broke not one, but two standing lamps and a perfectly good bookcase?"

Phoebe tugged at her black mask, adjusting the hole at her mouth. The fabric was sticking to the peachy lip gloss she'd so carefully put on while she told herself it wasn't for Sam. She just wanted to be pretty for her first major crime spree. Raising her hand in front of Nina's face, she jumped up and down.

"Christ. What, Barbie?"

"So, just a thought. And I'm merely thinking out loud here, but I feel this shouldn't go unmentioned."

"What's the fucking problem now, Phoebe? Did you only brush your hair for ninety-nine strokes before we left and you need a redo? Or do you have a chipped nail and we need to go back to Sam's so you can fix it? Wait. I know. Those black jeans make your ass look too big and you want everything to be just right when you commit your first fucking felony?" she mocked in Valley girl speak.

"Oh, no. I gave my hair an extra twenty strokes just to be safe, and you know my ass looks cute in these, Nina." Phoebe gave her backside a light slap. "It just hurts too much for you to say so. Anyway, I'm good to go on those fronts."

"You're funny. So much goddamn funny it hurts," Nina snarled, lifting her mask from her face in aggravation. Her deep dark eyes glittered in anger. Not an uncommon event where Phoebe was concerned. "So speak. Get to the point."

Her hands went to her hips where a walkie-talkie and, of all things, a pocketknife were attached to a belt around her waist. "When I tried to teleport today, and I swear on my unlife, I was thinking about Sam's bathroom. Swear it. Wouldn't it be cause for concern that instead of being surrounded by the warm glow of Sam's clay- and beige-colored porcelain and tile, I ended up in the bath fixtures aisle of Home Depot? I don't want to sound any alarms or anything, but that's a problem," she hissed, her every nerve raw and fragile. This was nuts.

Last night, it had appeared the only solution.

Tonight, she was sure it would just be easier to steal the Hope Diamond and turn it into a friendship bracelet.

Sam yanked his mask off, too, his luscious lips a thin line of grim. "Look, Phoebe, if you don't think you can pull this off, I'll do the wall thing and find a way to let you both in. We just thought it would be easier if we both managed to get inside, then let Nina get to a window we can open without having to break it. You know, no alarms, no SWAT team? Less attention drawn to the outside of the building is better."

"Not to mention," Nina groused, "it'll save me a chiropractic bill not having to haul your big ol' badonkadonk on my poor back if we end up having to hit a window two stories up because you can't get this asshattery power you have working."

Phoebe clenched her fists at her side, digging her nails into her hands. *Do not engage, Phoebe. Be the bigger person, Phoebe.* This had been her mantra since they'd awakened and began practicing her pathetically lacking teleportation skills.

That practice had led them to discover that Sam sucked at teleportation, and she'd done an equally dismal job at walking through a wall. Though, via her magically mystical vampiric wonders, the knot on her head and her blackened eye had healed in seconds.

Since dusk, like they were in some kind of vampire boot camp, Nina had barked orders and criticized her for having to chase Phoebe all over Manhattan because she just couldn't get teleportation right. Yet, even when Sam failed just as miserably as she did, Nina did nothing but encourage him with phrases like, "Fucking good try, Gigantor!" and the ever-popular, "Push, dumb ass! You know you can!"

At this point, after not one but five unsuccessful attempts to land in the right place via her vampire mind-meld, she was, as Marty had dubbed it, ass-fried. Yet, somehow, she'd curbed her temper. But her delicate lifeline was fraying as though it were being rubbed against something sharp with every snarky word her sister shot at her.

Between clenched teeth, she fought a snarl when addressing Nina. "Look, all I'm saying is, if I end up, say, on the Verrazano Bridge, I'll be no good to you, and if we hope to cover as much ground as O-Tech has by the plans we virtually stole from the inspector's office under cover of night, we don't need me screwing this up. All night

long you bitched about how time was of the essence. *In and out, Cat
Burglar Barbie*, you said. I'm just trying to get it right. Jesus. So cut
me a break, Vampire Master, okay?"

Sam let his head bow for a moment, seeking patience, a signal
she'd become familiar with when he'd been practicing his wall walking. "Ladies? Why don't we just give this a whirl and see what's what?
The worst that happens is we don't get inside and we have to find
another way."

Nina shook her head. "No. The worst is the two of you end up
ashes we have to dump in that fancy fucking chiminea Wanda has in
her backyard. That's the worst. So you'd better get it right."

Sam wrapped an arm around Nina's shoulder and pulled her hard
to him. "You're so much awesome. All supportive and encouraging.
I'm aglow with your love."

Nina flicked his shoulder, then pointed to the steel on the side of
the building. "Wall. Walk. *Now.*"

Phoebe's stomach sank. It was now or never.

Sam placed his shoulder against the building in preparation, bracing himself.

"Wait!" Phoebe all but shouted.

Sam and Nina gave her a pointed look while the wind whistled
about them and time ticked away.

"What's my handle again?" Jesus. She didn't want to forget what
name she was supposed to use when they corresponded on the
walkie-talkies.

"Little Mouth," Sam reminded her. "You know, so on the off
chance anyone is catching our frequency they won't have our actual
names?"

Oh, right. Phoebe rolled her eyes. Not only because she'd been
dubbed Little Mouth to Nina's Big, but because Sam had thought of
something so detailed like the possibility another entity could listen
in on their conversation on a walkie-talkie.

It was very *Alias*. Who used walkie-talkies anymore anyway? But he was a scientist. Maybe he'd done all sorts of factoring and statistics and come up with a probability she wasn't smart enough to consider. "Right. Little Mouth."

Dear God in heaven, she sent up a silent prayer. *Of all the days to not have a bout with my forgetfulness, now would be the shiniest one. Amen.*

"And I'm Gigantor," Sam said with an encouraging smile before he pulled his mask back down over his face.

"And why are we using walkie-talkies again? What if someone inside O-Tech hears us talking?" she fretted, wrapping her arms around her waist in a protective gesture.

"Because you said you suck at texting, nimrod, and we need a way to communicate when we split up to spread out this search," Nina grated, planting her hands on her hips.

Right. She did suck at texting. She always jumbled those crazy acronyms when she was in a rush, and her fingers never seemed to hit the right keys. AutoCorrect was not her friend, and if she was nervous, it would do them no service if she was LOLing when she should be OMGing. Thus, they'd decided on a lesser, if not totally outdated form of technology.

"The volume's on low, Phoebe, remember? The human ear won't be able to hear us. You know, vampire hearing?" Sam said, gentle and calm.

Phoebe nodded, her throat tight. "And what was it about all those security cameras again?"

Nina bent at the waist, placing her hands on her thighs before she looked up at Phoebe. "No one can see you on them because, unlike your reflection, the one I know you're thanking Vidal Sassoon you can still whip all that hair around in, you don't show up in pictures. Remember, that's why we took your picture? To check and see? It wasn't just to fucking see if you really do have supermodel skills, Phoebe. Now, please. For the love of all that's fucking holy, shut up and let's get moving. It's already midnight, and we've got a lot of ground to cover."

"So you ready?" Sam asked, ignoring Nina's urgent demand, his eyes focused on Phoebe.

Phoebe didn't trust herself to speak, so instead, she simply nodded.

Sam nodded curtly, then leaned back against the steel, aesthetically cold and imposing, and gave a tentative nudge to the wall with his shoulder. To everyone's relief, it disappeared inside the wall.

Now, if they could just get the rest of him inside without him taking out whatever was behind the wall, it was on.

Pulling her mask back over her face, Phoebe closed her eyes and thought of the image she'd seen on the plans for O-Tech's cafeteria. She attempted to imagine the tables that would line the area, where she'd land if she made it inside, how Sam had taught her to tuck her body inward in case she crashed into something.

Fear made her feet shuffle as her hand went to her neck. She tugged at the constrictive turtleneck and groaned. This would never work, and if they didn't find out what was happening to them, she and Sam were going to die. And it would be on her because she couldn't get this being a vampire right. She just needed a little more time. So no one would die.

Die. Oh, fuck.

"Listen to me, Phoebe," Nina whispered inches from her ear, low, seductively comforting. "Just concentrate on Sam. See him in the cafeteria. Picture him in your mind. Do you see Sam?"

Instantly, she was at ease. How odd when mostly Nina just made her want to spork her eyes out. But, yeah. She saw Sam. All hot ass and rippling muscles.

And she was seeing him on some sheets in his big king-sized bed. Ohh.

They were nice sheets, too. Egyptian cotton. Dark, delicious, smooth against your skin. Probably much like Sam would be. Double ohhh.

Did they have a king-sized bed in O-Tech's cafeteria?

"Not *that* Sam, Phoebe," Nina chastised, though her tone wasn't gruff. Placing her hand on Phoebe's shoulder, she squeezed it. "Picture the Sam who's inside O-Tech right now—exactly where you want to be. He's sitting at one of the tables, waiting for you. Can you see that Sam?"

And like when she'd landed in her kitchen, though she hadn't paid attention to the detail of it, the texture and feel of it, due to how frightened she'd been, she was just there. The darkness enveloped her, slithering over her skin like a sensuous lover, and when her eyes opened, she was in the cafeteria of O-Tech.

So neener, neener, neener, Home Depot.

Her eyes scanned the large room with its long buffet where the food was kept warm, and the cash register at the end of it. Picnic-style tables lined the walls and smaller, more intimate tables sat in clusters of twos and threes. As her eyes fully adjusted, she had to keep herself from gasping. Her vampire vision still astounded her, and it was an effort to not become startled each time she realized she could see in the dark.

"Phoebe?"

In her excitement, she launched herself at Sam, wrapping her legs around his waist and throwing her arms around his neck. "I did it!" she whisper-yelped against the knit fabric of his mask.

He tilted his head back while his strong arm braced her spine. "Nice job, Ninja Barbie," he teased.

Her legs went slack immediately, instantly embarrassed that she'd thrown herself at him. She slid down the hard length of his body, her eyes focusing on the top of his pecs encased in a black turtleneck. "So what's next?"

Sam pulled his phone from his back pocket and scrolled to the picture they'd taken of the building's specs. "First we let Nina in, then we split up and search every corridor—every door—and we use our super speed to do it. In and out. Though, I gotta say, even though I've said it before, I've been all over O-Tech, and unless there's something hidden that I somehow missed, I doubt we'll find anything."

He'd been voting down this venture from the get-go, and the more he assured them he hadn't missed some secret passageway, the more Phoebe had to wonder if they'd offended his sensibilities. Because he sure didn't love the idea that he could have missed something.

Phoebe put her hand on her walkie-talkie, preparing to find a window they could open for Nina to let her in. "Well, that's why we're all here. So we can give it a thorough once-over."

"Gigantor, this is Big Mouth. Let's do this, and do it now. Find a window."

Phoebe was the first to whip out her walkie-talkie, putting it to her mouth and pressing the talk button. "Roger that, *Big Mouth.*"

The static crackled before Nina responded, "Shut the fuck up, *Barbie.*"

Sam took her by the hand and pulled her out of the cafeteria, pointing up at a camera as they pushed through some double doors and headed out into the hallway that led to the basement stairs where they'd hoped to let Nina in.

They flew along the staircase, stopping short at the janitor's office where Sam claimed there was a window he'd once seen the janitor, Herb, blowing smoke from. She mentally crossed her fingers it was a window they could gain access to without having to break it.

Sam popped the door with ease and not too much damage to the door's handle, and shoved it open.

Her eyes flew past the bucket and the mop to the window where Nina's pale, beautiful face floated before them. Sam flipped the locks on it, and twisted the bolt, popping open the window and letting Nina climb through. She hopped down onto the desk below and jumped to the floor like a pale gazelle.

"Okay—I'll take the south wing. Sam, you go north. Powder Puff takes the east. We'll all meet up in the west wing if no one finds anything. And fucking remember, you see anything, anything at all—or anyone—you walkie-talkie me. No taking chances. No bullshitting around. I've got a serious grip on my strength. You two—not so much. Got it?" she inquired, her eyes dark and serious.

Phoebe nodded, turning away from them to dig her phone from her pocket to look at the picture of the plans for the eastern section of O-Tech, forgetting her fear for a moment and focusing solely on getting this over with.

Just as she made her way to the door, Sam's hand clamped on her shoulder. Eerily cool of palm, it still made her knees weak and her stomach jolt in excitement. "Phoebe, be careful. *Please.*"

Her hand found its way to Sam's and she let her fingers wrap around his for a brief moment. The cool digits soothed her, calmed her, and with that, she smiled beneath her mask. "You, too. Both of you," she whispered before she slunk out of the janitor's office and took a hard right, heading for the eastern staircase.

Alone.

Shaking off her rising anxiety, Phoebe slipped through the door and flew up the stairwell, reminding herself along the way—she wasn't exactly helpless here. She did have superhuman strength.

And that was a good thing, too, because wouldn't it just figure she'd run into a security guard.

One who wasn't supposed to be making his rounds for another fifteen minutes.

How unfortunate.

SAM sped up the northern staircase, pulling out his gun, one that had been tucked securely in his sock, and scanned the hallway through the glass window in the door. Tucking his piece to his chest with both hands, he slipped inside and plastered himself to the wall while his mind kicked into overdrive.

Fuck if he could talk those two hardheaded women into hearing a single thing he'd said about O-Tech. He'd worked here for three months. There was nothing to find.

And until he'd been bitten by a vampire, that's what all his reports had said. It was also the reason he'd agreed to go along with this batshit crazy plan of Nina and Wanda's. No one could get hurt if the worst that could happen was they'd end up in cuffs.

O-Tech was as exciting and worthy of an in-depth undercover investigation as a shoe factory. Yet, here he was. He couldn't very well have discouraged Nina and Phoebe with too much insistence or they'd have become suspicious.

At all costs, don't blow your cover, Agent McLean. You're there as a plant to be sure everything's on the up-and-up while you catch your breath, were the last words he'd heard before he'd gone in as Sam McLean, entomologist. All of which was true. He was Sam McLean. And he had once been an entomologist.

An entomologist who'd been seeking some respite from the crazy. So he'd jumped at the chance to take a job that probably wouldn't involve anything more dangerous than a microscope. He hadn't found a single thing about human testing anywhere in O-Tech. But . . . What happened to him could well have been a result of some experiment. Jesus. It made sense. It made sick sense.

If someone at O-Tech was testing some diabolical serum, powder, pill, whatever on humans, the O-Tech employees were damned good actors and actresses, because he hadn't witnessed even a hint of foul play. Nothing suspicious.

And he knew foul play. He'd seen plenty of it in his career.

In fact, just before the organization had been ready to pull him out for lack of discovery, he'd had the encounter with the strange woman and found himself a vampire, and he'd been stalling ever since. He'd bullshitted his way through three calls now, claiming he wanted to be as thorough as possible in an effort to keep them at bay.

Which was total horseshit, Sam thought as he rounded a corner and slid past one of several labs at O-Tech. Though stalling the organization meant buying time for himself and his new dilemma, it also reminded him he couldn't drag this mission out any longer without doing exactly what he didn't want to do. Arouse suspicion. It was time to call in and ask for some leave.

They'd buy it because he'd sell the shit out of his burnout from the job complaint, and the agency would close the case, letting him off the hook for a couple of weeks. Even if they did find something tonight, he couldn't report it now. Not in his new position as Agent Vampire.

But that didn't keep him from feeling like a complete shit.

He'd done lots of questionably moral things in his time as an agent for the FBI, and he often soothed himself that it was for the greater good. If the population at large were to know what he knew, mass hysteria would be the least of the government's worries. If they knew what had happened to him on this assignment—he'd be as screwed as some of the cases he worked.

In all his undercover work, he least liked deceiving people who were decent. Especially people like Nina, Wanda, and Marty.

Good people who in some crazy, loud, totally selfless way, gave up their everyday lives to throw themselves wholeheartedly into helping others who were afraid in situations that were unreal.

Others like Phoebe.

No one was ever going to believe this shit back at the agency. After all the years he and his colleagues had spent hunting the unexplainable, after never solving a single one of the bizarre cases they'd investigated, after being left to scratch their heads without ever finding a definitive answer to some of the crazy they'd seen, there was this. This paranormal Pandora's box. Who would have believed this was all real? All the leads, all the twisted shit he'd seen wasn't just some elaborate hoax or something one of the techs could explain away with a scientific fact. It was happening, and how ironic that it was happening to him. Maybe it was the universe's way of reminding him he'd begun to flail in his conviction that there really was something more out there?

And now, he was a vampire, and if the agency got wind of it, protocol would have him exactly where Wanda had openly warned Phoebe she'd end up. Somebody's guinea pig.

That thought brought to mind Phoebe and what could happen even if they survived this death-by-decomposition.

Sam was good at compartmentalizing—most of the time. He had quite nicely separated his duties to the agency and his emotions. He slipped into Sam the Bug guy's role as easy as he slipped his Stetson on his head.

He knew that guy—it was the guy he'd perfected over the years. Easygoing, affable, a little goofy. The real Sam had much darker shades to him, and those darker elements were usually what kept him from getting too involved. Though, even at his darkest, his failed one-night stand was totally out of character for him. He was on the job. He knew better. He never, ever gave in to his needs when he was on duty. But he'd been lonely. Period. Look what lonely had gotten him. A vampire and a couple of werewolves.

And Phoebe . . .

Phoebe had a vulnerability about her that, when mixed with her determination, made her one helluva sexy combo.

He'd been instantly attracted to her—something he couldn't claim had happened in quite this way in a very long time.

His stab at a one-night stand had been purely physical and completely impulsive—Phoebe was something altogether different.

It was bad timing on his part—to find himself stealing glances at her when she wasn't looking or imagining her curvy hips beneath his. To watch her soft lips part when she was concentrating and her auburn hair curve just below her chin. No matter how often he reminded himself he was still essentially on the job, he continued to find himself easily distracted by her beauty and her humor—even in probably the worst-possible situation, she still laughed.

And at whatever cost, Sam had to keep her not just alive, but out of the hands of the very agency he'd sworn to protect. It also meant, he couldn't go back to the job he'd been doing for ten years.

Then, as if things weren't already bad enough, he was going to have to come clean to the women of OOPS.

Right now, he was just going to be grateful that when he had to tell Nina and the others about what he really did for a living, he didn't just have vampire in his cache of badassery. He had a black belt in karate and black ops training on his side.

Because Nina was a badder bitch than any terrorist group as a whole he'd ever come across.

And still, it wasn't her violent nature that worried him.

It was the fact that he was going to end up breaking a trust she and the others had given him without qualm.

And that really blew some chunks.

CHAPTER
8

"Breaker! Breaker-breaker one . . . um. Damn. I can't remember the stupid numbers. I don't know! Just breaker!" Phoebe huddled in a corner, pressing her lips to the walkie-talkie. "Big Mouth, Gigantor—this is Little Mouth! Do you copy?" Phoebe whispered into the walkie-talkie, fear making her words rushed as she huddled in a quivering mass of freaked out in the corner.

Nina's voice crackled over the instrument Phoebe had pressed to her ear like it was her lifeline. "Jesus Christ. Yes. I copy, you mindless moron."

Sam's words slid into her ear, silken, and almost erotic—even in her panic, she was still able to make note of that. "Little Mouth? What's your location?"

"I don't know, but . . . please, drop the hammer, good buddies!" she whisper-yelled. That meant get here right now, according to the CB lingo she'd looked up online so they could communicate with subterfuge. At least she hoped she'd memorized it correctly. Because no doubt, she needed someone here STAT.

"Oh, I'm gonna drop the hammer, dingbat. Right on your air-head!"

"Little Mouth!" Sam's tone was urgent. "What's wrong? Where are you?"

"We got a bear!" Which meant she'd run into a security guard and/or cop. Or was that bear trap? Oh, Jesus. Her eyes flew in a wild scan of the room she'd landed in when she'd panicked after seeing the security guard. If she could still vomit, surely an ugly projectile wouldn't have been out of the question.

"A bear," Nina drawled, her sarcasm rich amidst the static. "Is it Yogi or Smokey? If it's Yogi, my apologies in advance. I forgot my fucking picnic basket. If it's Smokey, tell him to set you the fuck on fire with those matches he collects so I don't have to listen to you anymore!"

"Big Mouth, shut it! Little Mouth, what's happening?" Sam demanded, his rasping voice rough against her ear.

"We got a John Law right outside this door!" she yelped in return.

"Listen, *Convoy*, where the fuck are you? And tell me in English, Kris Kristofferson," Nina growled, her voice full of anger and a hint of anxious.

"I don't know!" Phoebe yelped. "But you two better highball it or we're gonna be in the pokey with a smoky!"

"Gigantor? This is Big Mouth. Find her before I rip her fancy salon hair out strand by fucking strand. Ten-four, *good buddy*?"

"Listen to me, Phoe, er, Little Mouth. Are you still in the east wing?"

"I don't know and I'm too afraid to look outside this lab."

"Lab? What lab, honey? There are no labs on the east side of the building," Sam said with insistence.

Honey? Had he just called her *honey*? Phoebe fought a full-on preen and tried to focus on anything but what was in the corner of the room. It would be lovely if she were afforded the time to bask in the glow that was Sam's endearment.

But, no—she had this to deal with. In fact, this—this was almost exactly like the time on *When the World Turns* when Pedro Montoya Federico Salinas had been found in a lab just like this one in an underground bunker in Old San Juan after his maniacal brother-in-law, Shawn Patrick O'Hara, put him in a coma.

She scrunched her eyes shut. "This is definitely a lab, good buddy. There are all sorts of vials of stuff, beakers, and a microscope and needles. So many needles!"

She could almost see Sam shake his handsome head in disbelief. "Okay. Stay calm. Is there a door to the lab? Can you see out of it?"

Phoebe slid along the wall in a crablike sweep, keeping her eyes on the door and not the thing in the corner. Pressing the button on the walkie-talkie, she nodded. "Yes. There's a window and a big bear right outside it!"

"What the fuck is a big bear, moron?"

"A security guard!" she hissed, her teeth chattering.

"How did you get into the lab, Little Mouth?" Sam prodded, his voice coaxing.

Oh. That. "I saw a security guard just as I came up the east side staircase. I must've freaked out and all I could think was I'm going to die in jail while some woman-beast with the title The Punisher or Bitch Maker beat me into doing her dirty jailhouse deeds. Not to mention, I hear the sheets in the pokey are really harsh on your skin. Then I began to think about my skin and how awful it would be if I couldn't have my coconut oil. I rub that all over my body to keep my skin smooth and glowing. Every single night. Anyway, it just felt worse than death to me—which is shallow and vain, I know, but I couldn't help it. And that put me here. The word death. I think. Anyway, it put me here. In this lab. With—with . . ." Oh, Jesus and a dead body, she just couldn't say it.

"With *what*?" Sam prompted with what sounded like strained impatience.

Phoebe jammed a finger in her mouth to keep from screaming.

She would not scream. Nina'd howl with laughter and that just wasn't acceptable. "With something heinous!"

"Heinous," Nina said in dry tones from her end. "What *is* heinous to Fluffy Barbie? Oh, noes. I bet she just found out her favorite hair gel is used to kill off tsetse flies. Aw, Barbie haz a sad now?"

Phoebe's last nerve disconnected from her sanity, and after much abuse, while she huddled in a corner, she blew her wad all over her walkie-talkie. "You know what, *Big Mouth*? That's enough, you mean, ornery, cranky, insulting, angry, bitch of the highest order—you can blow me! Do you hear me? Bloooow. Me. Hard! I'm sick to death of you and your put-upon bullshit. *You* did this to me. If it weren't for *you*, I'd have left your offices and probably never looked back, because you're a mean one, viper. I'm here because of *you*. You— you—*you*! So get the fuck off my back, you venomous bitch, and come find me, or I swear to the heavens above, I'm going to beat your ass with a sack of garlic and shower your stank with some holy water! Got that, Ghetto Barbie?" With a huff, she let go of the "talk" button and stuck her tongue out at the walkie-talkie, shaking.

There was silence from both parties concerned for a moment, giving Phoebe a moment to peek out the window of the lab and watch wide-eyed as Sam took out the looming security guard with a move she'd only seen in Jackie Chan movies.

Her mouth fell open. Wow. Entomologists were all sorts of kick-ass hot, huh?

Just as Sam pushed his way into the lab, Nina crackled on the walkie-talkie. "Barbie? That was a damn fine rant. One that fucking would have brought a tear to my eye if not for the fact that I can't cry, but I love to make people cry. Which is exactly what I'm gonna do to you when I get my hands around your scrawny, mouthy neck—"

"Big Mouth!" Sam shouted into the walkie-talkie. "Shut it and get here now." He gave Nina directions, pulling Phoebe to his side in a manner so protective it made her want to smile—and cling for dear life.

But she couldn't. Not with *that* over there in the corner.

Sam was the first to move, striding over to the corner, his hands on his hips. "What the hell is going on?"

Phoebe went to his side, clutching his arm but staying partially behind his broad back. "How did you find me?"

He rooted in his jean pocket and pulled out a silver clip she'd had to keep her hair up under her mask. It shined in the eerie light of the lab. "It must have fallen out when you were teleporting. It was by a door that led to an elevator I've never encountered before. So I took the elevator and pressed the only button it had. That brought me here."

Nina burst through the door to come up short behind them, skidding to a halt. "Who flattened the security guard?" she asked.

"Sam did," Phoebe couldn't help but gush. "It was like something out of a movie. He went all Bruce Lee on the guy. How did you learn to do that?"

He flapped a dismissive hand. "Took some karate lessons a long time ago. Plus, I am a vampire, right? All big and strong. It wasn't hard. We have other things to worry about right now."

"Holy fuck," Nina muttered. "Leave it to you to find something like this, princess."

Sam was the first to lean against the gurney.

The gurney with the dead body on it.

Covered in a sheet with nothing but the toes sticking out at the end of the bed, the outline it made was small, and probably female, if the red-painted toenails were any indication.

"Again, I ask, what the hell is going on? We make pest control, for Christ's sake." He peered under the bed and Phoebe followed his eyes as he scanned the countertops.

"What are we looking for?"

Sam shrugged. "Something—anything. Paperwork, maybe? I don't know. There's no computer anywhere—so clearly, they've just stowed the body here. Seems to me if they're really performing tests on human subjects, they'd have lab results, right? We need to see them. Maybe I can decipher what they're giving them."

As the horror of what she was seeing began to seep in, Phoebe found she had to will herself not to crumble.

Nina nudged her hard. "Hang tight, grasshopper. The last thing we need is for you to pass out."

Phoebe instantly straightened. As though on autopilot, she moved from behind Sam and went to the side of the gurney to begin searching the few cabinets on the wall as Nina began to sift through the paperwork on the various work surfaces.

Sam was the first to say what Phoebe was dreading. "We need to know who this is."

Each of the women stopped cold in their tracks when Sam's fingers went to the sheet that covered the body. Phoebe closed her eyes, then forced them open. She would not hide from this. No. This was a head-on kind of thing. No matter what, she was going to be conscious when and if they found out what had made them different than all the other vampires. If the answer lay in a dead body and O-Tech shenanigans, then so be it.

Sam's long fingers, pale and strong, pulled the sheet back, folding it to the body's waist. Nina leaned in, sniffing her for the scent of what they most feared. She nodded soberly with a curt bow of her head. "Yep. She's vampire. Damn it," she spat. Straightening, she stepped away from the gurney, pinching the bridge of her nose.

And that left Phoebe not so sure she was as all about the brave like she had been just seconds ago. She stumbled backward, knocking over a silver tray of gadgets, yet she couldn't tear her eyes away.

Sam was instantly at her side, gripping her at the waist. "Phoebe? What's wrong?"

Oh, God.

OhmyGod.

Nina grabbed her hand and squeezed it, giving her a good shake. "Phoebe, what the hell?"

Fear held her tongue. Terror rose and fell in waves of prickly heat along her spine.

Sam stood in front of her, blocking her view of the body. He cupped her chin, forcing her eyes to meet his. "Phoebe, talk to me, sweetheart."

She shuddered, over and over, a violent chill wracking her flesh. "I . . . Oh, God. I know her . . ."

Sam's voice rose enough for Phoebe, even in her horror, to realize it was urgent she answer them. "How do you know her, Phoebe? *Who* is she?"

Phoebe shook her head in denial, her eyes darting from Sam to Nina in frantic horror. God, no. They *were* testing humans. She knew that now as sure as she knew a fake pair of Manolo Blahniks. "She goes to the same doctor I do," she choked out.

Nina's face held instant concern, her eyes becoming hawkish, piercing hers. She pushed Phoebe's mussed hair from her eyes with gentle fingers. Fingers so tender, Phoebe had to stave off a dry sob. "What kind of a doctor, Phoebe?"

She winced, her hands trembling with violent, jerky twitches. "A neurologist."

Sam's eyes narrowed, his grip on her growing tighter. "For?"

She slammed her eyes shut, wanting more than anything to be able to do something as simple as gulp and avoid the pity she knew would follow once her secret was out. There was no hiding from this because it could help them discover the answer to what was happening to she and Sam. And even if it couldn't save herself—it might save Sam.

Phoebe opened her eyes and forced herself to look Nina and Sam in the eye. Her chin lifted, her words were steady. "Early-onset Alzheimer's."

* * *

WANDA brought Sam a bag of blood, placing it between his two hands and cupping them with hers. She squeezed his fingers and smiled the Wanda-was-born-to-nurture smile. "You okay?"

Sam's mouth tightened into a firm line. "I don't know what to say here, Wanda. Why didn't she tell us?" Damn. His gut burned, and whether it was the phantom pain of his long-gone humanness or not, he didn't know. He only knew it ached.

Wanda slid onto his couch, smoothing out her skirt to her knees. "I imagine because she didn't want anyone to know, especially Nina. But I'd bet that's why she looked for our vampire to begin with. Because she wanted to know her before she couldn't remember her," she said, her voice hitching to his sensitive ear.

If he still had a heart, he knew it would clench in sympathy. In dread. In sadness. Fuck. Where was compartmentalization when you needed it?

You're too involved, Sam. This isn't one of those cases where the end justifies the means. You don't just think she's beautiful in an aesthetic and you-won't-remember-her-the-moment-the-job-ends way. You think she's beautiful-beautiful. The kind of beautiful that brings with it emotions like sorrow, pity. This isn't Sam just sympathizing with someone who's been dealt a harsh hand. You got a whole other ball of wax up in here.

"She's so damn young, Wanda." He attempted to force the words out in a purely I'm-sorry-another-human-being-is-terminal kind of way. The bitch of it was, they didn't come out that way.

Wanda nodded, her sleek ponytail rubbing against the back of the couch. "She is indeed. Thirty-three, I think Mark said."

His disbelief had floored him back at O-Tech, and he'd lost his professional composure, making him surer than ever he liked Phoebe a great deal more than he should.

That they'd made it out of O-Tech without being seen after finding what they'd found, hearing what they'd heard, would always be a miracle as far as he was concerned. Every last lesson he'd been taught since he'd joined the agency had flown out the window with Phoebe's news.

The dead body he could handle. He'd handled plenty in his time.

The idea that Phoebe could have been mixed up in this before she'd been turned or that her body could have been the one on that gurney? Not so much. "What are the chances? I mean, really. *Thirty-three?*"

"It's very, very rare, I hear," Wanda replied, her tone somber.

"But there is good news, Master Samuel," Archibald offered, breezing into his living room with a frosty mug. He took the packet of blood from Sam and poured it into the glass.

"And what's good about any of this?" Sam asked, misery lumping in his chest.

Archibald pulled a towel from his shoulder and wiped his hands on it, his eyes wrinkled upward into a warm smile. "Miss Wanda hasn't shared with you the miracle of vampiric intervention?"

Sam's head cocked in Wanda's direction and she smiled, giving him a pat on the arm. "Phoebe doesn't have Alzheimer's anymore, Sam. Just like her heart isn't a living organ, essentially, neither is her brain. The disease that was damaging it no longer exists. I know, it makes no sense that you can be walking and talking without critical organs, but there it is."

And like a house had been lifted from his shoulders, instant relief flooded Sam. The science of it was extraordinary. The unbelievable miracle of it—better still. "Does Phoebe know yet?"

Wanda winked. "That's what Nina's in there telling her as we speak. Any second now, you'll hear the word *fucktard*, possibly followed by the harmonious strains of breaking glass. But fear not. I'll intervene if need be, and of course, Nina will pay for whatever she breaks over Phoebe's head. It might not be a bad thing to let the two of them duke it out so we can eliminate all the tension between them."

Sam let his head drop to his chest in gratitude to a universe that had, in some bizarre twist of fate, managed to save Phoebe. He tugged at his turtleneck, a renewed disbelief mingled with confusion making his head spin. He had several degrees and a postgraduate, yet still, he couldn't wrap his brain around the science of this. "This—*all* of this makes absolutely no sense."

"Hah!" Archibald shouted, swatting Sam playfully with his kitchen towel. "What does, sir? Has anything that's happened to you since your turn made sense?"

"True dat, Archibald. True dat." He paused for a moment, steepling his hands under his chin. "But here's a thought. We're not like the other vampires. What if this anti-aging cure all your ills doesn't apply to me and Phoebe because we're a different kind of vampire?"

"You may have different abilities, yes, and that could well be because of whatever's going on at O-Tech, but you're not breathing, are you? And yet still you walk among us," Wanda reminded him.

He smiled in irony. "Point."

Archibald crossed his arms over his chest. "Thus far, I've gathered this much. You found a dead female vampire, but no information on her other than what our Phoebe knows. There was no way for you to search the facility further due to the awakened security guard, whom Nina wiped clean of all memory, leaving us with no one to question. What I wonder is, why didn't she suffer the heinous death your mystery woman did?"

Yeah. He wondered that, too, as he sipped his evening feeding. "The only thing I can gather is maybe she managed to survive longer during the testing. Maybe she was a stronger candidate? She certainly didn't die by way of what you claim is a typical vampire kill. No wooden stakes through the heart—her head was still intact. If I could have just poked around more—maybe grabbed some of those vials in the room . . ."

"So thoughts on where we go from here, sir?" Archibald asked, handing him a cocktail napkin and pointing to the side of Sam's mouth, encouraging him to wipe it.

Sam couldn't help but hide his grin behind the swipe of the paper napkin. "Why do I get the impression you're really enjoying this, Archibald?"

Archibald gave him a sly smile with the rise of one bushy eyebrow. He clapped his hands together. "Because I am, Master Samuel! In my humble opinion, there's nothing quite like a good episode of *Murder, She Wrote*, and while I certainly understand to compare your situation with a one-hour drama is absurd, and quite possibly appears insensitive, I mean no disrespect. However, I will admit, I can't help but wait with bated breath for our next move."

Sam got it. Everyone was an armchair sleuth until they actually had to live it. "Well, I guess now we just have to get to that doctor and find out who that patient was and how she got to O-Tech. Phoebe didn't know her by name. She only recognized her from the office waiting room."

Wanda winced, rubbing her arms with her hands. "You took a picture of her with your phone to show them?"

The high he'd experienced a moment ago evaporated. "I did." And if he were smart, he'd send one to the agency, too. But he hadn't figured a way around keeping them from sending someone else in to help him. Someone who'd discover what had happened to him. Like maybe that prick Lewis who was always up in his face. What they'd discovered tonight was big. Big, and ugly, and clearly financed by some madman.

O-Tech was headed for some serious fallout if they could prove pest-control manufacturing wasn't the only thing going on there. People were dying. How he was going to blow that wide open and keep everyone safe became an insurmountable worry. *Focus McLean. Focus on one piece of the puzzle at a time.*

"And how do we get them to give us the information about this poor soul?"

"Leave that to me, Wanda," Sam reassured. He wasn't quite ready to tell them that he had a badge gifting him with credentials that would have him in and out of that doctor's office in no time flat.

Not just yet.

Nina had Phoebe cornered in Sam's bedroom, her face a mask of cold anger. "Why the fuck didn't you tell me?"

"Why the *fuck* would I?" Phoebe shot back. "Would you have whispered soothing words to me? Made me cookies and warm blood and tucked me in?"

Nina's full lips sneered. "Because, moron, it's important information. So why didn't you tell me?"

Because she'd rather be dead? Oh, wait. She was. Okay, because she'd rather live an eternity not getting to know Nina than have her sister want to know her because she felt sorry for her. "Would it have changed how you felt about me telling you I was your sister, Nina? Would it have made you feel sorry enough for me to let me into your nonexistent heart?"

Nina jabbed her shoulder with a sharp finger. "I guess we'll never know, will we? Know why? Because you *didn't* tell me, dipshit."

Phoebe jabbed her back, squaring her shoulders to make herself appear taller. "You know, it wasn't like I had a lot of time to do or say anything. One minute I was thinking we could have a cup of coffee and talk, and the next I was ass end down on Sam's fang. Since then, it's been a hundred miles an hour at warp speed. There wasn't really time for intimate chats by the fireplace and long walks on the beach."

"It takes two seconds to say, 'Nina, I have fucking Alzheimer's.'"

"Okay. You count. Ready, set, go. Nina, I have Alzheimer's."

"Not funny, Forgetful Barbie. Not even a little."

Fine. Not funny. Phoebe softened just a little, allowing one of her biggest concerns to fly freely from her lips. "I didn't want to start a relationship with you thinking I needed your pity. I also didn't want it to be the only reason you agreed to let me into your life—because you wouldn't have been in it for long before I didn't know who you were anyway." Jesus. That stung to say out loud. But it was the absolute truth.

Much like everything else, Nina made her regret opening up. "But you found me because you were afraid you wouldn't be able to look for me when your brain turned to oatmeal. So no matter *when* I found out, there sure as shit was going to be pity involved, short-cake."

She had no rebuttal for that. Yes, of course she'd intended to tell Nina, and still, there was even more to tell, but not before they'd at least found a way to connect. As of right now, they'd missed the connection mark by a planetary system. She'd had no idea her disease could affect anything vampiric, and since this had all begun, she most definitely hadn't wanted it to hinder their search for answers. In guilt, she averted her eyes.

But Nina wasn't going to let her off the hook. She cupped Phoebe's jaw, forcing her to gaze into her dark, menacing eyes. Nina's jaw was tight, her teeth clenched together. "Here's the score, cupcake. I'm not a nice person. I know it—everyone else knows it, too. I call it as I see it because life was once too short to fuck around. When you're a total bitch, it tends to weed out the people who'll conveniently forget to have your back when the shit flies. Now that my life's not so short, it's too *long* to fuck around, playing games and pretending things are something they're really not. I'm rude. I'm crass. I'm impatient. I'm so fucking honest some call me brutal. I also have a nasty-ass tongue I sharpen with a straight razor every day, and I don't like a lot of people. Some foolishly mistake me for being angry *with* them. The only thing I'm angry about is that people spend so much time being asshats on my life-dime. I just point that shit out to them—and, yeah, I do it with glee. But get this much straight. I'm not so much of a bitch I'd wish that special Alzheimer's kind of hell on anyone. *Anyone*."

Phoebe's throat was tight to the point of uncomfortable. Yes. Nina was all of those things. To a lesser degree, so was she, but she'd had a strong female presence in her life to soften her impatient edges.

Nina'd had only their father, which had left her with some very crude, and lacking, self-expression. "I was hoping by the time I was forced to tell you, we'd have been well on our way to establishing some sort of bond. Utter fool was I."

Nina chucked her under the chin with a sly grin. "You're not a fool because you have some disease you have no control over, Phoebes. You were dealt a shitty hand at such a young age, and that so sucks. But you're definitely a fucking fool." She rolled her tongue along the inside of her cheek. "Wanna know why?"

Just when she'd thought they were gearing up to have a squishy moment, Nina had a big pin at the ready to pop her bubble. "Oh, please. I'm sure you have a laundry list of reasons. Give them *allll* to me. Every last one."

"Because if you'd told me, I might not have been able to ease your mind about what could go down if we don't find some way to help you and Sam, but I could have at least lifted one burden off your designer shoulders."

Phoebe glanced at her pink nail polish, affecting a bored look. "My designer shoulders await."

"You don't have fucking Alzheimer's anymore, dingbat. You got a lot of other shit going on, but losing your brain matter ain't one of 'em. When you become a vampire, any illness, disease, what-the-fuck-ever, is cured. You can have unprotected sex until your vajajay shrivels up, because no disease can kill you, but you can't ever have kids. You age at the rate of ketchup dripping, so you're gonna be thirty-three for a really long time, and just like you don't have a beating heart or working kidneys, vampirism means whatever was eating your brain has stopped cold. But that's just the tip of the vampire iceberg. And *that's* why you should have told me." With that, Nina turned on her heel and stormed out of the bedroom, kicking Sam's jogging shoes on the way.

Oh. Sure. Put it all on her. Like it was her fault she had no clue she'd been cured of not just a long, agonizing, eventual death, but of, say, her period.

Phoebe's head shot up.

Hold up.

No more tampon shopping + getting her deposit back on the cremation she'd purchased + no more expensive neurological tests + the spared expense of anti-aging creams = jackpot, bitch! And maybe a quick vacay somewhere dark and sunless.

Score!

This was epic. Everything had changed in just a matter of seconds. With just one fang. God, the tears she'd silently wept each night since her diagnosis for the things she was destined to never experience.

Like Paris during fashion week. Venice in a gondola on a warm Italian evening. Buying her own home. A vegetable garden with fat, ripe tomatoes she'd make toasted cheese sandwiches with. Learning to sew. True love. Marriage. Wrinkles. Rocking chairs on a big front porch. Sitting in the buttery sunshine when she was seventy.

That was all gone now. Just gone—well, most of it anyway. Because of Nina. In essence, Nina had saved her from a death so callous and cruel, she couldn't fathom finding the right words to thank her.

"Phoebe?"

She turned to find Sam, strong, tall, and so breathtakingly handsome, in the doorway; if air still escaped her lungs, it would have done so on a wistful sigh.

Call it impulse or the rush of life that swelled through her literally undead body, or just call it plain old lust, Phoebe threw herself at him and planted a kiss on the lips that, when she hadn't been fearing for their lives, she couldn't stop thinking about since she'd found out they were straight.

And they were worthy of every sinful moment she'd dedicated to them. Soft but firm, lush and cool. Nom-nom.

Yet, the kiss that was supposed to be a simple peck, turned to something else altogether when Sam's tongue scoured the inside of her mouth, forcing her own tongue to taste his until she thought she'd faint from the delicious silky slide. The shiver he evoked from her body from the mere press of his lips was hot and hard, making her shudder against him, melt into him, arch her back with an almost feline growl. Her fingers clenched in surprise just as her legs turned to jelly.

And there it was.

The kind of kiss she'd sought for thirty-three years of her life, and until these last moments, thought she'd never have the chance to experience.

The kind of kiss that had Whitney Houston singing while Boyz II Men and 98 Degrees did the backup vocals in her head. The brand of kiss that left burning mental images of freshly fallen snow and windswept fields of wildflowers floating around in her brain.

There were clouds, too, white and puffy, drifting beneath their bottoms like cushiony chairs. Angels waved and smiled their fond approval at them as they floated by, still attached by their needy lips.

Harps played and rainbows appeared like a long stretch of colorful hills just waiting for her to skip to the end of them on winged feet.

The only thing missing was a unicorn.

CHAPTER
9

Oh. But wait. There it was. The unicorn. Just past the rainbow hills and windswept fields of multicolored flowers, his long, lovely mane lifting in the warm breeze, his majestic posture proud and regal.

"Phoebe?" Sam said against her lips, putting his hands on her forearms, forearms that had suspiciously crept up around his neck.

"Don't speak," she ordered in a dreamy state, letting her eyes slide closed again to recapture the bliss of the unicorn and harps. Her fingers twisted in his hair, the silken strands soft against her skin. She pulled his lips back toward hers, desperate for him to consume her, relishing the idea of his tongue in her mouth again.

It was in that desperate achy need that she made a decision.

Just this once, she was going to live in the moment—celebrate the joy of simply being alive.

Or undead alive. Whatever. Her thoughts were reckless and impulsive and headed to a place she didn't usually go without some cautionary thinking. Yet, this gift was to be celebrated—and celebrate she would. If Sam would just break out the party hats and horns with her . . .

But Sam lifted one corner of his mouth from hers, making her release a forbidden moan. Clearly, he wanted to shroud that moment in stupid morality and gentlemanly behavior. "If I don't speak, you won't be able to hear my misgivings."

She tamped down her inward groan, wanting to appreciate his integrity but hoping she could persuade him to join her in Inner Slutville where, if he'd just dip his toe in, the water was just fine. "Then that's a perfect reason not to speak."

"What kind of gentleman would I be if I didn't voice those to you, Phoebe?"

What kind of whore would she be if she just steamrolled his mouth shut with her lips and had her way with him?

And hey. Hang on there. Weren't his lax morals the reason he was a vampire to begin with? "Who said you have to be a gentleman?" she teased, pressing her hips to his and fighting the hot moan of need she experienced when she realized he was as aroused as she was. The fierce ridge of his cock drove against her, then pulled away, making her fight a squirm of anticipation.

"I said." Yet, Sam's palms continued to caress circles over her spine, making her arch against the hard shelter of his chest while she reveled in the magnified sensation of tingles he was creating.

His touch burned her, though his fingers were cool. His lips set hers on fire, though they were as chilled as the rest of him, and even though her senses were technically dead, the slightest graze of his flesh against hers felt like a million fingers touching her. It was the most intense brush of skin on skin she'd ever encountered. Her breasts swelled against his chest, unbearably achy. "What do you know?"

Sam's hands slid down her back, grazing her ass before returning to rest at her waist and tighten into a fist of restraint. "I know that you're experiencing an adrenaline rush. Your adrenal gland is releasing epinephrine—it's a fight-or-flight reaction to finding out you no longer have Alzheimer's."

She let her lips move away from his for a moment and cocked her eyebrow upward. "Thank God you explained the science of that. I don't know that I would have ever vampire slept again if you didn't tell me why and how my adrenal glands were in overdrive. It completely adds to the atmosphere, too."

"Phoebe," Sam's silken tones chastised. "I think you know what I'm trying to say here. The relief mixed with joy over what was technically a cure for your Alzheimer's is overruling your common sense and clouding your judgment."

"Who said kissing you means I have no common sense?" Or good judgment? What woman who was sane, straight, and possessed even half a hormone wouldn't want to kiss Sam McLean? That was good womanly judgment, if you asked her hormones.

Sam's chuckle was deep and rumbly. "Oh, no. That's not what I'm saying at all. Kissing me is totally common sense–filled. I'm a hot nerd. What I'm saying is I get the impression you're not normally the kind of woman who throws caution to the wind."

Caution was for whiners. Only the truly brave threw it to the wind. "And you deduced this how?"

Sam tipped her chin up with his forefinger. "You've got a calendar the size of one full wall in your bedroom, filled with what I'm going to assume is your client appointments. Oh, and booyah for nailing a gig with Master Z. He's pretty big in the rap world." He held his knuckle up for her to knock with hers.

She complied. "If you had any idea how hard he was to please, you'd know it was the coup of the millennium. All he does is complain about how he won't wear this color or that. The women in his videos can't be anything less than a C cup because he claims he has a good eye for hooters and he'll know if I've conned him with a double B. He's impossible, but he knows a lot of people in the industry. I'm not at the point in my career where people are knocking down my door to do video shoots or red-carpet events. Not yet."

Sam's head bobbed, and his finger lifted her chin in a gesture so tender she melted all over again. "I noted the importance of Master Z by the key you made along the side of the calendar. I'm guessing the red asterisks are the upper echelon of your clientele? And I also noted you have stacks of sticky notes lined up by color to within an inch of their lives on your desk, and your pens are assembled in that holder of yours by height. The pillows on your bed are so perfectly centered, I'd bet if I measured them, they'd have equal distance between them. And don't get me started on your closet. Those are all signs of someone who likes to plan and/or have a plan. Someone who likes to know where everything is at any given time—always. Not someone who acts on impulse and sleeps with a man she just met—even if he is a hot nerd." He grinned down at her, though his arms remained around her waist.

He made it sound so tawdry, as though he'd never considered tawdry. Hello. Decomposed one-night stand. Phoebe planted her hands on her hips and eyeballed him. "So, Mr. Observant, are you some kind of shrink, too? Wait, I know, maybe you're a profiler on the side, huh, bug dude?" she teased, barely noticing the stiffening of Sam's muscles.

His eyes shuttered. "Bug dudes are very observant because we observe bug behavior."

"What were you doing in my bedroom?"

"Mark offered to let me use your eye-makeup remover."

It was true. She did like to know where she was at. She had to know where she was at in order to keep her business running smoothly. Unhappy clients could be unhappy monsters. She'd learned that much as she began to deal with C-list celebrities. She also liked order and cleanliness and soap operas and the color pink.

So what?

That didn't mean she couldn't let loose every once in a while.

And Sam had just become her let-loose pet project. "I don't get the hesitation? I don't want to bring up a bad memory, but wasn't it you who was well on his way to a one-night stand when this all happened?"

He rolled his tongue along the inside of his cheek; a small tic pulsed in his jaw. "And look how that turned out. I'm now a vampire, and I turned you into a vampire, too. And our lives are decidedly at risk because of it. One-night stands aren't exactly my strong suit. Who knows the kind of damage I could create if I actually go through with it? Besides, who said if anything happens between us it'll just be a one-night stand? I'd be offended if I had a leg and some past performances to stand on."

Phoebe smiled up at him, knowing if her heart still could, it would skip. Even though her next words were going to have an extra put-out tone to them, she was secretly pleased he hadn't taken her up on her offer now that she'd had time to cool off. And he'd made a point. A good one. "So you're saying you won't sleep with me?"

"Not tonight and not with a houseful of people who have bionic hearing. What I am saying is, I like you. I'm attracted to you. I thought, even as I was on the floor like some pathetic broken toy at OOPS, that you were very attractive—"

"But the first thing you laid eyes on was what was under my skirt."

"No. That was the second," he reminded with a husky chuckle.

"Technicalities."

"Either way, once I was past the Stephen King–like properties of the evening's events, I found you very physically appealing. There's nothing hotter than a woman who has the balls to tell someone as scary as Nina off—not to mention, you can teleport. That makes you ridiculously hot."

She latched on to the front of his black turtleneck sweater, opting to give him one last test. "Ditto. So let's do this."

"Uh, no." He dropped his hands from her waist and took a step back.

Phoebe rolled her eyes, planting her hands on her hips. "Do women throw themselves at you like this every day, Sam? Is this old hat for hot nerds? Are entomologists all the rage? What's your hang-up?"

"No. Women don't throw themselves at me every day. Only once a week or so. Sometimes twice, but that's the exception, not the rule."

Phoebe wrinkled her nose in displeasure, pressing her hands to the edge of her sweater and smoothing it. "See. Me. Laugh."

Sam jammed his hands into the pockets of his jeans, his gaze serious. "Here's the hang-up. I really want to get to know you, Phoebe. I don't want to take advantage of you because we're in a life-or-death situation or because you're very vulnerable right now."

"You mean, even though we might die, and I could be the very last jar of goodies you get to raid, you still want to be a gentleman?"

"I do."

Big, girlie sigh. "Fine," she said with enough petulance to make Sam laugh.

He wiggled an eyebrow in the direction of the bench sitting under his bedroom window. "So, let's do it."

"Now?"

"You have anything better to do?"

"All right. What do you want to know about Phoebe Reynolds? Because I gotta tell you, I'm so boring, I'm like watching paint dry."

Sam took her hand and led her to a bench sitting just under his bedroom window. He patted a forest green pillow and smiled that delicious smile to encourage her to settle in. "Sit. We have a couple of hours before vampire sleep turns us into comatose vegetables. Let's talk. Life. Music. How old you were when you first shaved your legs."

Phoebe's stomach jolted when she sat on the pillow and pulled her legs up under her chin. "Fourteen, and it was like begging the Catholic Church for an exorcism. My mom was a tough nut to crack. She wasn't thrilled about me growing up."

"But you appear to have a healthy respect for her."

Phoebe cocked her head at him when she pulled the rubber band from her hair to let it flow loose to the tops of her shoulders. She ran her fingers through it and gave it a shake. "How would you know?"

"The pictures on your nightstand of the two of you. The birthday card from her that you framed. You looked happy in those pictures. You didn't look like your inner teenager was still grudging."

Phoebe's smile was of genuine love, making her forget how powerful Sam's observations were. "I'm not. My mom was so much great. I miss her every single day."

"How did she die, if you don't mind me asking?"

"She was going to die of exactly what I was doomed for, but she had a heart attack first." Phoebe's eyes shifted to the floor at the memory.

"You've had a pretty shitty lot lately, haven't you, Phoebe Reynolds?" Sam reached down and trailed a finger over her cheekbone, and she found herself allowing him to comfort her.

He plunked down next to her, taking her hand in his once more and smiling that infectious grin. "So, one of the most important things in life. Chocolate, vanilla, or strawberry?"

His question drew a quirk of a smile to her lips. "Ice cream?"

"Yep."

"What difference does it make? We can't eat it anymore anyway."

"I'm a firm believer in the ice cream theory."

"The ice cream theory . . ."

"The flavor you choose can be *very* telling. It will show me all your hidden agendas," he said, a somber tone to his voice, though his face hid a grin in the shadows of the lights peeking in from his window.

"Well, hell. Now I'm afraid if I pick strawberry, it means I'm some kind of nymphomaniac."

"It does."

Phoebe giggled, enjoying the firm caress of his fingers entwined with hers. "Then it's chocolate. Though, you wouldn't have known that by the way I steamrolled you like you were a Jimmy Choo vendor."

Sam frowned. "Damn."

"What?"

"Chocolate means you're a repressed serial killer."

Her head fell back on her shoulders in a snort of more laughter. "Then I guess Nina better watch herself."

"I'm a vanilla fan, personally."

"That's why we're here on this bench instead of in your bed, Sam McLean," she joked, not at all embarrassed that he'd turned down her invitation to rock his sheets. In fact, the more she adjusted to his rejection, the better it felt. And while his chivalry could all be an act, he'd prevented her from doing something out of character, and for that, she was grateful.

He tipped her chin up and smiled. "Broccoli or green beans?"

"There's a vegetable theory, too?"

"Oh, yeah. And it's even more important than the ice cream theory."

"If I choose broccoli, does that mean I was bullied in high school?"

"No. It means you're hotter than I thought you were."

She grinned, pushing a thick strand of her hair behind her ears. "Then, duh. Broccoli. Now it's my turn. Okay, heavy metal or classic rock?"

"Don't try to fool me, Ms. Reynolds. There's no music theory."

"No, that's true. I just want to be sure if I'm stuck in some car on a road trip with you I'm not forced to listen to Jimi Hendrix in the honeymoon stage of our budding relationship. You know, the one where everything you do is oh so adorable, but after six months makes me want to grind my fangs down with a band saw?"

He made a mock hurt face. "You don't like Hendrix? What kind of American are you?"

"The kind who can only take so many mindless, drugged-out

guitar frets before she wants to spork her eardrums out. And you can diagnose that answer however you like."

His shoulders sank comically. "You disappoint me. Wait, you're a Celine Dion girl, aren't you? All romantic and weepy. I should have known."

She used her free hand to flick him in the shoulder. "No. My heart does not go on and on. While I appreciate the greatness of her velvet chords, she's no Tom Jones."

"You mean, like the 'What's New Pussycat?' Tom Jones?"

"That's exactly who I mean. And if you mock my love of 'Delilah,' 'She's a Lady,' 'Help Yourself,' and 'I'll Never Fall in Love Again,' I might be pushed to find something made of wood and insert it into your chest. My mother loved him, and she passed that love down to me. I wear it with pride."

Sam tucked her arm under his and drew her close enough that she saw a vague twinkle in the deep brown of his eyes. "I can live with Tom. He is, after all, the king of the panty raid. A man has to respect that. I like punk—some techno. But I'm more a classic rock guy than I am heavy metal, and my first choice would be classical. Paganini, Beethoven, Vivaldi."

"You were a band geek, weren't you?"

"I was a violin geek."

"You can really play the violin?"

"I can really play. Someday, if you're kind to me, and you keep Nina from beating me up, I'll rock your socks off with my mad string skills."

So Yo-Yo Ma hot. "Television? Favorite shows?"

"Huge fan of detective shows. Especially old reruns of *Murder, She Wrote* and *McMillan and Wife*. Also a big *Burn Notice* fan. You?"

"Soap operas. They're my guilty pleasure."

He popped his lips. "I'd have never guessed. I should have been suspicious when all you talked about was Alejandro Esteban Juarez

Iglesias's love child with Dr. Marina Deveraux. How was I to know they weren't friends of yours?"

Phoebe giggled. Okay, some of it was absurd, but it was a comforting absurd. "When my grandmother watched me after school, I'd come home, and she'd always have a plate of freshly baked cookies, a glass of milk, and her finger to her lips to shush me because she was watching her 'stories.'"

"Some fond memories, I gather?"

Phoebe's smile was wistful. "So fond I can't put it into words." She gave a shrug to ward off the losses she was feeling so distinctly in her life right now. "Favorite book?"

"Is *Hustler* considered a book?"

"Only if you skip the centerfold and learn all the big-boy words from those supposed articles they boast. And it's not like it's *Breastie Babes*. I would have instantly lost respect for you."

Sam chuckled. "Phew. Then I'm good to go. *Breastie Babes* is so low rent. So why personal stylist? Or is that a stupid question, considering even your face mask was the exact shade of black as your jeans tonight?"

Her smile was fleeting. "After a rough, rebellious period in my life when I discovered I really wasn't doing the grunge/goth look any favors, I let out the real me. I love fashion, makeup, hair. All the things girls love, except I never had the vision or creativity to create any designs of my own, and I hate to sew. But I do know what looks good on people. I know what's flattering to all different types of body shapes, colors, et cetera. But try telling that to your college-minded mother. So I got a marketing degree, decided I didn't love my boring office job, and fell into personal stylist by way of Mark, who was forever telling his friends about me at the day spa he worked at. I did a bunch of makeovers on the weekends for a while and word got around. So I saved my makeover money while I worked my day job, and three years later, here we are. Mark and I went into this

fifty-fifty, and just recently, we've been getting some more presti-
gious clientele."

Sam smiled his approval, and she basked in the glow. "Impressive.
A self-made, up-and-coming millionaire."

"Well, I wouldn't exactly label me millionaire, but I'm not in the
local shelter, and it hasn't been without its battles. There are those
who say my job is frivolous. I'm not curing cancer, yada, yada, yada.
But if you feel better about how you present yourself to the world,
how you feel about you, inside and out, I don't see the shallow in
that. I see the joy in finding someone's self-esteem and teaching them
to make good use of it. And I can still climb a tree, so don't think
for one second because I love the color pink I can't wallop your ass
at a good game of touch football."

Sam's finger wrapped around a strand of her hair, twirling it
about his finger, sending a wave of awareness along her flesh. "You
are an odd dichotomy of feminine tomboy, Phoebe Reynolds. I
admit, it fascinates the shit out of me to watch you get up in Nina's
face like some kind of gangster out to cap her one minute, and in
the next fix your lip gloss. Fearless and sexy rates high on my list of
likes."

Everything about Sam rated high on her list of likes. "So why
entomology?"

Now Sam's smile was fond. "My seventh grade science teacher,
Mr. Evans. I was, for lack of a better word, a real assclown as a kid.
My parents didn't know what to do with me. I was forever in the
principal's office. But Mr. Evans changed all that when he decided
to harness my energy in a positive way and throw me into his after-
school bug-collecting program. His theory was that I didn't need a
good grounding, I needed a hobby. So short of ending up in deten-
tion for six months after I let the pet frog loose in his class to impress
Mary-Margaret O'Shea, I had no choice. I think my interest came
at first out of respect for him. He didn't want to get rid of the prob-

lem by booting me from class, and he was the first teacher who cared enough to realize I wasn't being challenged academically. He saw my hijinks were a result of total boredom, and he was right. Shortly into that year spent with Mr. Evans, he encouraged the school to test me and I was placed in some gifted classes because of it. The rest of it just fell into place. He taught me a healthy respect for looking deeper into things we don't always understand on the surface. So while bugs are mostly just annoying, I feel like they get a bad rap when some of them do nothing but good for the planet."

She frowned. "Yet, you work in pest-control research?"

"Well, there are bad bugs, too. They destroy crops, carry viruses. So I consider myself an advocate for healthy human to bug relationships."

Phoebe's head had begun to drift toward Sam's shoulder. He smelled delicious and warm—and above all else, safe. "How old are you?"

"Thirty-eight."

"Favorite movie?"

"*Zack and Miri Make a Porno*."

Her eyes were so heavy, but she wasn't ready to let this intimate moment go just yet. "Of course. After your chosen reading material, how could I have thought something as boring and without meaning as *Terminator* was your thing?"

"I like a good comedy. Life's too short to not have a good laugh."

His words whispered a faint but distinct sort of disappointment in life. But how much disappointment could an entomologist have suffered? "Newsflash, Mr. McLean. Our lives aren't so short anymore."

"Well, let's hope that's true, Phoebe Reynolds."

Boo, hiss. Reality. Phoebe slumped against him, not only fearful, but fighting that bone-deep weary she'd unsuccessfully fought the night before. "I'm very afraid, Sam."

He trailed a finger along the bridge of her nose. "I'm man enough to tell you, I am, too, Phoebe. What's going on at O-Tech is very scary indeed." Sam detangled himself from her slumber-heavy body and scooped her up. "For now, Vampire Barbie, it's time for all good undeadlings to be in bed."

With a swift few steps, he was placing her on his big bed with a tender touch. Phoebe latched on to his sweater and pulled him to her, pressing her lips to his ear, and letting his silky dark hair tickle her nose. "One more thing before I pass out."

His eyes gazed down into hers, deep and lovely when he bracketed her body with his hands; his smile was doting when he pulled the covers under her chin. "What's that?"

"Favorite cereal . . ." she muttered, wanting to pull him closer when he lifted his head, but unable to move her arms.

His grin was devastatingly handsome, even from beneath her rapidly closing eyes. "You want me to say Fruit Loops, don't you?"

She managed a husky giggle. "No. That would mean you're a sex addict, and my nymphomaniac strawberry ice cream would definitely conflict with your Fruit Loops sex addiction. Never the twain can meet—not unless it's in a seedy, back-alley hotel where the bed gives you massages for fifty cents."

Sam let his lips drop low, so close to hers, if she had an ounce of energy left, she could easily capture them. "Peanut butter Cap'n Crunch."

No way. That was her second favorite. Second only to Frosted Flakes. And she wanted to say so, but her lips were in not-gonna-happen mode.

Her final thought before she fell into this strange vampire sleep was how warm a simple connection to Sam by way of cereal made her feel.

That and the light kiss he pressed to her lips.

A kiss that held promise. One she hoped they had the chance to explore.

*   *   *

"So did you get it?"

Sam flashed a manila folder at Phoebe, and smiled. "Did you doubt I would?"

She slumped down in the passenger seat of his SUV, obviously fighting the pound of her temple from the late afternoon sun. Her fingers went to her nose, where Nina had slathered on sunscreen. Sam could sympathize—his head ached, too, and his skin stung, but it was bearable.

A full eight hours of sleep really did do a vampire good. Less than that and you were just treading water until the lifeboat arrived. His senses were muted and dulled by it, and that wasn't acceptable. Not now.

She nudged him, making him want to take back last night, pull the car over, tear off her cute outfit, and drive his tongue between her legs. Clearly, those senses weren't so dull. "How did you get past Nurse Ratched?"

Sam started the car with a quick turn of his wrist. "Nurse Ratched?"

"Yes, Nurse Ratched. You know, the beast who mans the desk like she's manning a nuclear warhead?"

He grinned, pulling out into traffic, his eyes twinkling with amusement from behind his dark sunglasses. Sam kept his eyes on the road, forcing himself to look anywhere but directly at Phoebe. He couldn't tell her he'd flashed his FBI ID to get what he wanted. It hadn't been. What was hard here was lying to everyone.

He had to hope that Dr. Hornstein's nurse, whom he made an imaginary date with for the first of next month after he got back from Russia, wouldn't contact the FBI until he didn't show up at Antoine's for dinner and a bottle of Chianti, her favorite wine.

That's when she'd realize he'd conned her and try to contact his superiors. While he'd used one of the fake IDs he'd had made when he wanted to keep the powers that be from knowing he was investigating off the clock, it wouldn't be long until they put two and two together and figured out he was one of the only agents in New York right now.

Until then, it was their little secret that Nurse Leona had copied this woman's files and handed them over to Sam with a flirtatious smile. That should buy him some time to tap into some decidedly shady resources and not tip off the agency while he was at it. "I gave her the infamous Sam McLean smile and she was like buttah, baby."

"So many gifts bestowed upon you. How do you do it?" she teased, flipping open the folder to scan the files in it, her long, slender fingers folding back the thick ream of paper.

"It's the geeky-hotness burden I bear."

Phoebe grew silent, her mouth falling open as she thumbed the files and read. A mouth he wanted to devour while he slammed her up against a wall and drove his aching cock into her.

Thank Jesus for vampire sleep. Had he been human, after last night, he'd have never slept with all the mental images of Phoebe running around, offering herself up naked in his head. With vampire sleep, you didn't have a choice in the matter. You passed out. Period. Which left him unnerved.

Because of his training, he was a light sleeper, always at the ready, always prepared. The only consolation he took in this vampire thing was that if someone did attack while he slept, more than likely, it wouldn't be with a wooden stake.

Still, he had to be careful. He most especially had to be careful with Phoebe. To sleep with her was not only dangerous to her emotions and probably his, too, but dangerous to his cover. When they made love, it would be only after he told her what he was doing in New York at O-Tech to begin with and showed her that Sam the Entomologist was just a part of a personality that had more complexities than a strand of DNA. He wanted her to know the real Sam before she slept with him. It was the single decent thing he could do in all of this mess.

The pang in Sam's gut, the one filled with burning apprehension over her reaction to his undercover status, reared its ugly head again. Yet, he managed to tamp it down when Phoebe said, "Her name was Alice Goodwin, she was sixty-two, and she was diagnosed with Alzheimer's. Oh, dear God. What are they doing to these people, and what a coincidence that of all the people to find dead, it was someone I knew. Why would she be at O-Tech?"

Sam forced himself to remain silent. He had not a single clue. How random was it that Phoebe had known this woman? And, yeah. What had Alice been doing at O-Tech? "Maybe she knew someone there? Worked there?"

"Not unless you hire hairdressers at O-Tech."

"She was a hairdresser?"

"She was. Retired and living in Brooklyn."

"Yet, she was seeing a specialist in Manhattan?"

Phoebe's auburn nod was slow. "She was referred to Dr. Hornstein by a Dr. Barry in Brooklyn. Dr. Hornstein's one of the best neurologists in the country. My physician referred me to him after I was diagnosed. Anyway, she has no emergency numbers listed, no family if the notes here are right."

"You have a home address listed in there?"

"I do." She read it off to him, her plump lips distracting him.

"I say we give it a flyby," he said, typing it into his GPS.

"Like detectives or something?"

His hands clenched the steering wheel, but he managed a charming smile. "Detectives: The Night-Dweller Squad."

Phoebe giggled that giggle that created a warm spread of something in his stomach. The stomach he wasn't supposed to be able to feel anything in anymore. Her laughter was tender and husky, sweet and soft, and it did things to his nonexistent heart that hadn't occurred for him in a long time. Not since Helene.

She dropped the file on her knee and gave him an impish grin. "Very *Starsky and Hutch*. But promise me this, I get to be Hutch. Starsky was just icky hairy."

"Fine. But I'm not wearing one of those disco shirts."

Suddenly, there was hesitation in her voice. "But wait, what if we get caught?"

"We're vampires, Phoebe."

"I'd like to say I'd forgotten that, but with all this sunscreen on my nose, it's impossible."

"How are you feeling about it today? You've taken this entire thing like a total champ. I'm expected to because I'm the man, but according to Nina, women usually cry. A lot."

"That's only because Nina would point and laugh if I did."

"So this is a one-upmanship thing?"

"No. It's a pride thing. Crying won't get me anywhere. What's done is done—or maybe it all hasn't sunk in just yet. There hasn't been a lot of time to do much of anything but look for answers. But don't go thinking I wouldn't like to sit in a corner and have a good bawling session over the fact that there'll be no more blueberry cheesecake for me."

"How do we know that for sure? Maybe because we're potentially manufactured vampires, we can still eat. We can do things other vampires can't—like see our reflections."

"That's hopeful at best, Starsky, but unfortunately I know for sure we can't eat anymore."

He'd considered testing the theory, but the worry something would debilitate him and keep him from protecting Phoebe kept him from attempting a cold beer. "You didn't."

"I did. It was just a little sliver of that delicious cake Archibald made last night. Coconut cream, I think. It smelled so good baking, I thought, what's the worst that can happen? The worst is, you spend an hour worshiping on your knees over a toilet. Which, by the way, for a man, you have the cleanest toilet I've ever seen."

He fought a chuckle. "Couldn't keep it down, huh?"

Phoebe winced, making a face. "The second it went in was the second it came right back out. Can I tell you the kind of grief counseling I'm going to need because I can't have a Snowball? So if we find the pricks that did this to us, I say you let me at 'em. The least they could have done was given us more of a perk than just eternal life." Her voice hitched at the last of her words, and Sam knew why.

The words *eternal life* gave them both pause, driving them each into silence. Fuck. He had to figure this out. If their vampirism was related to the dead Alice Goodwin and she was related to the woman who'd shown up on Phoebe's doorstep, they had to move fast. Who knew how long between the time that woman had been turned until she died had been? What if they were only days away from decomposing—hours—minutes? And why hadn't Alice decomposed like his feeble attempt at a one-night stand had?

When he had a moment alone, he'd call Stinky Malone, one of his most reliable, albeit crooked agency resources. Stinky knew how to keep shit on the down low.

For years Stinky had hacked into government sites with classified information on suspicious events labeled *paranormal* by the government. Most only had inconclusive findings, but Stinky knew how to get to them. Maybe, now that he knew something was definitely going on at O-Tech, Stinky could help him out—fish around—something.

Sam pulled his iPod from his jacket pocket and plugged it into the stereo in the car. Music always helped to calm his frayed thoughts when a case got too hectic.

Tom Jones drifted through the speakers, and from the corner of his eye, he saw Phoebe's lips turn upward, again leaving him ridiculously pleased. He'd downloaded them just before they'd left in a lame, schoolboy attempt to impress her with his listening skills.

She burrowed into the passenger seat; the glow of the setting sun casting a peachy haze over her auburn hair and creamy skin. Jesus, she was sexy. "Are you wooing me, Mr. Vampire?"

He gave her a nonchalant shrug. "You can't woo a woman with Tom Jones. It's inconceivable."

She tucked her stylish dark brown trench coat around her chin and smiled. "You can if it's this woman."

He gazed out the window and made a left at the next street. "Let's put the woo on hold for now because I think we've arrived."

The brownstone they drove past was well kept and swept clean of the early fall leaves. Trees surrounded it, now barren and bending in the wind. A set of wide steps lined with potted mums led up to a locked door with an intercom system. One they'd probably need to be buzzed into.

Phoebe glanced at him, concern on her pretty face. "Why aren't we stopping?"

"Because, Detective Hutchinson, if Alice Goodwin and the woman I was bitten by are connected to us via O-Tech, who knows who could be hanging around, looking to keep us from finding out what's going on. So we park a couple of streets away—you know, to keep our cover?"

"Ohhhh," she said, patting his arm with a smile and a nod. "Good point. You're pretty good at this."

Sam fought a grunt. "I watch a lot of TV on my downtime."

"You mean when you're not fending off hordes of women?"

"That can become trying for a hot geek like me. We need our rest to fight the hordes another day."

Sam parked the car two streets over in a grocery store parking lot behind a Dumpster he could smell every piece of garbage in.

Phoebe hopped out, gagging. She covered her mouth with her arm. "Okay, vampire smell-a-vision officially sucks. So what's the plan?"

The plan was to find a way to get into Alice's brownstone without having to use the front door. He held out his hand, one she almost always willingly took. His fingers curled around hers, and he tugged her smaller frame to his. "I think we're going to test the theory that we have the ability to jump—high."

Phoebe frowned, tightening the belt on her coat. "Can't we just break in? We did that at your place just fine. Or why don't you wall-walk?"

"That was because we weren't going to arouse suspicion at my place, and I don't know the exact location of her apartment. I don't want to walk into the middle of the wrong apartment. A brownstone, if it's the typical type anyway, tends to have just a few apartments. So people know each other pretty well. We don't want anyone to see us or be able to identify us."

Phoebe wrinkled her nose. "Okay. I propose that when this is all done, you know, if we live, we go out somewhere. Anywhere. Like a place that doesn't have a TV, because you're far too good at this breaking-and-entering, felonious-acts thing."

If she only knew . . . Sam smiled at her suggestion, then tugged her along behind him, their footsteps silent against the wet pavement. It took them all of ten seconds to walk a quarter of a mile through the back alleys leading to Alice's—still a source of wonder for Sam.

He approached the backside of the building, and for a moment, rethought his plan. He should have dropped Phoebe back off with Nina where she'd be safe rather than risk someone harming her. It had been hard enough to convince Nina he could handle the doctor's office. If something happened to Phoebe, she'd chew him a new asshole. Even he, trained in the art of war, was just a little leery of the Nina-nator, as Marty called her.

Phoebe looked up at the brownstone while she stood beside Sam. She gave him a nudge. "I say we go for the roof, break the exit door lock, and tap the stairwell."

Sam grinned down at her, unable to help some misplaced sense of pride at her willingness to bust into a brownstone not just in heels, but balls to the wall. "Wow, who's the amateur detective now?"

Her almond-shaped eyes twinkled. "Alas, I'm a single woman, living with a gay man. We do a lot of *Psych*. Mark won't admit it, but I think he has a crush on Corbin Bernsen. Anyway, do you think we need a running start?"

"I don't know. When Nina showed us how, she was in the air without much effort at all."

Phoebe let go of his hand and crouched low on her haunches. "I feel very Bionic Woman right now," she joked before she was up and gone—completely out of his line of vision.

Sam mirrored her crouch, lunging upward with so much ease he almost wished the guys back at the agency could see him.

He landed with light feet on the rooftop, caught a glimpse of Phoebe's smug, pleased grin, one he was about to return but didn't quite manage.

Instead of smiling in return, he blacked out.

CHAPTER 10

Phoebe tore her phone from her jacket pocket and hit the app on it for Twitter. Why wasn't anyone answering their phone? For the love of 911. It wasn't like they were in a vampire state of emergency or anything. Shouldn't everyone have their phones manned and at the ready?

She held her phone up and squelched a screech. No bars. Perfect. She used her thumb to frantically find the location of the icon to text—the one Mark had shown her like only a million times—and bit off another scream. If they got out of this in one piece, she was getting the phone for kindergartners, with big directions and easily understood icons.

Sam's limp, pale body made her force herself to focus. What had Nina gone on and on about this afternoon before they'd left to go to Dr. Hornstein's office? Twitter and Facebook. Yes! A secondary way to get in touch with them, if she couldn't reach them by phone or text.

Nina had said, if all else failed, tweet or Facebook the OOPS account, and if she didn't see it, some person-demon-otherworldly creature Phoebe had yet to investigate named Darnell would. Locating the big Twitter icon, she pressed it and prayed the instructions were simple.

She held Sam's head in her lap with one hand, lifting his eyelids to see if he responded. Thank God she'd been practicing her crappy texting skills. She forced herself to calm and began to type, ignoring the quiver of her fingers and how pale and unmoving Sam was.

Clotheswhores @OOPS Help! Where r u? Answer phone. Man down! Make that 2!

She bit the inside of her lip, running her hands over Sam's forehead and brushing his hair out of his face. Her gaze strayed to another man, who lay on the far corner of the roof in a crumpled heap. When her phone vibrated, she almost cheered out loud.

OOPS @Clotheswhores Barbie? Is that u?
Clotheswhores @OOPS Yes! Gigantor backed out. I have a situation. Help!
OOPS @Clotheswhores OMFG! Backed out of what? Did that motherfucker stand u up? Will club 2 death. Buy Louisville. Best wood for clubbing deaths.

Phoebe frowned at her phone in confusion, then clamped her teeth together. Damn you, AutoCorrect! She retyped her text with shaky fingers, glancing worriedly at Sam.

Clotheswhores @OOPS No. He's black now!
OOPS @Clotheswhores Jesus. He can change colors? Now he's Chameleon Vampire?
Clotheswhores @OOPS No. Sam is BLACKED out

OOPS @Clotheswhores WTF? What r you 2 shitheads doing? Didn't I say come right home after doctor?

Clotheswhores @OOPS STFU. I'm a bug girl. Can take care of myself.

OOPS @Clotheswhores Which explains y you're tweeting me for help, BUG girl.

Clotheswhores @OOPS Stop bitching and get here!

OOPS @Clotheswhores Where's here, brain surgeon?

Phoebe typed in the address and prayed Nina would hurry. No sooner had she tweeted Nina back than a tall, portly man appeared out of nowhere with a shimmer of light and, she'd swear, a faint tinkling of bells. Chains with gold medallions swung from his thick neck, and he wore a blue football jersey that hung low over baggy jeans tucked into high-top Nikes.

His gravelly voice was cheerful in contrast to his enormous stature. "Don't be afraid now, Miss Phoebe. I know all about whass happenin'. I'm Darnell—sho nuff nice to meet ya, shawty." He held out a hand so large Phoebe was sure he'd crush hers. Yet, his grasp was gentle and warm to her cool fingers. "Nina sent me cuz I can get here quicker than her. She'll be here any minute, I 'spect."

Phoebe wasn't going to dwell on how he'd arrived out of thin air, nor would she dwell on the fact that, as she recalled, he was a demon. Which was bad, bad, bad, according to her Bible study teacher.

Why fret over yet another paranormal experience? Werewolves were supposed to be vicious animals, if you allowed books and movies to dictate your beliefs. Yet, Marty, in all her fluffy hair and half-off designer clothes, was anything but vicious. And Wanda? She was like the Grace Kelly of halfsies. Regal, elegant, diplomatic. So that a demon that resembled The Notorious B.I.G. had appeared out of thin air came as almost no surprise.

The enormous bear of a man stooped low, the heavy gold chains he wore around his neck swaying in the frigid air. His scruff of shortly cropped black hair clung to hers when he leaned in toward her. "C'mon, now," he encouraged, kneeling beside she and Sam. "I'll get him while you tell me what happened, a'ight?"

Darnell had an instant charisma, an immediate reassuring quality to his tone and mannerisms that left Phoebe feeling safe. "We were trying to get information about the dead woman we found the other night at O-Tech. She lives in this building."

Darnell hoisted Sam's big body over his shoulder like he was a rag doll and patted him on the back like one would an infant. "Sammy here got the name of the lady from your doc, right?"

Phoebe nodded, her eyes skirting the man across the roof. The man who hadn't moved an inch. "Sam said it probably wasn't a good idea to go in through the front door in case we were seen. So we decided to test our vampire skills and jump up onto the roof, break into the exit door, and hit the stairwell to get to her apartment. Sam got to the roof just fine, but almost the second his feet hit the ground, he blacked out. Just crumpled."

"And the dude in the corner? What happened all up in here?" Darnell thumbed a finger in the man's direction.

She trembled, despite the fact that she couldn't really feel the cold anymore. Her tremble was for the fear of the unknown. "He was already up here when I got here. He caught me by surprise and grabbed me from behind. So I took him out." Like she was David Carradine reincarnated, in fact.

And it had taken nothing more than a good upward swing of the heel of her hand. The moment the stranger's hands were on her, she'd reacted in a blur of color and limbs. The powerful surge she'd experienced when Nina had cornered her at Sam's had returned tenfold, and it was both frightening and exhilarating. Yet, she had no idea why he'd jacked her from behind or who he was.

But she'd smelled him. Just like her big sister had taught her to.

Darnell chuckled, flashing teeth so white they glowed in the dark. "Hoo-boy—you a fiery one like yo sista, huh? Nice job, Phoebe. Give ol' Darnell a knuck." He held out his fist full of gold rings, and Phoebe knocked it with hers. "You okay otherwise? You feel a'ight?"

The landing of another pair of footsteps had them both turning to find Nina coming at them with a sour expression. She stomped up to Phoebe, looming over her in the way of the badass. "Didn't I tell you two to fucking come right home if you got that file from the doctor, Buffy Junior? Goddamn it. I knew I should have gone with you two twits. I should have never fallen for the 'leave it to me, I can be very charming when I need to be' bullshit Sam fed me. And you, Powder Puff Barbie," she said between clenched teeth, "quit following Sammy around with your cootchie-la-la and your lusty lady-lumps and listen for a change. If he wants to have his ass slaughtered, then that's on him, but the hell you'll end up whacked, too."

Before Phoebe had the chance to react to all that sisterly love, Darnell wedged himself between the two women while Sam's body hung limply from his shoulder. He put his free hand on Nina's arm and patted it. "Chill, honeycakes. Phoebe here, she took a dude out. Looks to me like she capped da dude purty good, yo. She got it covered."

It was as though Darnell was the Preparation H to Nina's hemorrhoid. Upon his words, instantly, her angry features relaxed and she smiled.

Smiled.

Phoebe gave a surreptitious glance around the rooftop in search of one of the four horsemen. Surely one of them would ride up on his trusty steed and wipe them all out. The universe had to be at risk if Nina was smiling. Though, even in the midst of yet more chaos, Phoebe couldn't help but think that her sister's smile made her even more beautiful, if that was possible.

She gave Darnell a slap on the back. "I told them not to do anything but get that file. So what are they doing here?" Nina asked him, sweet as the day was long.

"They's lookin' for clues to that dead lady y'all found. This is where she lives. But we got more trouble than jus' Sammy blacking out. Look over yonder." He lifted a chubby finger over his shoulder.

Nina followed Darnell's eyes to see the heap of limbs across the rooftop. Her nostrils flared, but Phoebe's hand was instantly in the air because she'd smelled it, too. "No, don't say it. Vampire, right? Bad vampire."

Nina nodded her agreement, jamming her hands into the pockets of her hoodie. "Jesus Christ, Darnell. It's like vampocalypse these days. What the hell is going on? How many people has this asshole gotten his hands on?"

A long, low moan made them all swing around. Phoebe was the first to react, her feet moving toward the stranger with that bizarre blur of speed she was still adjusting to. She knelt beside him, rolling him over and fighting back a scream of horror.

God. No. Not again.

Like the woman in her apartment, the man she'd taken out just moments before writhed in pain and began screaming his terror while his body shuddered in violent jolts. His face, one that didn't look like it was more than fifty or so, was wreathed in a mixture of horror and pain.

Nina was at her side in seconds, tearing off her hoodie and throwing it at Darnell. Her grunt in Phoebe's ear was a muttered, "Here we go again."

Darnell set Sam down, putting Nina's discarded hoodie under his head, then put a hand on Nina's back, his expression under the surrounding streetlights painfully grim. "Lawd have mercy on us all."

Phoebe didn't have time to ponder the irony of Darnell's plea upstairs due to the fact that the man began the same agonizing struggle the woman who'd bitten Sam had. Twisting his body as his skin began to deteriorate, he moaned.

Darnell was the first to react, dragging the man to his lap, pulling him close, and rocking him, digging the heels of his Nikes into the roof's surface to keep the stranger near. But even Darnell, as large and imposing as he was, had trouble keeping the man, a quarter of the size of him, calm and still.

Nina and Phoebe automatically both positioned themselves at either end of his body. Nina's lips moved to his ear. "What happened to you? *Who are you?*" she whispered, though her words weren't harsh, nor did they hold any sort of angry determination to garner information. Instead, like before with the woman in her apartment, she soothed, cajoled.

The man's body stiffened, and Phoebe, with the lingering memory of the woman who'd bitten Sam still fresh, prepared for the end with frustrated defeat.

Tears fell from Darnell's eyes in fat, salty drops, splattering down his nylon jersey, something Phoebe couldn't quite fathom. "Ol' Darnell's here for ya, man. You let go, brotha. Let go now. Go where it's good," he cooed as they held him.

"Did this happen to you at a place called O-Tech?" Nina pressed one last futile time, her face full of both distress and sympathy.

Yet, like before, he was too far gone to answer. And when his flesh began to melt away from his body, still, no one let go. When he screamed the scream of the terrified, each of them uttered nonsensical words to soothe him.

As his screams silenced and he turned to ash, after the fluttering gray particles of his remains floated up and away, no one moved for a few moments.

Darnell stared at his empty hands in grief-stricken silence.

Nina, still on her knees, leaned forward on her elbows, letting her head sink to her clenched fists.

Phoebe's head dropped to her chest in defeat. She fell forward on the palms of her hands, letting her forehead rest on the bend in her arm.

A hand, cool and familiar, pressed to her back, but she didn't have the energy to be startled. "Phoebe? What happened?"

And then she was lunging into Sam's arms, desperately needing the sweet relief of tears, but only managing a dry, hacking wheeze.

"No," he said against the top of her head, his voice husky. "Not again."

Darnell was the first to rise, helping Nina to her feet, then wiping his cherubic cheeks with a handkerchief from his back pocket. "I ain't nevah seen nothin' like dat in all my years as a demon. Not even in hell itself. Don't never want to again. I say we find the motha-effers and take 'em out but good."

"If we could just find them, Darnell," Nina seethed into the wind. "If we could just fucking find them."

Darnell held his hand out to Sam. "I'm Darnell, by the way. Came here to help your lady when you blacked out."

Sam shook it and gave him a grim smile. "Much appreciated. So is that what happened to me? The last thing I remember is seeing Phoebe had made it to the rooftop."

Phoebe nodded against his wide shoulder. "You made it to the rooftop, and then you just collapsed. Why did you pass out like that? What happened?"

He shrugged his shoulders and avoided Phoebe's eyes. "Not a clue. Maybe some residual vampire shifting stuff?" Sam pointed a foot in the direction of the man's ashes and changed the subject. "And this? Another one?"

"Just like the last time," was Nina's disgruntled response.

"Were you able to get anything out of him before . . ."

Phoebe shook her head, burrowing closer to Sam, fearing his collapse was a sign the disease was beginning to rear its ugly head.

"No," she whispered. "And it was just as horrible as the first time, in case you were wondering."

Sam kept her close when he surveyed the area. "No identification on him, either, huh?"

Darnell shook his head after a quick scan of the rooftop with a cluck of his tongue. "Sho don't look like it. I think we need to get to this lady's apartment and see what we can see. I don't nevah, evah wanna do somethin' like dat again."

"You mean like with us," Phoebe couldn't help but point out, numb with fear.

Darnell chucked her under the chin and flashed her a sympathetic smile. "I mean most especially with somebody as purty as you."

Nina pushed her way past them with a grunt. "That's not going to fucking happen as long as I'm here. So let's tap this broad's apartment and try to find something—anything that'll help us figure this shit out." Nina began to walk toward the roof's exit door but stopped midstride. She stared down Phoebe and Sam. "And the two of you, do me a fucking favor. Don't be tools. If I tell you to do some shit, just do it, and don't question me. It pisses me off."

"I'd bet even world peace would piss you off. So tell me, Nina, what doesn't piss you off?" Phoebe, afraid, worried, and on edge, asked with a taunt.

"Not a lot. But we've covered that ground, haven't we? So I'm gonna let your ignorance slide because you've just had one of those traumatic experiences. But that doesn't mean I'll cut you a solid forever. Which means you should tread lightly with your ballerina slippers, Buffy Two." Nina stomped off in typical manlike fashion.

Phoebe's fists clenched and her temper soared. Nina deserved a good swift kick in the teeth, and she was going to be the first to do it. Oh, and fuck taking the high road. She was fine with Low Avenue if it meant she could rip Nina's hair out follicle by follicle.

But Sam grabbed her by the waist and pulled her up against him tight. He leaned down and whispered in her ear, "Now, now, Phoebe. You're not looking at the bright side here."

"The bright side?" she asked between clenched teeth, refusing to allow herself the luxury of pressing her ear to his lips in favor of staking a bitch through the heart.

His chuckle was low. "Well, yeah, you silly. She didn't call you *Barbie* once. That's progress in familial communication, if you ask me, yes?"

"I'll give you Barbie," she muttered fighting her way out of his grip and doing some of her own stomping to the door. "Let's get this over with, and do not linger, boys." With a muffled hiss of rage, she flung the door open and stalked down the flight of stairs.

DARNELL managed to get into Alice's apartment without incident, and somehow they'd all made it inside without being seen. While they sifted through her personal items, each lost in their own thoughts, Phoebe fought to block the image of yet another poor soul lost to whatever was going on.

Instead, she tried to take in her surroundings and the small but tastefully decorated apartment, from the crocheted blanket in dark blue and gray slung over Alice's corduroy couch to the tiny glass tabletop dinette for one in the corner of the room.

There were few pictures of Alice with anyone but a golden lab who, according to the date on the urn on her coffee table, had met his fate earlier in the year. Though, her walls were littered with pictures of her many clients. Clients who had cancer and had come to her from various charities that offered help to women and children who needed to be fitted for wigs or transition a hairstyle befitting their newly grown hair.

If the pictures she had and the client letters she'd framed were any indication, Alice Goodwin had been a kind, loving, hardworking woman who'd deserved to die with dignity. Instead, she'd not only been diagnosed with one of the most undignified diseases there was, but she'd been used as some kind of guinea pig.

Disgust flooded Phoebe—sorrow, too—as she leafed through Alice's appointment book. Though Alice was single, and had what appeared to be no living relatives, she had been loved and her life, if her full social calendar was on target, had been happy.

"She was part of a book club," Phoebe spoke out loud when she found a notation for an upcoming meeting. "Books That Bite, it's called. How ironic their chosen reading material is paranormal books. Anyway, they meet next Tuesday. Maybe someone from the group can help us? Maybe they know what was going on with her?"

Though, if Alice was anything like Phoebe, she'd probably kept her condition to herself, and that would only make things more difficult for them.

Sam's head popped up from his place on the couch where he'd set a plastic tote with Alice's bank records. "If we don't find anything tonight, it's a place to start. Damn, she seemed like a pretty nice lady. She had a modest retirement fund, if her bank statements are correct. No credit card debt, and she was planning a trip somewhere if this last statement is any indication. What a damn crappy end." He ran his hand over his hair, displaying the disgust Phoebe was feeling. "Sometimes, this jo . . . life," he corrected, "sucks."

Nina paused her rifling in Alice's kitchen cabinets and glanced at Sam as though she was going to speak, but Darnell, shoulders deep in a bookcase, whooped a yelp of joy. "I think I got somethin'!" He unfolded a packet of papers with a shake of his hand. "This here Alice was applyin' for some kinda clinical trial for her Alzheimer's. She got a bunch o' forms all filled out right here."

"A clinical trial?" Phoebe said in surprise, rushing to Darnell's side to look at the forms he held.

Her hands trembled when she took them from Darnell; her eyes went wide. "This was the same trial Dr. Hornstein offered to me . . ." She reached a hand behind her to keep from pitching backward. Each clue they found reminded her how close she was to what was happening.

Somehow, she kept managing to skirt one fate only to find herself involved in another. Her balance failed her, but Darnell was instantly behind her, pressing a beefy hand to her spine.

Sam crossed the room in two strides, reaching for her while Nina trounced across the floor. "When was this supposed to start?" Sam asked, clutching her hand in his.

Her voice shook when she finally spoke. "Dr. Hornstein said he had connections and he could help me get into this very exclusive trial, but it was controversial at best. Though, he did tout some pretty impressive results. I didn't fill out the forms because I wasn't sure if I wanted to participate or not. As desperate as I was to even just stall the Alzheimer's, I didn't want to do it with only one eye while I was hooked up to life support. I didn't have time to look into it thoroughly—so I don't know when or even if it started."

Sam's eyes narrowed when he put a finger to his lips and closed his eyes as though he were formulating his thoughts. "Hold on. You don't have any surviving family do you, Phoebe?"

"Not unless you count fashion apocalypse here." She made a face at Nina. "And I didn't list her on any of the forms as a contact. I was offered the clinical trial entry just before I found Nina. So, technically, I only have Mark, who's like family."

"That's it!" Sam shouted, dropping Phoebe's hand and pacing. "The clinical trial. I'd bet my left nut whoever is responsible for what's going on is doing it under the guise of these clinical trials. Think about how easy that would be. Or easier, I should say. Both you and Alice had no family—so it wasn't like anyone was going to come looking for you if you disappeared, and even if, say, Mark did, there'd be nothing he could do because he wouldn't have access to your medical files. Sonofabitch. You were all disposable. I can feel it in my gut."

"Hold up, man," Darnell said. "Those forms say Alice was goin' to some clinic here in Brooklyn. O-Tech's in Manhattan. How'd she get herself all da way over there and dead to boot when she did it?"

Sam's lips formed a sneer, so unlike him, Phoebe noted, it made even Nina pause. "I don't know, Darnell. But I know I'm right. Call it gut instinct or whatever, but I'm right. Maybe they were sending candidates to this clinic in Brooklyn and farming them out to O-Tech, or maybe that's just where they're stashing the bodies, but what better way to find test subjects than to give them hope for a disease that's so hopeless? Goddamn bastards," he swore with a snarl, jamming a fist into the pocket of his jeans.

Nina made an angry grunt, her eyes scanning the forms Phoebe held. "Fuck. This just keeps getting better and better. So now what?"

Sam placed his hands on his lean hips, his eyes glimmered. "We send Phoebe in."

Ahhhh. Bait. She could be bait. To murderers. Madmen. Total nutballs. Oh, sweet mother of all things holy. "So you want me to join the clinical trial?"

Sam's expression was hard, making Phoebe cock her head. He was usually so easygoing and lighthearted. But this Sam had a vibe she didn't understand, a hard current of something . . . "Yes. That's exactly what we do. You've got all the forms, right?"

Phoebe gave a hesitant nod. "I do."

"You already have the diagnosis, and your doctor deemed you a candidate—all we need to do is get you into wherever it is they're performing the tests."

Fear swept over Phoebe. Go figure. "I don't want to poke holes in your *Miami Vice*–like plan, but what good am I going to do? Sure, I can get inside, but I don't know the first thing about chemicals and beakers and all that medical stuff we saw, Sam. They're obviously not going to give me the laundry list of ingredients they're using to test these poor people with, and I wouldn't know what the ingredients were even if they did." Panic had begun to set in again, deep and foreboding.

When Sam answered, he was all goodness and light again. "No, honey. I don't want you to go in, go in. There'll be no *Charlie's Angels* for you. I just want you to join the trial and get the address for where this is going down. The rest will be up to me."

Relief flooded her. God, he was super-duper dreamy. Virile. Smart. Funny. Sexy. Sexy. Seeeexy.

"I dunno, Sammy," Nina said, intruding upon her inward fangirl gush. "I'm not so hip to the idea that they could find out about Phoebe. What if one of those goons comes looking for her? What if they fucking decide to come get her when she doesn't show up? I'ma hafta slap a bitch if that happens. So, tag, you're the bitch, Sammy."

Sam began to pack up Alice's bank statements while Darnell straightened the bookcase. "Do we have any other choices, Nina? I'd rather risk them knowing *of* her than not find the answer to this and let her *die*."

Okay. Sam was officially dreamy napalm. Damn her fears, her inexperience with a solid felony, her misgivings. He was willing to do whatever it took to keep her from dying. Mad-ass hot. That's what he was.

Nina slapped Sam on the back and smiled with a sinister glint to it. "She dies, you die, dude."

Darnell chuckled, husky and low. "Aw, now, Nina, stop harshin' the man's vibe. He's jus' tryin' ta do what he feels is right for his ladylove. You gone and forgot what thass like?"

But Phoebe didn't hear Darnell proclaim she was Sam's ladylove as much as she did the threat that Nina would kill Sam if something happened to her. Her eyebrow rose. "Was that sisterly concern I just heard?"

Nina flipped up her middle finger, pale and threatening. "No. That was if-they-find-you-they-might-find-us concern, Presumptuous Barbie."

Phoebe would have risen to the bait if she weren't getting so good at this emotional-reading thing. She found, in the madness, she was spending more time really hearing the intonation of people's voices, really listening to the inflection and change of pitch.

That had been concern in Nina's, and while she was prideful enough to refuse to allow Nina's rejection to show outwardly, she wasn't going to pass up the opportunity to revel in any small indication Nina was warming to her. She sauntered over to Alice's window and flung it open. "Was not," she taunted in a tone that teased. "You liiike me. Oh! You know what this reminds me of?"

Nina rolled her beautiful eyes. "Christ. If it's one of your stupid soap opera references, it's nothing like it. I'd kill a bitch before I'd let her hold me hostage in some convent while she slammed my man. Trust that shit."

Phoebe shook her head with a coy smile. "No, it's not like that, silly. I don't even know your man. Who's my brother-in-law, by the way. It's more like the time on *Guiding Sunrise* when Sierra Madson finally, after a twelve-year search, found her sister Arianna living right next door to her. Arianna didn't like Sierra at all when she found out they were sisters, but when danger struck in the way of the Bowler City serial killer, she had Sierra's back. Which just proves, you don't want anything to happen to me. I'm growing on you, Nina, and I know that cinches your panties, but really, what doesn't, Warrior Barbie?" she asked with a giggle before she jumped out the window to the back alley, narrowly escaping Nina's screech of fury.

She smiled when she landed like some graceful version of a one-hundred-forty-five-pound cat.

Nina liked her.

Heh.

CHAPTER 11

"I can't turn my brain to the off position," Phoebe said from her place on the bed. Freshly showered and in a pair of sweats Mark had brought for her along with some of her other clothes and cosmetics, she'd propped herself up on Sam's pillow while she waited for vampire sleep in his darkened bedroom.

Sam gave her a drowsy glance from the bench under his window where he'd been sleeping since this had begun and he'd offered up his bed like the gentleman he was. "It isn't your brain that needs turning off—it's that pretty mouth," he said, though his sleepy words were filled with amusement. "But before this vampire sleep-by-comatose assault gets us, you really did a number on that guy on the roof, huh? Way to go."

She knew how to defend herself—she'd spent a lot of time using her fists before she'd learned her lesson. But it didn't make how utterly mortified she was any better.

She'd used her vampire powers to take a weak, dying fellow manufactured vampire out. "I'm not too proud of that, Sam. He had to have been weak and desperate at that point, and now he's dead, too. But we have no idea who he is or why he was at Alice's. Though, I'd bet he was following the same trail we were. So not only did I beat him up with my fierce from-the-hood skills, he spent the last minutes of his life being launched across a rooftop."

"You're right. I'm sorry. And unfortunately, his identity is a question we may not have the answer to anytime soon—or even ever, honey."

Yet, she couldn't stop the worry from rolling over her in waves. She'd tried to put together any sort of connect the dots to this madness, and she still wasn't sure it had to do with patients for the clinical trial. "Do you really think this is the answer? The Alzheimer's patients? That we were just easy targets for these monsters because no one would care if we dropped off the face of the planet? That if I had been a part of the clinical trial, I would have ended up like Alice?"

Sam's words were instantly soothing, his tone gentle and sympathetic. "I do. It's only a hunch, though. I just looked at the common denominators the minute you said you'd been offered the trial. But I don't think that's the case, in reference to you dropping off the face of the planet, Phoebe. I think Mark would move heaven and earth if something happened to you. If his clucking over you like a mother hen tonight was any indication of how he feels about you, I wouldn't put it past him to hunt the bastards down and take them out. In fact, I wouldn't put it past him to take out Nina, if it meant protecting you. And that's saying something."

Phoebe shivered despite the fact that it was only a phantom reaction to the fear that she'd come so close to ending up like Alice Goodwin and that poor, unidentifiable man on the roof.

Though, the way things stood right now, they both could end up like that anyway. "But it's like you said, he wouldn't have gotten very far because he's not a relation. So had I gone first, Alice could've been me. And I know that's a shitty thing to say when a perfectly decent human being is dead. My thoughts should be with Alice. Yet, I can't help but focus on the fact that this could have happened to me if I hadn't hesitated about the trials. There would have been no one to take up for me because I'm essentially alone." Her eyes squeezed shut tight. Okay, she wasn't entirely alone. She did have Mark and . . .

Oh, God.

The clock was ticking and still she hadn't told everyone everything.

She heard the rustle of Sam's jeans as he moved on the bench, felt the sink of the mattress beside her when he sat at the edge of the bed. Without a word, he enveloped her in his arms, and she let him, resting her head on the spot where his chest met his shoulder.

Sam placed his chin on the top of her head. "We'll figure this out, Phoebe. We've got a solid lead now."

Without realizing she had, she wrapped her arms around his waist. "Listen to you, *Baretta*, with your fancy detective terminology," she teased, then briefly wondered at the slight stiffening of his body. But that didn't last long. Not when a tendril of heat was finding its way to her belly, warm and stoking a potential fire.

"I just mean we've got something to go on now."

"But it isn't a lot. We could be all wrong about the connection between the clinical trial and us. And if we are, we're back to square one . . ."

"If this is what I'm thinking, if this Dr. Hornstein really is using this clinical trial as a cover, he'll rush your application through for the chance at nabbing another test subject. If what we suspect is true, this will all be over before you know it. Trust me on that."

Right then and there, it hit her. Hard. In the gut. Without warning. "I don't think I'm ever going to relax again. Who could relax after finding out there really is a boogeyman, Sam? Nothing's the same anymore. Nothing. The entire world's changed after what's happened to us. We're vampires, Sam. Sweet baby J, vampires really exist. They really drink blood. They really live forever. They have friends that are werewolves and demons. Demons who wear bling and high-top sneakers. Who would have thought—"

"Favorite soap opera?" he muttered against her forehead, pulling her tighter to him.

"Don't try and distract me. We're in the middle of a crisis and you want to talk something as superfluous as soap operas? We're vampires. Vam-pi-res," she sounded out. A vampire. She was a vampire, vampire, vampire. Phoebe clenched her teeth. Teeth that included fangs. Fangs, fangs, fangs.

Fangs, fangs, bo-fangs, fee-fi-fo-fangs.

Fangs!

Oh, Moses and the Red Sea.

Sam pulled her into his lap and cradled the upper half of her body. "Hey. Focus on me. *Favorite soap opera,*" he insisted, tweaking the space where her waist and hip met.

She squirmed in his embrace, ignoring the rush of heat he created in every naughty bit she owned. "I guess it should be *Dark Shadows* now. You know, to show solidarity for our people."

"Stop dwelling and stick to the here and now. Current favorite soap opera."

She shook her head with a giggle. "I can't choose. They're like kids. I love them all for different reasons."

"Wishy-washy at best, Ms. Reynolds. Okay, name one place you've always wanted to go but haven't had the chance to." His hands palmed her back, rolling circular motions over it.

She tried to snuggle closer without being incredibly obvious, yet fight the sensual climb of heat he was creating by putting her hands on his chest. "Italy. Venice in particular. I want to ride in a gondola. I'm hoping I'll live long enough to teleport myself there. The dream before this all happened was to sort of *Eat Pray Love* the Italian/India/

Bali experience. You know, like the movie where Julia Roberts goes to Italy, eats her way through the country, gains twenty pounds?"

"I vaguely remember it," Sam muttered, his hand moving to her lower back area.

"But seeing as I can no longer eat, and I'm not a fan of sweating it out in an ashram or giving up my moisturizer for the *pray* portion of that dream. I'll stick to a gondola."

When he answered, his voice had turned to hot chocolate, slipping over her frayed nerves and warming the cold, fearful depths of them. "I'd ride in a gondola with you."

Somehow, their lips had become but inches apart. Sam's eyes glowed in the dark of his bedroom, churning with emotion. "Sam?"

"Yeah?"

"I think I'd better sit up."

"Are you uncomfortable?"

Oh, on the contrary. She was on fire. Nothing about it was uncomfortable.

He shifted, swinging her around and pulling them up to the head of the bed where he could brace himself against the pillows. Her legs straddled his lap, falling to either side of his strong thighs. "Better?"

What wasn't better about being in Sam's lap while his man-bits of pleasure were so close to hers she could scream from the heat of it?

"So where were we? Moisturizer and ashrams."

"Gondolas."

"In Italy," he husked out, the tips of his fingers grazing the exposed flesh where her sweatshirt had risen above her pant line.

That just a simple touch of his fingers was making her skin burn like he was the match and she was the gasoline caught her off guard. Every nerve ending responded to his touch in surround sound, and while she'd enjoyed plenty of sex in her time, a mere touch had never had so much magnification.

Oh, if this was just a taste of what was to come when you experienced sex as a vampire—he should just stake her now. Right now. Otherwise, she'd surely die of the pleasure.

Cupping her face, Sam drew her to him, his lips so near every line in them was magnified. "Phoebe?"

"Um, yep?"

"We shouldn't be doing this," he whispered, lining her lower lip with his tongue.

She fought to keep her eyes open. "Hey, you said no, rejected me like one would reject an undercooked piece of chicken at a bar mitzvah, and I went without balking. No is no. Even for girls."

His teeth gleamed in the glow of the city lights outside his window just before he nipped the corner of her mouth. "Like I said, we shouldn't be doing this. You know, *touching*."

Phoebe flapped her hands at her sides all while her insides turned to mush. "This is me not touching you."

"But I'm touching you," he drawled, slow and hot.

"Guilty as charged."

Sam let his fingers caress her cheekbone, lighting small fires on her cool skin. "I *shouldn't* be touching you."

The attempt to keep her voice steady was going to be an effort, but she made it anyway. "I guess that depends on who you ask."

"But I really want to touch you. We have a dilemma."

"Okay, so could we make a choice here? Touch. Don't touch. Do me. Don't do me. But choose. I mean, if I miss this because of the attack that is vampire sleep, someone's going to pay. Ball's in your court. Go."

Sam's lips grazed her jaw. "I wanted to wait."

For what? The second coming? "For?"

"The courting process."

Court this. "Then we'll have to wait a little while longer while we figure out if we're going to die. After that, I'm free as a bird. Get back to me then. I'll pencil you in."

Sam's groan was one of frustration when his mouth almost

touched hers. "I wanted to take you to a movie. Bring you flowers. Candy's out, but I'd bet I could manage to put a bow on a packet of blood with Marty's help."

"Dreamy." Soooo dreamy.

"I wanted to watch TV with you. Read the Sunday paper with you. Maybe take a moonlit stroll in Central Park with you."

Flares of white-hot heat assaulted Phoebe when he took to nipping her lips again. Add in his words, words that touched every romantic bone in her body, and she was headed for a puddle of butter. "Was this all going to occur before you made your slick nerd bedroom moves on me?"

"Well, that was the gentlemanly plan."

"We'd have been dating into the next millennium. Maybe we should double up and do blood and Sunday papers together as sort of a combination package?"

"I wanted to court you in the way you deserved, Phoebe. With all the trimmings."

Tingles rippled up her spine at his gravelly admission. "And now?"

"Now I want to do that *and* run my tongue all over your body."

"All at once? Central Park will never be the same." She clamped her lips together to prevent a moan while he slid his tongue over the shell of her ear. Hearing those words was like finding out Chanel had named her their sole heir.

When she leaned into him, kneading her fingers into his hard chest, he let out a sharp hiss. "I want to throw you down on the bed, rip off your sweats, and make you scream."

Er, pause. Some honesty was needed here. "I can at least relieve you of one stressor. Here's the thing. I'm not much of a screamer. Just so we won't have any lingering disappointments between us. I'm not very noisy when I . . . you know . . . Doesn't mean it's not good, just means I'm stealthy."

Sam lifted his head from her ear, his eyebrow cocking upward in arrogance. "Oh, I think I can make you scream."

Phoebe planted her hands on her hips and rolled her neck at his challenge. "Was that like a double-dog dare?"

His grin was cocky. Deliciously cocky. "Maybe."

Fine. It was on like *Donkey Kong*. No one dared Phoebe Reynolds. A double-dog dare was like challenging her to a duel at dawn. She yanked her shirt up over her head, thankful she'd left her peachy lace bra on. "Then I double-dog dare you."

Sam pulled his shirt off, too, with a defiantly amused gaze. "Good thing it wasn't a triple or I'd have had to make you scream twice."

"Hah. As if. Okay, Sam McLean. I triple-dog dare you to make me scream twice. May the force be with you." With swift fingers and her own pair of amused defiant eyes, she hooked her thumbs into the top of her sweats, lifted off his lap and yanked them down to her ankles, shoving them off each foot.

Sam grabbed her at the waist and planted her even closer to his chest. "I'd venture to say I could probably prompt three screams out of you. And maybe even a beg for mercy."

With the flick of her fingers, Phoebe popped the clasp at the front of her bra, pulled it off, and threw it at him. "Like I'd in a trillion years beg for mercy. Do you have any idea who you're dealing with McLean? I was the baddest ass in the land from kindergarten right up until graduation, buddy. You're really giving your nerd prowess some serious ego. I hear a lot of hype, but I'm not seeing a lot of proof. Your serve, ninja geek."

In a blur of his new vampiric skill, Sam drew her to him, their chests flush, her nipples hard and driving against his cool skin, making her gasp out loud. His mouth went to her throat, his tongue, oddly hot in contrast to the rest of him, silken and raspy, ran over her needy flesh.

Sam cupped her breasts, full and achy; they responded in kind, swelling and filling his hands. He tweaked her nipples between his fingers, rolling them to hard peaks, making her moan in delight. He nipped at the skin of her neck, trailing downward until he reached the top of her shoulder.

Phoebe's head fell back at the exquisite pleasure he wrought when his lips found her nipple, cool and smooth, then surrounded the tight bud, drawing it deep into his mouth.

The place between her legs burned, ached, grew damp as her hips drove down against the hard ridge of Sam's cock, still encased in his jeans. Her fingers dug into his thickly muscled shoulders when he alternated between her nipples, biting them with gentle nips, swirling his tongue over them in long drags.

She pulled him closer, wanting to absorb the deliciously agonizing feel of his mouth on her. When he finally released her breasts, he slid under her and rolled her to her back. Her legs dangled off the side of his bed while she watched him strip his jeans off and drop his boxer briefs.

Under the heated black cover of the last remnants of the early-morning hours, she began to appreciate the gift of vampiric vision. Sam's body, lean and sculpted, stood in proud, unabashed beauty. His wide chest led to a lean waist and even leaner hips.

Those hips had that sharp indentation of muscle, proof of hours spent at a gym. His thighs, thick and taut, sprinkled with dark hair, flexed when he leaned forward and pulled her panties off with a rough yank.

If her pulse could race, Phoebe was sure it would when her eyes strayed to his cock, thick and hard; the sight of it made her groan in the kind of anticipation that left her shaking.

And then Sam was kneeling in front of the bed. He said nothing, but when Phoebe's eyes would have slid closed, his commanded her to watch him. Dark and hooded, his intent was written in them when he lifted her thigh and slung it over his shoulder.

Her fingers went to the blankets on the bed, clutching the fabric with a trembling grip. Her upper body strained against the feel of his hair caressing her abdomen, brushing against the skin of her legs, taunting her, teasing her.

And now, she did want to scream. She wanted to scream at him to drive his tongue into her so deep she'd die of the pleasure. She wanted to end the agonizing bliss he wrought from her while he trailed wet kisses on her quivering flesh.

Yet, she fought it with clenched teeth, and when he finally drew his fingers between the slick folds of her flesh, still, she didn't scream. But her hips bucked upward and the heel of her foot crashed against Sam's shoulder, his touch was so intense.

His thumbs moved to spread her flesh, one hand slid beneath her ass to lift her upward, yet still, he didn't slide his tongue against her aching clit.

And Phoebe found herself fighting another scream of frustration—fighting a wail of pent-up need, a plea to Sam to drive into her.

But then his mouth was on her, consuming her, licking the strip of exposed flesh, savoring it with a hot tongue. It took Phoebe by such surprise, she reared upward against his mouth, mewling as he lavished her clit with the slickness of his wet tongue.

Sam pulled back for a moment when he seemed to sense she was close to the edge. Her head thrashed against the bed in protest, her hands went to his head to draw him back to her, but Sam suspended the moment by kneading her upper thighs.

Trailing his fingers over the tight curls between her legs, he moved in agonizing inches toward her clit, circling it before dragging his finger downward and inserting it into her, catching her by surprise.

And then his mouth was on her again, sipping at her swollen clit as he drove his finger into her time and again.

It was more than Phoebe could take. The sweet-sharp pain deep in her belly, the hot flares of spiking heat began to torment her. The need for satisfaction became bigger than her, and that's when she let go.

With a scream.

It hissed from her throat, and she managed to catch it only by placing her knuckle in her mouth and the brief realization everyone out in the living room and guest bedroom would hear her.

Sam drove his finger into her and she rode it with wild abandon, whimpering, clenching her muscles, relishing the astounding impact a vampire orgasm had.

Sanity had just begun to return when Sam lifted himself from the floor and hovered over her. He smiled, but it wasn't filled with the kind of victory she'd expected. Instead, it was decadently sinful when he pushed her knees upward and lingered between her legs.

He let his cock glide between her wet folds, teasing her, slowly bringing her back to the place she'd just left.

She reached between their bodies, marveling at how cool his skin was when she grasped his cock and wrapped her hand around it.

Sam's smile went from tormentor to the tormented in one long draw of his hard shaft. His moan of pleasure fueled her, drove her to return the favor he'd bestowed upon her.

But Sam wouldn't have it. He lifted his hips away from hers, pulling back, grabbing her hands and circling her wrists above her head.

There was a pause, a moment when the thought of turning back was now or never. The silence between them pulsed with thick suspension. Seconds had passed, but they felt more like days.

His deep chocolate eyes met hers and then, his decision made, he was in her, driving upward, entering her with such fierce force, Phoebe had to cling to him to keep herself beneath him.

Never had such exquisite pleasure accosted all of her senses in quite the way Sam inside her did. He stretched her, filled her, made her hips clash upward toward his.

Lips met, mouths clung and meshed, tongues clashed and warred. Flesh melded with flesh as their chests fused together.

Sam let her hands go, wrapping them around his neck, then sliding a hand beneath her, cupping her ass, driving her hard against his groin. The scrape of his pubic hair against her swollen clit sent a molten shot of desire deep within her belly; it pulsed outward, making her arch her neck to deepen their kiss.

That now familiar need he'd evoked in her when his head was between her legs began the steep climb to relief. Phoebe responded by hooking her ankles around his waist, riding the ever-growing pang of desire until she was ready to explode.

Sam's muscles tightened to rigid proportions, each sinewy plane of his sculpted body reacted, and Phoebe knew he was as close as she was.

His lips were suddenly at her ear, nipping the lobe, swirling over it with a wet glide of his tongue. Her nipples tightened when he commanded, grinding the words from between teeth clearly clenched, "Come, Phoebe. Come *now*."

The hot, gravelly tone of his voice, the demand to do his bidding drove Phoebe over the edge.

And there was another scream when her orgasm ripped from her body and raced over her overstimulated nerve endings. The wave of pleasure was so distinctly sharp, so clearly defined, it swept over her in one rush of sensation.

They bucked together, their hips crashing, their skin flush. Sam hissed in her ear, nipping at her earlobe before straining to take that one last drive of his cock, forceful and demanding.

The silence as they each went boneless was almost eerie. How odd not to hear the crash of breath or the harsh rasp of needy lungs seeking air.

Sam cradled her against him, brushing her hair from her face. "So excuse me. Do you hear that?"

Her smile was as sleepy as her question. "Hear what?"

"The resounding echo of your screams. Not one, but two, Ms. I Double-dog Dare You." He chuckled against her forehead, letting his lips graze it.

She ran her hands over his broad back, luxuriating in the dips and planes of his muscles. "I don't want to throw stones, but I *triple-dog dared you.*"

"I couldn't wait any longer. That's just how vixen-ish you are."

"Don't you try and sweet-talk me just because I'm sexual napalm, pal."

He chuckled down at her, pressing a kiss to her lips. "Fine. Next time, it's four. I owe you one."

There was going to be a next time? She bit the inside of her cheek to keep from squeeing her joy. "And I believe there was a beg for mercy in there. So, I win. You lose."

"I'm happy to concede. So is it me, or is it completely off the wall that we're not doing any heavy breathing?"

"It's not you. It's weird not to be out of breath."

"Or sweaty."

Phoebe smiled, no doubt, dreamily. Hah. No boob sweat. "I think I'm okay without the sweat. But I get your meaning."

"And no wet spot."

She giggled. "The crazy. It just keeps coming."

"Do you think every vampire before us has had this conversation when they first experienced sex as a vampire?"

"Yes!" a voice yelped. "There are adults out here talking, kiddies. Now shut the fuck up and quit acting like this is some kind of amusement park and you two are the Tilt-A-Whirl!" Nina bellowed from the living room.

They both muffled their laughter in each other's necks. Sam whispered in her ear, "But woo and hoo. Vampire sex is the shiz, huh?"

"No lie."

"However, we have a problem."

Phoebe frowned, giving him a drowsy pout. "Is this the regret portion of vampire sex is the shiz?"

"Hell, no. I don't regret a damn thing. But I will regret something."

"You mean tomorrow—like morning-after regret?"

"No. That I'm finding it hard to keep my eyes open and you'll be all bent out of shape that I didn't appropriately utilize our afterglow."

"I don't think I'll have any right to complain."

"Because?"

"Because I'm going to do a totally man thing and pass out in two, three, one . . ."

As the deep, dark call of vampire sleep swept over them, they didn't disentangle their bodies—entwined, still locked in the last vestiges of their lovemaking.

Though now flaccid, Sam remained inside her, and her last thought was, she could do this every night with him.

For eternity.

"So, vampire, where are we tonight?" Marty asked, threading her hands through her hair and plunking her poodle Muffin down on Sam's couch. She'd come to share a babysitting shift with Archibald so Nina could catch her breath and on the off chance reinforcements were needed should trouble arise.

Nina's eyes were dull with defeat. "I don't know, Marty. I sure as shit don't know."

Marty held a hand up and frowned, her wedding ring gleaming in the lamplight. "Hold up. I didn't hear an ounce of sarcasm in that statement. Who are you, and where's the real Nina, poser?"

"The real Nina's experiencing what some might call a life struggle," Wanda offered, sitting down next to them and dragging Muffin into her lap.

Marty cocked her head, her blue eyes wide. "A life what? Nina? *Our* Nina? You mean she hasn't beaten the struggle out of someone to find the answer yet?"

Wanda shot Marty an admonishing look and shook her head from behind Nina to signal it wasn't the time to razz their friend. "We've got trouble, pal. Not just a little, either." Wanda went about explaining where Sam and Phoebe's situation was now and the events of the night.

Marty's mouth fell open, but she instantly closed it. She put a hand on Nina's knee and squeezed it. "We'll figure it out, Nina. We always figure it out. I know it looks grim, but we've been to grim and back."

Nina grabbed for Marty's hand and clung to it in a rare act of true fear. "I did this, Marty. I fucking well did this. Those people in there could die if I don't do something to save them. *Die*. I mean, Jesus Christ."

Wanda stroked Muffin's head, running her fingers along the top of the poodle's lavender T-shirt that read, DOES THIS SHIRT MAKE MY BUTT LOOK CURLY? "It isn't just you that has to do something, Nina. You're not in this alone. We're in this together."

Nina scoffed at them both. "The hell I'll let you two ballerinas end up hurt because of me. You're officially fucking sidelined. This is my stank to deal with."

"The. Hell. It's like Wanda said, we always go in together, Nina. Period," Marty reminded her with a stern tone. "That's what OOPS is about. And Phoebe's your sister. She's family. We don't abandon family. You didn't abandon Casey when Wanda needed you and Casey's life was at stake. So was Clay's," she said, referring to Wanda's sister and Clay's plight to untangle himself from a mate he'd never wanted to begin with.

Nina threw Marty's hand back at her. "Yeah? Well, usually, when we go in together, I didn't create half the problem. We've got an equal interest in saving the client, and Casey's shit was on Clay. He spilled demon blood on her. It had nothing to do with Grace Kelly here. This time, it's on me. If I'd have chilled out like you warned me to, Princess Phoebe wouldn't be here today."

Marty and Wanda both stared at each other. Simultaneously, they reached out to one another's chins and, using their index fingers, pushed them upward.

Marty nudged Nina's knee. "Is that remorse I hear, Nina? Accountability? What the hell's happened since I saw you two days ago?"

"I saw a dead body, no, three now, and the kid has—or had—whatever, Alzheimer's—early onset. So, yeah, my out-of-control temper saved her from dying from some crippling fucking disease, but it ain't gonna save her from the shit that happened to that dude on the roof at Alice's or what happened to Alice Goodwin. That shit's on me. I knocked her into Sam because I felt threatened."

Marty's look was of the unfathomable. "Hookay, shut the front door. You're owning up to pushing Phoebe into Sam, not to mention, you're owning up to feeling threatened? You are not Nina Blackman-Statleon. No effin' way, imposter. Maybe she's one of those manufactured in the likeness of Nina vampires, too. So stop the crazy train, I want off."

"Shut the fuck up, Marty. It is so me. I can feel like shit, too. So just let me, all right? Christ, you're like one of those yippy terriers, always humping my leg. I did this because I didn't want to believe my father loved anyone other than my mother. It made me want to crack her stupid Barbie head over my knee when she told me. But what she says is true, and what Wanda says is true, too."

"And that is?" Marty asked, her eyes full of concern.

"That it's not Phoebe's fault my father did her mother and fell in love. My mom was gone. At least gone in the sense that she'd fucking abandoned me for some crack. I don't know the exact timeline on the shit that went down between Phoebe's mother and my father. I just know my dad did another chick. And that was all I could hear out of Foofie Barbie's mouth."

"And you felt betrayed," Wanda coaxed. "Maybe even a little jealous that you weren't the only apple of his eye?"

Nina let her chin fall to her chest. "I was hacked off at the idea my father had a whole other life. He was gone a lot when I was a kid. I guess some of that time was spent with Phoebe and her mother, and it pissed me off that it could have been spent with me and Lou."

Marty reached behind Nina and gave Wanda a poke with her finger. "Wanda, hold me up, friend. I'm winded. Admission of guilt from Nina is one thing, but displaying emotions of remorse and jealousy—out loud? I expect to hear the clop of hooves as one of the Four Horsemen lands right here in Sam's living room."

That Nina didn't respond to Marty's wisecrack made her instantly pull her friend's hand back into hers. "Nina, if it takes an army of us, I'll find a way. *We'll* find a way. I don't know what the way is, but I'll figure it out. We'll all figure it out."

Nina slid down on the couch and let her head rest on Marty's shoulder, pulling her hoodie around her face.

Marty drew Nina to her chest, letting her chin fall to the top of Nina's head, stroking her cheek while Wanda laid a gentle hand on her friend's arm.

Muffin climbed into Nina's lap, pressing her head to her longtime, under-the-table scrap-feeding friend's chin before settling in and curling her body into a tiny ball of fur.

And they all sat that way—in silence, in fear, in thought—for a very long time.

CHAPTER 12

Phoebe woke with the usual start. One she was still getting used to. The one where your eyes flew open and you were instantly awake and aware of every single, minute detail. It was better than any shot of double espresso she'd ever had.

She reached a hand out to lever herself off the bed and bumped into something—something hard and cool.

Sam.

Last night slammed into her memory in the way of carnal images and vivid Technicolor flashbacks. Phoebe sat for a moment, savoring the memory. Savoring Sam's still sleeping body next to hers. She peeked at him from hooded eyes, taking in the thickly muscled lump next to her. The way his arm was flung up over his forehead. The strange, yet alluring lack of any rise and fall to his sexy chest.

And then it sunk in.

Best day ever!

Best sex ever.

It was like tripping over a pair of brand-new Louboutins on the sidewalk, mint, in package, totally in her size, while on her way out of Tiffany's after being declared the hundredth shopper and scoring a shopping spree.

Boom, baby.

Sam's hand snaked out to grab her wrist and pull her to him, making her gasp in surprise. She fell on his chest with a chuckle and smiled up at him. There was no awkward morning-after vibe between them—at least not on her part. It was like they'd always done this.

"I've decided you shouldn't be our decoy," he whispered against the top of her head, tightening his grip on her waist and molding her body to his.

Phoebe stiffened. "You've got a better candidate in mind?"

She felt the shake of his head and the clench of his jaw. "No. I just gave it some thought, and I've decided we can find another way. Whatever, whomever is doing this is insane. A sick bastard psychopath. I don't want to risk you getting hurt or someone finding out you're not the old Phoebe with Alzheimer's."

"Wow."

"What?"

"I must be a helluva lay."

Sam's finger traced her jaw with a lazy swirl. "Such a lady."

Her chuckle was morning-husky. "Always."

"And you've drawn this conclusion from?"

"The fact that we only just had our first tryst last night and already you're pulling the caveman overprotective act."

Sam scoffed in her ear. "I'd hardly call me a caveman because I don't want you deader than you already are. I wouldn't want any of you to end up hurt because we did something foolish."

She pulled away from him, rising on an elbow and smiling down at him with a raised eyebrow. "So you're saying I'm not a good lay?"

His eyes narrowed. Clearly, he was losing his sense of humor. "I did not say that at all. What I said was, sending you into the middle of this is too dangerous—or have we forgotten that woman at your apartment or the guy last night on Alice Goodwin's roof?"

"You mean your one-night stand? Oh, nay, Mr. McLean. I haven't forgotten," she teased, tucking the sheet around her.

"And have you forgotten my one-night stands tend to end up in ashes?"

"Am I now classified under one-night stands?"

Sam's eyes, deep as always, took on that warning hint to them. "You know what I mean, Phoebe. Stop deflecting and listen to me."

"Who's deflecting? You do whatever you have to do to come to grips with the fact that not only are you behaving like I'm now your property, but that I'm going to do this whether you want me to or not. As for me. I have a late-afternoon doctor's appointment to make—and I've got a date with some spray tan. You know, so I don't look like a vampire? So while you worry, I'll go make sure Marty picked up what we need."

He gripped her arm, his urgency was less understated now, and the charm Sam usually spewed an order with was strained. "I said no. It's too dangerous. If anything's going to happen to anyone, it should be me. I started this—so whatever they're testing, torturing people with, I should be the sacrifice. Period."

"Sam?"

He smiled—wide and endearing. "Yes, cupcake?"

"You're an entomologist. You're about as helpful here as this personal stylist is. You study bugs. You're not exactly qualified to do some undercover sting. Our skill sets are pretty much on par with each other's. You play with squicky bugs, and I play with clothes. Hardly a covert couple of operators. But if I don't go in, who will? I'm the only viable candidate we have, and BTW, I'm not all that much like Alice anymore. She went in a human. I'm going in a vampire. So let's leave this episode of *Twenty-four* and be realistic, Jack Bauer. If I can find out who's in charge of fixing my eternity, you can bet I'm down with some spying."

Now he shook his head. Like he could tell her what to do. "No, Phoebe. You're not going anywhere. I'm not kidding."

Phoebe rolled under his arm in a swift move she'd learned in a self-defense class and hopped off the bed, glaring down at him. "Sam? Me, neither. So do you wanna do some naked vampire v vampire here—or are you going to stop being ridiculous and let me get ready?"

His mouth formed a thin line. "We're going to have our first fight. Right here. Right now." Sam tapped the empty space she'd left when she jumped off the bed.

She wiggled her fingers at him over her shoulder while she sauntered her nakedness toward the door. "Perfect. But prepare your battlefield, amateur. Because I was on the debate team my senior year. You do not want to mess with this mouth."

Sam sat up on the bed, the muscles of his chest and arms flexing with tension. "Bring it."

Brushing her mussed hair from her eyes, she asked, "Are you daring me again? Haven't you learned anything after last night?"

He crossed his arms over his chest. "Consider yourself dared."

She planted her hands on her hips, her expression purposely cocky. "Ohhh. You know what this reminds me of, don't you?"

"Some guy named Alejandro who has a Catholic priest for a father and twin brothers born in sin who've been cryogenically frozen in the Arctic circle?" he mocked.

She wrinkled her nose. "They weren't cryogenically frozen, silly. I can't believe you remember me telling you all of that at Nina's."

Sam's already razor-sharp cheeks sucked inward. "I remember *everything* you say, Phoebe."

She flapped her hands at him, heedless that she was naked. "No, funny man. That's not what this reminds me of. This"—she jabbed her finger in the air—"reminds me of the time Skye Summers from the *Willful and the Beautiful* had to sacrifice the love of her life, Dante St. Croix, and marry an obsessed Colombian drug lord to keep Dante from being shot. Dante was a total brooding, angsty stupidhead, who just couldn't admit he loved Skye because she was rich and he was a chicken farmer's son. So you know, the usual 'I love you, I hate you' nonsense ensued. For months. Months, I tell you. So many months I wanted to choke Dante with his ridiculous pride while he tried to get his degree from an online Internet college so he could get a fabulous job and impress Skye who really didn't care about how poor he was anyway. If he'd just told her what he was doing every night instead of letting her think he was with that utter whore, Penelope Winslow, everything would have been just fine. But noooo—it went on for a millennia. Of course, there'd be nothing to watch if they'd resolved it too quickly. But that's neither here nor there."

"What *is* here or there, Phoebe?" Sam asked, clenching his fists in his lap.

"What?"

"The point. What's the point here?"

"Right. Anyway, the Colombian drug lord obsessed with Skye was sick with jealousy about her love for Dante. So he kidnapped Dante. Oh, it was brutal to watch. The hostage situation went on for days and days while Skye's brother and police chief captain, Felix Caulfield, tried to negotiate both their safe returns. Then there was this huge rescue attempt, which totally failed. It was one of those scenes like right out of a horror movie, where you're screaming, 'Don't go down in the basement, dummy!' What a botched job that was—everyone ended up dead and Felix was left in a coma. Oh. It was so ugly. Anyway, Dante told Skye he'd rather die than let her marry that swine Carlo Gonzales."

"And how, in your pretty little head, does this situation even remotely resemble Colombian drug lords, sacrificial marriages, and shootings?"

"Well, first there's your pride. I think your pride is a little wounded because I'm the one doing the saving. You're not used to disruption in your quiet life, but if there is one, you like to believe you should be the one to handle it. And then there's what Dante said to Skye when she told him she was going to go through with it to save his life."

"Pray tell, what did Dante say, Phoebe?" he asked, not bothering to hide his sarcasm.

"Exactly the same thing you did."

He cocked an eyebrow, his lips flirting with an amused smile. "Which was?"

"The word no. Well, it was more than no. It was a sort of don't-you-dare kind of thing."

"So let me guess: Against his express wishes, Skye married Carlo to keep Dante alive and, in the process, managed to spite him, too?"

"You bet your undead ass she did." Phoebe strolled out of the room to the tune of Sam's growl.

She was a vampire. It was more ammunition than poor Alice Goodwin had been equipped with when she'd gone into this clinical trial.

And she had teleportation on her side. If something went wrong, she'd just zap herself out.

She sent a silent prayer up that if she did have to zap herself out—she wouldn't land in like Botswana. Or God forbid, The Cheesecake Factory.

Fuck. That would be a real slap in her blueberry-cheesecake-lovin' kisser.

"HAVE I said I don't like this?" Sam ground out as they gathered one street over from Dr. Hornstein's.

Phoebe pulled her arm from Sam's with a hard yank and tucked her hair back up under her red beret, straightening it and her large black purse, which held the forms they needed to get her into the clinical trial. "I only have so many fingers and toes. I've lost track of the number of times you've said you don't like this, Sam."

"Last count was twenty-two and a fucking half in less than thirty minutes. You stopped him cold midsentence last round of Phoebe v Sam," Nina said, slapping Sam on the back with a laugh. The sharp crack of her hand against his leather jacket made Phoebe's ears ring.

"Dude, look. I don't like it any more than you do. But she's only handing over the forms to the doc for right now. It's not like they're going to throw her in some van and kidnap her. It's a doctor's office— in fucking Manhattan at rush hour. No way they can get her out of here without us seeing it. She'll be fine. And FYI, it's only five o'clock. I don't get up until at least seven for anybody. Which means I'm pissy. Know why? Here's why. I was up half the night listening to you two get your humpback beast on. That makes me cranky. Count yourself among the goddamn lucky I don't need as much vampire sleep as I used to. So shut up, for shit's sake. Let Phoebe do her thing, and we'll all go home after she's done and plot our next move to take over the world with some blood in those fancy glasses Arch likes so much."

Sam's lips thinned for the second time in less than twenty minutes. Phoebe had discovered this was a sure sign he was losing his patience. He didn't do it often. So when he did, it meant something.

He ran a hand over the brim of his black Stetson. "I really think you should bring someone in with you, honey." His words held a plea to them, and he'd softened them in order to get her to do what he wanted her to do.

She fought to maintain her stance. Um, no. This was their one shot. She was taking it.

Phoebe's head cocked. She crossed her arms over her chest, folding her gloved hands in the crooks of her arm. "Bring who in with me? You mean like you, Mr. Hot for the Head Nurse? How will we explain that to the woman you made a move on just so you could get Alice Goodwin's files?"

Sam's head dipped in impatience and he sucked his cheeks in so hard he created deep caverns on either side of his mouth. "Okay. Then take Nina," he growled.

Phoebe rolled her eyes and pushed past Sam to make a break for it, but he stopped her. In frustration, she yelped, "No! No one else is exposed to this. We can't afford to have anyone else associated with this mess. They think I don't have any family. You don't suppose Buys Clothes at the Five and Dime Barbie can get away with saying she's my friend, do you? We look too much alike, Sam."

Nina snorted and made a face. "Please. We do not either look anything alike. I'd fucking rather be Marty than look like you, princess."

Darnell spoke for the first time. His round face was full of devilish glee when he gave Nina a shoulder bump. "I dunno, Nina. I think y'all look a lot alike. Only difference is Miss Phoebe's got red hair and a nicer tongue. Oh, some blue eyes, too. She's like Nina-light."

Phoebe clapped her hands together in finality, smiling in Darnell's direction to thank him for his support. "And there you have it. We're like twins, Nina. Love it. Now, I'm going in. I'm going to hand over the clinical trial forms, talk to Dr. Hornstein, and come right back out. Forty-five minutes—an hour tops. Can you go on existing that long without me, Sam, or do you want me to text you kissy faces so you know I still like you?"

Sam grabbed her by her upper arms and forced her to look up at him. His handsome face was semi-hidden under his black Stetson, but she knew beneath that brim were worried eyes. And an odd sort of urgency that wasn't like Sam at all . . . "Knock it off, Phoebe, and pay close attention. Any sign of anything out of the ordinary, even a hint of suspicion, and you get the hell out. Got that? Use whatever form of the getting you have to in order to do it. Or I'll blow this whole ridiculous sting thing wide open by rushing the place."

Phoebe relaxed in his tight hold. "Again, thank you, Jack Bauer slash buddies with bugs. Now go somewhere that's not here, and quit worrying."

Lines of concern wreathed Sam's face. "Do you have your phone?"

"I do. And my Mace, for those sticky occasions like when a human tries to take on a vampire."

"Sarcasm. Not lovin' it right now." He glared down at her to show her how little he loved it.

For a moment, Phoebe paused and really listened to the urgency in Sam's voice. She was getting better and better at learning how to use her ability to sense emotions. For instance, much like she had back at Alice Goodwin's apartment, she knew Nina was worried for her. How deep that went was another story entirely, but it was there.

But Sam's tone didn't just display worry—it was something more. Something she couldn't put her finger on. So she decided to ease up with the taunting. "Look, Sam. I promise to be careful. I have my phone, and if I need you, you'll know. Plus, if things get really hairy, I'll do what Darnell taught me and picture him in my mind. He'll appear out of nowhere in his white whip like the knight in shining Nikes he is, and all will be well. But please let me do this without worrying about anything but getting it done. I don't want to go in anxious and freaked out if there's no need for it. You're only making this worse with your fretting. Look, the clock is ticking. We have no idea how long we have left to live. Let me try and find out. *Please.*"

Scooping her up, Sam placed his lips on hers and left a hard kiss on her mouth, one that caught her by surprise but melted her just as if they were alone and not about to embark on some potentially dangerous shenanigans.

Nina poked her face between them. "Hey, vampires two point O—lay off the fucking canoodling and let's get 'er done. You'll be late for your appointment if you don't move your fat ass, Phoebe."

Sam let her go with obvious reluctance, dropping her to the ground with a caveman grunt of displeasure.

Phoebe threaded her fingers through his and gave them one last squeeze before letting go. She had to hope he understood that this simple form of communication between them meant something. To her. To her heart. That she wanted to come back to him in just the way she'd left him—because that meant they could continue this exploration thing. Today, she'd discovered, she wanted that almost as much as she wanted to find acceptance with Nina.

Sam held up his hand to his ear and made a sign for the phone to signal she should call him, his face grim.

Phoebe nodded her consent.

Just as she tried to slip past Darnell, he gave her a bear hug, thumping her on the back with his large pawlike hand and whispering, "You be safe now. You need me, member what I tol' ya. Just think me up. Picture my ugly ol' puss in yo head. I'll be there, a'iiight?"

Phoebe cupped his jaw and gave it a quick pinch as he let her drop back to the ground. "A'iiight."

As she swept past her sister, Nina clamped a firm hand down on her shoulder, her fingers trembling ever so slightly before she let go, giving Phoebe a shove in the direction of the doctor's office.

Without another word, she moved down the sidewalk at a rapid pace, remembering Nina's advice to keep her feet in time with the flow of other people's footsteps so as not to arouse suspicion.

At the door of the glass building that held Dr. Hornstein's office, she paused, taking in her ridiculously orange spray tan against the deep red of her wrap coat.

She saw the fear in her eyes; the protective eyewear couldn't hide it, and she had to remind herself once again that she was only dropping off some forms. No big thang.

Before she'd settled on personal stylist as her bread and butter, she'd dreamed the dream most young girls do. She was going to run away to Hollywood and become a famous actress on *Saved by the Bell*. Mario Lopez, of course, was going to be her on- and off-screen husband.

She'd done a school play or two in her time. Okay, so she didn't exactly get the part of Sandy in *Grease*——but girl walking the high school halls, carrying her binder with purpose, as she'd been billed, was acting, too.

She could do this. She could fake her way through this. She certainly could summon up the terror of her now distant diagnosis with no trouble at all. She could remember the agony her mother had suffered at the very hands of the same disease Phoebe had once thought was going to be her death sentence as well.

If she recalled the horror of her mother's illness, then finding out she, too, had the same disease, she'd put method actresses across the land to shame.

So shit on you, Mrs. Swarkofsky, for not giving me the part of Sandy. No way had Mindy Mifflin looked better than she did in that spandex/Lycra concoction Olivia Newton-John had worn.

Wrapping her hand around the door handle, she yanked it open with purpose and headed toward Dr. Hornstein's suite on the third floor.

Look at me, I'm Sandra Dee.

So.

Here she was.

But where the flippin' hell was here?

When Nina's words came back to her, she cringed. *It's not like they're going to throw her in some van and kidnap her.*

Oh, realllly?

She'd beg to differ.

Somehow, that was exactly what had happened. She'd handed her forms to Nurse Hawk-of-Eye and waited until she was called to see the doctor. They'd chatted quite pleasantly for a few minutes about her finally making a solid decision to give the clinical trial a shot, and waited some more while he allegedly went to make the appropriate phone calls to set up her appointment with the doctor in charge of the trial.

Then Dr. Hornstein came back in, told her the clinical trial was a thumbs-up but she couldn't begin for a week while she took some pretrial drug to ready her for the testing. She was sure he was going to whip out his prescription pad, thus thrilling her due to the fact that it meant maybe whatever he was going to give her was something that would lead to what they were doing to these people.

But instead, he gave her a pill and watched as she pretended to take it, but rather shoved it under her tongue.

He left. She spit the pill out and palmed it, throwing it in her jacket pocket for later inspection. It wasn't like she could have swallowed it anyway. She waited some more, until there was a stirring outside her examining room door, probably unnoticeable to a human ear, and a voice she couldn't attribute to any of Dr. Hornstein's staff spoke. "She'll be out cold in about twenty minutes. We'll take her from here."

A sedative . . . More of that familiar jolt of panic sped along her spine while she scanned the room for her purse to text Sam. Yet, her inspection came up dry. They'd somehow lifted her purse without her even knowing. It had probably been while she'd worried over the possibility Dr. Hornstein was going to want to examine her with his shiny stethoscope, which would lead to him discovering she had no heartbeat.

The bastards. She had a hundred bucks in cash in her wallet.

But why examine her when they were just going to kidnap her?

The next thing Phoebe heard was the distinct shuffle of feet and clearly the preparation to take her wherever it was they were taking her.

Go figure, more panic had set in, and instead of fighting her way out of the office like the ass-kicking, mind-reading, teleporting vampire she was, Phoebe opted to lie down and play dead. She fell back on the table, closed her eyes, and waited, forgetting to picture Darnell in her mind or to utilize her rather fluky teleportation skills.

But as a guy with the bulkiest shoulders she'd ever encountered jammed in her gut first put a pillowcase (one that was definitely under her required thread count, by the smell of it) on her head, then carried her fireman style to the most unoriginal escape vehicle ever, Phoebe formed a plan.

Which, now, as she reflected, was just a little Jack Bauer *24*-ish on her part. The nerve of her accusing Sam of pretending to be something he wasn't. She'd apologize the second she was free of her Walmart-purchased pillowcase.

If she could just pretend she was unconscious for long enough to find out where they were taking her, she could teleport out, or think up Darnell, and she'd be able to find out who was in charge of vampire-mania.

Now, what felt like hours later, Phoebe fought to remain calm as she played dead beneath the pillowcase they'd slapped over her head and lay as still as possible on the cushiony table. Her thoughts went back and forth over the decision she had to make. Kill Dr. Hornstein for being a part of this—or Nurse Hawkeye just because she was such a cranky bitch.

Her ears strained to hear any movement, but wherever she was, it was as silent as a church after Easter Sunday services.

Phoebe's nostrils flared, sniffing the air through the fabric of the harsh pillowcase. No one was in the room with her. Of that, she was sure. She tugged at the harsh fabric, lifting the bottom edge of it to peek out.

"Ms. Reynolds?"

Uh, dear person in charge of magical, mystical, wondrous vampire pow-ers. What the ever lovin' fuck? I thought my nose was supposed to be so sensitive I could smell a sale on a Vera Wang dress from a hundred miles away? Someone in your department has clearly fucked up, and I'd like to lodge a complaint.

Love,
Phoebe the Captured

* * *

DARNELL flew toward them, his Nikes stomping the pavement as the chains around his neck slapped his broad chest. It had been just over an hour when Sam decided he couldn't wait anymore. He was going to break down doors and knock some heads together and find Phoebe. While he seethed, Nina had texted her three times with no response.

Just shy of ripping Nina's head off while she held him back, Darnell went in after Phoebe, but the look on his face as he rushed toward them didn't look good.

Darnell stopped short of Nina, out of breath. She clamped a hand on his shoulder, giving it a shake. "Dude—where the fuck is she?"

He shook his dark head, leaning forward with his hands on his knees. "They sayin' she ain't nevah had no appointment with them. I looked round as best I could, but I didn't see her all up in there. She jus' gone, Nina!"

Sam slammed his fist against the side of the building they waited by, pushing it visibly through the wall in his anger.

Nina was quick to yank it back out, latching on to his arm and giving him a hard shove. "Dude! Knock it the fuck off before you get caught doing a David Blaine, and help me think."

"I told her!" he ranted, anger ripping through his gut. "I've had a bad feeling about this since last night. Jesus Christ, what the hell was I thinking sending her in there?"

Darnell had finally caught his breath. His moon-shaped face was pained when he attempted to soothe Sam. "Aw, Sam. Now you cain't blame yoself, brotha." He held up one chubby finger, glistening with a gold ring that spanned his entire hand and had the initial *D* sprawled across it. "First, yo. Nobody knew it was dangerous. Phoebe was just goin' in ta hand over some forms. Ain't nothin' dangerous 'bout some paper. Second, ain't no one can tell that little lady what she cain't do. You saw her. She was goin' in no matter what. So don't you worry—ol' Darnell's gonna find her."

"Fuck!" Sam yelped into the growing darkness of the chilly night.

Nina rammed the heel of her hand into his shoulder, her features pinched in anger. "I said lay the fuck off with the martyr crap, dude. It was a good plan. No one had any idea this shit would go down. Now keep it on the down low or I'm gonna take you the hell out. Quit pissin' in the wind, whinin' for your woman, and let's think."

Sam held up his finger to pause Nina's chatter. His mind was made up. "Give me a second." Sam took quick strides away from Darnell and Nina; yanking his phone from his jacket, he dialed a number he should have dialed a long time ago. The one he'd avoided for fear his agency would find out, and he'd put everyone at risk.

Stinky Malone picked up on the first ring. "Sammy? S'up, FBI guy? How's my favorite secret paranormal agent man? Found any suspicious paranormal activity lately?"

He clamped one hand down over his Stetson to keep it from blowing off his head as the wind picked up. "This paranormal agent man needs something. So don't talk, just listen. Some shit's gone down. I need you to hack into a computer system for me."

"What's in it for me?" he singsonged in his nasally drone.

"The gift of *life*."

"Damn, Sammy," he drawled, slow and lazy. "You've never threatened to take me out. That's never been our game, cowboy. Do you even remember the game? I lead you on. You appease me and whisper sweet nothings and sites that need hacking in my ear. I behave like the computer genius cock tease I am. You try to win my favor with flowers and candy like the info-needing bitch you are. Oh, and cash. Lots of it. Unmarked. In a bank account of my Cayman Islands and/or Swiss choice."

Sam's fist tightened into a ball of fury. It was all he could do to keep his head on straight. Phoebe was gone. There was suddenly nothing else but the danger she was in and the sheer terror he'd lose her. Sam the FBI guy, calm, cool, compartmentally capable was gone.

This thing between him and Phoebe had happened quickly. This attachment to her didn't even creep up on him—it hit him full in the face. It was irrational and way too soon to use words like *commitment* and whatever else came with wanting someone in your life permanently, but there it was.

And the fuck he was going to miss out on that.

Gripping the phone, Sam spat into it. "Shut. The. Fuck. Up. Stinky, and pay attention," he said between clenched teeth. "You will do exactly as I say minus the game or I'll hand your ass over to my department so damn fast, you won't know your dick from your sweaty peanut-sized balls when I'm done. There'll be no more living in your mother's basement, surfing Internet porn, and planning world domination using Popsicle sticks for props while your creepy online friends with user IDs too long to pronounce help you rape me for some cash, weasel. Got that? Now do what I tell you, and do it now, or I'll spend the rest of my life hunting you like the fugitive you are. Clear?"

Stinky's voice went soft with a quiver. "Jesus, Sammy. I was just kidding. What the hell's gotten into you?"

Though Stinky hacked for cash, he was basically harmless, albeit a harmless criminal. His crimes didn't hurt people in the physical sense, maybe more like fiscally. He was just a skinny, scared kid whose genius had been mocked his entire life. If the kids who'd beaten his ass in school could see his bank account, they might rethink their days spent wasted pushing Stinky around.

Nowadays, he was omnipotent on the Internet, not to mention a master at hacking some of the most secure sites in the world. And wanted in more states than Sam could count without losing track and having to start over. Stinky could hack Hornstein's account while he solved a Rubik's Cube and deciphered the theory of relativity.

Sam had used Stinky's hacking skills on more than one occasion without department permission. He couldn't blame him for falling into the familiar pattern of their cash-for-services-rendered banter, but he'd picked a damn bad day.

Fighting for the control he was usually a sensei at, he gritted his teeth. "Stinky? Now's not the time. Listen, and get it right the first time, because if I have to say it more than once, I'll chew you a new asshole with my laser scope. Dr. Philip Hornstein. A neurologist in Manhattan. Get into his patient files. Get in now. Find a woman named Phoebe Reynolds. In fact, find anyone with the diagnosis for Alzheimer's. Then call me back with whatever you got. You have fifteen minutes or I come drag your ass up the stairs of your mother's house in Queens and make her a very rich woman."

"You know where I live?" he squeaked.

Sam's eyes narrowed. "Now I do. Fifteen minutes, Stinky. *Fifteen*." He clicked the phone off with a hard press of his finger to the touch screen only to find Nina, her eyes flashing and hot with anger, pinned on him.

She cracked her knuckles, her smile full of menace, her eyes hot and angry. She clapped him so hard on the back, he stumbled forward, falling into the building's brick wall. "Sammy, Sammy, Sammy," she cooed. "I get the feeling when you used the word *department*, you didn't fucking mean Macy's—you know, like *department* store? Which means, I gotta yank your Mr. Twinkie off. With my teeth. While you beg for mercy."

CHAPTER 13

Nina came at him like a freight train, driving into his gut with a head butt so brutal it slammed him directly into the brick wall of a bodega. If he hadn't been practicing, he wouldn't have been able to control driving his body straight through it. Rain began to fall in cold sheets of ice, plastering Nina's hoodie to her head and bouncing off Sam's Stetson.

She pinned him against the wall, and he let her, smelling an anger so rife he could have chewed on a piece of it like a cow on cud. "So when were you going to tell Barbie, Sammy?"

His eyes captured hers with a direct gaze, but he kept his hands at his sides, catching Darnell's hesitant gaze just over Nina's shoulder. "As soon as I could be sure she was safe."

Nina threw her middle finger up under his nose, butting his chest with her angular shoulder. "Oh, fuck you, Sam!" she roared. "Is that even your name, you goddamn liar? Do you really play with bugs, or is that just a crock of shit, too?"

"Keep the lies to a minimum," he said, choking on the words so often drilled into him. "Yes. My name is really Sam McLean and I was once really an entomologist—before I entered the FBI. Though the apartment we're staying in isn't mine and neither are the people in the pictures on my wall." It was all just a part of another elaborate cover. He caught sight of Darnell just over Nina's shoulder, looking to help, but Sam held a hand up to stop him. Nina deserved a piece of him.

"So now you're some kind of undercover narc, working for a super secret division of the FBI that investigates paranormal activity."

"You heard?"

Nina jammed the heel of her hand against his chest. "You stupid shit. Yes, I heard. Vampire hearing, Supernatural 007. Oh, and nice touch, Mulder. You got a Scully lurking somewhere around here? You know, so I can fucking kill you both at once and save myself some time?"

Time to lay your cards on the table, Sammy. He was getting sloppy because of his attachment to Phoebe, and that aside, his FBI career was over anyway due to his latest life change. Not that it mattered. It was probably over from the moment he'd met Phoebe anyway. "Look, Nina. I was sent into O-Tech to do a job. Sometimes they send us into places like O-Tech undercover to be sure everything's on the up-and-up and they're meeting FDA regulations. You know like the undercover agents they put on airplanes in case of terrorism? It's a random plant. I was getting tired of the crap thrown my way in the paranormal division that never amounted to anything. I needed a break from the people I thought were kooks. I fit the bill because I have a degree in entomology. My undercover work had nothing to do with testing some crazy drug on humans. The worst I thought I'd find was maybe some drug smuggling. Not drugs tested on humans. That any of the rest of this happened was all just a coincidence."

"And this coincidence, Sammy, did you happen to mention any of it to the jackoffs you work for?"

"No."

Nina rolled her head on her neck and sneered, flashing her fangs. "Yeah, and why was that? Because if you told them you're a vampire, too, they'd slap your lying ass into some lab somewhere and turn you into exactly what you're trying to prevent happening to more innocent people to begin with. You're the enemy to us, shithead. Not to mention, you're sleeping with the FBI's enemy. But the real dilemma is, once you were the hunter, now you're the hunted. Sucks when the shoe's on the other foot, huh, *vampire*?"

His jaw clenched. "Which is exactly why I haven't reported it to my superiors, Nina. If they knew about me, I couldn't protect you. I can't protect Phoebe if I'm locked up in some highly classified government facility."

"Fine, but you know what else that means, Sammy? It means we can't look over our shoulders if we have no clue something else, aside from all the decomposing, rabid vampires, might be coming for us. What the fuck is wrong with you?" she shouted as rain pelted them in sheets of prickly ice. "What if one of your schleps came looking for you and found us, too? How can we protect ourselves if you didn't even give us the fucking chance? I don't much like being lied to, but I like being blindsided even less, dude. You're subject to clan rule now, and the clan won't like this shit. I can promise you that much."

He still hadn't moved an inch. Letting Nina have control of this conversation was only fair. "The clan doesn't have to know if you don't tell them. I didn't do this solely for selfish motives, Nina. No. I didn't want to hurt Phoebe. I knew I'd have to tell her eventually, and of course, she'll think everything I've told her so far is all just part of my cover. But if I reveal what I know, and the agency gets ahold of it and finds your connections, even the remotest one, it's not just me that's screwed. It's all of us. *Together.* So, yes, I lied. Yes. I'd do it again to protect all of you. And let me just make mention of this—aren't you the women with full-fledged ads in magazines and don't you have a website, Twitter, and Facebook accounts? Might I remind you, you're not exactly hiding the existence of OOPS."

Nina ran her tongue over her lower lip, her eyes gleaming slits in her head. "Yeah. And here's the fucking beauty of that, Sammy. Let's say one of the nutballs that calls us on a daily basis actually got someone interested in taking a look at what we got goin' on. Let's say they got someone like *you* to look into it. What the fuck would you have found when you showed up? Three chicks in a nasty, damp-ass basement office—one really pissed off and a little pale, one who dresses like she's Audrey Hepburn, and one who looks like she just came fresh from a Badgely whoever-the-shit Mischka photo shoot with a cute, fluffy poodle. Three *women*—women that they'd label crackpot wing nuts like the dudes that chase UFO sightings and tell people aliens abducted them. Do you really think they'd take us seriously? We'd be the desperate, bored housewives. You'd all go back and have a good laugh over brewskies—and we'd snark you for being stupid. It's hiding in plain sight, Sammy. The only people who take this seriously are the people it really happens to."

Point. Nina was right. No one would have taken women like them seriously. So he remained silent.

"So back to you, Mr. 007. You don't suppose your people won't come looking anyway now that they've lost contact with you?"

Oh, he'd covered that base, and covered it but good. For the moment. "There's nothing to come looking for at this point. I took leave when I told them there was nothing to report at O-Tech. They let me because they clearly aren't suspicious, and they knew I was fried from the job overall."

She poked him in the chest with a finger akin to the end of a drill. "But you're worried now that you're pushing your luck and soon they'll want to reassign you or some shit?"

Sam's nod was curt. Yeah. He was worried. "Which is why I was going to suggest we move to my cabin upstate tonight. Not even the agency knows about it."

"Because then, you'll be just like all of us paranormals. Hiding away from the dicks at large. Boy, you covered all your goddamn bases, didn't you, FBI guy?" She rolled her tongue in her cheek, posturing.

Sam lifted his Stetson and ran a hand over his face, welcoming the rain on his skin. His disbelief had begun to subside, but the utter astonishment reared its head once more. "Who knew this was really a possibility, Nina? I've been a part of the program for over ten years and we've done a lot of investigating, but I don't think, even in my wildest fantasies, I thought any of it was true. I thought. I dabbled. I toyed with theories. I considered, but most investigations led to nothing but wild speculation. Sometimes there are no investigations to be had aside from the cranks, and we send in the rookies to handle that. Which is why everyone who's a part of the program is offered the opportunity to do various forms of undercover work. So you don't burn out. I've done all sorts of undercover work. Narcotics, missing persons—the gamut."

The harsh wind swept over her sodden jacket, making it ripple and stick to her. "So you being at O-Tech really had nothing to do with suspicious paranormal activity? If you're lyin', I'll kill you."

Sam shook his head. "Nope. It was just a random check. Me ending up bitten was all just some crazy coincidence I still have trouble believing. That vampires and werewolves really exist is beyond surreal. Not to mention, you're not—correction—*we're* not the animals we've been led to believe. Of all the suspicious reports we've investigated over the years, none of them led me to remotely consider you were shopping at malls and writing romance novels. Who knew you were all just big cuddly teddy bears with sharp teeth?"

Nina clucked her tongue, the tension in her face easing a bit. "First, never call me fucking cuddly. Second, dude, I feel you. I get it. Never in my wildest did I think this shit was real until it happened to me, either. I still wake up sometimes and think it's crazy-ass. But here we are. But not giving us all the information so we can protect ourselves if someone comes looking for *you* is bullshit. Not to mention like a death wish. It doesn't take much more than a trip to the goddamn produce section of the grocery store for some garlic to immobilize us, Sam. We might be pretty fucking scary with all these powers, but if people knew how easy it would be to break us—we'd be broke-ass."

Sam's lips thinned. She was right. He said as much. "You're right. I was wrong."

She flicked the brim of his hat with her finger, sending the rainwater gathered there flying in all directions. "You put us all at risk, Sammy. Today, I don't fucking like you like I did yesterday."

He nodded his agreement, glad she'd begun to ease off. "I wouldn't vote me in as class president, either."

"Oh, I would, fo sho, Sam," Darnell finally chimed in, his smile wet as the rain battered it, his face full of relief. "I bet you got some mad-ass leadership skills."

Sam smiled, but it was filled with irony. Yeah. He had those, and now he didn't want them anymore. "Thanks, Darnell."

"So the cutesy, nerd-is-the-word Sam McLean who's goofy and charming was just playing at it. He's really slicker than black ice and a trained killer, too. Nice, you shit. You totally had me."

"Damn it," he mocked, scuffing the heel of his boot against the glistening pavement. "I can't seem to do charming without goofy. All my superiors say so. That's why I never got the cool international jet-setting gigs. Because my charm just isn't suave enough."

"Bet you look good in a tux, though, man." Darnell held out his fist to Sam, who knocked it.

"It's my job, Nina. No. I'm not as goofy as the Sam you first met who wore a red sparkly dress and heels. But it wasn't all an act. However, I am the Sam who wants everyone's secret to remain safe at all costs. Even if it means revealing myself."

She shook her head back and forth with as much clear irony as Sam was feeling. "I so fucking want to hate you right now, but your coolness factor just went back up a notch."

Sam smiled again. "*X-Files* fan?"

"Long before any of my own shit went down. Now, when I watch the reruns, I giggle my ass off because you all don't have a fuckwit's clue."

Oh, irony. "Tell me about it."

Nina took several more steps back, jamming her hands into the pockets of her jeans. "So what're we gonna do here, Gigantor? How are we gonna fix this so Phoebe doesn't think all that slamming each other was just part of your cover? She's a girl. That's exactly where she'll go, brother."

Again, he couldn't hide his astonishment. "You really don't think it's part of my cover?"

She rolled her beautiful eyes and scoffed. "What kind of FBI agent are you? Don't you have a notepad with all your facts and lame misinterpretations about my personality type written in it? You know, right next to your laser scope? I know it's not an act, fuckwit. I can read minds, remember?"

"Then why didn't you know about me sooner?"

Rolling her tongue in her cheek, Nina clucked her tongue. "I know you'll find this hard to believe, but I've got a code of honor— we all do. I don't get all up in your brain matter without reason. Like when that woman was dying and we needed answers. I use my evil powers for good."

"Honorable."

Her arched eyebrow rose in arrogance. "Unlike someone I know."

Sam winced. "Fair."

Nina's eyes assessed him. "Phoebe's gonna shit a Kenneth Cole."

Yeah. Maybe even a MAC lipstick or two before it was over. "I've been here once before."

"And what happened?"

Helene. They'd been college sweethearts. But not after she'd decided having a family with someone who carried a gun and pretended to be people they weren't was too dangerous for her. "Oh, she dropped me like I had the clap."

Nina nodded. "You loved her?"

"I did."

"You love my sister?"

Whatever this emotion was, it wasn't like any other he'd had before. "I think I'm beginning to. I think you are, too."

She waved a dismissive hand at him, flinging water in his face. "Oh, bullshit. Leave me out of this. And what the hell is it with you dudes and a chick in heels and a designer skirt?"

"We're gluttons for punishment."

In a matter of seconds, she was back in his face with one last threat. "You'd better tell Phoebe, and tell her soon. Or I will."

"I never doubted it."

"Good." She paused, then smiled. "So, this super-secret branch of the FBI—you seen any aliens? Bigfoot, maybe?" Nina's coal black eyes sparkled with mischief.

Now his eyebrow rose. "Would I win back some cool points if I said yes?" he teased.

"Not unless you could get me a lunch gig with them. Oh, and Mulder. He was sick-hot."

Sam laughed, and it was genuine. For the first time since this had all gone down, it was the kind of laugh he hadn't had in a long time.

But there was still Phoebe. The woman he wanted to protect from the people he'd once thought he was helping to keep the world safe with.

And she was missing.

The moment of light banter passed and his gut began to burn with fear for her again. Where the fuck was Stinky with that info?

"So this Stinky? Do I have to hunt his ass down and fucking kill him for information? Or will he really call back?"

Sam glanced at his watch. "Oh, he'll call back in ten, nine, eight . . ." His voice drifted off when the phone rang.

Shrill and jarring him to his core.

A slender man, fabulously easy on the eye, with the bluest eyes Phoebe could ever remember seeing, stared down at her. His blond hair was slicked back to within an inch of its life, and his white coat was pristine. Beneath his lab coat, he wore a pin-striped shirt in navy and silver, followed up with a red tie. His clipboard rested against his ribs, a Bic pen dangling by a piece of white yarn swaying back and forth.

She slid to a sitting position, swinging her legs over the side of the hospital bed and scooted to the far side of it.

"Ms. Reynolds? How are you feeling?"

Stall, Phoebe, stall. And stop hatching ridiculous plans in your head like you're Siobhan from O'Hara's Faith. She was neither Irish nor blond and busty—or a cop slash escort with cancer of the brain. "Well, I don't know. How would you feel if you had this"—she held up the pillowcase like it had leprosy and wrinkled her nose—"thrown over your head. What kind of kidnappers are so callous they'd use anything less than four-hundred-count thread? I'm insulted by this cheap liaison."

His eyes danced with amusement. But it wasn't the kind of amusement that was gleeful. It was the cat-and-mouse kind of amusement. "My apologies for your harsh entry to our program."

She smiled—probably just a little too bright—while she hooked her feet together at her ankles and let them swing. "Accepted. And now, I think I've decided I'd rather lose my mind to Alzheimer's than spend another minute on this bed—in this room. Who's in charge of paint round here? The blind?" From the bright orange walls to the lone metal chair, there wasn't much that wasn't hideous about her holding room.

He chuckled, thin and high, reaching for her wrist. Phoebe snatched it away.

"Ms. Reynolds? You'll want to cooperate from here on out. Now I need to take your vitals. Please remain still and calm until I'm done."

Vitals? Good luck with that. Her feet hit the floor with a slap. Damn them. Her heels had fallen off when Thor had been a caveman carrying his pelt to the van. No purse and no heels made for a very disgruntled Phoebe. "Um, no. I said I want to go home. So call me a cab, saddle up the horse and carriage. Whatever it takes, McDreamy."

"I don't understand, Phoebe," he drawled, cooing her name, the smile wreathing his lean face easy and relaxed. "I thought you wanted help with your disease? I can't help you, if you won't let me."

Her eyes narrowed. "Where am I?"

"At the clinical trials, of course."

As her thoughts began to form, she realized she hadn't been in the back of that nasty-smelling van for long. Tops, maybe ten minutes, some of which had been spent with the car standing still. Wherever they were, it wasn't far from Dr. Hornstein's. Speaking of—what a lying, Hippocratic-oath-taking, donkey-ball-sucking pig. "And *where* is that? You know, like an address. In case I change my mind and want to come back. I'm abysmal at directions, and that isn't just my Alzheimer's talking."

"Somewhere safe where we can begin your journey to health without interruption."

"Well, I've decided I like having Alzheimer's. It's not such a bad thing to forget stuff. I'd like to forget my credit card bill—my weight—my senior prom date. That was an event best left in my box of nightmares. What I was thinking when I said yes to Dickey Callum can only be described as momentary insanity. Oh, and that dress I bought at some cute shop in the village because it was on sale for twelve dollars. Made my ass look like the side of a big red barn.

So I'll just be on my way. No journey to health necessary. Now let me out of this room."

"Phoebe, don't make me call for help." He walked toward the wall, his finger hovering over what she supposed was a button for an intercom.

She shrugged her shoulders with indifference. "Call the National Guard, if you like. But if it's that heathen who slapped me over his shoulder like I was a sack of potatoes you're calling, could you at least ask him to use deodorant? He smelled like a goat."

"How unpleasant." He turned to press the intercom, cool as a cucumber.

Before she gave it a second's worth of thought, Phoebe jumped off the table in a haze of movement, grabbing his finger and bending it backward, making him drop his clipboard with a mewling squeak.

Booooyah! Her inner *Fight Club* screamed. *I am vampire two point O. Hear me roar.*

Clamping her other hand over his mouth, Phoebe reminded herself, physically, she was the superior being. If need be, she'd fight her way out of here. Whatever was on the other side of the door was anyone's guess, but she was damned well going to have the chance to find out. They needed answers. She was in the maniac's lair, and finding the head maniac was crucial.

Rolling her neck to loosen up, she decided to recall all the threats her sister had lobbed at her recently. They'd aid her in putting on her best performance of a lunatic ever.

With a final glance skyward, Phoebe had one last thought.

May the power of Nina compel her.

Phoebe jerked the doctor's neck hard, hearing the crack of his fine bones and the stretch of sinew as she twisted it. "So here's the thing. If I were you, I wouldn't press that button. Because not only will I break off your finger, I'll eat it as a precursor to, say, *your balls.* Nom-nom." She leered, making her eyes wild.

He bucked against her as she dragged him backward, but she

stilled him by clamping her hand tighter over his mealy mouth. "So, let's talk, yes? Nice and calm—or I'll make good on my promise. Now, if I let go of your mouth, and you whine like the sissy la-la disappointment you're turning out to be—it's on. Got it?"

He nodded against her hand before she threw him into the chair, remembering to temper the brute force with which she did it like Wanda had lectured her. He slammed against the metal, slipping to the floor with a moan.

And there was to be no killing unless absolutely necessary. Also the word, according to Wanda. So if this nutball were lucky, he'd only leave limping—maybe bruised, and it was totally okay to draw blood as long as she'd reached a level where she could resist temptation.

Yet, seeing this insidious jackass made Phoebe see red. Which was a lovely color on him—especially if it was dripping from his head. She fought for control. After all, she made a promise to Wanda. Even when Nina had encouraged her to kill first, ask questions later, she'd sworn to Wanda she'd always abide by vampire protocol.

Phoebe crouched down on her haunches and glared at her captor. Giving him as little information as possible would be key to keeping herself and the others safe until she could call in the cavalry.

The trick was, she had to ask the right questions so he'd give her some answers without catching on to how much they'd found so far. "Where am I and who are you, Dr. Horrible?"

"Who are you?" he whispered, fear lacing his tone. Even his perfect hair quivered, leaving Phoebe feeling the stiff breeze of omnipotence.

She smiled again, summoning up one of Nina's menacing smiles that were anything but friendly. She dragged a finger down the side of his face, reveling in his cringe as she taunted. "Oh, silly. You know who I am. I'm Phoebe Reynolds. You know, your walking, talking lab rat with early-onset Alzheimer's and good hair? Didn't we establish that when I filled those forms out in triplicate to qualify for Frankenstein's eighth grade science project? God, that was a chore,

FYI, and invasive to boot. But back to the dealio at hand. Who are *you*? And I'd answer fast or who knows what organ I might go for first. I'm all about the sneak attack." She poked him in the kidney and giggled, throwing her head back in abandon.

His lips thinned and his chin lifted in defiance.

She slid down next to him, folding her legs under her, and nudging his shoulder. "I don't want to quash your romantic dreams of playing the tough guy here, but let's be serious. You're just not cut out for the part."

With fingers that almost missed their target due to her speed, Phoebe managed to snatch a handful of his hair in her hand and jerk his head to her lap. His whimper of fear was delicious. His eyes, wide and afraid—delicious-er. "See? Clearly, you're no swarthy swashbuckling match for me. So let's do this."

Yet, as she talked her smack, the realization hit Phoebe again. She didn't know what waited for her outside that door. And if he didn't answer her, she'd have to make good on her threats.

Still, he remained silent, closing his eyes as if to pretend she wasn't really there. "Are you really going to make me blow my anger-management recovery? Do you have any idea how many sessions I had to go to to get my crazy temper under control? Swear it. If I lose my fifteen-year chip—there's gonna be an organ harvesting right here in this room. God, they're so bloody. And the mess? Your cleanup crew'll be in here till day's end unwrapping your entrails like a Christmas present. So speak, douche bag—or *die*."

Just like old times, Phoebe, eh? It was uncanny how easily she'd fallen back into the role of predator. She hadn't threatened a life in years. Not since Mark's trouble their junior year.

Because there were lives at stake, she hoped whoever ruled the universe would forgive her.

Looking down at this strangely handsome man, she saw he still wasn't budging. She flashed him a coy pout. "It doesn't have to be like this, you know. You, silently valiant. Me, really hacked off by it. We," she gritted out from between her tightly clenched teeth, giving his hair another hard yank, "could have been such good friends." Her final words were a scream in his face as she rose, dragging him behind her to cross the room and attempt a peek out the door.

She tried the door handle only to find it was locked. Of course. Why not ruin her manicure, too? They'd all but stripped her of her girly goods anyway.

A hard yank, and she popped the door open, poking her head out to see rows and rows of fluorescent lights lining a crude, cement ceiling. Cocking her head, she listened until the good doctor struggled again.

The shake she doled out was hard, silencing him. She hissed instructions at him. "Again. I don't want to remind you, but a hero you ain't. So why ruin a perfectly good shirt trying to get away from me?"

The hall was clear for the moment.

What to do, what to do?

Kneeling down, Phoebe gave him one last chance. She drew him up close to her face. "How do you feel about sharing now? It's your last opportunity before your life light hits the skids."

The words he finally did utter chilled her to the bone. It was when she knew she'd been made. "Dear God, you're not breathing." His blue eyes shimmered in some sort of twisted excitement and his lower lip quivered. "You're one of them!" he screamed, a scream flavored with a dash of bizarre delight.

Ugh. Cover blown.

If there were Angie Dickinson awards to be handed out—she was going to miss this round of *Police Woman* 2012.

Without thinking twice, Phoebe dropped him to the ground with a solid right hook to the side of his head. His eyes rolled back before his shiny blond head lolled to one side and he was rendered unconscious, if she was judging correctly by the speed of his sluggish pulse.

Dragging him to the bed, she hurled him onto it and covered him with the sheet before racing to the door. A quick glance outside told her the coast was still clear, but it wouldn't be for long once someone realized the doctor was missing. She swooped up his clipboard and shoved it under her arm before stepping out into the hallway.

On swift feet, she launched down the long, tunnel-like corridor in far-reaching sprints. Pipes lined the ceiling above, but she only caught brief glimpses of them as they whizzed by her line of vision.

The goal here was to find something—*anything*—that might help them stop the agonizing process they were headed for.

Oh, and get the hell out with the information while she was still upright.

Double doors caught her eye when she made a left after hitting a dead end. Voices coming from behind the doors raised the hackles on the back of her neck.

Her legs trembled. Her hands shook, but she couldn't force herself to look inside the window. Maybe what they needed to figure this out was just behind this door. What if there was nothing they could do to stop the decomposition from happening? What if there was no answer other than the obvious.

Death. With a capital D that rhymes with C and that stands for casualty.

She ran trembling hands over her face and waffled.

Jesus, Phoebe, a voice inside her head scorned. *What would Nina say? This is just my personal thought, but I think her rant would be brought to you by the letters F and B, and it would go something like this: Get it together, Fuckwit Barbie!*

Oh, fuck Nina and her name-calling. She wasn't the one who was damn well in here all alone with no idea how to get out, and worse, shoeless. So let Nina call her whatever she liked. She wanted out.

But out wouldn't solve anything. This was the closest anyone was ever going to get to this madness. And there was more than just her to consider. She might have found a reprieve for her Alzheimer's death sentence, but there was a new vampire death threat to take its place. If something happened to her, what would happen to . . .

No. She would not allow that thought to play on her fears.

Steeling her determination, Phoebe called upon her will of iron. The one her mother said would be the death of her.

Hah. No truer words.

Inching along the wall, she clung to the clipboard like it was her lifeline and craned her neck.

And then she saw.

The clipboard clattered to the floor, making a sound so brittle against the cement floor it vibrated in her brain.

She had to close her eyes and force them back open again in order to process what was in front of her.

Could just this once, the ongoing horror of this freak show not involve any more images that might have to stay with her for an eternity? Why did everything have to be so *Nightmare on Elm Street*?

When she finally opened her eyes again, it was still the same mind fuck.

A man lay on a table, split wide open from stem to stern. Tubes from every direction spilled from his gut and arms. Lights flashed, monitors beeped. She had to shove her fist in her mouth to keep from screaming her revulsion and focus on her mission.

Phoebe shook off her rage for the inhumane treatment of this poor soul and made her eyes take in the interior of the room.

If she was seeing right, it was an elderly man, his arm was hooked up to some kind of monitor, and an IV line threaded its way to the front of his hand, dripping fluids at a slow pace. He had those thingamajigs stuck to his head and attached to what Phoebe guessed was an EKG. His wispy, white hair floated down past the edge of the gurney and his gnarled hands were relaxed.

Two more men in lab coats surrounded the gurney while another sat at a computer and typed. Printer paper spewed from a printer in thick, endless stacks. Vials of what appeared to be blood sat in containers in the far corner of the room where yet another man looked into a microscope, examining the samples.

She didn't know what any of the monitors were meant for, nor did she understand any of the words she saw clearly on the computer monitor. None of them made sense, making her wish she'd at least spent part of a semester in chemistry not half asleep.

Though, what she did see clearly was one thing.

The man on the table.

The man on the table who was *talking* to the doctors surrounding his bedside.

CHAPTER 14

"Stinky?" Sam barked into the phone while rain pummeled the pavement at his feet. "Whaddya got, and it better be good."

Stinky's sigh was shaky before he spoke. "Holy fuck, cowboy. What the hell have you gotten yourself into?"

"Tell me what you've got," he ordered while Nina paced in time with a worried Darnell.

"Oh, my friend, the stank I've got. Look, here's the score. This Dr. Hornstein? I found shit for shit on his office comp, but I hit the mother lode when I tapped his personal PC. It took me a minute, but I followed a couple of IP addys and . . ." He paused on a grating sigh. "Never mind. It's too involved for your all-brawn, cowboy mind to absorb, Sammy. Let's just say, no one's safe from Stinky Malone's superior hacking skills. *No one*."

"I'd clap, but my hands are going to be too tied up wringing your fucking neck if you don't get to the point and stop tinkling your own chimes!"

"Whoa-hoe. Easy there, Violent One. I got your back. Anyway, he's got all sorts of files labeled *Project Eternal Clinical Trials*. It sure the hell isn't an FDA-approved trial, and that means something hinky's goin' down with these bogus trials. Serious hinky. Which is why I'm guessing you're calling me to begin with?"

Stinky's brilliance was going to be the death of him one day. Sometimes, he just knew too much. Right now, he was valuable to many people. He'd better keep it that way for all the secrets he knew. Sam couldn't afford to reveal too much, because if the op presented itself, Stinky'd sell him out. Which meant, if the FBI came looking for him via Stinky, he'd spill with the first loaded syringe they waved under his nose. He'd never make the fingernail-pull round. "Get to the point, Stinky."

"Each one has a name attached to it, and they're all what considers candidates for this bogus clinical trial he invented for his Alzheimer's patients. And they don't all have Alzheimer's. A couple of 'em are just terminal. But they're not just *his* patients, Secret Agent Man. He's in on this with a couple of other freaks. Which makes sense if these people are disappearing. If they all disappeared from one doc's joint, eventually someone's going to find that a little too coinkydink. One of the dudes works at some hospital in the emergency room, but he doesn't have a private practice. The other one's a retired oncologist, if I'm reading this doc's version of a sentence right."

Instantly, Sam was on alert, his grip on the phone tightening. "How did you know these patients are disappearing, Stinky?"

Stinky's response was one of disgust for Sam. "Well, the word *expired* on three of the files sort of tipped me off. I can't believe how underestimated I am. I don't have a high IQ because I'm a dummy, Sam. I ran a comparison of all the potential candidates' files, another one of my too-technical-for-your-simpleton-brain-to-wrap-around programs I use, and I found two common denominators. One was, none of these poor fucks had any family. There's always less red tape that way because it isn't too many friends they'll give out patient files to. You know from experience, they don't even like to give 'em to the cops without a whole bunch of rigmarole. Two was, they're all headed for the Highway to Heaven but this one. I'll be damned if I can figure out why she was chosen for the trial. She has nothing in her file other than she bit it. No contacts. No medical history—no stats—not shit, and I can't find a damn thing out about her. Not a one. But the notes in this file say she's knock, knock, knockin' on heaven's door."

Fuck. Three people dead. Alice Goodwin, the guy at Alice's apartment, and his one-night stand. He had to wonder if the third person was the woman who'd shown up at Phoebe's apartment. "Names. I want all of their names," he spat.

"Alice Goodwin, Raymond Schaffer, and Meredith Villanueva. Meredith is the chick with no history."

Sam staggered back as if he'd been hit in the chest. He leaned against the side of the building, absently watching the rain run off the arm of his jacket while he composed himself. "Are you *sure* about the name Meredith?" Had someone else escaped and they didn't bother to record it? If there were only three that quite possibly made Meredith the woman who'd died in his arms . . . But Meredith Villanueva couldn't have been the woman at the apartment . . . Yet, it made sense if Stinky couldn't find any history on her . . .

Once more, Stinky was offended. "Well, I'm lookin' right at it, and last I checked, my high IQ came with literacy skills."

He'd have to table his astonishment at hearing that name for later. It was more important to find Phoebe now. "What's the timeline on these people entering the bogus trial?" He was hoping, in the midst of everything else, to get some perspective on how long they had before both he and Phoebe, quite possibly, died like Meredith and Raymond had.

"A week and a half from the time Alice and Raymond entered the trial until they were of the doornail persuasion. Meredith doesn't have an entry date—just an exit. November first."

The day he'd shown up on OOPS's doorstep.

Leaving them at best, another day until decomposition. "Who's in on this with Hornstein, Stinky? Names. I want goddamn names." Names so he could find the fucks and rip their throats out with his bare hands.

"I don't have any names yet, just the initials. TDB. No clue what they mean, either."

The initials on his memo pad from O-Tech. Shit. "A location where this is all goin' down? You have one of those, Stink?"

"Not yet. But I'm on it."

"So what did you find at O-Tech?"

There was a pause, and some keyboard clicking and then Stinky said, "Now that's the strange thing here. I didn't find a damn thing. They're right as rain, pal. Not a solitary blip. No files that look even a little suspicious. I can't believe it myself, but O-Tech is legit. They really are in the business of pest control. Don't find that often in my line of work. Can't find a single connection between O-Tech and Dr. Crazy Train."

Then why had Alice Goodwin's body been at O-Tech and why had the woman who'd shown up at Phoebe's place been there, too? "And what did you find on Phoebe Reynolds?" Sam had to force her name from his mouth without going into a fit of rage. Yet, alerting Stinky to his involvement with Phoebe would only give him the opportunity to rat him out if Stinky needed to save his own ass.

"She's thirty-three. Diagnosed with early-onset Alzheimer's. What a shitty rap at such a young age. She's single, and marked as a possible candidate for the trial. But the funny thing about her is, she *does* have family. Finding them took some digging, too. Her mother and father are dead, but she has a sister—"

"Right," he muttered, cutting Stinky off. A sister who was going to gnaw off his limbs from the bottom up if he didn't find Phoebe.

Stinky must not have heard his interruption. His voice droned on with more facts about Phoebe. "Her sister's twenty and lives in Highland Hills. You know, that facility for long-term brain injuries? But that wasn't in her patient files. I found that by hacking into her personal PC."

Sam's eyes went wide. Phoebe had another sister? Nina tugged at his arm with impatience. "Tell the dork, if he doesn't have a location for the kid, I'm going to sniff his genius out and eat his brains. Got that, Smelly?" she yelled into the phone, stalking up and down the sidewalk.

There was laughter from the other end of the phone. "You got a partner now, Sammy? She sounds saucy. I thought you worked alone?"

He held up a hand to Nina to thwart her. Darnell saved him by putting one of his big paws on her shoulder and pulling her away. "No. Not a new partner. Listen, are you sure about the info you just gave me?"

"One hundred percent. Phoebe's sister, Penny Reynolds, was in a hit-and-run when she was ten. Got nailed on her bike right on her street. They never caught the shit stain. Kid's paralyzed from the waist down, and suffered brain damage she never fully recovered from. Needs care twenty-four-seven, but she's semifunctional. I found a bunch of emails from the director of the facility to Phoebe. They went back and forth about who'd take care of Penny when Phoebe couldn't anymore because of her Alzheimer's. This Phoebe was worried about how she'd pay for Penny's care when she bought the farm. She's a pretty decent chick, for the most part, not bad lookin', either. No record other than some fighting and mandatory counseling way back in high school, and I really had to dig to find that. No tickets. Nothing. She lives in Manhattan, personal stylist . . ."

Stinky's voice warbled in Sam's ear as he rambled on about Phoebe's stats.

He wasn't the only one with secrets. But his gut assured him, Phoebe's reasons for keeping this so close to her chest were much different than his. She'd kept Penny from Nina due to Nina's outrage—her anger at finding out she had one sister was a lot. Two would have sent her over the brink.

She'd done that to protect Penny until she thought it was safe enough to tell Nina. In the same way she'd kept her Alzheimer's to herself. She was looking out for everyone concerned, revealing only what she had to in increments to consider all the emotions involved in finding out about Penny.

This wasn't just about saving herself, it was about saving herself so someone could always be around to look after Penny.

Christ.

He brought his focus back to Stinky's voice. "Stinky! Shut up. I don't need to know the woman's shoe size. I need you to put a track on Phoebe Reynolds's phone. Find it. Find it now. While you're at it, send me everything you've got. All the files on the expired patients and potential candidates, every single note this freak's written, and anything else you can get your hands on."

"Dude—I'm smart, but I'm software smart. I don't know a whole lot about some of the medical crap this guy's got goin' on. How the hell are you going to figure out what this all means? You want me to send it to my contacts?"

"With my degree in chemistry." God willing. He'd gotten that degree early on in his life by the hair of his chinny-chin-chin sandwiched in between frat parties and the FBI recruiting him. "And none of your slimeball contacts. Got it? One word, you breathe wrong about any of this to anyone—I'll find you Stinky Malone. You and your blow-up dolls."

"Shut. Up. So you're not just some cowboy from Wyoming with overdeveloped trapezoids? Sammy. You been holdin' out on me, playin' dumb all these years?"

"Stinky?"

"Boss?"

"Find Phoebe's damn phone and call me back with a location. Five minutes." Sam clicked the phone off with a terse finger.

He wasn't much for praying, but his eyes went heavenward anyway. Hat in hand, rain beating down on his head, Sam prayed.

* * *

"THAT'S her!" someone yelled from behind.

Phoebe's head swiveled on her neck, taking her eyes off the horror before her just before the barbarian who'd brought her here slammed into her, knocking her into the double doors, leaving her face-first on the floor.

The screech of metal as she crashed into the wheels of the gurney, taking out two of the men in white lab coats with her, bounced off the walls of the room. Surprised howls followed suit.

Clearly, Conan hadn't expected her to react so quickly. At least not judging by the look of shock on his face when she grabbed the leg of a chair, brought it high over her head, and cracked it over his back.

She smiled at the satisfying crunch the metal against his flesh made.

But like all jarhead twits who couldn't admit defeat, he was right back up, lunging for her while the weasel she'd tried to get information out of screamed, "She's one of them! She's strong, Yuri! Immobilize her! Someone get the sedative!"

Faintly, and just before this Yuri rammed into her, wrapping his arms around her waist and hurling her into the far wall, dislocating her shoulder, Phoebe realized whatever they were getting to immobilize her had to be a cocktail specially made for vampires. They'd created something that was powerful enough to stop a vampire and it wasn't garlic or a wooden stake?

Badass. Sucked to be her, but badass.

She couldn't let them get near her with it or it was curtains.

As the thug grabbed her by the neck and lifted her off her feet, still completely unaware he wasn't keeping her from breathing, she noted her left shoulder sagging awkwardly. Her eyes darted to the victim of these animals, fearing he'd be hurt in this weird science version of the WWE.

Someone rushed in and wheeled him out as quickly as the thought came to Phoebe—enraging her further. Just who in the fuck did these people think they were?

Rage rather than fear motivated her next move. She went slack, closing her eyes and playing a pretty decent imitation of a rag doll, if she did say so herself. Okay, so it wasn't the coveted role of Sandy in *Grease*, but sticks and stones.

The beast that smelled like an elephant's ass chuckled. Just like all good trained seals do when they think they've slain the dragon, er, vampire. And she let him revel in his manliness, dangling limp and feigning helplessness.

That is, before her eyes popped open and she flicked his large, red nose with her good hand. "If your big, greasy paw leaves a mark on my neck, so help me Jesus, it'll be your head. I bruise easily, thug."

His beady black eyes, smushed between his nose and his forehead, opened wide, confused. "What the hell?"

Phoebe rolled her eyes in disgust, letting her good shoulder sink. She plucked at one of his fingers, bending it back in the same fashion she had Dr. Nutball's. "Vampire, stupid. We don't breathe. As in, so much air between your ears you have genuine cyclonic value, you're wasting precious energy here, *Yuri*. I know you'll find this a big, fat disappointment, but this doesn't hurt." She pointed to his hand and gave him her win-a-client-over-with-charm smile. "Not even a little. Neither does the shoulder you so carelessly dislocated. And yet, I have to ask myself. What would your mother say about you beating up a woman?"

But he didn't have time to answer with her knee lodged in his groin. She didn't even need to brace herself to get enough leverage when she swung upward. He crumbled like a fallen house of cards, his scream of pain ringing in her ears when she fell to the ground, hitting it with the slap of her bare feet.

She was up in half a second; head down, she scooped up the clipboard just outside the door and made a break for it, leaving behind two unconscious men in white lab coats with the hope she'd find the man they had on the gurney. How she'd get him out of here or if he could even be saved was something she couldn't dwell on.

Finding him was.

Stopping but for a moment, without thought, she backed up against a wall, placing her good hand on her mangled shoulder and slamming it against the hard cement. The sharp crack didn't even make her wince.

Behold the wonder of vampire.

Then she was running again, racing in the opposite direction, away from the room the doctor held her in and down another corridor, where she flew past room after vacant room. Where the hell had they taken him? Her eyes skittered across the dank landscape before her, locating an exit.

The cement tore at the skin of her feet when she skidded to a halt in front of the door, but she didn't feel it. The only thing she was feeling was the rising panic at her inability to locate that poor man.

Flinging the door open, she lunged up three flights of steps to the next available door and, without thinking, burst through it, ripping her skirt.

She looked down in disgust, slapping her hands over her thighs. Goddamn it all. As if trying to escape this hovel wasn't bad enough, she had to do it while her ass hung out, too?

The indignity.

Vaguely, as she tallied up the damage to her personal items— phone, purse, a hundred bucks in said purse, manicure trashed, shoes left like orphans in some parking garage, and now her skirt—Phoebe realized someone owed her a makeover.

And again, as with all things shiny, she was so distracted by her torn skirt, and the peek of panties the rip revealed, she lost her focus.

So, so, so much bad when you were the hunted.

Four enormous men formed a barrier in the middle of the white-tiled hallway she'd just entered, and they didn't look like they were lining up to do the electric slide. In front of them stood the doctor, a gun of some sort in his hand, but it wasn't the kind of gun you saw on television. It was huge—like a child's water gun, with a round green nozzle attached to the end of it. More than likely, whatever was in that gun meant to immobilize her would have a spray effect, thwarting her from rushing at them.

Her eyes assessed the situation, giving them a fierce once-over. And from out of nowhere, she couldn't help but think this was a lot like the time Arizona Caulfield from *Mercy General* found herself locked up in a psyche ward because the dastardly, revenge-seeking Victor Hemp found out she was his half sister. A half sister who was due to inherit a fortune unless she was diagnosed mentally incapacitated.

Of course, that meant Victor would get everything and Arizona would be left in the dirty, state-run hospital for the rest of her life with no one to save her. Arizona made a daring attempt at escape, only to end up dead after a heated chase, resulting in her tripping over a chair and falling through a window ten stories up.

In reality, the actress who played Arizona had just wanted off the show. Rumor had it, the powers that be wouldn't indulge her fetish for expensive champagne and the request that only yellow M&M'S adorn her dressing room each day.

But still. This was a lot like that. A. Lot. And Arizona was a really nice name.

"Phoebe? I'll give you one last chance to surrender. You know there's no way out, right?" Dr. Handsome called. He held out his hand, and smiled—serenely—patiently.

Her eyes darted in a mad attempt to find an escape. "You ripped my skirt," she accused in an effort to stall. *That's right, Phoebe, make 'em sweat Tim Gunn style.*

The lovely blond man with no name clucked his tongue. "Would it make you happy if I offered to buy you a new one?"

Well, yeah. It had run her forty bucks. She really had to lay off the felonious acts when she was wearing something so cute. Phoebe pouted with a coy puckering of her lips. "Maybe. And what about my shoes? My phone? Do you have any idea the money they charge when you have to replace a phone? It's like a mortgage payment."

He inched closer, his footsteps soft. "I promise to look into it."

Before or after he hacked her open while he dispersed social niceties? She fought a shiver of fear, squaring her shoulders. Shoulders that ached from being slammed against the wall.

Wait, that couldn't be. She wasn't supposed to feel pain anymore. She'd just jammed her shoulder back into place like she was as tough as any member of the Vampire Fight Club.

Oh, wait! Maybe it was that phantom pain Marty had talked about. She only *thought* she felt it. Still, it wouldn't make her sad if someone were kind enough to grab her a bottle of that delicious mint and vanilla massage oil she could only find at Bed Bath & Beyond and give her a good rubdown.

Before she could again find something shiny to distract her mentally, several things happened at once. Four large, hygienically dysfunctional men were rushing her and Dr. Loon was aiming his super vampire gun.

At point-blank range.

With a will of their own, knowing there was nowhere to run, instead of facing her attackers, her uncooperative eyes slid closed.

And then it was done.

SAM jammed a finger to the touch screen on his phone and bellowed, "Stinky? That was five minutes and twenty-eight seconds. I got some new asshole to chew!"

The pop of gum snapped in Sam's ear. "You know what would solve all your problems, Sam? Herbal tea. Chamomile, maybe. You're always so wound up."

"Speak, and it better be good!" he demanded with a roar.

Static crackled over the line. "You'll never believe it."

"And you'll never believe the damage I can do to your esophagus with just one blow."

"She's at O-Tech, dude."

His look of disbelief alerted Nina and Darnell, who'd been pacing the pavement, waiting on Stinky's call. "But you said there's nothing going on over there. Swear to Christ, Stinky, if you're pluck-ing my ball hairs, I'll take you out in your sleep," he snarled while precious minutes ticked away.

"Hey, Cowboy Sam! This is not bullshit. I tracked her phone to O-Tech. If she's still got her phone, she's inside O-Tech!"

Sam's lips formed a sneer. "You'd better be right, Stinky—or it'll be your scrawny ass!" Clenching his fist, he held on to his phone, resisting the urge to throw it when he ended the call.

Nina was at him like some fierce mother cub. "Where the fuck is she, Sam? Is she okay?"

Cool, Sam. Keep your cool. It's the only way to get anything accomplished. He eyed Nina, letting warmth seep into his gaze. "I don't know if she's okay. I just know her phone's at O-Tech."

"Hoo-boy. We got some high IQs to beat down, then, huh?" Darnell whooped, stomping his sneakered foot in a puddle.

Nina shook her head, her wet hoodie sticking to the sides of her face. "What in the ever-lovin' fuck is going on here? I thought your friend Smelly said there was nothing to find over there?"

"Stinky. His name's Stinky. And that is what he said. But if Phoebe has her phone, she's at O-Tech. Stinky may be a greedy twerp, but he's almost never wrong on a location."

Nina cracked her knuckles. "Then O-Tech it is, and I promise you, one hair on Fluffy Barbie's head outta place, and someone's gonna have a shitty day," Nina said from between teeth so tightly clenched Sam wondered how she'd managed to spew the words.

He nodded his consent.

Just one hair was all it would take.

One hair.

"WANDA?"

"Phoebe? Oh, sweet heaven, Phoebe! Where are you, honey? Are you all right? Did they hurt you? I'll kill them myself if they put one itty-bitty finger on you!" Wanda cried.

Thank God she'd remembered the number for OOPS. Without her phone, she was lost, which, if you asked her, was a sad state of affairs. Back in the day, if you didn't know your phone number by heart, speed dial wasn't an option, but screwed was.

But she'd picked up the phone a hundred times at least to make that phone call to Nina when she'd found out it was where she worked. Now she was grateful not only to have memorized it, but that she remembered if no one was in the OOPS offices, the call would be rerouted to their cell phones.

"Phoebe? Honey, answer me!"

"I'm okay, Wanda," she whispered against the mouthpiece. "But could you maybe come get me? I feel so incredibly weak, and my legs just don't seem to want to cooperate." It hit her the moment she'd landed and she'd just barely managed to dial the phone she was using now.

"Ohhhh, you need to feed, Phoebe. It's been hours since you last drank. That's what the problem is, honey. Where are you? Are you safe from harm?"

Phoebe gave a glance over her shoulder at her surroundings. "I can't remember the last time a Wamsutta comforter set, complete with sheets and two matching pillows, was unsafe. But you just never can tell with the way things are made these days."

"Phoebe?"

"Yes?" she muttered, glancing up at the kind elderly woman who'd allowed her to use her cell phone, but only after Phoebe had convinced her she was absolutely not an alien from the *beyond* part of the store's moniker. And it hadn't been all sunshine and lollipops while she'd convinced her, either. At first, the woman, a woman who appeared so harmless, yet had rapped her over the head with her new toilet bowl scrubber like she was playing for the Yankees, had been skeptical.

And really, who could blame this poor, unsuspecting shopper? Phoebe had quite literally fallen from the sky on top of a pile of towels shelved in the middle of the aisle, bounced off them, thereby hitting her head on the edge of the display, and somersaulted head-first into this fine citizen's carriage.

"Phoebe? *Where* are you?"

"I'm a little embarrassed."

"Well, you can be embarrassed after I pick you up, too, if you'd like. Choice is yours."

"Um, Bed Bath and Beyond. Conveniently located right down the road from Sam's apartment, in fact. In the comforter aisle." The last place she'd thought of before she'd zoned out of that clinical trial hell.

"Say no more. Don't move. Auntie Wanda's there."

From her place in the carriage, Phoebe located the "end call" button and handed the phone up to the woman with the kind face with sheepish eyes. "Thank you. I'm sure your kindnesses will come back to you tenfold."

Placing her hands on the edges of the cart, she lifted herself up with shaking hands and willed her last ounce of energy to allow her to climb out.

That the loud rip that followed her exit made an entire store full of shoppers turn around was just par for the course in this vampire's day.

Standing in your underwear in the middle of Bed Bath & Beyond, barefoot, with smeared mascara and a torn nail was certainly not the worst that had happened to her today.

Certainly not.

SAM burst through his apartment door, with Nina and Darnell directly behind him, heading straight for Wanda. "Where is she?"

he demanded in the authoritative tone he often used when he needed answers out of a suspect.

Wanda held up a hand and gave him a haughty raise of her eyebrow. "I'm sorry, Sam. Did you just ask me a question like I'm some kind of terrorist subject to your interrogation?" She landed a finger in the soft spot between his armpit and his shoulder and drove it into his flesh. "Never, ever, *ever* talk to me that way, Mr. McLean, or you're going to find out what happens to a lady when she goes batshit wild."

Nina cackled her clear enjoyment, shedding her wet hoodie. "I don't like admitting it, Sammy, but Wanda's a crazy-assed psycho when she gets loose. So go be a big boy now and take your lickin' like manly men do."

Archibald rushed in, putting his stout body between Sam and Wanda and handed him a wineglass of blood. "Sir? Drink or you'll be no good to anyone, especially our battle-weary Phoebe."

He took the blood and nodded his thanks, zeroing in on Wanda. Seeing her anger, he gave her a humble gaze and fought the impulse to tear through the apartment to locate Phoebe. "My apologies. Would you *please* tell me where she is?"

Wanda put her hand on his arm, her eyes only a little less confrontational now. "Slow down, Sam. She's taking a bath. Give her a few moments to gather herself."

Sam fought the urge to set Wanda aside and asked, "Did she tell you what happened?"

"She did. And to say it was dreadful is like classifying Nina under the category *gentle as a lamb*. It was akin to purgatory. I mean, I've heard things—and trust me when I tell you, I've seen things. But this, Sam? This was . . ." Wanda shook her head, sorrow in her eyes. "Now, she hasn't had time to process all of this properly. But she will, and when she does, we need to be there for her. What we don't need is you rushing in there and demanding answers. I absolutely will not have you interrogating her like some suspect until she can work this out. I can tell you whatever you need to know for the moment, Mr. Undercover."

His nod was curt. Wanda knew. Cue angry female number two. "Nina told you all of it, I gather?"

Her arms crossed over her chest. "All while you were on the phone with Smelly."

"Stinky," he corrected over the rim of his wineglass, giving her a direct gaze.

"Like there's a difference?" was her stiff-lipped question.

"And you're rightfully angry."

Wanda's finger jabbed the air, and her face, tight and angry, glowered. "Well, I can tell you, I'm not in love with this latest development, but I'd bet I can't add any more recrimination or hurl any nasty words at you that haven't already been lobbed by Nina. She does come in incredibly handy from time to time—especially when it comes to an angry WTF. So for the moment, I'll save my rant with my extensive vocabulary for another time. Just know that Wanda the Halfsie is *not* pleased, and she's not afraid to share her displeasure in the way of snarling and fangs should you have the audacity to become arrogant! However, given your motives, and the idea that your feelings for Phoebe are genuine, I'm going to grant you the gift of time heals all wounds."

Sam's shoulders relaxed. "Noted and appreciated."

Wanda's face broke into a wide smile. "So, we have some ass to mutilate, yes?"

Archibald clapped his hands together and chuckled. "Ah, the chase begins! Oh, sir, I realize your boots are quite deep in the stench of manure where the ladies are concerned, but I hope they'll forgive my fascination with your place of employment. An FBI agent, Master Samuel? It's brilliant. Truly. You are quite covert. I would have never guessed. It's pure genius how you present yourself as some mild-mannered scientist with just a dash of absurd. Why, it's almost Superman-esque, don't you agree, ladies?" He looked to Nina and Wanda in his excitement. They each gave him a sour expression.

Archibald straightened and cleared his throat, his face returning to the decorous, composed expression he wore. "Right, then. I'll just go back to the kitchen, where a lovely glazed peach tart awaits our Darnell. Come, demon," he directed Darnell with a hand to his elbow. "We shall pour ourselves a fresh glass of cold milk, and you can tell me all about Agent Sam." He winked before exiting the living room, chuckling in soft fits of laughter.

"I really need to see her, Wanda. For myself."

Wanda softened again. "Of course you do. You have a lot of splainin' to do."

Sam winced, setting his glass on the end table. "Does she know?"

Wanda's eyes widened in disbelief and she wrinkled her nose. "Are you kidding? After what she fought her way out of today—I wasn't going to be the last bit of pile on. No. I didn't tell her. I'm leaving that up to you because it's on you. And I'll let you see her. But one word, one squeak of discontent from her, and I'll hear it. And you won't like it when I knock that door down and emasculate you. So don't make me. Now before you go in there, let me fill you both in on what happened. She'll need to get this all off her chest in her own words, I'm sure. But the kind of trouble we're up against needs to be thought over. You'll need to absorb it. At least Nina will. I imagine you see things of a similar nature in your line of work, Sam. Regardless, we need to talk this out as a group."

Sam nodded, forcing himself to put on his agency face as he listened to Wanda relate what happened to Phoebe and keep his thoughts from straying.

When Wanda finished, Sam sat stone-faced. He'd seen some shit in his time. Definitely. Serial killers, pedophiles, terrorists—the scum of the universe. But he'd never seen the kind of shit Phoebe had.

Wanda leaned into him, her pretty eyes inquiring. "Now do you get it?"

He let his head drop to his folded hands and nodded. "I get it. I have to see her now."

"Remember what I said," Wanda warned, though it was without the harsh undertones of before.

Another nod, and Sam was rising, dropping his Stetson on a coat hanger before pushing his way into the bedroom.

The bathroom door was still closed, and he thought to turn away for a moment, but he needed to see Phoebe. Hold her. Smell her hair. See for himself she was at least physically unharmed.

And then he'd tell her everything.

He gave a light rap to the door with his knuckles. "Phoebe? Can I come in?"

The gurgle of water in the tub sloshed and the door popped open.

Sam took two steps inside and had his first glimpse of her, sitting in the darkened bathroom.

Up to her eyeballs in bubbles, her auburn hair pulled up into a knot at the top of her head. Her creamy skin was streaky from the spray tan, but her eyes, wide and full of so many emotions he didn't know where to begin to list them, made his gut ache.

Her vulnerability in that very moment would stay with him for as long as he lived.

And it was his undoing.

Sam put both feet inside the bathtub, cowboy boots and all, and sat on the edge. Reaching for her, he dragged her to him, soaking wet, molding her to him, heedless of anything other than feeling her against him. Lifting her, he pulled her from the bathtub.

Water dripped to the floor, leaving puddles at his feet and along the edge of his sunken-in tub.

Her arms went up around his neck and her frame relaxed against him.

Sam pressed his lips to the top of her sodden head, and closing his eyes tight, he rocked her.

CHAPTER 15

They sat that way for a long time until Phoebe was able to speak, her voice raspy, and answer Sam's unspoken, yet totally clear desire to talk. "I don't think I can right now," she whispered, wishing futilely for the cleansing flow of tears to wash away her horrors. She clung to him, letting the soothing strength of his arms seep into her tired body.

"You don't have to," was Sam's gruff answer.

She lifted her head, her eyes searching his. She wanted to tell him. She wanted to purge the images by putting them into words. She wanted to find respite from this terror. "Sam? I . . ."

Sam shook his head, brushing the wet hair from her eyes with tender fingers. "Don't."

Phoebe broke then, dragging Sam's head down, pressing her lips to his with a fevered need to feel him inside her. The affirmation of life or unlife, whatever they were calling it—she needed it.

Now.

She was ravaged from the inside out. Torn apart for leaving behind that man.

Solace.

She needed to find solace. She needed to find a safe harbor to set aside her emotional turmoil and just feel.

Her hands grabbed fistfuls of his thick hair, twisting her fingers in it, tugging his lips to her mouth, forcing them to melt into hers. She heard his moan, felt the delicious scrape of his tongue against hers, tore at his shoulders in the effort to take his jacket off.

"Phoebe," he said on a rasp, gripping her shoulders with fingers that dug into her flesh. "Before we . . . I need to tell—"

She quieted him by pressing her lips closer to his and grabbing at the lapels of his jacket. "Don't say anything. Please. *Please*," she begged.

Sam's harsh, needy groan echoed in the bathroom, his hands tightened over her slickly wet skin, pulling her entirely out of the tub so they stood together. Water washed down off his clothes, dripping in rivulets to puddle at their feet.

He ran his hands over her skin with hard palms, pulling her to him with a grunt, shrugging out of his wet jacket while she popped the buttons of his shirt with shaky fingers as their lips meshed. Sam's tongue, deep in her mouth, left her legs weak, her knees shaking with need.

Phoebe pressed her cheek to the damp skin of his chest before she slid down his body, kneeling before him and yanking the buckle of his belt free. She used her hands to shrug his jeans and boxer-briefs down over his thick thighs, her lips caressing the muscles in them as she went.

She backed him against the opposite wall by wrapping her arms around his thighs and giving him a nudging. And then she took in the brilliance of his beauty—his jeans around his ankles, his boots still on his feet. The hot sight of his desire made her quiver, and the deep ache he'd created at her very core began once again.

Sam's hand immediately went to her head, threading his fingers through her wet hair, letting his head fall back on his shoulders.

And then she was enveloping him, taking a long drag on his cock, running her tongue along his thick hard shaft, shivering when his husky moan settled in her ears. Trembling fingers engulfed his engorged flesh as she drove down on him, twisting her hands to slide up and down and follow the path her tongue had taken.

Sam's hips jutted forward with a hard jolt. He drove his cock into her mouth, tangling his fingers in her hair, grinding against the press of her tongue before he pushed her away with a grunt.

His hands grabbed at her shoulders and dragged her up along his hard frame so that she felt every inch of his cool flesh along the way. Her nipples tightened to sharp points, scraping against his chest with delicious friction. Her breasts ached for his tongue to swirl the heated tips.

As though Sam could read her mind, he hauled her upward until their noses touched, slipping his tongue into her mouth for one more taste. Their eyes connected in a hot gaze and lingered for a moment, and then he was setting her on the edge of the sink's vanity, sliding his mouth along her neck until he made his way to her breast and found a nipple, swirling his hot tongue over it.

Phoebe bucked forward, wrapping her arms around his head, reveling in the molten achy heat between her legs.

Sam used forceful hands to spread her thighs, driving them apart before slipping his fingers into her wet folds and entering her.

Colors flashed before her eyes upon the impact, impact she couldn't get enough of. She lifted her hips to rock against him, sliding her ass to the edge of the counter so he'd go deeper while his tongue lashed her nipples. The heel of his hand rubbed against her swollen clit, making her head thrash and a harsh sound slip from her throat.

Just as that spiral of white-hot heat began to reach its peak, driving her sensitive nerves to a frenzied need for orgasm, he left her breasts and kissed his way down to the tops of her thighs before removing his finger.

Phoebe whimpered her discontent, but when Sam laid his head on her thigh, closing his eyes and wrapping his arms around her waist, she realized, this brief flicker of seconds ticking away was meaningful.

When Sam spoke the words that gave definition to the moment, Phoebe Reynolds fell in love.

For the very first time.

"If you'd been hurt . . ." he mumbled, vulnerable and harsh in one bold statement.

She ran her hands over his hair in understanding, trembling and just as vulnerable as he was.

But Sam didn't linger. It was as if he needed to touch her continually to reassure himself she was really all right. His head dipped between her legs and his tongue was on her with rapid speed, licking, sucking, devouring every inch of her exposed flesh until she did exactly what she'd dared him to do just last night.

She screamed.

At the exquisite pleasure his tongue swirling over her clit in slow strokes created.

At the bone-deep need only Sam had ever evoked in her.

At the way he loved every inch of her flesh with such powerfully desperate need.

Her back arched as her hips bucked upward, driving against Sam's face until the sweet-sharp release eased.

Yet, just when the tension had begun to ease in her body, Sam scooped her up, wrapping her legs around his waist and sitting on the counter.

He sat her on top of his cock, and with one swift upward thrust so forceful her body jolted, he entered her, making her cling to his neck. Hands at her waist, Sam drove upward harder still, stretching her, filling her, and leaving behind an ache that would have been painful if not for the heat.

That damn wave of molten lava washing over her, making her

want to scream, it was too much yet not enough. The swell of him inside her consumed her, drove her to a mindless pleasure she would never be able to describe.

Phoebe made herself memorize every inch of his hard back, her hands roaming freely over it as the tension between them built. She explored his arms, clenching and unclenching her fingers to revel in the ridges of his flesh.

Sam's hand explored, too, cupping her breasts, tweaking her nipples, gripping her hips hard until he sensed she was at her breaking point.

Relief was but a hard stroke away, yet Sam teased until Phoebe felt the ripple of his muscles, the tightly coiled flex of his tendons.

The moment between them suspended for mere seconds, and then she was falling, driving downward on his delicious, rigid cock until her teeth clenched and nothing else but release mattered.

They came together, hard, hot, greedy with pleasure. They took from each other. They gave to each other in a split second of spiraling relief.

Phoebe was the first to cave, sinking into the hard shelter of Sam's chest and pressing her cheek to his.

He reached up and bracketed her face, kissing her closed eyelids, her cheeks, the tip of her nose.

"Yay again for vampire sex, huh?"

His chuckle rumbled in the bathroom. "Yay again."

Lifting her head, Phoebe gazed into Sam's dark eyes so full of so many things she wasn't quite sure she could read them all. "Are you okay?"

Rising with her still around his waist, Sam made his way into the bedroom and set her on the bed. He plopped down next to her, dragging his soggy boots off and kicking his wet jeans to the floor.

He pulled her to him, running his hands along the space where her waist met her hips. "That's my question you're stealing there. But it's one I'm too afraid to ask you because after what Wanda told me . . . Well, I only experienced it secondhand, and even I'm not okay."

Her lower lip trembled when she let her head fall to his shoulder. The deep, gut-wrenching anguish she felt over transporting out of there before she'd been able to help that poor soul began anew. "We have to go back. We have to help that man. I won't ever sleep again if we don't help . . . Oh, God . . . what they were doing to him. It was . . ." She fisted her hands together to keep them from trembling. "I don't even know who he is, but he's being tortured and I don't even think he realizes it, Sam. I don't know if he has Alzheimer's but if he does, he must be so far gone, he doesn't know what's happening to him. They were *laughing*, those vile pigs. Laughing and chatting with him like everything was damn well normal. Like throwing your guinea pig a social interaction bone is all part of the job. He was split wide open, Sam . . ." She squeaked his name, then pressed her fingers to her eyes to wash away the ungodly images.

Sam tucked her head under his chin. "I heard, honey."

Phoebe's voice cracked when she said, "But I've got to get him out. I won't be able to bear it if we don't. I'm not even one hundred percent sure where he is, but we *have* to find him."

"I've got someone on it."

Her head shot up. "Say again?"

"I said, I've taken care of it."

Phoebe paused with a frown. Took care of what? "You did what? How can *you* take care of this man's fate?"

Sam set her away from him. "How about we talk about this tomorrow?"

Phoebe watched Sam's eyes evade hers, then return to her face. "Uh, no. Yeah, yeah. I've been traumatized and you don't want to push poor, scarred-for-life Phoebe over the edge, but now I want to know what you mean by, you've *got someone on it*. Who could you, the bug guy, have on something like this, King of the Geeks? Mothra? The Fly?"

"About that . . ." Sam took her hand, lacing his fingers with hers.

Phoebe's antenna was on red alert. The intonation of his last words implied guilt. She knew they did due to the fact that Archibald had told Wanda a little white lie about who'd eaten all of his angel food cake. He'd feigned no knowledge of the cake thievery and told Wanda to ask Darnell if he'd finished it.

That was because he didn't want her to beat him down about his very human cholesterol numbers and how high they were his last trip to the doctor. And when he'd fobbed the cake eating off on Darnell, Phoebe had heard the guilt in his words.

She let go of Sam's hand. She'd heard guilt. "Yeah. About that?"

"Look, this can really wait until tomorrow. You need to rest after today, honey."

"Oh, no. Don't you go deflecting with concern for my battered soul, *honey*. Spill, McLean. After today, I can take whatever you got."

"So. It happened like this . . ."

"*What* happened like what?"

"How I got to O-Tech in the first place."

Dread filled the pit of her belly. And then the conclusion jumping began. Oh, Jesus. He was somehow involved in this manufactured vampire thing. He was a maniac, too. A hot maniac, but a maniac. Oh, hell. He was a maniac she'd wonked to within an inch of her undead-edness. And he was in this room with her. How could Wanda and Nina let her be in a room with a maniac? What the shit kind of got your back was that?

Wait. Maybe that was too much? Perspective. Phoebe fought for perspective.

She straightened her shoulders, pulling the comforter over her naked body as though it were a shield she could use to protect herself from whatever Sam was going to say. "So. How did Sam the Entomologist get to O-Tech?"

His eyes were clear and direct when he looked at her. "He got there through the FBI."

"Like some FBI bug-study program?" Oh. Well, then. What was the big deal about that? Relief flooded her.

Sam closed one eye and popped his lips, scraping his hand through his hair. "Um, no."

Relief officially gone. "Go in for the kill, Sam. Just say it."

"I'm an undercover FBI agent. I work for a division of the FBI specializing in the investigation of suspicious paranormal activity."

"You mean like *Fringe*?"

"Well. I prefer to think of myself categorized more Mulder from *The X-Files* than Olivia Dunham, but, yes. It's a very similar division," he said. Calm. Organized. Due a punch in his stupid, handsome face.

Her hand went to her chest in a formerly human reaction. She was winded and she couldn't even breathe. "Does Nina know about this?"

"She does. So do Wanda, Darnell, and Archibald."

Nice. How very all in the family. "And you still had your junk to work with in there? Nina didn't rip all your business off with her teeth?" she asked with disbelief as she thumbed over her shoulder in the direction of the bathroom.

"There was a moment I was sure that's where we were headed, but she let me explain."

"Booyah for her."

Sam sat silent, his eyes contrite.

He was good. But of course he was. Sam McLean was practiced at keeping everything under control, wasn't he? He was practiced at lots of things that had to do with the word *under*, now wasn't he? "So you've been undercover all this time?"

"Yes."

"Investigating suspicious paranormal activity at O-Tech?"

"No. Not exactly."

It all started to make sense. The caution he'd used about breaking into O-Tech. The way he'd made sure no one could find them on some unknown frequency by using walkie-talkies instead of their cell phones to communicate.

The hesitance he'd displayed at going into O-Tech despite their united vampiric strength and various powers. The way he'd covered all avenues when they had to break into Alice Goodwin's apartment by parking a couple of streets over. The way he'd led her to believe that he'd just watched a lot of detective shows in his time and that was why he always knew exactly what to do.

But Starsky had a secret, didn't he?

The. Motherfucker.

So what did *not exactly* mean? Forget it. She didn't want to know. She'd been used up one side and down the other in all forms of the word.

That was the only *exactly* she was sure of. Rising from the bed, she pulled the comforter with her, yanking it so hard she knocked Sam over. "You know what, Sam. I'm not sure I want to know what the word *exactly* means to you. In fact, I'm sure of it. Keep your *exactly* to yourself!"

Still, he remained calm, using words he purposely made distinct, probably hoping to penetrate her haze of anger with rationale. "I'd like it if you'd let me explain to you what I meant by that, Phoebe."

Then something else hit her. He'd been pretty Jackie Chan at O-Tech that night. He was an FBI agent trained in the use of force—or whatever they called it. He played with guns and he played at being something he more than likely wasn't. Like an entomologist. Winged things, her ass!

But he hadn't just faked his job—he'd probably faked his feelings for her. She'd seen enough TV to know the things those spies did to keep their covers.

As the pieces of Sam's deception came together, she realized the worst thing of all. He'd put them all in serious danger. If Sam investigated people just like them—what would the FBI do when they found out about Nina and Wanda and everyone involved in this mess?

Her finger slashed the air and her eyes zeroed in on him. "Hold up. Does the FBI know about us? Do they know about you?"

Sam's eyes were sheepish and full of supposed remorse. But who knew if that was really remorse, or he was just playing at remorse because it was his job? "No, honey. They don't know about any of this. I took some leave."

"You mean they don't know *yet*—that's what you mean, Sam! But what if they'd come looking for you? They would have found us, and then what? What happens when they do finally come looking for you?"

Sam held out his hand to her with more irritating-as-hell calm. "If you'll just let me finish explaining—"

She gawked at him, her eyes bulging. "What could you possibly have to explain? The facts are simple. All this good-old-boy, goofy, down-home charm was a total act right from the start. You didn't have some desk job at the FBI, Sam, or you wouldn't have been karate chopping your way to that lab that night at O-Tech. You don't play with bugs, you play with guns and murderers and suspicious paranormal-activity makers!"

"No, Phoebe, that's not true. I do play with bugs. I mean, I am an entomologist, and if you'd just let me explain everything to you, you'd better understand what I've been doing at O-Tech."

She shook her head, backing away from him when he rose to reach for her. "Ohhh, no, pal. Don't you do the whole calm, rational, she's-the-crazy-one-here FBI bullshit with me! No. No. Not gonna fly. There's nothing to explain. I mean, how do you explain that you knew something was going on at O-Tech, Sam? How do you explain using me as your decoy today so you could get the job done? How do you explain pretending to be on our side when you investigate people just like us? People just like you, you lying, bullshitting, moth lover? How do you explain throwing down with me like we just did? All part of the paranormal investigation, Sam? So you can report back on paranormal nookie? Fuck. You!" she screamed, grabbing for her clothes and flinging his bedroom door open.

As she stood in the doorway, she narrowed her eyes at him. "You know what this is like, Sam? This is just like the time Leticia Rothwell on *Sedona* found out her brand-new husband Yanislov Bertowski was an international spy. Oh, he was good, too. Just like you. He was charming. Funny. Endearing himself to everyone around him. He had this goofball air about him just like you. But really, he was a cold-blooded killer who'd sack any chick he had to, kill anyone in order to get the job done. That's what *this* is like."

Sam planted his hands on his still nakedly lying hips. "And did Leticia Rothwell forgive Yanislov Bertowski, international spy, for lying to her and only *sort of* pretending to be something he really wasn't?"

She threw her head back and snorted a mocking laugh. "Nope. You know what she did to him, *Sam*?"

"I'm all anticipatory."

"She slit his throat!" Slamming the door shut behind her, she stalked off into the kitchen, ignoring the open mouths of her so-called got-your-back crew.

SAM rubbed temples that really didn't hurt with cool fingers that couldn't really ease something that wasn't there.

So. That had gone well.

He dug through his dresser drawers and located another pair of jeans. Sliding into them, he fought to keep himself from jamming the drawer through the wall.

And by the fucking way, he wasn't the only one with secrets. She had a lot of nerve calling him a liar when she had another sister.

Is that really the same thing, Sammy? Really? C'mon, bro. She didn't lie about it. She just didn't tell you yet. Now I bet she's glad she didn't tell you because it would be just one more person she'd have to worry she'd put in danger.

So it was a lie by omission. Same damn difference.

No, Sammy. Very big difference.

His phone rang, making him forget the nagging voice in his head. He stalked to the bathroom and dragged it out of his jacket pocket, glancing at the screen.

A text message from Stinky that read,

Incoming, cowboy. Found your third victim. Sending her pic and some seriously hard-to-locate stats. Thank me in the way of the dude who flies a radical kite. Thank me a lot. ☺

Sam clicked on the link Stinky had sent him, forcing himself to focus on putting this all together.

He scanned the files Stinky sent, skimming the contents.

When he reached the end of more medical jargon than he could process all at once, he saw the picture Stinky had attached of Meredith Villanueva.

Oh, good fuck.

"MISS Phoebe?"

She let her cheek lay on the steel countertop, refusing to raise her head while she swung her legs from the stool she sat on. "Yes, Archibald?"

"I'd so love it if you'd indulge my overprotective nature and partake of more blood. You're still a new vampire, and today was quite draining. You must nurture your vampiric health by feeding it. Often." He set a glass down in front of her, then leaned forward and pressed his cheek to the countertop, too.

Their eyeballs met. Hers sad. Archibald's warm with understanding.

"Miss?"

"Yes?"

"Might I offer some advice from an old, interfering man?"

Deflated, she said, "You might."

"I think Master Samuel, while a two-faced, unforgivable cad of a liar, isn't entirely without redeeming qualities. I think he's nothing like your Yanislov Bertowski."

She winced, twisting a strand of her hair around her finger in embarrassment. "You heard?"

His round cheek grazed the countertop in a swishing up-and-down motion. "Oh, indeed. Even those of us not blessed by your audible good fortune heard, miss. It was unavoidable. My apologies."

Her eyes darted to the underside of Sam's kitchen cabinets. "Accepted."

Archibald nudged her arm with a chubby finger. "Have you heard the entire story of our Sam's journey here to you?"

Yeah, yeah. She'd heard. "Yes. Wanda told me. He wasn't really investigating paranormal activity at O-Tech. It was a random FBI check. He's really an entomologist. He really was coincidentally bitten by a vampire. And he's not so bad. He was just looking out for all of us. Blah, blah, and blah." She repeated the story Sam had fed Wanda and the others in wooden tones.

The lines on Archibald's forehead deepened when he smiled. "Do you doubt his sincerity, Miss Phoebe?"

"Like I doubt I'll be wearing the latest swimwear on a beach in St. Tropez next season. I think he needed me to get into that clinical trial, and I don't believe he took some leave from the FBI. I think this craziness could make FBI history, and Sam wouldn't mind some of the glory for discovering it. That's what I think." And she did. Mostly. Okay, she was waning. So?

He clucked his tongue. "Ah. Well, then, there's no point in delving any deeper into this conversation, is there? He's a cad of the worst order and the moment his impeccable skills as an assassin are no longer needed, we shall stake him through the cold blackness of his nonexistent heart!"

The very idea actually pained her. Phoebe finally giggled. "Are you going to stick up for him, Archibald?"

Archibald smiled again, teasing. "Oh, no, miss. I'd rather watch that dreadfully arrogant Bobby Flay than ever offer my support to such a heathen. It's unthinkable."

Arch was just wowed by Sam's cool factor. It hadn't gone unnoticed that this sweet manservant enjoyed a good cop show. "You think that he's an FBI agent is cool."

"The coolest, miss."

"State your case, Arch."

"Well, if one were to summon even a little sympathy for such a monster as our Sam, I would suggest we reflect upon the fact that the moment he became a vampire, he lost his job and became the hunted right along with all of you."

"He could have told us that, Archibald. He *should* have told us that. He put us all in danger. What if some of his paranormal goon investigators had come looking for him?"

"You'll get no argument from me, Phoebe. He's despicable. However, I wonder how involved he thought he would be with all of this. By the time he realized something suspicious was going on with your turnings, he was already hip deep. While I do agree he should have revealed this much sooner, he was facing a prominent life decision. One that would take away his income and the job he clearly loved. But it's also my understanding that he called his superiors the moment he could to tell them there were no suspicious findings at O-Tech, and then he took some overdue leave."

She'd heard it all—this extolling of Sam's virtues. "But he pretended he wanted to get to know me, Arch. He . . . We . . . He was just keeping his cover. Something I'm sure he's done a million times before. Not to mention, he let me go into that clinical trial like some lamb to slaughter."

"Aha!" Archibald tapped the counter with his fingertip. "On this I have to most respectfully disagree with you. Samuel absolutely did not want you to go into your foul doctor's office. In fact, he protested quite vehemently once he'd thought through his impulsive suggestion. I heard him say as much to you. It was *you* who insisted there was no danger. Certainly, on top of everything else, you didn't expect him to anticipate they would ambush you? And about that ambush, miss . . ."

Yeah. About that. "What about it?"

"While I commend your heroic gesture to storm the castle walls, I must remind you of something. You could have gotten away from your captors at any point before they took you into this facility of horrors. You are a vampire, Phoebe. It would have taken nothing more than one splendid right hook to escape them before you were on the inside. My suspicion is you chose to go in on a fact-finding mission. Would I be incorrect in my assumptions?"

Guilty. Guilty. Guilty. "No. No, you're right. I chose to go into the lair because we needed to find something that will help us stop that awful decomposition thing. I had no idea it would be so . . ."

"Ghastly?"

"That's at least one adjective I wouldn't turn my nose up at."

"And you think Sam did?"

"Did what?"

"Know it would be so ghastly? Know they would rip you from that doctor's office so callously?"

All of this reasoning sucked, but she was teetering nonetheless. "Point. But that doesn't change what he did to . . . with . . . You know what I mean."

"Your wall-rattling consummation?"

Her eyes fluttered shut. She'd known Sam for only a few days, and she'd been cranking him like he was the last man on earth. It probably looked horrible to a gentleman like Archibald who came from an era that was chaste, to say the least. "Yeah. That. He should never have let me believe he was someone he wasn't. That he cared about me in any other capacity but a way into that clinical trial."

"Thus, I must ask you, you don't think he could have gotten you to agree to his plans minus the rattling of walls? You want this to end as much as he does, don't you? You want the same answers Samuel seeks. I believe, whether the two of you were intimate or not, you would have, as you young people say, taken the hit anyway."

Point. Point. Point. Fucking point. Okay? "You just like him better than me because he's like all your detective show dreams come true and all I can offer is suggestions on what your most flattering color in manservant suits is."

Archibald chuckled before running his finger down the length of her nose. "I will not deny Master Samuel's appeal is just a notch above yours in that particular department. But this is what I'm really saying, Miss Phoebe. Sam had secrets he certainly should have revealed to all of you much sooner in this game."

Phoebe snorted.

"However, I don't believe he did this with malice or to save his own hide. I believe he did this to keep you all safe while he figured out what to do to keep his colleagues as far from you all as possible until he found what will save the two of you. You do realize, if his agency found out about all of you, they'd find out about him. He'd be locked away somewhere, as is protocol, according to Sam, and then where would you be? It was better he kept this an inside job."

She rolled her face on the counter so her forehead was at the ready for the head banging she shouldn't waste a second longer avoiding. Yes. That made perfect sense. Damn perfect in all its sense. "I lost my temper, didn't I?"

Archibald held two fingers together and grinned. "I would offer the words *just a smidge*."

But he could still have been lying about how he felt about her . . .

"And as an aside, I can't remember ever hearing a man in such distress as I did your Samuel when he thought he would never lay eyes upon your beauty again. Oh, the phone calls back and forth between himself and Mistress Wanda. Loud, miss. Very abrasive."

"Really?"

Archibald's eyebrow rose. "Really, miss. And now, while this chat has been lovely, I believe I'm quite disoriented."

Phoebe popped up, hopping off the stool and helping Archibald to a standing position. She gave him an impulsive hug, one he returned with an awkward pat on her back.

"I'm off, miss. Kojak awaits!" Archibald rambled off to the guest bedroom, leaving Phoebe to stew in his wise words.

Yes. Sam had lied.

But she'd been lying, too.

Both of them had done it in order to protect someone.

And she had to come clean with Nina and Sam soon in order to keep Penny safe.

Soon.

SAM grabbed one of his disposable phones and punched in the number for Harlan Luftkin. Another of his more questionable contacts, but without a doubt, his most trusted, despite his tawdry past. While he waited for the call to connect, he sifted through some of the DVDs Archibald had left in his room that Nina and Phoebe had missed when they were cleaning up after the apartment was burglarized.

One in particular caught Sam's attention—a blank one that was mixed in with his movies.

But he forgot all about it when Harlan answered on the first ring. "Sammy?"

"Yeah. I got trouble."

"Name it."

Words were something Harlan didn't do much of. It was what Sam liked most about him. He cut right through the bullshit and went for your throat. "Penny Reynolds. Twenty, in a wheelchair. Highland Hills long-term care facility in New York. Get there. Just watch for now. Keep it on the down low unless shit gets heated. Whatever it takes, make sure she's safe until you hear from me. Also—I need low-key manpower on a Mark Boyer, Manhattan. Keep your distance. He's easily freaked out, but not in the direct line of fire for right now."

"You givin' permission for me and my friends to play with our guns?"

"Balls to the wall, Harlan. Take out any fuck that gets in your way except the staff at Highland. No collateral damage."

"It's like fucking Christmas and Charlie Manson's birthday," he quipped, his southern twang accenting the word *birthday*.

"Then merry, merry, happy, happy," Sam said before clicking the phone off.

Pulling his shirt over his head, Sam shrugged it down over his waist and reached for his gun.

While he'd scanned the files Stinky had sent him, something had occurred to him. Something that should have occurred to him much sooner than four hours after Phoebe's harrowing entry into that clinical trial. His emotional attachment to Phoebe—the total center she'd become of everything for him—had kept him from looking at the big picture from all angles.

One huge fuck-up on his part? The freaks had Phoebe's phone and her purse, and every one of them was listed as a contact in there.

Surely she'd called Penny from that phone any number of times, and now they could locate her apartment, too. Thankfully, Mark, after the scare of that first night, had decided to take their cat and go stay with a friend when Phoebe had packed it up and come to his place.

If they wanted to lure Phoebe to them—Penny was a sure bet. Harlan was the best he had to offer. The best candidate for getting the job done swiftly and silently with no remorse for the effort. Harlan would die before he gave Sam up out of some misguided belief he owed Sam his kid's life.

Sam had never looked at it like that. It was his job to save people. Harlan's people included. But right now, he was glad Harlan was on his side.

Fuck. He could really use some skilled backup right now.

PHOEBE sat in a ball on the chair, her legs tucked up under her, thinking. Sorting through this mess. When Sam entered the room, his large frame blocking out the dim light they left on for Archibald, he paused in front of the chair she sat on. His face no longer held the handsome, open beauty it had once held. It was set with determination. Hardcore determination.

"Where is everyone?"

"Oh. Look. It's the FBI guy," Phoebe poked. Her chat with Archibald had eased most of her anger—not all, but most.

Leaning over her, Sam placed his hands on each arm of the chair and forced her to look at him. "I'm going to say this once, Phoebe, and once only. I tried to explain to you. You didn't want to hear me. I did this to protect you and everyone else. The less you knew about why I was here, the better. Whether you approved of my judgment call or not. There it is. *Deal*." He pushed off the chair with a jolting shove of his hands and a hard set to his jaw.

Her eyes shot upward, meeting his two flecks of black granite. This was not the cute, cuddly Sam of twenty-four hours ago. The one whose eyes she could get so lost in. This was FBI Sam. Hard. Cold. With a plan.

But he was right. So she caved. "You're right. Our differences aside, we have some real problems to deal with. And there's some-

thing I have to tell you—all of you. Before this goes any further."
The knots in her stomach twisted at what she had to do next.

"You mean about your other sister, Penny?"

Her eyes flew open while her fingers clenched the edges of the
sleeves on her sweater. "You know?"

"I'm the FBI guy. I know everything." His sarcasm dripped into
the air between them and oozed all over her.

Phoebe held up her finger. Why was it okay for everyone else to
be angry with him? According to Wanda, Nina had torn into him.
"First, lay off the sarcastic, put-upon crap. You caught me totally off
guard, and it's been, in case you missed the part where I almost
bought it, a long damn day. Plus, you did lie to me. Second—if you're
going to wander around with a stick up your ass because I called you
on this—wander around somewhere else. I'm not going to have you
covertly attacking me. Be a man and give me the courtesy of saying
it to my face!"

Sam shot her a look of disbelief. "You mean, shoot straight,
Phoebe? Like you did with me about your sister?"

Oh, foul. Big foul! "My sister was none of your beeswax, buddy!
And she certainly didn't affect anything that was happening to us.
Unlike the fact that you work for the fucking F-B-I!" she shouted
between clenched teeth.

"Then *why* didn't you tell us about her?" Sam insisted like the
skilled interrogator he was.

And it made her cave with the guilt that had been eating her up
since this had begun. He might as well have shone a flashlight in her
eyes and threatened to make her talk.

Phoebe let her head fall to her heavy chest, the misery welling
up in her like a dam ready to burst. "I kept it from Nina because it
was enough that I had diagnosis death hanging over my head. I wasn't
sure she could handle that and a brain-damaged twenty-year-old who
needs constant care. Nina didn't handle *me* very well. So I figured
after this was all over, we'd part ways and she never had to be the

wiser. I love Penny like nothing and no one on the planet. She's my heart, and she's my responsibility for as long as I'm still here. She's one of the very reasons I get up in the morning, and I won't allow anyone to shun her the way Nina shunned me. She's sweet and unassuming, and loves everyone with no judgment. Sometimes to her detriment. She doesn't have the ability to understand when she's being mocked. Nina would do nothing but frighten her. And aside from that, everything got so crazy, I didn't know where to begin. I'm sorry."

"She's taken care of," was his terse and still cold response.

Phoebe nearly swooned with such relief, she had to grab the edges of the chair she sat in. "Meaning?"

His chiseled jaw lifted. "Meaning I've got someone watching her day and night until this thing breaks."

"Oh, God. No, Sam. You didn't call the FBI in, did you? To send someone in to protect her? They'll crucify you!"

"They'd crucify *us.* And no. It's not FBI, but it's someone I trust implicitly, and no one you need to know anything more about. Just know I've covered Penny and Mark's safety."

Fear crept back up her spine, and the image of that poor man flashed behind her closed eyes. Penny's sweet, sweet face floated in front of her eyes, too. Gentle, unassuming Penny, with eyes just like Nina's and the thwarted mental capacity of a ten-year-old. "You don't think they'll go after Penny, do you? How could they even know about her? I've kept her existence very quiet." She jammed her knuckle in her mouth to keep from screaming.

Sam's eyes flashed a streak of concern like the old Sam would. "They have your phone, Phoebe. I'd bet you've called her a hundred times from it. It wouldn't be hard to find her—and no doubt, you're on their most-wanted list. If you talk, let's just say, they're not gonna want that to happen. So they'll do everything in their power to find you and eliminate you."

Oh, good. More death. If they didn't get her one way, they were sure to get her another. Overwhelmed, especially at the thought that Penny could possibly be hurt, she pleaded with Sam. "Why don't we just go to the police, Sam? We need more help. You can't have this all on your shoulders. It's too much."

Nina strode back into Sam's apartment, her phone in hand, her mouth twisted into a snarl. "Because if we fucking do that, the tables will turn, and those douche bags'll give us up just like we're giving them up. So while we might save that poor guy's life in the middle of all that shit, we're fucking an entire community no one knows anything about—and not just our own community. That's why. Besides, we've handled shit like this before. It might not have been as fucked up, but we've taken on plenty of assholes since the freaky-deaky began. We can take on more."

Sam held up a hand to thwart Nina. "We have a lot to consider, Nina. A lot more than just us at this point. First up, we need to figure out where the hell this is going on."

Phoebe pressed the heel of her hand to her forehead. "Because I transported out to, of all places, Bed Bath and Beyond before I could figure it out, right?" God. She could just kick herself for panicking like that. Massage oil. How, in all that dire, she'd conjured up the idea of a massage instead of the training ground for a team of skilled ninja assassins would haunt her forever.

Nina gave her head a gentle shove. "You shouldn't have been there to begin with, nitwit. We told you—anything suspicious, get the fuck out. I think a pillowcase over your head is a little on the suspicious side, don't you, Brainy Barbie?"

Phoebe fought to keep the anger out of her voice. Okay. She'd made a bad choice. "I just wanted to help. And if I hadn't taken that pill, Dr. Hornstein would have become suspicious."

Nina tugged a strand of her hair. "No. He would have thought you chickened the fuck out and then he probably would have tried to kidnap you later. You know—the kind of later where we would have been there to beat his ass bloody?"

Sam placed a hand on Nina's shoulder and squeezed, though his face was still all business. "Ease off, Nina. It's done. Here's the second part of this. The part that worries me. I know who the woman was that showed up at Phoebe and Mark's that night."

"Who?" everyone said in unison, including Darnell and Wanda, who'd joined them.

"Her name's Meredith Villanueva. Stinky couldn't find anything on her at first, but he did a little digging and he came up with some things we need to be concerned about. I knew her name the second he said it, but I've never seen her before. Not many have. She works alone, and her identity is one of the most protected in my field. It was a standing watercooler joke with us whether that was even her real name. She's a legend at the agency. She's a legend for a reason. Meredith's undercover skills are, bar none, some of the best in the world."

"But wait a second, Sam," Wanda said, her brow furrowed. "If all of you at the FBI know of her, why didn't they tell you she was in the middle of this mess doing undercover work?"

Sam's face was dark and cloudy. "Because she's not FBI. She's CIA."

FBI. CIA. And Meredith had been almost DOA.

So many acronyms.

So, OMG, and BTW, enough already with the madness, and just as an FYI, this was not a ROFLMAO kind of fun.

CHAPTER 16

Phoebe finally found the words to speak. "So your one-night stand was a CIA agent? Don't all you acronyms ever talk to each other? You know, communicate so everyone's on the same page?"

Sam clenched his jaw, but he still didn't directly address her. Instead he spoke to the entire group. "I don't know what happened. If you know anything about our agencies, you know, while we respect each other's work, we don't always love when someone else treads on our turf. My purpose at O-Tech was innocuous. I wasn't there to necessarily find anything at all that was of the magnitude this is. I was just burnt out from the job and needed a break from the crazy." He gave Phoebe a pointed look before saying, "And according to Stinky, O-Tech's clean. Which is exactly what I reported just a week ago. But that Meredith was there means there really was something big. I suspect she found that something big in the same way you did, Phoebe. What happened after that is all just speculation."

Nina cracked her knuckles. "Does this mean we're gonna have

more letters of the alphabet breathin' down our necks, Sammy? You know, like the CIA?"

"If Meredith was in deep cover on a long-term assignment—that might be what buys us some time. You have specific contact times—usually weekly—and if you don't send out a distress signal, you're on your own to get the job done. It's only been a week since Meredith disappeared—that wouldn't draw a whole lot of attention, but I make no promises. She was pretty far gone by the time she got to us—if she didn't contact someone, it was only because she was half out of her mind in pain. It looks like it would take all reason away. Even CIA reasoning."

The panic Phoebe kept forcing down rose again, and this time, she couldn't stop her fear for Penny from spewing from her mouth. A fear that almost immobilized her. She'd promised her mother she'd take care of Penny at all costs. If it were the last thing she did, Penny would be safe.

Her hands gripped the chair's arms when she jumped up, her legs shaking. "We have to go back in there, Sam! It isn't just about that man in there anymore. None of us are safe until we catch those bastards. Oh, my God! What if they find Penny? She can't defend herself—she's still like a child! She trusts everyone!"

The room went silent, all eyes trained on her.

If gulping were still a verb in her world, it would've been audible.

Nina was the first to cross the room with furious feet. She stood in front of Phoebe with narrowed eyes. "This Penny? Bet she's not your pet gator. She's gonna be one of those big surprises, right?"

Phoebe shot Nina a guilty look, but she remained silent.

"Answer me, Phoebe," Nina roared, her face a mask of yet another level of angry. She whipped up a hand in her sister's face. "Wait. Lemme ask in a way you can relate to. So, is this gonna be one of those surprises, Phoebe? You know, like on fucking *As the Days of Our Bold and Beautiful Loving Hope Turns*—or whatever the fuck you call that crazy shit you watch. This is where the suspenseful music plays and some chick named after something stupid like a town in Georgia does the big secret reveal, right? One of those secret reveals that pisses her sister with the very cool name right the fuck off?"

Phoebe lifted her chin, but she didn't back down. She would not apologize for Penny. But she would own the last of the secrets she'd kept with her head held high. "Yes. Yes, it is."

Nina's lips thinned, turning as white as her skin. She pointed in the direction of Sam's bedroom, giving Phoebe a nudge. "You? Get in that muthafucking bedroom and get the fuck in there *now*. Wanda? Come with. I'll need a witness when the clan wants to know why I killed a bitch!"

Wanda was instantly at Nina's side, taking her arm. "Oh, no. We will do this like adults, if I'm going to have any part of it. Your temper's gotten us into enough trouble as it is, vampire maker. Next you'll be turning Phoebe into triple vampire. So you will remain a lady, or I will beat you into one." Turning to Phoebe, she muttered from the side of her mouth. "March, young lady."

Phoebe's eyes sought Sam's for a brief moment, pleading for support, but he chose to look away. Instead, he directed his gaze to Darnell. "Let's go sit down. I have to read the rest of the files Stinky sent. I could use your help, man." He slapped Darnell on the back, and the two of them headed toward the kitchen.

Leaving Phoebe and Nina the Human Guillotine alone.

Phoebe plodded into the bedroom on reluctant feet, but she kept her head held high and her eyes on the only thing that would save her from Nina's wrath.

Wanda. Jesus and a Tiffany's box. Thank God for Wanda. She was probably the only thing between her and a beating by roped garlic.

Wanda stood by the bench under Sam's window, her eyes scanning each of the women. "Girls, I'm going to say this once. Keep it clean. And if you want to pummel each other like nothing more than common thugs—I will hit you with my shoe. Hard. Often. With so much glee." She rolled her hand in a forward motion. "Carry on." Plunking down on the bench, she crossed her legs and smoothed her skirt over her knees, giving them both a beaming smile.

Nina surprised Phoebe when she didn't instantly attack. There was no rushing her this time. Instead, she let the seconds tick by with her displeasure, making Phoebe sweat.

It was like experiencing *the look* your mother gave you when you knew you'd gone too far, but she wasn't ready to offer the spoken words for how too far was.

Which had then, and obviously now, always made her ramble stupidly. "Look, Nina. I'm sorry I didn't tell you. I didn't know *how* to tell you. I was so afraid, and caught up in this mess, that as the ball got rolling, I just . . . I don't know! Penny was just one more pressure to add to this huge mess. You had a lot on your plate. I didn't want to add to it. No one knew about her—not even the doctors I was seeing."

Nina remained stone-faced, her eye trained on Phoebe with a look of such disappointment, she felt an acute sting.

Her instant reaction to her sister's stoic silence was to launch an attack. "And you did this to me to begin with. You never would have had any reason to know about Penny if you hadn't pushed me. So this is sort of all your fault." Ah, deflection. Welcome back to the fifth grade, Phoebe Reynolds.

Wanda clucked her tongue and shook her finger. "Phoebe," she said in that kindergarten teacher way she had. "Tsk-tsk. Unfair. Yes. This was Nina's fault. Established. Every bit of information withheld after that's on you, sugarplum."

Nina held up a finger before putting it against her pursed lips. "Shut up. Shut up now. *Who* is Penny, Phoebe?"

And there it was. There was no way to avoid it. So she just said it. "My sister. Your sister, too, if you want to be technical."

Wanda pretended to cough to cover her gasp, and then she muttered a warning growl. "Nina . . ."

Instead of going for Phoebe's throat, Nina put her hands behind her and felt for the edge of Sam's bed, sitting down. "Say it. Tell me fucking all of it. Do it without whining and carrying on, or I swear to you, Phoebe, I'm going to smash your face in."

Phoebe instantly backed down. This Nina. The one who spoke words that were relatively calm, and succinctly enunciated wasn't the openly angry Nina. The one who made threats that were, for the most part, just empty threats. She had no doubt Nina could do some damage, but she'd never follow through on one of her I'll-pull-your-dick-through-your-belly-button war cries unless she absolutely had to.

But this Nina? The one who hadn't called her Fill in the Blank Barbie but *Phoebe*, wasn't the Nina who yelled and carried on at a very predictable level of ire. This was a bone-chilling Nina.

She was also a Nina whose world had been turned upside down—a Nina that was feeling the true sting of betrayal by the father she'd so loved. Huge chunks of her life were now accounted for in a much different way than she'd thought, and it had defeated her. Sadly, Phoebe read it. In her words. In her actions.

And for the first time since she'd met her sister—Phoebe hurt for her. She hurt for the Nina who'd been kidney punched by one secret after the other.

Sitting on the edge of the bed near Nina, Phoebe put her hand on her sister's stiff arm and began. "Penny is twenty years old. She was late in life for my mother and our father. A total surprise, but not one that wasn't a happy one, if you heard Mom and Dad talk about it. She was conceived just before Dad died. He knew about her, but he never had the chance to meet her."

"So one less secret he didn't have to keep, right?" Nina sneered, though it was a weak attempt at hiding her sadness.

Phoebe's response was quiet, measured. "My mother didn't know about you for a long time, Nina. Not until just before Dad died, according to her. When he told her, she wanted to incorporate you into our lives, and I *know* she would have loved you just the same way she loved Penny and me. Whether you liked it or not. I think Dad was about to give in . . . but then he died. I only found out about this just after my mother was diagnosed with Alzheimer's two years ago."

"Your mother had it, too?" Nina choked out the words, stiffening her spine.

Phoebe's nod was tight, her eyes hot and grainy. "She said she told me about you because she didn't want me to be alone when she . . . was gone. I don't know why she never tried to find you after Dad died. I think it's because she was too busy trying to keep it together for Penny. And then Penny had a horrible accident and . . ." Her voice choked on the words of that terrible moment in time.

Nina's head shot up so fast the bones in her neck cracked. "What happened to her?"

She retold the events of that devastating day her mother had called her in a state of hysteria when Phoebe was just twenty-three.

She'd known the moment she'd heard her mother's voice, one that was rarely prone to raise even an octave, that something awful had happened. "Penny needs twenty-four-seven care. Her brain injury was more than I could handle and manage work at the same time after my mother passed. Without help, without someone to take her for her physical therapy and all of the things required to care for her, I decided to use the insurance money my mother left me and the money I made from the sale of our old house to put Penny somewhere where she would be cared for properly until I could hire someone to live in with us full-time. I did try to keep her with me. I tried so hard. Mark helped, but finding good, reliable help was almost impossible. I'd come home from work to find she hadn't moved from her wheelchair all day—"

"She's in a wheelchair?" Nina asked, her voice unusually thin and shaken.

Wanda moved to sit near her friend, pulling Nina's hand to her lap, silent tears streaming down her face, catching the streetlights from the window.

Phoebe's stomach tightened at the question. Whether it was really there or not, she still felt the bitter ache in her gut when it came to Penny's condition. "She is—one she's so self-conscious about around other people her age, it makes me want to lay down and die. She wants to be like everyone else, is all. And who at ten doesn't? She also has the mental capacity of a ten-year-old, and she always will. It's the brain damage. But she's the sweetest thing in the whole wide world, and my heart. She's trusting and loving and—and—if—" Her words broke again. She squeezed her eyes shut to relieve the grainy pulse of them.

Nina's eyes, penetrating Phoebe's right through the skin of her eyelids, forced her to open hers. She took Phoebe's chin in her hand. "Who fucking did this to her?"

Phoebe bit the inside of her cheek. A regret she'd always live with. If living was what she was doing when this was all over. "We never found out."

Nina's fists clenched. "The fuck better hope I never get my hands on him." She paused, then closed her eyes and rolled her head on her neck before she spoke again. "And you didn't tell me about this, why, Phoebe? Forget all the other bullshit about how angry I was about finding out about you and give me the real reason."

Sorrow burrowed deep in her soul. "Wasn't I enough, Nina? It wasn't bad enough that you knew nothing about me—add in my Alzheimer's and ice that cake with Penny? As difficult as you are, even I didn't think that was fair to you. But once I saw your reaction to me, I didn't want Penny to be shunned, too. There really was no point to telling you about her. I figured once this was over, we'd part ways and it would be done with you never the wiser."

Nina's eyes narrowed. "You better not have done this because you're ashamed of her—or I'll kick your ass, Phoebe."

How odd that she'd thought Nina would be insensitive to Penny, but also that Nina thought she hid Penny away in shame. "No! No. It's nothing like that. People can be very cruel. I've experienced it firsthand

and so has Penny. She might be disabled, but she still understands when people stare at her or make rude remarks. She's not deaf. Just disabled. Sometimes when I take her out for the day, kids . . . They just don't understand—some people just haven't taught their children about differences. But I hurt for her. So much that I want to beat all the mean kids up at the park—which is ridiculous. I'm the adult."

"I'm fully in control of myself at all times, and I'd want to do the same, Phoebe," Wanda offered, her eyes warm and sympathetic.

Nina flashed a hand between them. "And the assholes from this clinical trial know about Penny how? I thought they thought you had no family?"

Her hands twisted in her lap. Because she'd done something foolhardy in her surge of *I am vampire, no one fucks with me*. This was all her fault. "Sam said it's because they have my phone. The hospital's in my list of contacts. I never, ever listed her on any of the medical forms I've filled out—which is probably why they didn't think I had any living relatives. But she's there . . ."

Nina nodded, but her teeth were clenched. "Fuck, fuck, fuckerly, fuck."

"Sam said he has someone looking out for both her and Mark. I don't know who, and I didn't ask questions. But I trust that he's done what he said." Even if she wasn't so sure she trusted anything else about him.

"I won't feel better until *I* know she's safe," Nina spat. "End of."

Phoebe let her eyes fall to the floor. "Anyway. I'm really sorry. She's all I've got. There's nothing I wouldn't do for her. *Nothing*. I just wanted to protect her."

"From big, bad me," Nina seethed, some of that familiar anger seeping back in the way of apparent self-recrimination.

"Oh, Nina," Wanda said with watery tones, wrapping her arm around her friend's shoulder and giving it a squeeze so hard Nina bucked forward. "While I don't condone Phoebe not telling you, talking to you isn't exactly like sitting down at a Gandhi-Oprah hosted tea party, sweet face. It's more like taking a meeting with Ted Bundy. So don't pull the martyr stuff, miss. I call foul."

Nina flipped her the bird, but she followed it with a smile. "Fair enough, but fuck you anyway, Wanda."

Wanda chuckled, reaching over to squeeze Phoebe's hand. "You've had a lot on your plate, Phoebe, but no more secrets. Got that? Auntie Wanda's not terribly fond of surprises, okay? We can't protect what we don't know is *ours*."

That Wanda had used the word *ours* made Phoebe's eyes sting. For the first time since her mother died, she didn't feel as alone in the world. "That's all of it. I swear." The tight knot in her chest began to subside.

Nina nodded with a firm shake of her head. "So, after the commotion in here, and the phone call from Siberia telling me to ask you two to keep it the fuck down, obviously Sammy told you about his shit."

Phoebe looked down at her hands in her lap. "Too much?"

Nina laughed with a hoarse snicker. "Even I let him explain, Melodramatic Barbie. Christ."

Her chin fell to her chest, her head shaking from side to side. "I said *fuck you* to him." And now she regretted it.

Nina snorted and clapped her on the back. "Yeah, I heard, badass. Honest to shit, I just don't get how we can be related," she remarked, her tone dry.

"What?"

"You swear like a sissy-la-la. Jesus. Work on that. I can't let anyone know you're my sister till you get that shit worked out."

Phoebe tamped down her excitement at Nina's use of the word *sister*. "Well, you are legend. Promise I'll work harder to live up to your legacy. Either way, I was just so angry with him for lying. And even if it was to protect us, it was a serious thing to keep from us."

Nina slapped Phoebe's thigh. "Agreed. On all counts. But then, you're just as guilty, Clandestine Barbie."

Wanda chuckled at Phoebe's silence.

"But don't think for one of your girlie seconds I didn't tell him as much either. Because I did. While he was pressed up against a wall and my fist was all up in his good-looking, I'm-so-innocent face."

Oh, she totally got that. "When it hit me that all that cute, Care Bear cuddly he throws around like it's free for the taking was just an act, I felt like I'd slept with a stranger. I know we haven't known each other long, but what attracted me to him was how sort of corny he was. I went into it with the hot nerd and came out with a cranky FBI agent. Now I just feel dirty."

Nina clucked her tongue in response. "You should, for all the screaming you two do in here."

Her cheeks would stain bright red right now if she were still human. "Is nothing sacred with you people?"

Nina tugged on Phoebe's ear. "Not when you have vampire hearing. And FYI, Betrayed Barbie, Gigantor didn't use you to do anything. You did that shit all on your own."

Her disgust with herself for even considering going in alone mounted by the second. "I know. I know. Archibald, in all his cheerio, Sam's an FBI agent, told me as much. I jumped the gun. I get it. But I'm just not sure the Sam out there, the real one who won't even look at me, is one I'm going to like as much as I did before I knew he was an FBI agent."

Nina tapped her with a light fist to her arm. "So you don't like dudes who'd do anything to protect their chicks?"

"And their family members?" Wanda chimed in with a wink and a giggle.

She still wasn't convinced. After some time to think about it, she'd come to the conclusion that when she'd offered herself to Sam like some sort of love-starved idiot, he'd stalled her because of his job. That he'd responded to her let's-get-it-on vibe just meant he was a man. "It still doesn't mean he meant what he said to me. He made this big thing about how he wanted to get to know me before we . . . But that was a different Sam. Wouldn't you call me Fuckwit Barbie if I just jumped right back in, eyes wide shut?"

Nina shook her head, pulling her legs up under her. "Nope."

"Did you get a bad batch of blood today? Has it turned your brain to oatmeal?"

"You forget what I can do. I can read minds, twit. Yeah, he added another element of danger to this bullshit by lying, but he ain't lyin' about how he feels about you."

Oh, again.

"And," Wanda added with a warm smile, "he certainly wasn't faking his feelings when he was calling my cell phone every twenty seconds to see if you'd somehow gotten back here. I know fear when I hear it, and he was afraid, Phoebe. Though, I'm sure he'd caveman that up and call it hesitant."

Nina lifted Phoebe's chin with a finger. "Look, kiddo. I'm gonna be straight up with you about something here. Sam digs you. He didn't want to at first, and that was probably the game he was playing when he said he wanted to take things slow. Now he doesn't want to because it just makes everything more complicated, but he's not lying. Am I cool with what he did? Not so much, but I get his reasoning. The less we all knew, the better. I think he stopped protecting his cover and started protecting you a long time ago. Not just you—all of us."

She was weakening. "How refreshing to know I'm not just some pawn in his paranormal game."

Nina leaned back on the bed on her elbows and stretched. "Figures you like soap operas. Knock it off with the drama. No. You're not his big supernatural coup or whatever other lame crap you've thunk up in that pretty head of yours."

Phoebe batted her eyelashes at Nina and tilted her chin toward her shoulder with a coy smile. "You think I'm pretty?"

Nina's eyebrow rose, her expression bored. "I think you think you are. I'm just a playa in your game, yo."

"Would it be weak of me to tell you how relieved I am about Sam?" Phoebe asked, running her hands over her eyes.

"Yeah. So don't."

Phoebe smiled. "Okay. I'm relieved."

Nina palmed her head and gave it a light shove, but she followed it with a smile that was so close to warm, it almost made it to her eyes. "That's because your cootchie-la-la's all singin' a happy tune."

"I think it might be more than that." Which really worried her. Despite the Sam out there, the one who was anything but cuddly, she still found him ridiculously irresistible.

Nina clucked her tongue. "Then I guess we'd better fucking figure out how to fix this so you have the chance to find out if it is."

There was that shooting stab of fear again. "What if we don't?"

"Then I'll die tryin'."

"That's unequivocal."

"What is?"

She gave her sister an astonished look. "You actually know what that word means?"

Nina held up her fist. "You know what this means?"

Phoebe clapped her hands and snorted. "You like me."

Nina made a face. "Oh, the hell. I don't like you. I don't like anyone. We've been over this. Tell her, Wanda."

"You like me," Wanda teased, pinching Nina's cheek.

But Phoebe cut her off. "No, no. You like me. You don't want to, but you do. You've discovered, once you got past all that rage, that we're a lot alike. I'm just better dressed and I have a handle on my fits of rage."

Nina's face held a question. "How did you fucking do that anyway?"

"What?"

"Get a handle on your fits of rage."

Phoebe grabbed one of the throw pillows from Sam's bed and tucked it under her arms. "I wasn't always the girlie-girl you see before you. In fact, I was a lot like you. Sullen, moody, angry, badly dressed. It was a phase that came as quickly as it went."

"Because?"

"Junior year. I beat Danny Krackowski to within an inch of his pathetic, useless life for beating Mark up. He beat Mark so badly, he ended up in the emergency room with four stitches and a fractured wrist. He didn't want to tell me who'd done it because he was afraid of Danny and his spineless thugs, but I knew. I knew because Danny cracked on Mark all the time because he's gay. I also knew because Mark managed to bite him and he had the bite marks on his arm the next day at school."

"And you flipped? Okay. So you're not that much different than me. I'd slap a bitch if anyone even considered touching one of these two fruitcakes." She thumbed her finger at Wanda.

Phoebe's look was far away as she remembered that day in the cafeteria. "I flipped like I was Mary Lou Retton going for the gold in an Olympic floor exercise. I lost my shit. Right there in the cafeteria. I cornered Danny and rammed my binder up under his jaw—I don't remember a whole lot after that. I just remember there was a lot of screaming and the word *stop*—or something. But I couldn't hear anything. I just wanted Danny dead. And I don't just mean that like when someone uses the euphemism *I'd rather see you dead*. I mean dead-dead, and I wanted to be the one to do it. I'd always had a temper, but to be honest, when I came down from that quest for the kill and Danny was a bloody mess on the floor, crying at my feet between lips that looked like tires on a four-by-four, it scared me."

Nina shrugged her shoulders. "He was a dick. He deserved it."

"That's neither here nor there. I ended up suspended for two weeks, and as part of my reinstatement to school, I had to go to counseling. I didn't go willingly, but if you knew the first thing about my mother, you'd know for all her pressed faux silk shirts and makeup, she was as much of a badass as you. You didn't talk back to my mother and plan a future afterward. So I went, and the first

couple of sessions I sulked. I whined. Once I even went in my paja-
mas because my mother came in to find I was still asleep when it was
time to leave. So she dragged me out by my ear, slapped me in the
car, and dropped me off. But then I learned something."

"Bed head sucks at the counselor's?"

Phoebe grinned. "I was just angry."

Nina cocked her head in question. "About?"

"Our father."

Nina nodded her head but said nothing. Though, Phoebe sensed
Nina had some residual anger with their father, too. Part of that
anger had to do with the secret life he'd led.

"I was angry because he died the day before he was supposed to
come and take me to a father-daughter dance. But I didn't know he'd
died trying to get to the dance. I showed up in a dress my grandmother bought me. Mom even let me put lipstick on. I had a princess
dress with big puffy pink sleeves and a skirt that twirled, and I waited
on that curb for three hours—while other girls' dads swept them
inside a room filled with big disco balls and fancy big-band music."
And just saying it out loud now still hurt.

Nina slouched, letting their upper arms rest against one another.

"But Dad didn't show. I found out through that counselor that
even though rationally I knew it wasn't his fault, somehow I'd made
it his fault. Because I didn't see him much more than once a month.
Our time was always limited when I did. I didn't know he had
another family somewhere else. I'd grown up with only occasional
visits from him anyway. But the dance meant a whole night with
him. Just him and me. I'd spent two months building it up in my
mind—and then it was gone, and when there was no chance for
another dance, it hurt."

"So enter Spiteful Barbie. The one who was never going to dress
up and be pretty for anyone ever again," Nina theorized like some
undead therapist.

Phoebe nodded with a sad smile. "That summer, everything changed for me. I went the whole nine. Black nail polish, lipstick, thick eyeliner, black clothes, ripped jeans. I did my version of grunge slash goth proud. I didn't shower. I rebelled against a lot more than a bar of soap, too. I was just short of cutting myself. No one really talked to me because they were afraid of me to begin with. Except Mark. He never stopped being my friend—even when he called me an epic fail from *The Rocky Horror Picture Show*, Mark was always my friend."

"So what did this counselor do to change all that? Did he Dr. Phil boot camp your ass?"

"Mr. Macintyre had the kind of family I'd always wanted. A whole family—a nice wife, two kids, a dog, and a big house, a backyard with a tree swing. But he told me something that made me realize nothing is perfect. His son was a meth addict. A counselor's son— one who had so many awesome things going for him that he just couldn't see because he was angry. He made me realize that a family is never perfect and it doesn't have to have both parents in it to make it happy. He helped me grieve the loss of Dad properly instead of bottling it up and letting it explode. That's not to say I don't still have a hot temper—I just get how to control it.

"Techniques and shit, right?"

Wanda clapped her hands. "Techniques, you say, Phoebe? Can we write them down? No. Let's give them their own Word document. We'll laminate it and hang it up on the walls of OOPS."

Phoebe laughed. "Yep. You wanna learn a few, Nina?"

"Fuck no. I just wouldn't be Nina if I wasn't a raving lunatic."

"I wouldn't be Barbie Vampire if not for Nina the Raving Lunatic," she reminded her.

"Heard and ignored," Nina snarked.

Wanda threw her arms around the two of them and hugged them hard. "Good talk, girls. Look at what we've accomplished. But there's still one wee, little matter Nina has to clear up. So while we're all hearing the 'Circle of Life' song, Nina, I do believe you have a bit of a secret, too."

Phoebe's eyes narrowed in Nina's direction. "You have a twin, don't you? Good gravy, there are two of you."

Nina's lips pursed. "Nope. But you have a grandmother. Her name is Lou, and if you fucking upset her even a little, I'll break your Barbie feet. Got that?"

Phoebe's eyes went wide, but then she smiled. A grandmother. Oh, that meant fresh-baked cookies and milk and . . .

"And stop right there," Nina warned. "She ain't the kind of grand-mother that's breaking out the hand mixer. She cooks once a week, and it's the worst fucking pot roast you'll ever eat in your entire life. But you'll eat it, spit it in a napkin like I do and pretend Chef Ram-say cooked it, because if you hurt her feelings, I'll beat you like a dirty rug."

Phoebe's fingers trembled. She had a grandmother . . . "Wait. She's not a vampire?"

Nina flicked Phoebe's hair and made a face. "No, moron. She's a little old lady who likes game shows, butt-ass ugly Hummel figurines, and those stupid soap operas you dig. She forgets to put her teeth in her head, like, all the time, and she refuses to let Greg and me move her into the castle to live with us because she's probably more stub-born than twenty mules. She likes her *things*, as she calls them, and she won't part with shit. Even though we have enough room in that tin can to fit a small Guatemalan village. And she has no idea we're paranormal. None. Don't fuck that up."

Phoebe grinned. She didn't care if Lou liked naked poker.

Nina cackled. "She likes that, too."

"What?"

"Naked poker. It makes me want to yark my lunch, but there it is, yo. She has a group of cronies she hangs out with at the senior center, and the geriatric cruise director caught her organizing a game of naked poker last year. Jesus, it was embarrassing."

Wanda giggled, putting her hand to her mouth. "You should have seen it, Phoebe. When Nina told Lou it was *strip* poker, Lou scoffed and said why waste time at her age praying for a losing hand when they could just start out naked?"

Phoebe didn't even care that Nina had read her mind. She wanted to know this person. She wanted to belong. "Can I meet her? I mean, will it be too much? I don't want to upset her."

Nina's white teeth glowed in the darkened bedroom when she smiled. "She raised *me*. There isn't a whole lot that upsets her. She's a rock. So, yeah, you can meet her. Which means I'm handing the pot roast torch to you, cupcake. We'll swap days every other week. If you're not on time, she makes you clean her dentures. It's nasty shit."

She was going to be enough of a surprise. She'd wait on telling her *grandmother* about Penny. "I promise not to mention Penny."

"The fuck you won't," Nina protested with a frown and a crack of her knuckles. "It's not the kid's fault she's jacked up, Phoebe. I know people are assholes all the time about shit like that. But that won't ever happen as long as I'm around. Stop fucking hiding her because you think you have to protect her from us. Besides, Lou'd clap you in your head if you didn't. Lou'd wanna know about this. She's no pansy-ass. She'd never forgive you if you didn't tell her her Joe had more than one kid. She'll be shocked, but she's a tough old bird."

But the reality of their situation crept back in, tainting her joy at finding out she had a grandmother. "Well, if things go south, you won't have to worry about giving up your pot roast night."

"Nothin's goin' anywhere. Believe that shit," Nina assured her.

A brief knock on the door made them all turn around. Sam poked his head in, his face still as hard and unforgiving as it had been twenty minutes ago. He tipped his Stetson up to view them. "Ladies? We have a location for where Phoebe was. Now we need a plan."

Phoebe couldn't stop herself from visibly shaking.

But Nina put her palm over Phoebe's hand and gave it a squeeze before rising. "C'mon, kiddo. Let's go kick some freakazoid ass. I got another sister to meet."

CHAPTER 17

Everyone gathered in Sam's living room with the kind of tension you could taste on your tongue—each one of them locked and ready to load like coiled springs.

"So here's the score," Sam addressed them, his face openly hard and determined. "You *were* at O-Tech today, Phoebe." His eyes briefly touched hers before resting on the group.

Nina slapped her thigh. "But we searched that damn place up one side and down the other. How the fuck?"

Sam lifted his Stetson and scratched his head. "According to Stinky, and some plans he found for O-Tech dating back to the late sixties, O-Tech had underground tunnels running beneath it. They were sealed off as some kind of hazard a long time ago before it was O-Tech—or so everyone thought. Apparently, it wasn't a big deal to knock out one damn wall to gain access. It was just *one* damn wall, and if that security guard hadn't woken up when he did, we were two bloody feet from it," Sam growled. "Either way, I think I also have the answer to the initials Meredith wrote on my memo-pad. TBD is the owner of O-Tech. Whoever it is, they bought the company back in late 2008. Total takeover. Stinky's still working on what those initials mean, but it's when the wall was knocked out. Stinky found some records from a wrecking company in Jersey that did the job. I'm going to take a leap of faith and figure the person who bought O-Tech had the wall removed."

"And all this to create vampires. Who the fuck is crazy enough to want to be a vampire on purpose?" Nina asked in wonder. "I gotta ask myself if they realize they'll never eat another chicken wing again."

Sam planted his hands on his hips. "You don't think for one second the government wouldn't if they could get their hands on something like this, Nina? I can think of a million different people who'd take the opportunity. But for right now, I'm not as interested in motive as I am in finding the crazy bastards and finding out what Phoebe and I have to do to keep from ending up dead."

Phoebe sat silent while Sam spoke, watching him in all his FBI element. His face was sharper, tension filling each muscle movement in his jaw. His eyes were hawklike and intense, his posture rigid and taut like an arrow just waiting for its bow.

He was virile and smart—and all the goofiness was gone. The succinct edge to his words, the defined way he explained things wasn't anything like the Sam she'd gotten to know.

Yet, it added a whole new element to her fierce attraction to him. One she had to set aside for now—in lieu of that crazy thing called death.

Wanda popped up from the couch, tucking her knee-length sweater around her slender waist. "Have you figured out how they did this, Sam? How they managed to find a way to manufacture vampires?"

Sam rolled his tongue in his cheek. "Stinky found some antiques dealer in Lafayette, North Carolina. I don't know how he does what he does, but he traced the origins of the original formula these freaks have back to this guy's store. The guy sold this recipe for vampire to a woman who paid cash for it. The antiques dealer had no idea he was selling anything more than an antique. This formula, or whatever you want to call it, was in some old jewelry box in a hidden trapdoor. Stinky says it's some ancient relic written in bits and pieces of a language that's a linguist's wet dream. Some pretty powerful people hunted the black market for years to find it. And this woman just walks in and buys it like it's toilet paper. His description of her was pretty vague—blond and hot could be anyone, so we're SOL there. All I have is a picture of the jewelry box—but when Stinky did a search on it, that's what he came up with. Archaeologists speculate the jewelry box is just an urban legend."

Phoebe shivered, though she managed to ask, "So someone, in essence, cracked this ancient code and started making vampires."

Sam's nod was curt. "It would have to be someone pretty rich. It takes a lot of money to hire linguists and create the kind of labs you described, Phoebe. I've got Stinky searching those initials right now to see if they match anyone with that kind of liquid cash available to them."

"Any word on the name of that man I saw today?" It was all she could do to speak the words. Darnell came up behind her and placed a gentle paw on her shoulder.

"Nothing yet," was Sam's grim response.

"So now what, Sam?" Wanda asked around her fingers—fingers that Phoebe detected a slight tremble to.

"Now, I go in."

"Not alone, brotha. Ain't no way ol' Darnell's lettin' you jump into that batch a crazy without backup. Not happenin'. You might be a badass, but you only one badass. I'm like two badasses fo the price a one." He smiled, patting his belly with a wink.

Sam shook his head with a firm "not a chance." "*No.* No one else but me. Don't get me wrong, I appreciate the love, but I'm the one trained for this kind of thing. Add in my vampiric powers, and I'm more than enough to take them on and take them out. *All* of them."

But Wanda was the first to voice the most important factor of all. "Yes. We absolutely have to go in and get that poor elderly gentleman Phoebe told us about. But to what end? You can't go in there and take everyone out, Sam. I know you can't call your buddies in on this and have the abominations simply arrested for fear those men will give Phoebe away. But you can't just aimlessly kill them or we may never find what we need to reverse this, Sam. You need one of those Dr. Frankensteins to give you an antidote."

"If there even is one," Phoebe muttered without thinking. "Obviously, project Build a Vampire's been a bust so far."

"I'll bust a head until someone figures it out," Nina gritted.

Fear crawled back up Phoebe's spine as yet another realization hit her. Really, where would she be these days if she didn't have some good old terror to munch on at snack time? "But what if you black out again?"

"Yeah. So it's settled. Me and Darnell go with—and don't fucking try to pull the brave FBI guy shit with me," Nina said. "You need someone there if you flip out, Sammy. I'm the biggest, baddest bitch in the land. So when do we go in?"

"No way I'm letting you go alone," Phoebe said, though the words were wobbly—it wasn't happening without her. She wasn't going to sit here and wait to find out if they'd killed Sam and her sister just so they could save her. Who was she to be granted the gift of eternal life while everyone else sacrificed?

"*Sit, Phoebe,*" Sam demanded as though she were his subordinate, pointing to the chair.

She stiffened her spine, pushing past Nina and Wanda to confront him. "*No, Sam.* The hell I'll sit by and let you all be slaughtered! I'm going with you. I know you think you're the best candidate because you're a trained badass, but you won't be so badass blacked out on a floor. Or have you forgotten Alice Goodwin's? I'd bet, with all the maniacal genius they have running around in that place, and after I showed up there and they know I'm one of their creations, they've got plenty of people just waiting to take you out. The more manpower the better."

Sam shook his head—the kind of shake that brooked no argument. "You will stay here with Wanda, Phoebe. You'll stay or I'll make sure you stay, and you won't like it."

A spike of anger shot up her spine. "Who do you think you are? You can't tell me what to do! This isn't some FBI sting where you call all the shots, and I'm not your peon!"

Sam's face went dark, and as good as she was getting at reading emotions, he was on his last strand of patience. "I'm the guy who knows you have a sister who needs you, Phoebe. If I'm slaughtered— it'll only hurt my parents for a little while. But they're self-sufficient, and they don't need me to take care of them. Penny *needs* you to take care of her because you're all she's damn well got. And don't forget one little thing. They only know *you're* a vampire. You'd be the weakest link. But they don't know about me or Nina and Darnell. Now quit wasting my time with your bravado. Sit down. Shut up. *Do not* open that mouth of yours again. You will stay here, Phoebe—even if it means I have to knock you out to do it. Final word."

Phoebe's eyes flashed hurt, angry, indignant, but Nina was quick to grab her by the arm, swinging her around with a jolting shake. "Knock it the fuck off, Phoebe. Sam's right."

"What good will I be to Penny if I do the ashes to ashes, dust to dust thing?" she shouted, yanking her arm from Nina's grasp.

For the first time since she'd met Nina, her face had a plea on it, and it stopped Phoebe cold. "Because if Sam finds something to stop this and he doesn't get out—if I don't get out—we've got Darnell to bring whatever the fuck it is back to you. I did this to you, Phoebe. If anyone bites it, it should be me—it *will* be me. And if we don't come back, then you've got a shitty job to do. Go see Penny one last time and tell her people who will love the living shit out of her are gonna take real good care of her. You can't let that happen without seeing her, warning her. She'll be afraid if you don't tell her who Wanda and Marty and the others are. I won't have her afraid, Phoebe. Not anymore."

Penny. It was the surest way to make her sit up and pay attention. If something happened to her, and she didn't have the chance to tell Penny, she'd never understand that Phoebe would never leave her if she didn't absolutely have any choice. She'd rehearsed the going-to-heaven speech a million times when she thought Alzheimer's was going to rob her of her mind. And she'd been the one to tell Penny their mother was gone in much the same manner.

Phoebe's eyes instantly went hot and grainy, her trembling fingers ran over them, and her voice hitched when she turned to Wanda. "You'd take care of Penny for me?" The words squeaked from her lips.

Wanda's eyes, always so clear and alert, were filled with unshed tears. She cupped Phoebe's face with her soft hand. "Of course I would, Phoebe. We *all* would. She'd never want for anything. She'll always, always have us. She'll have more uncles and aunts than she can shake a stick at, and a grandmother I'll make sure she knows. She'll eat pot roast and watch soap operas and the Game Show Network, and Lou will love her to pieces." The last words were directed at Nina, who lifted her chin and averted her eyes.

"And don't you worry none 'bout that park," Darnell said, his voice thick. "Ain't nobody gonna talk smack 'bout Penny round ol' Darnell. 'Cause I'll set their overalls on fire."

Phoebe reached for Darnell's hand and brought it to her cheek, closing her eyes. "Thank you," she managed to whisper. Then her throat became so tight, she could only shake her head. These people didn't know Penny. They weren't even really related to Nina—yet, they extended themselves, gave of themselves so selflessly, so openly that if this did all end, Penny would be surrounded by people who weren't just invested in her physical well-being, but in her soul's well-being.

Squaring her shoulders, Phoebe manned up, but she still avoided Sam's eyes. "Okay. You're right. I'll stay."

Nina knocked her in the head with a flat palm and smiled. "Good Barbie. Now quit with the doomsday shit and wish us fucking luck."

Instinctively, she knew Nina would never stand for a sappy out-pouring of emotion—or a long, tearful good-bye. Instead, Phoebe tugged either side of her hoodie, praying she could keep her tone calm and level. "Don't go and get whacked, okay? It would really suck if you didn't have the time to like me even more than you already do. And you owe me a game of Mystery Date. Maybe even a Barbie Dream House playdate." Trailing a finger across her sister's cheek, she smiled.

Nina grabbed her finger, giving it a gentle squeeze before brushing it off. "I'm never gonna like you, Baby Sister Barbie, and the only thing I owe you is a round of Rock'em Sock'em Robots, so I can vicariously beat your ass without being hassled by the PC paranormals in my life. You need to feed. So go find Arch and get the fuck out of my hair."

Before taking Phoebe's hand, Wanda reached for Nina, wrapping one arm around her neck. "You don't come back? I have to hunt you down in the afterlife. If you think I'm the burr in your saddle now? You don't want to know me if I have to move heaven and earth to find you in my heels. Got that, Mistress of the Dark? Be safe. And kill those vile bastards." Pressing her cheek to Nina's for a mere moment, Wanda closed her eyes and inhaled, then led Phoebe off toward the kitchen.

Sam, bent at the waist, placed a gun in his sock. No matter how angry—no matter how hurt she was that he was going out of his way to extend the life of her punishment for not giving him a chance to explain—no way would he leave here without one last thing.

Placing her hand on his back, Phoebe knelt down in front of him and cupped his face, her eyes filled with so many things she'd like the opportunity to say to him someday. "Don't go ruining my chance to fall in love with you by kicking the vampire bucket. Got that, Sam McLean?" She didn't give him the chance to answer. Instead, she pressed a fervent kiss to his lips and rose to follow Wanda into the kitchen without looking back to gauge Sam's reaction.

It didn't matter. It only mattered that she'd unabashedly shared her feelings. No one was leaving here without clarity.

Yet, each step she took away from Sam on feet made of lead quite possibly could be the one step that drew her closer to losing him forever.

THEY stood outside the steel and glass walls of O-Tech. Snow had begun to fall in thick flakes, sticking to sidewalks and making visibility low. Heavy drops of moisture slapped at Sam's face, adding an irritated edge to his pre-mission jitters. Jitters he couldn't shake.

He'd done this kind of thing a hundred times before. His gun was locked and loaded. He'd gone over the mental version of how this would play out. He'd briefed Darnell and Nina as if they were his own men, with verbal diagrams and orders. They had a loose plan. Who needed a tight one when you were a vampire? The plan didn't allow for every possible scenario, but statistics and probabilities had to fall further down the list of priorities in light of the imminence of the situation.

The only thing left was to just do it.

Yet, the stakes were much different this time. This time it wasn't just some hostage's life on the line—someone he only knew on paper via details and a thorough though impersonal investigation.

It was Phoebe's life, and in turn, Penny's future.

And there was no way around the gut-wrenching fear he was fighting with each inch that drew them closer to the end of this chaos.

No doubt, these people had to be taken out. No question, he'd have no qualm being the one to do it.

But what if they didn't find the answer they so desperately needed? What if the heinous death Meredith had suffered was inevitable for Phoebe?

His jaw hardened. Then, by hell, it wouldn't be before he took out the fuck that was responsible.

Regret stabbed at him. He should have told Phoebe how he felt before he left. He should have pressed his lips to hers one last time—savored the fullness of them. Told her that no matter what, he'd make sure she lived. That he wanted to live, too, so they could explore this new life they had to live together.

But words weren't something he was good at. Sam the Entomologist was much better at them.

Sam the FBI guy had secrets and private horrors and the occasional night sweats.

Nina clamped a hand on Sam's shoulder, her face grim. "How much time do we have, Sam? Did Stinky tell you how long it's been since Alice and Meredith had been turned before they bought the golden ticket? And don't sugarcoat the end game. Just fucking say it so I know what we're up against."

Sam looked at his watch, then down at Nina, his lips a thin line of bleak. "If what Stinky said holds true as far as the records go for us like it did the others? I've got a couple of hours max. Phoebe? Maybe another twenty-four. I don't know how the symptoms begin or if it just blindsides you. But who knows—maybe the strain of this vampire virus has grown stronger in us." *Hopeful, Sam. Very hopeful.*

"Or weaker," Nina spat his fear out loud.

"So we goin' in to kill—or we just gonna have some fun with them—maybe hand 'em over to the clan?" Darnell asked, cracking his knuckles. "I don't like the killin', but I'll do what we need to to shut 'em down. They know 'bout us—wouldn't surprise me t'all if they'd give us up to yo superiors to make a deal to save their wussy hides. Cain't have dat, now can we?" Though it was the truth, Darnell's face still betrayed his concern over taking another's life.

It was clear he was pained by the idea. It was all over his round face. An odd predicament for a demon, and if Sam had more time to dwell, he'd ask Darnell how that had come to be.

Instead, Sam ran a hand over the gun at his waist in a familiar gesture. "It's a case-by-case situation. If you have to take them out, Darnell—do it. Don't hesitate. They wouldn't. Nina, you, too."

"Okay, boss," Darnell agreed with a grim nod. "So we better get on up in there 'fore somethin' worse happens. The second you get in there, ya think me up. I'll be right behind ya."

Sam's phone rang, revealing Stinky's number. "What?" he barked into the phone, ready to jump out of his skin.

The clacking of a keyboard ticked in Sam's ear. "Cowboy? Meredith Villanueva was a board-certified neurologist—which is why she was in the middle of this shitastrophe, but she wasn't just a neurologist, she was one of the best spies in the world, if the underground word I'm hearin' is right. She was CIA. Whatever was goin' down underneath O-Tech was big."

A neurologist. Now it was coming together in his mind. The last piece of the how and why she'd been at O-Tech. Even though most of the information was redundant, it only proved to Sam just how valuable Stinky was. "So is this phone call to tell me the CIA's on its way?" They'd be crawling all over the place, leaving them no chance in hell to find the answers they needed.

Stinky shifted in something Sam guessed was leather by the sharp crinkle. "Naw, man. Relax, Super Spy. No rumblings from the CIA. Trust that. But it won't be long. She's gonna miss her date with her handler for tomorrow. And, Cowboy? I still can't figure out what the hell these Dr. Frankensteins are doing. This formula's uncrackable. You had any luck?"

Sam's eyes went cold. Yeah. Like he'd tell Stinky if he had. He heard the curiosity in Stinky's voice betray the nonchalance he was hoping to purvey.

The old Stink-man was throwing his line into the lake and hoping to come up with a big trout. One he could brag about during a good geeky-gossip session. Sam kept his voice light and grunted. "Have you seen that chicken-scratch, Stink? I don't know what any of it means. Guess it's true what they say about doctors and their hand-writing."

Stinky paused for a moment, as though he didn't believe Sam, but he let it go. "Right. Doctors. So what's next, Sam?"

"Next? I go grab a cheeseburger and you shut your face. One word leaks out I was poking around, and your mother's basement's going to look like a bloodbath of body parts."

He sounded an offended snort. "I do not live in my mother's basement. Jesus. Why does everyone stereotype the brains in an outfit that way? It's damn unoriginal. I live in my *father's* basement, FYI—" Stinky stopped short.

Sam chuckled, giving it a sinister edge. "I'll remember it's not your mother's basement, but your *father's* when I come to kill you, Dwight Eugene Tann-en-baummmm," he drawled Stinky's real name. "Oh, and I'll do it in *Queens*. Later, Stink." Sam clicked the phone off to the tune of Stinky's mewling, shoving it back in his pocket.

Nina sidled up to him, moving from foot to foot—cagey and cranky. "Will that little shit narc on us? I'll sniff his brainy ass out and kill him."

Sam couldn't worry about that right now. He had to prioritize his uncertainties. Stinky was the least of them. "I won't make any promises. I don't kid myself Stinky can't be bought by the highest bidder, but for right now, he's too afraid to get overconfident. We need to get in and out before he bleeds into cocky."

Darnell crossed his arms over his broad chest. "So we ready, boss?"

Sam hesitated again. "I'll say this one last time. This is dangerous. Stuff doesn't go down the way it does on TV. I'm trained to do this. If I don't bring you back alive, Phoebe will hunt me down in the afterlife. I can do this alone."

Nina was the first to react by flicking his Stetson with a sharp snap. "Fuck you, Sammy. Stop showin' your ass. Just because you have a gun and some special-op-Navy-Seal-Green-Beret-whatever-the-hell crap on your résumé, doesn't mean you're the only one who can kick some nasty booty. I don't just play a badass on TV. I *am* a badass. Darnell's no slacker, either. We're in, and we don't come out until we *all* come out—or we all *don't*. Either way, it's team vampire-demon. So put up and shut up, and lead the fucking way." She waved her hand at the building.

Darnell slapped Sam on the back and shot him a genuine smile. "What the crazy lady said."

Sam's nod was curt, but his appreciation for their loyalty was bigger than he'd ever properly find the words for. "Then we're in."

They each turned to make their way to the wall Sam had entered the last time, plodding through the snow, heads down, when Sam's phone rang again. He ripped it from his pocket and barked, "Jesus Christ, Stinky. What?"

"It's Harlan, man," was the thick-drawled response. "I'm gonna say this straight and waste no time, Sam, and then I'm gonna hang up and go hunt down the rat bastards and kill 'em. *All* of 'em. They got to the kid before I did."

The click in Sam's ear, signaling the end of Harlan's call, was like a sonic boom.

"PHOEBE? I know this is an utterly absurd request, but please, sit down." Marty, who'd just arrived, patted the place on the couch next to her.

But Phoebe couldn't rest. She'd paced since Sam and the others had left. Her chest was tight as she went over and over in her head her last moments with Sam. She alternated between that stark image and Penny's sweet face flashing before her eyes in vivid memory. The conversation between Wanda and Marty flitted in and out of her ears in choppy bits.

Marty rose, setting Muffin on Archibald's lap, and began to pace with Phoebe. She latched on to her hand, walking back and forth with her, rubbing soothing circles across her skin. "Okay, so bring me up to speed while we wear a path in Sam's floor, would you, Wanda?"

"Sam has some crazy contact named Stinky . . ."

Wanda's retelling of the story became a buzz in Phoebe's ears while she brought Marty up to date. Bereft, she forced her shaking legs to keep moving while she prayed.

But Marty stopped dead, yanking Phoebe to a halt along with her. "Say again?"

Wanda scooped Muffin up and hugged her tight. "A jewelry box. This secret, crazy, whatever code, formula thing these monsters have was in the bottom of a jewelry box. It's apparently, in my very crude explanation, a recipe to create a vampire that's centuries old. A woman, who obviously doesn't shop at Target, picked it up for a song in North Carolina at an antiques shop. Isn't that the most ridiculous thing you've ever heard? There's some urban legend about this jewelry box being a high-dollar, black-market coup. All sorts of billionaires are looking for it. Sick. It's just vile!"

Marty's face went ashen. She gripped Phoebe's hand so tight, it made her wince. "Did you say a jewelry box?"

Wanda bobbed her head. "Look." She held up her phone. "Sam sent me the picture."

Marty's roar was high and keening, her pretty features twisted, her hands at her gut. "Oh, my God, Wanda! Oh, my God!"

Wanda's expression went from forced calm, to panicked. "What? What's wrong?"

Marty's chest heaved as she sank to Sam's couch. She covered her eyes and sucked in gulps of air with raspy wheezes.

Phoebe knelt in front of her, clasping her wrists. If one of the three least likely to freak paranormals was in freak-mode that meant alarms should be sounded at a DEFCON 5 level. "*What*, Marty?" she pleaded.

When she lifted her head, her blue eyes were a confection of icy fire. She grasped Phoebe's hands, squeezing them with such strength, if she could feel the pressure, it would have made her cry uncle. "I know who the bastard is! I know *who's* responsible for this!"

Like personally? Phoebe had to wonder. Because wow. It was time to find new social circles to travel in.

CHAPTER 18

"They have Penny?" Nina hissed, her fist held high at her temple.

Sam rolled his shoulders, fighting back the urge to ram a fist of his own through something. "Yes."

"Well, now, thass fo sho enough, ya feel me?" Darnell roared into the wind, his beefy fists clenched and raised to the sky. "Ol' Darnell don't play when they snatchin' the babies!" His beefy finger pointed in Sam's direction; his black eyes were chips of granite. "You get yo head together now, Sammy, and you get on in there through that wall. Do it now and think me up. I got me some criminal butt to whoop!"

Sam didn't speak another word. Yet, his head swam. One phrase ran through his mind over and over. *They had Penny.* These fucks wouldn't take the chance Phoebe'd die before she could get to the police. They would do whatever it took to lure her to them and they'd kill her because she knew too much.

He rammed himself against the wall in a haze of fury, driving his shoulder into it like some possessed linebacker, but to no avail.

Instead of falling into the wall and landing in his desired location, he slammed back against the concrete ground, kicking up snow in white, billowy puffs.

Nina dragged him upward, brushing him off. "Dude. Concentrate. I want to get to her as much as you do," she warned, her sloe eyes riddled with worry.

He shook off the hard landing and focused, aiming for the cafeteria just like the last time with but one mantra. *Save Penny.*

Sam's entry to the cafeteria left him almost crashing into the same table Phoebe had narrowly missed.

Phoebe. He had to save Phoebe. He *would* save Phoebe.

Closing his eyes, he summoned the image of Darnell. Enormous. Covered in gold chains. Generous. Loyal.

With a shimmer Sam would have sworn was just a play of light if he hadn't seen the evidence of Darnell's out-of-thin-air appearances before, Darnell was there. He gave Sam the thumbs-up sign, and they headed to the spot Sam had shown them on the new plans for the underground portion of O-tech Stinky had sent.

Letting Nina in was as easy as it had been the first time, and on silent feet, they were in.

That he'd missed this secret location all the while he'd worked here could only mean he was burnt out. He'd missed things the agency would have had his head for, and it had everything to do with his careless stupidity. While he had no choice but to reevaluate his future career plans due to his strange upgrade in life, now he really had to admit it would have been over anyway. A fuck-up of this magnitude would haunt him forever, and leave him at a desk job if he was lucky, at least until they found out they had a vampire FBI agent punching a keyboard.

Passing through doors, and forging up flights of stairs, Sam forced himself not to dwell via the martyr system while they located the elevator Phoebe had found. With but a silent look between the three of them, a look that screamed a million emotions, Nina pressed the button and stepped into the open doors as Sam and Darnell followed her.

All three of them watched the floors descend—somber—determined.

Into the belly of the beast.

Now Wanda was the one pacing as they texted Sam, Nina, and Darnell what Marty had told them. If nothing else, according to Marty while she was on her way out the door and headed for O-Tech, a bitch was goin' down tonight, and when she did, Marty wanted to be the one to put her down.

Phoebe shivered, going over the information Marty had shared in fits of spewing rage.

Someone would pay tonight.

Someone would bleed.

Someone would die.

And all Phoebe could see in her head was Sam and Penny. Nina. Darnell. The man who'd been so violated. Fear welled up in her throat, nearly choking her, gluing her feet to the floor, cementing her hands together. She should be with them. In the midst of this chaos, she should be helping create order.

Archibald placed a shawl around her shoulders, pulling her to him for a moment and whispering with fierce conviction, "I, too, shall see to Mistress Penny's well-being. Never you fear, Phoebe, for there will be an abundance of love. She will bake cookies with a manservant who has cooked for kings. She will learn the manners of a proper lady from a dutiful servant who has raised duchesses and dukes from wee seedlings. She will laugh in the sunshine—wear ribbons of the finest silk in her hair. She will walk in the park with me as her faithful caregiver. She *will* and more. And I shall never, ever let harm toward her ladyship come to pass."

Leaning back against Archibald, his weathered hands at her shoulders, she clung to them before letting her head drop to her chest. Her eyes drifted closed—and she pictured Penny with Archibald.

In the sunshine at the park with buttery shafts of golden light shimmering on her long, dark ponytail captured by a streaming, pink ribbon.

Laughing. Smiling. Loved.

With those vivid images of a Penny free from the confines of nurses and doctors in her head—Phoebe slipped away.

Like literally.

SAM shot a curt nod over his shoulder at Darnell and Nina when they hit the end of a long hallway, signaling them the coast was clear. If what Phoebe had said was fact rather than described from her heightened fear, they should be close to the room where they'd held the man. If she'd counted right, there were approximately five doctors and a big goon with a Russian name.

If . . .

Fuck. There were too many ifs.

But he didn't have a choice. It was now or never.

Slipping down the hallway, Sam rounded the corner with Nina and Darnell close, locating the double doors of the room Phoebe had described. He held up his hand for them to wait while he listened—assessing the situation.

The distant rumble of muted voices made Sam stick a finger in his ear and lean in. Yet, the harder he tried to get clarity on the words he knew he was hearing, the less he was able to makes sense of them. It was like listening to a conversation held underwater. What the hell?

Then something occurred to him. Something that wrenched his gut. His senses—his vampire senses—were beginning to fail him.

And so it began.

Nina's hand touched his back, making him whip around. Her

intense eyes connected with his in concern, but Sam just shook his head, cocking it to give another listen.

Though strangely warbled, Sam knew the tone of the voice he heard. Knew it as if he'd heard it all his life. As if his ears had been made to respond to that voice alone.

Phoebe.

They had Phoebe. In that room full of horrors she'd described so vividly to Wanda. It was all he could do not to gag.

Which meant someone's death was imminent. At his hands. And it would be so ugly. So ugly and painful.

PHOEBE popped her eyes open; grainy and hot, they scanned her surroundings while she fought a chronic throb in her head.

Hoo-boy. So this wasn't good. Not good at all. If Sam and Nina found out she was here—that she'd disobeyed their super orders, even if it had been a complete accident—she was probably worse off than if she ended up fireplace-kill.

She slammed her eyes shut, tightening the shawl Archibald had given her around her shoulders, ignoring the fact that she was actually feeling the cool chill of the room, and wished herself back to Sam's apartment.

Please, universe, if you have any mercy at all, get me back to Sam's because Nina's gonna kill me.

Opening her eyes again—she jammed a knuckle into her mouth. Her eyes flew to the door in fear. As though her parents were going to walk through it and catch her sneaking out of her bedroom window.

Except, there were much bigger worries than some lame parents and a good grounding lying just outside that door.

She had to get out before she was caught.

Yet, something shoved in the corner of the room caught her attention. The head of the poor man—the same man who'd been gutted like a market fish—poking out from beneath a white sheet on the same gurney he'd been on when she'd seen him earlier. Her hand instantly went to him; trembling, she pressed her fingers to his scarred neck. Deep sorrow tore at her, clawing, clinging to her every nerve ending. Goddamn these animals!

"No, no, noooo!" she almost screeched, the words slipping unbidden from her mouth before she was able to stop them. Phoebe choked, covering her mouth. "Oh, my God. I'm sorry," she cried into the still of the room. "I'm so, so sorry. I tried to get here in time. I swear . . ." She dry-hacked, pulling the sheet back up over his face, rambling words to console someone who could no longer hear her. "I'll find out who you are. I'll do whatever that takes. *I swear* I will. I'll make sure you're buried with the respect you deserve. But not before I hunt these motherfuckers down and rip them to shreds. In your honor, I promise you, they'll all die before I leave this earth. They'll die and it will hurt—so bad," she hissed out.

Footsteps caught her sensitive ears just as a rush of singeing heat attacked her flesh. How was she experiencing any kind of sensitivity after not having felt a thing since this began?

Phoebe winced, her eyes frantically searching for somewhere to hide until she could assess who was walking down that hallway. A closet . . . She remembered a closet where someone had hung their lab coat.

Her head whipped around to locate it and she made a mad dash for it, reaching for the handle and twisting the steel until she broke the lock on it to lunge herself inside.

Her eyes adjusted to the darkness of the interior of the closet with vampiric ease.

And that's when she saw Penny. On a gurney just like the one the man had been on.

She would rip these animals apart—shred their intestines, puncture their lungs with her own teeth—if a single hair on Penny's head was disturbed.

Knee-weakening relief attacked her legs when she saw the rise and fall of Penny's chest. She was asleep. Thank God, she was asleep.

Phoebe pulled Penny's limp hand to her cheek, scrunching her eyes shut and clinging to it. "Everything's okay, honey," she forced out. "If you can hear me, everything's fine because I'm here. I love you, Penny. *I love you.*" Tucking her sister's slender hand under the blanket, Phoebe actually prayed they'd sedated her for what was to come. She didn't want Penny to witness the brutal end she planned to dole out to these bastards.

The voices grew louder, as did the buzzing in her ears, and the endless pounding in her skull. Sparks of white-hot flames began to poke at her skin like molten embers from an open bonfire would if you stood too close.

She tamped down a cry of fear when a searing pain hit her square in the stomach. She bit the inside of her cheek to squelch a sob.

And she listened. Squirming in her own skin, she listened for the animals to file in.

Because when they did—she'd kill them all. She'd take every single asshole out in order to keep Penny away from these monsters.

"DUDE!" Nina whispered hot and fierce against Sam's ear. "What the fuck is wrong?"

Sam clasped his head, gritting his teeth—the buzzing had turned into a rapid-fire banging in his brain and a shooting pain attacking his chest almost disabled him. He couldn't think clearly for the pandemonium erupting in his body. "It's fine. Just listen," he ordered, grinding out the words. "Phoebe's in there. I hear Phoebe." If he had anything left in him when this was over, he was going to kill this woman who'd so captivated his heart.

Darnell nodded with a vigorous bounce of his head, his eyes screaming his worry, his voice low and chilling. "Yeah. Thass her a'ight. She talkin' to somebody. We need to get to gettin' here. Now!"

Nina's eyes burned with anger when she cocked her head to listen, too. Her fists wadded in clear fury. "I'm going to eat Bad Listening Skills Barbie for lunch, goddamn it!"

Sam ignored everything but getting to Phoebe. "We need to move!"

But as with all good plans—and in Sam's vast experience, sometimes a covert op was a lot like those horror movies you watched and the soap operas Phoebe had compared their situation to—you really did need someone to be your audience so they could scream, "Look behind you, you dumbass!" Especially when you did something stupid like forget to cover your back. *You're really slipping, Sammy* . . .

In flashes of white coats, muddy work boots, and the craziest most convoluted gun Sam had ever seen, they were caught and a warning was sounded.

"I wouldn't move, if I were you. I know *what* you all are, and with one spray of these guns, you'll be extinguished," a voice taunted from behind, gleeful and filled with hatred.

Someone slammed into each of them, dropping them to their knees with the sharp crack of bones when they hit the cement floor. Sam instantly clasped his hands behind his head, encouraging Nina and Darnell to follow suit with his urgent eyes.

His first concern was Nina and her mouth. He shot her a warning glance, and she flashed her murderous eyes at him but said nothing.

Large, callused hands grabbed at them, yanking them upward and forcing them to move toward the very room they'd planned to storm. Those bizarre guns pressed to their backs, the wide nozzle ends jammed close against each of them.

Darnell stumbled on the strings of his high-top shoelaces as he walked, his eyes vivid and hot with an emotion that was a stark contrast to the twinkle usually written in them.

Nina's jaw was tight—flexing and grinding as she so obviously fought the urge to control her rage. Sam couldn't help thinking how proud Wanda would be that Nina was showing such unbelievable restraint. Her anger was so thick, it seeped out into the air—it was palpable—nearly visible and wildly chaotic. And still, she remained silent.

In the name of Penny . . .

They were launched into the room with the double doors, skidding and sliding until they stopped short of the far wall.

Nina's nostrils flared, her eyes meeting Sam's as she directed him to the closet.

Fuck. Phoebe was in the closet. He could smell her perfume— the same pear-scented perfume he'd reveled in when they'd made love. If she could just stay put.

"Turn 'round!" someone gruff with poor diction roared.

As each of them turned to face their attackers, Nina was the first to react. In words. Those words that could cut you to the quick or simply cut out all the bullshit. "*You?* It's you?" She threw her head back and laughed, her mouth wide—the cackle was meant to mock, to debase. When her head lifted, her eyes gleamed just the right kind of crazy. "Oh, you motherfucking, spineless, ass-licking freak. You'd better hope whatever you got in that gun works, panty wipe. 'Cause if I get my hands on you, I'll rip your limbs off, and while I do? I'll pick my fucking teeth with your skinny-assed bones!" she screamed, straining against the hands Sam and Darnell had each placed on her arms.

The man who Nina had verbally assaulted swung the freakish gun Phoebe'd described wide and cracked Nina under the jaw with it.

Darnell growled, but he held his tongue while Sam's blurry eyes assessed. Two thugs plus the blond man. Clearly the brains of the outfit. Three guns total. Three guns with foreign ammunition he had no idea how to stop.

The gun pointed at them, glaring and white. "Oh, Nina," the doctor Phoebe had depicted so vividly admonished. "Still so *classy*. Tell me. Have you given up on the word *fucktard* and graduated to the big-girl name-calling?" He flapped a hand at her and smiled—charming, cold. "But that's neither here nor there, now is it? In fact, I encourage you to lob any and all protests. It makes for a much more invigorating kill."

Nina growled, making Sam latch on to her arm while a bone-jarring pain ripped through his arm and headed straight for his temples. He fought a grunt—fought it like if it were ripped from his throat, he'd explode into a million pieces. And still, the question remained. Who was this man? How did Nina know him?

The placid face of the blond doctor made Sam take great pause. This was the face of a madman. His expression was devoid of anything—even the joy he claimed he would take in killing them.

He was the worst kind of sociopath, if Sam was reading him correctly. If the classes at the agency he'd taken were proof, there'd be no reasoning—no deal making, no distracting.

The only hope they had left was the element of surprise from behind.

Fucked would probably be the best adjective Sam could give this scenario.

They were fucked. There was no one left—behind or otherwise.

IT wasn't just fear that tore at Phoebe—it was a shredding, screaming pain, crawling all over her body—upward until her scalp was on fire. Yet, she clung. Who was this man Nina clearly knew? How could she possibly keep them from pulling the triggers of those guns she knew they had trained on them. On Sam.

Her hands blindly grabbed at the interior walls of the closet; her fist went to her mouth to keep the howling scream from pushing its way out of her throat at bay.

Realization crashed around her. This was it. What was happening to her right now was what had happened to Meredith and Alice and Raymond Schaeffer.

But it was going to happen before she got Penny to safety.

No. No. It would not. By all that was holy, she would stop this. Think, Phoebe—think. Surely there's a soap opera scenario you can call on.

Think, damn you. What would the great Leticia Halloway from *Eagle's Crest* do?

"So I guess you want to know who I am and what I've been up to?" the blond man asked. "I'd only consider that a fair request. After all, I will be the one to help you meet and greet with your maker. Clearly, you should have a name to grudge on. Nina and I know each other, er, socially," he said with clear disdain. "But we'll get to that later. So for now, shut up. Got that?" He winked at her.

Nina grunted, but Darnell held her fast, pulling her to his padded side.

Nina knew him? All this time and it was someone the women of OOPS knew?

He ran the tip of his finger along the top of the gun with a sensuous pass, like it was his lover. "First, the why, and I'll be brief. Not long ago, maybe four years or so, my world fell apart. I blame one person, and one person alone. That person will, along with all of you, die a heinous death. Much like the ones I've already doled out to that CIA agent Meredith, who was foolish enough to think she could stop me and save my test subjects."

He spread his arms wide, the crinkle of his lab coat shredding Sam's eardrums. "This is Project Eternal. A project that was four years in the making. Four years of hatred for one woman who took everything from me. Now, some would call me diabolical or crazy— whichever adjective most makes you comfortable. I just call me awesome sauce. But I can't take all the credit. I didn't do this alone. I had help from someone who almost hates this person as much as I do. Almost. Though, she only lost some silly man over what happened. But a grudge is a grudge—no matter the source. Some of us seek retribution out of scorn—and others, others like me? They seek it out of *revenge*."

Sam knew better—he knew not to react—but again, it was that damn woman in the closet who kept him from keeping his highly trained mouth shut. "I know the drama of this is what you've been living for—but could we get to the point? I have a helluva headache. And, yeah, yeah. You're the genius responsible for that. I'd tip my hat to you, but I think my arm might fall off if I lift it."

The blond man smiled. "I like you, Sam the Cowboy, is it? That's how Phoebe has you listed on her phone. Very manly hat, by the way. Tell me, Sam, how did this happen to you? I'm all sorts of intrigued." He swept a hand up and down Sam's length. "And don't bother to deny you're one of my maniacal creations. I can smell it."

Smell it . . . no. Sweet Jesus, no. Sam warred with his disgust when he gave a subtle flare of his nostrils. "A woman—beautiful, so beautiful. She bit me at a Halloween party."

"Gorgeous dark hair and the most vivid eyes anyone's ever seen?"

Sam nodded, short and quick, because when he moved his head, it felt like it would explode. "That was her."

"I can see how her beauty would have captivated you. That was Meredith the CIA agent."

"Wow. CIA agents come hotter than Hades these days, huh?" Sam joked.

His face went on instant alert. He flashed the gun at them. "Smokin' hot," he agreed with a cold chuckle. "At least that's what her handler thought."

Sam forced his face, a face that was bleeding fire by now, to go blank. "Her what?"

He nodded his perfectly coifed head. "So, she bit you? How brilliant. That had to have been the rabid stage of the serum. It happens fast, as you'll soon see. She was really quite something, this Meredith. A neurologist—brilliant. In fact, she contacted me. She really had me believing she was just a poor little rich doctor who traveled in elite circles unavailable to most—which was how she claimed to know of my inquiries. The tales she told about hanging on to all that beauty were quite impassioned. Damned determined to bring us down, and she came close. I can't tell you the luck I've had—it's like the fates are on my side. I happened to catch her here one night, quite by chance, and from behind. As you're aware, that's always the best way to sneak up on would-be assailants. Anyway, I double-dosed her. You know, to be sure her demise would be quicker than the average life span of a test subject. Then I took her phone, and her handler and I, one I'm almost sure she was in love with, have been sharing the most delightful texts back and forth. Her demise came much more quickly than the last two subjects. On the off chance you were wondering why you haven't met your fate *yet*."

Sam gritted his teeth. Damn. At this point, he'd have even settled for some CIA love showing up—clearly, that wasn't going to happen now.

Moving closer to Sam, he asked, "I know from Phoebe's phone contacts that she's Nina's sister—one I presume Nina didn't know about. Or if she did, she certainly didn't share the information with anyone. But how did you and Phoebe find each other, Sam? How did she end up just like you, Nina? I know the connection lies with the lovely Phoebe—who looks just like the beautiful but foulmouthed Nina, but I don't understand the connection? Expound. *Please*."

"For the love of fucking Christ. You, too? I do not look like her, freak," Nina seethed.

Sam jumped in—desperately trying to get a handle on the shooting pain invading his body in ugly waves and keep Nina from inciting their captor. "I turned her."

He looked aghast, his blue eyes dancing. "Purposely? Surely your aggression couldn't have begun so quickly? It usually doesn't happen until just prior to death. Have you been having fits of aggression, Sam? Could this be a new strain?" For a moment, the cool facade faded, as though he were worried every precaution hadn't been taken before he utilized his madness.

Sam didn't want to reassure him everything was going to be just fine, but if he kept him talking . . . "It was an accident. Your evil genius remains firmly intact."

His face couldn't hide his overwhelming relief. "Good to know. And shall we talk about irony? How circle of life is it that Phoebe happened to be a candidate for my Alzheimer's trial and she ended up being involved with all of you, Nina? It's like the gods handed me all of you in one fell swoop!"

Darnell finally spoke, and when he did, it rasped from between his lips like it was torn from them. "God's gonna hand you somethin', brotha, and it ain't gonna be a key to heaven's gate."

The man's head whipped around, staring up at Darnell, he eyed him closely, pressing his gun to his chest. "What are you, anyway? I can't pinpoint it."

Darnell's eyebrow rose when he stooped to the man's height. "Yo worst nightmare, little man. Yo worst evah."

He scoffed at Darnell. "I think my nightmare beats your nightmare," he said on a chuckle. "Anyway, the point, right? We need to have one so you can all have whatever therapists call it."

"Closure," Sam fairly spat, his eyes drifting above the man's head to the door that had opened but an inch.

Phoebe . . . He sent her a harsh signal with his eyes. However, Phoebe being Phoebe, she ignored it as her fingers clung to the edge of the door. Fingers that, if he was seeing correctly past the knife in his head, had tips that were turning gray.

"Yes! That's the word. Closure. So here's the short of it. After my world fell apart due to this *woman*, I decided if I couldn't beat them, I'd join them. So I learned a great deal about the paranormal. I studied. I watched. I played nice with everyone. So nice, I think I earned my place in the dictionary right under the word. While I studied, I learned of a folktale. One even the paranormal world thought was an urban legend. A formula to create vampires written by some pathetic scientist who sought to find a way to bring his wife back from the dead."

This was similar to the story Archibald and Dmitri had relayed. It was true. Jesus.

"What people didn't know was this formula wasn't just some legend, it was real. Imagine my joy. Through my various filthy-rich connections, I managed to locate it. I didn't do it without help, but I found it. In, of all places, an antique store. The word was, this formula was in a false bottom of the scientist's wife's jewelry box. One he'd given her just before she died of some disease that no longer exists. Lo and behold, it took a couple of years, but I bought it for a song while I laughed in the faces of those who mocked my sheer determination."

Nina shifted on her feet, prompting the two goons to raise their guns. "Seriously, dude. All this drama just to what? Make fucking vampires? You could have just come to me, shit ball. I'd have bitten your chicken neck for free, *freak*."

He took the barrel of the large gun and lifted Nina's chin with it, making her fangs flash. "Now you know that would never do, Nina. You, in all your angry rage, would have drained me. And everyone else in your strange little community? They shun me because of what that bitch did to me. I'm always the last one chosen for paranormal dodgeball. It hurts, you know. And why would I turn to one of you? You and all of your 'We Are the World'–like clan rules. I don't want to have to follow your strict guidelines for the undead or pack laws or whatever else you've all concocted, so I'm forced to blend with society. I've never been very good at blending. I stink at hand-holding and songs like 'Kumbaya.' I want to create my own society. Now you know what that means, don't you?" He paused dramatically, waiting.

"I know! I know!" Sam chanted, unable to stop the flow of words shooting from his mouth. It helped keep the searing agony from eating him alive while he kept an eye on that door Phoebe kept opening in painfully slow increments. "You're going to wipe out the vampire population with your fancy spray guns, right? That means you've found a way to not only create vampires but kill them, too. In a way that's sort of a mass killing instead of risking your neck trying to take them out one by one. Damn, buddy. That's actually kind of cool. So much *Fringe*, it hurts." He tapped his chest with a finger that had turned a dark gray.

He cocked his chin over his shoulder. His smile was cock-tease-ish. "Sam—you're brilliant. Really. I've found a way to not just eliminate vampires, but the paranormal world at large. If I wanted to eliminate only vampires, I'd just spray holy water, silly. No, Sam, the woman who did this to me isn't a vampire at all."

The woman who'd done this to him . . . Who was this woman if it wasn't Nina?

"Anyway, I'm so glad you came to me and I didn't have to come get you. That was next on my plate, and it was a task I was dreading. But Phoebe's phone gave me everything I needed to know, including her sweet sister Penny's location. I guess if Phoebe's your sister, Nina, then Penny's yours, too. God. You're all just like that bitch that forced my hand. Trailer park dwellers—the lot of them—even that Wanda who pretends to be classy but is really just a whore. The world will be a better place without the likes of you."

Nina growled with a high-keening screech that left Sam's brain on fire, making a lunge for him, but Darnell dragged her back, wrapping his wide hands around her waist while her feet dangled. "I swear to you, you fuck, if you hurt her, I'll eat your balls off all the way from the afterlife!" she howled, the pain of Penny's captivity deeply ingrained on her face.

The man cracked Nina in the jaw with the gun again—hard, making her head crash back against the wall. "No. I rather think you won't do that. You won't have the chance. One drop of my version of Paranormal-Out, and you're a goner, Nina. All of you are."

Talk, Sam. Talk. It doesn't matter what you think you know about the complexities of a subject's personality. It doesn't matter what you think you've read just from observing them. Talk. All sociopaths love to have their work validated.

Validate—fast while Phoebe sneaks up behind them.

Leaning back against the wall, Sam fought the wild jolts of electricity pounding into him and asked, "So you didn't just create a vampire. You created a super vampire. Stronger than the vampires already in existence, right? Again, I gotta give it to you. You're pretty smart."

He nodded his blond head. "It was incredible, really. I'd never seen anything like it until I watched it actually happen. My creations are stronger, faster—"

"And they can walk through walls," Sam cut him off. "Ask me, I know. It's like every fifth grader's fantasy."

"You flatter me, Sam," he preened. "That was in the early stages of the project. Raymond could walk through walls, and Alice, wow, Alice. If only she'd lived to reach her potential. Not only could she walk through walls, but she could teleport herself just like Phoebe. Fascinating."

Sam bit back a howl of pain, his neck muscles straining from the effort. "So why did you pick these people? Any special requirements? I mean—do they have some sort of rare gene. Are they all geniuses?" he inquired.

"Geniuses? Hah. No, Sam. Not one genius in the lot but Meredith, who as you know, was a plant. I picked them with one criteria in mind—no one would care if they were dead. No one important, anyway. Also, because I'm just that kind of guy, I chose test subjects who were doomed anyway. Destined to die of one thing or another. Phoebe was a ridiculous, impetuous mistake, and I told Philip that— you know, just the second before I killed him. We'd already taken one of his patients, Alice, as it was. Two missing from his office was just a little too coinkydink, don't you agree?"

Sam nodded—each movement a special hell. "He sure didn't think that through, did he?"

"Ah, what can you do, though? Philip was overly excited and leaned toward impulsive to begin with. Yet, he was brilliant and he had scads of money. So I let it slide. There wasn't anything I could do about something that was already done by the time I arrived here and found Phoebe. Anyway, I wanted semihealthy candidates. Though, I do admit to stooping to the scourge of society with him over there." He waved the ridiculous gun at the gurney in the corner. "He was homeless, and so irritating. He begged for money every day by the coffee shop I frequent. Everyone was always feeling sorry for him—he made more money than if he'd bothered to get a job, for heaven's sake. Lazy! I can't abide the lazy." It was the most animated Sam had seen him since he'd caught them all. The meaning behind that was simple—he was a sociopath who, rather than tolerate a pet peeve, would simply eliminate the pet peeve.

Keep him talking, Sammy. "So, I suppose you've perfected this thing so well, you can reverse the effects of the decomposition? Like an antidote or something? I'm just curious. You don't have to tell me, if you don't want to. But really, who am I going to tell? I watch a lot of TV. I mean, a lot. Love detective shows. Hope they have them wherever I'm going when you end my misery. All those detective shows always have one. Sort of a twelfth-hour save." *Please, Jesus. Let there be an antidote.*

"Oh, definitely," he said on an easy smile. "I definitely have an antidote. If Meredith hadn't helped Raymond, our first test subject, escape, I would have injected him with it. Naturally, that would have been after we gathered the initial injection's test results. He would have been eliminated, no doubt, but only after we'd perfected the serum. Alice was our second victim. She had the misfortune of turning up in the wrong place at the wrong time. She never made it past the first phase after the injection because Meredith went all CIA on us and tried to rescue her. She was rather caught in the cross fire and ended her journey much sooner than we'd planned. But this man over here in the corner. The one Phoebe witnessed— he was who we finally got it right with." Kissing the fingers of his hand, he cooed. "Perfection. We turned him and just as decomposition began, we brought him back. That's when we knew we were good to go. It's also when I took out everyone else involved with the project. No fuss. No muss."

Which explained why Alice's body had been in an O-Tech lab . . . "Well, I'll die much happier knowing you'll be right as rain. I mean, if things were to suddenly go all *awry*. Not that they would. You have us pretty well cornered. But just in case," Sam said on a smile that made his face feel like it would split apart.

The blond man's eyebrow cocked. He pursed his lips. "Is this the point in our story where you've given me a hint, and I should pay closer attention, but I'm so egomaniacally wrapped up in the retelling of my coup, I don't catch on?"

"Oh, you bet your fucking life it is, Terrence Bradford Douglas— it—most—definitely—is, *brother* mine!" a female voice screamed from the doorway.

That's when it hit Sam.

TBD.

The initials Meredith had put on that memo pad. Sam fought the war his skull and his brain were having to piece together memories of a conversation he'd had with Marty just after he'd been turned. She'd said that during the chaos of her turning werewolf, someone had kidnapped her and tried to kill her. That someone had been her half brother. A half brother who wanted her dead because she was part heir to Bobby-Sue Cosmetics.

Marty was the woman in this maniac's equation?

CHAPTER 19

Marty screamed the words from the open doorway, leaping across the room in a flash of trendy boots and knit-sweater dress, landing on this Terrence's back with a wild cry while Archibald pushed his way into the room in front of Wanda and Darnell. He began to scatter gunfire from, of all things, a machine gun, covering their paths. The two men dropped like flies, blood spattering in rich drops of crimson.

Marty clawed at Terrence, pulling his head back and driving her fist into his face. "You worthless piece of shit. I'll kill you!" she keened, her eyes wild with anger.

Once more, as in the movies, just when you thought it was safe—all hell was destined to break loose, and it was always when you were at your absolute shittiest.

Someone, somewhere was screaming, "Grab the gun, you fucking idiot!" over some buttered popcorn and a double gulp Pepsi.

Sam stumbled as two more men appeared in the doorway and Archibald opened fire. Yet, the bullets he sprayed like he was coating a pan with a nonstick aerosol bounced off them. They were strong and they were vampire, if the way they lifted Darnell off his feet was any indication.

That was when they flew at Archibald—three of them. Sam didn't have time to reach for one of the scattered guns—he couldn't see them, but he launched himself across the room at them, knocking Archibald's elderly body into a wall and out of their way.

Wanda was the first to grab at the pile on, her face hot with red anger. Her hands were balled fists. She latched on to one of the goon's shirts and lifted him off the floor, hurling him across the room with such ferocity cement from the walls scattered, spraying hard debris.

Nina was right behind her, grabbing two of them at once, running with their bodies clenched in her grip and jamming them hard against the wall with a warrior cry.

Darnell looped his arm around Sam's waist and threw him upward to a standing position while the hot pain assaulted him, driving him to grit his teeth. "We have to find the antidote! Find the antidote! Get it to Phoebe!" he roared over the loud crash of yet another thug Wanda couldn't keep down smashing to the floor.

They were like Whack-A-Moles. The moment they were down, they were back up again. "Vampires!" Sam bellowed in a hoarse rasp. "They're all vampires!"

A cluster fuck of vampires, he thought while, head down, he ran for Phoebe, who was dragging herself across the cement floor.

Leaving clumps of her hair behind in a trail of auburn streaks.

IF she could just get to the fancy gun. *Get to the gun, Phoebe.* Open fire on these shitheads just like when Larissa Corleon Monaco wiped out all the bad guys after they took everyone hostage in the hospital on the short-lived *Manhattan.*

Of course, Larissa, at least not that she could remember, hadn't been losing pieces of her flesh when she'd sprayed the terrorists who were trying to get to the vicious mob boss, Marco Anthony Botti, with her mega-gun.

Falling to the floor from the stinging, debilitating pain, she reached outward, the tips of her fingers blackening as she clawed the floor. Each scrape of the cement tore at her falling flesh. Each inch she moved ripped at her skin, making her bite back screams.

Get the gun, Phoebe. Get the fucking gun.

Her hands touched the cool white enamel of one; latching on, Phoebe dragged it to her—each inch it moved, a slow agony—each tendon in her hands and arms ripping and tearing.

Kill the bad guys, Phoebe. Kill the bad guys before they hurt Penny.

The mantra replayed in her head as she dragged herself across the floor, managing to lift her knees and press into the wall for leverage. She rose on legs that were a hundred years old judging by the heavy, wobbly feel of them, then lifted the gun with arms that aged before her eyes. Phoebe pulled the lever and aimed with fingers that felt like they were in the flames of a roaring fire.

And she screamed—screamed with her last bit of energy. "Get out of the way, Nina!"

Kill the bad guys, her brain screamed when she took out the first goon who had Nina by the neck. His wailing, high-pitched scream cut through her ears like a knife. But it was over in an instant when he crumbled to the ground in a smoky pile of flesh.

Kill the bad guys roared in her head when she aimed it at the shit stain who was grabbing Archibald by the arms.

But she was losing her grip when she set her sights on this man Terrence. A man Marty and Nina knew. The gun fell to the floor in a clatter just as Terrence threw Marty into the far wall. Her scream wasn't of pain, though. Phoebe knew it was born of rage.

Sliding along the wall, her eyes caught on Marty, who'd once more gone for Terrence with a werewolf howl so piercing Phoebe winced.

Marty's body drove into his with such force he fell to the ground.

Then she was on him, screaming, "You sick, sick bastard! Tonight, you die, motherfucker!" Spit flew from her mouth, her eyes were wild with rage when she grabbed onto his lab coat and smacked his body down against the floor.

But Terrence was stronger, if what Phoebe had heard was right, and he easily flung Marty from him, knocking her into the cement wall.

"He's vampire, Marty! The motherfucker turned himself!" Nina screeched, fighting off the two remaining animals to claw her way to her friend, who had hit her head so hard she was slumped against the wall.

"Phoebe!"

Sam—it was Sam. She'd smile, but her teeth falling out was probably next, and the last thing she wanted someone to remember when she was on her deathbed was a toothless Phoebe. Chic even in death, baby.

Sam pulled her to him, his right hand black and beginning to crumble. "Hold on, Phoebe! Hold on!" he bellowed, the deep grooves in his handsome face chipping away. "Don't you dare do this to me, Phoebe—suck it up, Barbie. Don't you dare leave this world before we read the Sunday paper together!"

No sooner were the words spoken than Terrence rushed Sam, latching on to his back and hauling him off Phoebe, his eyes alight with his newfound strength.

He picked up the gun and aimed it at Phoebe, the smile on his face serene.

Out of nowhere, and where he'd found the strength, Phoebe would never know, Sam blindsided Terrence, smashing into him and taking him down with a roar.

Pain made Phoebe rear up, her back arching while the black tendrils of scorching heat ate at her. Nina scooped her up off the floor, pulling her close when she caught sight of a woman entering the closet where Penny was. No. No. No!

She clung to Nina's neck, fighting back the scream her throat wanted to open up and roar from the sheer agony. "Pennyyyy!" she howled. "Leave me, Nina. Leaave meeee! Get Penny! Closet—she's in the closet!" The words she bleated from her lips sounded like someone else, and in her haze of agony, as her body began to fail, she had but one thought.

Save Penny.

SAM landed one good right hook to Terrence's face, so sharp and quick, his trainer would have smiled. But Terrence was stronger at this stage of the game of Sam's decomposition.

Until Darnell grabbed the scruff of Terrence's neck with one hand and pointed the vampire ray gun at his face with the other. "Who's yo nightmare, now, brotha?" Throwing Terrence down on the ground, Darnell cornered him, pressing the gun to his sharp jaw.

"Antidote," Sam rasped from a parched, inflamed throat. "Get the antidote!"

Marty came up from Darnell's rear and pushed him out of the way. "Give it to me, Terrence, or I'll have him kill you! Do you hear me, you whiny piece of shit? I'll watch you squirm your way to the grave and laugh while I do the Riverdance at your pathetic funeral." She reached down and grabbed either side of his lab coat, dragging him upward until their noses touched. "Give it to me, brother—or I'll gnaw your little testicles off right here!"

Terrence's eyes, glazed with anger, searched Marty's. "You should have just gone away, you whore! I despise you and your filthy spawn! I despise you for sitting across the table from me at *my* father's house. I despise you! If I could have gotten my hands on your disgusting, screaming toddler, she would have been my first guinea pig!"

Marty slapped Terrence so hard the muscles in his neck cracked, echoing in the room. "You speak her name—breathe her existence—and I'll choke you with your own needle dick!"

"Marty!" Nina screamed from the other side of the room. "Get the fucking serum now!"

Marty shook Terrence hard, rattling his fangs. "You've got two seconds to give it up, Terrence, or I'll give Darnell the word!"

"Miss Marty!" Archibald yelled from across the room amidst the debris of vials. "I think I've found it!"

Sam willed his body to cooperate; arm after decomposing arm, he fought his way across the floor, his hair falling along the way in black chunks, his flesh protesting, burning, disintegrating. He had to get to Terrence. He had to make him give them the antidote.

Wanda screamed across the floor in a clack of heels, her hand clasped around a vial. She kicked Terrence from Marty's grasp and fell to her knees in front of him. "Is this it, sissy-man? Is this it, Terrence? So help me God, if you don't give me the right serum, I'll cut your head off myself and play a game of kickball with it!"

Screams. All Sam could hear was Phoebe's screams. He had to get to her. Had to tell her . . .

Terrence smiled up at Wanda, eerie—blank—devoid of even the thrill of the kill. "Oh, that's it, all right. But there's only enough serum for *one* person. So choose, bitches! Choose between them!"

"Phoebe!" Sam screamed, long and dry, the crackle of his voice ugly in his ears. His fangs ached, pushing outward, making communication almost impossible. "Give it to Phoebe!" Her ear-piercing screams tore at him—worse than the demons inside him ever could. "Phoebe," he panted, clasping Darnell's ankle as the last of his fingers began to crumble. "Get it to Phoebe . . . Penny. *Penny needs her . . .*"

NINA clung to her shoulders, rocking her, crooning in her ear. "Hang on, Phoebe! Just hang on! Don't you dare fucking leave this earth before you have the chance to make me fucking shop with you!"

Her body bucked against Nina's, writhing with the pain. She tried to free herself, but Nina held fast. "I'm sorry. I'm sorry I didn't know about you. Jesus Christ, Phoebe. I'm sorry. Just hang on. Hang the fuck on!"

That was all she needed. The last bit of acceptance from Nina. "Penny . . ." she wailed, clawing at Nina's hoodie, her eyes sightless for the torture. "Take care of Pennyyyy . . . Save Sam. Please, Ninaaa—save him, too . . ."

The burning. Oh, God in heaven, the burning—it streaked across her skin in hot colors, in blazing white ribbons of electricity.

Please, she prayed with her last coherent thought. *Please, let it end soon.*

"Nina! Hit the closet and get the bitch who's got Penny!" Wanda ordered with a frantic demand. She took Phoebe from Nina's arms, pulling her close to her chest. "I'm here, honey. I'm here. I'll make it better," she cooed against the top of Phoebe's head. "Hold her down, Marty! For fuck sake, keep her still!"

Phoebe struggled against Wanda's tight grip, hearing their words but fighting against them anyway. It burned. It burned so much she wanted to crawl out of her skin.

"Phoebe, listen to me! Open your mouth—open it, damn you!" Someone pinched her cheeks, forcing her mouth open and letting out what she prayed would be her last scream before it was over.

The taste on her tongue was cool and thick. A balm in the burning mass of blisters her mouth had become. "Phoebe, listen. Listen to me," Marty cooed, dragging her hands over Phoebe's face, soothing her. "Let it happen, honey. Please, stop struggling. It's okay now. Shhhh. Nina has Penny, and it's okay."

The pain screeching along her body skidded to a halt and entirely evaporated. Just like that, Phoebe sat up with a shot, narrowly missing Marty's head. "Penny! Where's Penny?"

"Got her!" Nina yelled from somewhere sight unseen.

"Ladies! Sam! We got ta help Sam!" Darnell bellowed from the opposite end of the room where she could clearly see he held one of those guns to Terrence's head.

Pushing past Nina and Marty, Phoebe rocketed across the room to where Sam lay. He writhed, and Phoebe fought a scream, for she knew his pain well. Brushing her hair from her eyes, she dropped down beside him, wrapping him in her arms. No. Please. Not this way. "Oh, God, Sam! Darnell—get the antidote!"

"There is no more, you stupid bitch!" Terrence cackled from his place on the floor next to Sam.

It was all it took for Phoebe to let Sam go and fall on Terrence. She yanked him upward by the hair. "Make more, you slimy fuck!" she screamed so loud it hurt even her ears. The demand tore at her throat, ripping from it with force.

His eyes gleamed the venom that had eaten him from the inside out for all these years. "There's no time. He's going to die, you whore! He'll die like the rest of them!"

From the corner of her eye, Phoebe caught Terrence's slender, pale fingers reaching behind him while Sam shook, crumbling before them.

Her eyes caught a flash of white, registering a stray gun lost in the scuffle. His speed was such that she only had time to scream, "Shoot, Darnell! Shoot the motherfucker!" before ducking for cover and pushing Sam out of the way as a loud splash gushed from the gun's barrel.

Terrence's wails mixed with Sam's—high and howling. The anguish in both their wails spurred Phoebe toward Sam.

She crawled to him, pushing Wanda from him, pulling him into her arms, making a split-second decision. He'd given her the last of the antidote. He'd given his life to save hers, and she'd do whatever it took to save his.

She had nothing to lose. Healthy vampire plus not-in-such-good-shape vampire could equal diluted but upright vampire, right?

She pulled him to her, tearing at her shirt and revealing the one spot on her neck where her blood had once pulsed. Without thought for what it could mean, without concern for anything other than saving Sam, she yelled at him, "Bite me, Sam! Do it now!" Phoebe cupped his head, yanking it back by clutching his hair, and placed her neck against his protruding fangs.

Sam twisted, arching upward when she drove his fangs into her neck, his muscles straining and flexing—pushing at her, pulling into her, fighting against her until he stilled and lay against her breast in a lump.

The sting of Sam's bite was a million things at once. Hot bliss, agonizingly sweet, but sharp and painful, and she fought to keep her balance.

Yet, Sam lay so still. "Sam!" Phoebe cried, giving him a hard shake. "Don't you dare do this to me after all this, you shit. You didn't even say good-bye to me, you—you stupid, prideful man. I can't get to know FBI Sam if he's dead. So don't be dead. Please, please, please don't be dead," she begged on a dry sob, scrunching her eyes shut to ward off tears that would never fall.

Then Wanda was kneeling beside her, rubbing her shoulders, resting her chin on Phoebe's head. Marty, too. Both of them silent— silent because they didn't want to speak the unspeakable.

Nina fell to her knees beside them. She wrapped her arms around her sister, pressing her forehead to Phoebe's back, rocking her. "Stop, Phoebe. Stop now. *Please,*" she whispered hoarsely.

"I don't know what you did, but I reiterate my original vampire concerns. If it involves choosing teams or sparkling in the sunlight, I would have preferred death," a muffled voice said.

Nina fell against Phoebe in clear relief. She reached around Phoebe and tugged a lock of Sam's hair. "Swear to Christ, dude—no sparkling."

Wanda hiccupped, swiping a thumb across her cheek with a watery smile. "Not funny, Sam McLean."

Phoebe looked down into Sam's face. Whole, pale, without a single scratch on it. She bracketed it with both hands. "You gave me the last of the antidote. You saved me," she whispered, pressing her lips to his. "You're like the wolver to my rine. The bat in my man. The Alejandro to my Constance."

"I don't know who Alejandro is, but I'm going to be the pin in your bubble," Sam snarled, pushing his way out of her embrace and sitting up. He cupped her cheek, fingering the tendrils of her mussed hair. "I told you to stay put, Phoebe. What the hell were you doing here?"

Her hand wrapped around his wrist with a chuckle. "It was an accident. Swear it. I was pacing and worrying about you and Penny and the others, and bam——"

But sharp screams stopped Phoebe from further explanation. Everyone turned their heads.

Nina rose first, brushing her hands on her dirty, blood-spattered jeans. "Shut the fuck up, whiner, or I'll give Arch the signal!" she yelled in the direction of the closet. She answered the question on everyone's faces. "The other half of this dynamic duo. Arch has her at gunpoint."

"Who?" Phoebe asked, rising with Sam's help. "Who are these people?"

He pulled her tight to him, holding her close, the strength of his embrace making her smile. "Long, long story. But Terrence is Marty's half brother."

Phoebe gasped against his chest. "In all the commotion, I wasn't sure I heard Marty right. So he's the brother who tried to kill her back when she was turned into a werewolf in the first place?"

Marty chuckled, straightening her dress. "The one and only. The woman is Alana—a jealous pathetic clinger who once thought my husband should have been hers. She was in on my kidnapping the first time, too. Yet, still, she hasn't learned, I'll always be the badder bitch."

Penny. She was in the closet with Penny. Forgetting everything, Phoebe strained against Sam. "Penny!"

Nina held up a hand and crossed the room, popping open the closet door to reveal Archibald holding the most beautiful blond woman Phoebe had ever seen at gunpoint. She snatched the woman up under one arm, and gingerly lifted a sleeping Penny, limp and still unaware, across the other.

Archibald rushed in to take Penny from Nina, pointing to her wheelchair for Nina to set her in. He placed a blanket over Penny's lap, cradling her head with his hand. "I'll take her, miss. You"—he eyeballed the blond—"make sure this guttersnipe never sees the light of day."

"Oh, look. It's Hooters Gone Wild. You were in on this with Terrence, too?" Marty sneered, circling the woman Nina slammed to the ground like she was a sack of potatoes. "Everyone? This is Alana. Alana? Meet everyone who wants you dead."

"I bought the goddamn jewelry box, you twit! That formula is mine!" she cried, rearing upward, her lithe body long and lush. "Whatever it takes to get rid of you so Keegan will come back to me—where he belongs!"

Marty crossed her arms over her chest, staring down at the woman. "I should have known, you jealous bitch. Jesus. How many times do you have to lose to me before you remember you're pathetic? Isn't it like a slap in the face every time?"

"She's gotta go, Marty," Nina said with deadly calm, leaving Phoebe shivering against Sam.

"Leave her to me," a booming voice sounded. A handsome man, tall and wide, stopped just short of this woman Alana's sobbing form. "I'm Keegan Flaherty. Marty's husband. Pleasure. I'm sure we'll have more in-depth conversations at some point now that you're part of the ever-growing fold. Until then, I have business to take care of."

Marty's face went from infuriated to beaming in a split second. "Hi, honey! Thanks for coming. As you can see, we have a problem. Honest to God, never in a million did I believe that jewelry box story Helga told us was true."

Keegan smiled at her with blatant love written all over his tanned face. "Leave it to you to actually listen when it involves the word *jewelry*."

Marty ran a loving hand over Keegan's forehead, ruffling his hair. "Okay, off with you. Give your wife a kiss, and please, this time, throw the pack book at her, huh?"

Dropping a kiss on his wife's lips, he smiled down at her. "You sure you got this?"

Marty rolled her blue eyes. "Of course, silly. Shoo. See you at home later. Tell Hollis I'll come in to kiss her good night."

Keegan nodded his dark head. "I'm out," he said before stooping and grabbing Alana's arm. Throwing her over his shoulder while she screamed her rage, he nonchalantly sauntered through the door.

Darnell clapped Sam on the back and chucked Phoebe under the chin. "So thass all she wrote, folks. I'm all for gettin' on outta here now, if y'all don't mind. Don't like the killin' t'all." His huge brown eyes held sorrow—remorse for what had to be.

Nina's eyes gleamed, mirroring Wanda's. "You guys go. We'll handle this shit."

Phoebe looked to Sam in confusion.

He pressed another kiss to her lips. "The evidence, honey. We have to be sure no one gets their hands on the formula—and clean up the mess." His eyes went to the man in the corner of the room, his gurney haphazardly smashed against a file cabinet.

"You go, too, Sammy. You had one shitty night. You both need to feed and rest. Go. Go fast before I hand you a broom and a dustpan," Nina teased.

Phoebe grabbed Nina's hand, her chest tight with gratitude. "Nina—"

"Don't even, Sentimental Barbie. I don't do sappy, teary bullshit. It's over. Now get the fuck out before you start with the crap about how I like you. Because I don't." Yet her harsh words were tempered with a smile. One that was genuine. Honest.

Phoebe stuck her tongue out at her. "Do so. I heard you, Nina, when . . . when I was—"

"Spewing body parts all over the floor?" Nina joked on a snicker.

Phoebe nodded, smiling. "And I'm never going to forget it. Never." She gave a strand of Nina's hair, covered in dust and debris, a tug. *"Never."*

She pinched Phoebe's cheek. "Yeah, yeah. Now get out. You two have some shit to talk about. Hoo-boy, do you have some shit to talk about."

Wanda gave a hesitant look to Nina, then ran a finger across her throat. "Not now, bloodsucker."

Sam gave them each a worried glance. "Talk about?"

Nina gave him a hard punch to his arm. "If I was you, Sammy, I'd fight for the right to pick out the china. You should have at least one fucking thing that's all yours and yours alone."

Marty flicked a finger at Nina. "Shut up, Mouthy McMouth."

Nina flipped Marty the bird. "Fuck you, Marty. They're gonna find out anyway. Might as well be now."

"Find out what?" Phoebe asked.

Nina clucked her tongue. "First—way to problem solve under so much fucking pressure, kiddo. Having Sam bite you was genius. I just wish we'd considered that as an alternative when that lady Meredith and Raymond were kicking the bucket. Second, you know that genius problem-solving thing you did to save Sam?"

Phoebe tilted her head. "You mean let him bite me?"

"Yeahhhh," Nina crowed. "Know what that means in the world of vampire?"

"Is this the equivalent of me giving her my letter jacket?" Sam asked, his eyebrow raised.

"No, dummy. It's the equivalent of you giving her your balls. You two"—Nina pointed at them—"are officially mated—for life. So go celebrate. But hurry the fuck up and get it over with before I get back. I'm goddamn tired, and the last thing I wanna hear is the two of you screaming 'Give it to me, baby' while I fucking get some shut-eye."

And then she cackled in true Nina form.

*   *   *

Phoebe curled against Sam on his bed. Okay, it wasn't his bed. It was the FBI's, but for now it would do. Her stretch was content—sated. Penny was sleeping peacefully at Highland Hills, where no one even knew she'd been gone, while Darnell hovered over her like a mother hen, with strict instructions from Archibald to keep her safe until he was there to orchestrate her discharge.

Nina, Marty, Wanda, and Darnell had all returned safely from O-Tech after cleaning up and taking the man, who'd turned out to be homeless, to a place where he'd be given a proper burial with the respect he was due for his suffering.

Greg, Nina's mate, had taken on the task of making sure every last piece of evidence, every last traceable bit of the formula, and anything relating to Terrence's madness was destroyed. But he'd only done that after meeting Phoebe and giving Nina the kind of hell that left her mumbling words about divorce by rope of garlic beating and big trees in their backyard with limbs that would make nice sharp wooden stakes.

"Well . . ." Sam drawled in a sexy coo.

She closed her eyes, pressing her nose to his chest, savoring the scent of him—still here—with her. "Well, what?"

"Do I call you *Mrs.* McLean?"

Straddling him, Phoebe chuckled when she wrapped her legs around his waist, rolling her hips against the rigid flesh of his cock. "I prefer Mrs. 007 or even Mrs. FBI, but I'm okay with McLean, too," she teased, running her tongue over his lips.

He sipped at her mouth, sending hot shafts of heat to the place between her legs. "I really didn't want to lie to you, Phoebe."

She grasped his cock between her hands and lifted her leg to slide down on it for the second time since they'd consummated the strangest union ever. Sam groaned his pleasure. "I know. I know. Ditto for me. I get that you were trying to protect me—us. So let's not rehash.

We have other things to do. Like figure out where we're going to live, how we're going to make a living, and whether you leave the toothpaste cap on or off."

Sam's fingers slipped between them, cupping her sex, he used his thumb to part her folds and swirl her clit in tight circles. "I most certainly do not leave anything off."

Phoebe fell forward on him with a gasp of delight. "That's so good . . . to know," she purred as he took her stiff nipple between his lips and licked it.

He slipped his hand from between their bodies and wrapped it around her hip. "I hate doing laundry," he said from around her nipple.

The slow storm Sam created in her every time he was inside her began to stir, stretching her, teasing her, filling her. "Me, too. Let's just throw the dirty stuff away and buy new."

"Sounds like an excuse to shop."

"You'd rather me naked?"

"Duh." He growled the word, thrusting upward, making Phoebe jam her hands into his thick hair.

"What about dirty dishes?" she hissed, the spiral of electricity dragging her down. "Do we throw those away, too? Ohhhh . . ." she purred when he touched that spot that never failed to bring her instantly to orgasm.

Sam wrapped his arms around her back and drove into her a final time, capturing her lips and slipping his tongue between them. Their groans mingled in satisfaction before Phoebe collapsed against him.

"Where were we?" he asked in his husky afterglow voice. "I got distracted."

"I can't remember."

"Then it couldn't have been that important."

"Right now, nothing's important but the fact that Penny is safe, and we're still not breathing."

Sam chuckled, caressing her cheek. "You were really something in there, lady. Talk about thinking on your feet. I never would have considered biting you as a way to save me."

"There but for the grace of a Manolo Blahnik," she muttered against his neck. "It just seemed like simple math. And forget me. Hello. You gave up that antidote for me. Now that was true chivalry. Thank you. *Thank you,*" she whispered, her throat tight.

Tucking her closer, Sam snuggled down under the blankets with her. "Geeks so rule."

"No argument here. No argument here," she muttered, drifting off into vampire sleep.

Happy. Safe.

SAM gave Phoebe a look of wonder from smoldering brown eyes.

Phoebe shook her head as they both sat on the bench by the window in Sam's bedroom.

After they'd gone to discharge Penny from Highland Hills for good, he'd decided they couldn't stay in his FBI cover apartment for much longer before someone came looking. A good long talk with the others and they decided, for the time being, he and Phoebe should get out of Manhattan for a little while until things cooled off. Nina had volunteered to take Penny and also allow them time to get to know one another.

Phoebe, an organized planner by nature, had taken to gathering the few things that really were Sam's to pack while Penny napped, and waited to meet the rest of her family members.

It was then Sam found the stray DVD he'd forgotten after his phone call with Harlan. When he'd popped it into his laptop, both he and Phoebe had gasped.

The DVD was from Meredith Villanueva—beautiful even battered, and in obvious agony as she fought the pain tearing her body apart to leave Sam a message. The clue that would have solved this whole thing had been right here with them all the time.

"My name is Meredith Villanueva, and I'm an undercover agent for the CIA," she spat through teeth elongating even as she spoke. Her dark hair was matted and surrounded her pale face in clumps. Each word she spoke was an obvious effort—one she appeared determined to get through. "I leave you this message in a rare moment of clarity so defined I'm almost afraid I won't finish in time to tell you everything."

Phoebe's hands shook right along with Meredith's when the CIA agent steadied Sam's laptop screen. "After attending a Halloween party at O-Tech in order to gain after-hour access to a laboratory hidden beneath the building where I was hired to help research a test study titled Project Eternal, I did something horrible tonight to you, Sam McLean." She paused then, letting her head fall to her chest. There was a hissing noise, one that made Sam cringe, for it was surely the attempt to quell the scream that agonizing burn taking over her body would accompany.

Her glazed eyes focused in on the camera again, red rimmed and wide with such obvious horror Phoebe put her head on Sam's shoulder and scrunched her eyes shut. "In my rush to help a woman escape the madman who'd injected us with a centuries-old virus located via the black market, I mistakenly chose you as an escape. I used you, Mr. McLean, to get me out of O-Tech, unaware of your intentions due to the side effects of the virus. My antenna for subtleties was, quite simply put, dulled by the effects of the virus, and thus I apologize for any misunderstanding. Upon reaching our destination, the pain I was experiencing was grave indeed. I never meant to bite you, Mr. McLean. It was an absolute accident and a result of my artificially induced uncontrollable urges for which I take the fullest responsibility. To my utter horror, you're now infected, too."

Sam's head had dropped low then as Meredith continued. "My attempts to rouse you were to no avail, but I couldn't leave you to"—she choked on the next words, then straightened her spine like any well-trained CIA agent would—"like the others. To awaken alone and frightened in this new state of suspended life. Things become quite blurry for me after we met and I realized what I had done. During this strange haze, I somehow lost track of you. Yet, my next memory is of finding your identification. I located your home via your driver's license and your place of work via your O-Tech badge, I shall continue to make every attempt to find you and any pertinent information regarding your location until I can no longer . . . search. Forgive that I've rifled through your things as I searched for clues in order to determine if there was someone you might contact in this dire time of need. Please, *please* know, Mr. McLean, had there been any other way, had my senses been on full alert, I would never have caused you so much irreversible pain. There is, as of now, no turning back for you. If you're seeing this, then you know I speak the truth. I pray you get this message, Mr. McLean. I pray there is an answer for you, as there is none for me. I will continue, for as long as I'm able, to search for you—help you. If you find this message and you're still among the living, find one Terrence Douglas Bradford. Find him. His name leads to all roads . . ."

There was a scuffle as Meredith clamped her hands on her head and knocked the screen of Sam's laptop and then there was silence. Dead and black on the screen in front of them.

Her loyalty to the job was something to be celebrated. Yet, no one would ever know what she'd sacrificed to try to stop Terrence. "So she found out where I worked and put herself at further risk by getting back into O-Tech to try and leave me a note. That explains why she had my memo pad. She, even in her state of undoing, was trying to cover as many bases as possible to get the information to me," Sam said, his tone solemn with admiration.

Phoebe's lower lip trembled, but she was unable to move. This woman's incredible act of noble bravery left her humbled. "I can't believe she was still coherent enough to make that, let alone find you. She looked like she was in incredible pain. She was one tough lady. So brave."

Sam ran a hand over his chin, still shocked. "I couldn't figure out how I got to OOPS in the first place. I guess I'll have to chalk this up to fate. . . But if Wanda and Marty hadn't found me . . ."

Fear spiked along Phoebe's spine. "Maybe Meredith actually knew about OOPS? And technically, according to Wanda who'd intervened during their argument, Phoebe had allowed another vampire to drink her blood. Even though Sam had been a dying vampire at the time, the sharing of blood still left them mated—unofficially anyway. The only thing missing had been someone to officiate their bloodletting. Which, also according to Wanda, was an easy fix. Do you really think it just some crazy coincidence that you ended up there?" The idea that even one person in the CIA knew about her sister and the others and might take it seriously made Phoebe's legs tremble.

Sam shook his dark head. "My gut tells me if she did know, she had far more important things on her mind than investigating three women who run a supposed paranormal crisis hotline. If she was at all suspicious about or thought it was an organization to take seriously, she didn't have time to think about investigating it anyway due to the state she was in. I think I'll call coincidence. OOPS isn't far from O-Tech. Whatever happened between the time I was bitten and when I arrived at OOPS might just have to remain a mystery."

Phoebe wasn't sure if Sam was just attempting to soothe her fears by placating her or he really didn't believe Meredith knew about OOPS. She couldn't let herself go there. Instead, she asked, "Why do you suppose she didn't contact the CIA for help?"

"I have to think it was partially that she wasn't thinking clearly. Terrence obviously had her phone. He taunted us with the fact that he'd texted with her handler. But then I wonder if it wasn't for the same reasons I didn't contact the FBI," he offered, his eyes haunted with the endless variations that could have ended this all so much differently.

Pulling him down to her lap, Phoebe didn't say another word. She didn't pry. Instead, she stroked his head and closed her eyes.

And he was grateful. So grateful.

NINA knelt in front of Penny's wheelchair and tilted her chin up to gaze at her sweet round face. "Well, look at you. You look just like me, you know?"

Penny reached a finely boned hand out and lifted a strand of Nina's hair, twirling it around her finger. "Like you," she repeated in her soft childlike voice.

Phoebe hovered behind Nina, worried Nina would reject the one person in the world she loved unconditionally. She wanted to be at the ready if that was going to happen. Penny would cry for days if someone took something of hers—something as simple as a hair band or a toy.

To be unwanted by Nina would crush her gentle soul, and in turn, crush Phoebe. "She doesn't talk very often, and it's usually just in fragments," Phoebe rambled. "But she understands everything you say. What goes on behind those eyes when she listens amazes me."

Nina whispered conspiratorially in Penny's ear. "Whaddya say we tell Phoebe to take a hike and we go sit over there by that big window of Sam's? We can watch the snow; it's pretty, right? Oh, and I dig a coloring book. Bet you do, too." Nina pointed to the table that held coloring books and crayons Sam had purchased that morning. "That cool with you?"

Penny gave her an awkward, lopsided smile due to her partial facial paralysis. "Cool."

Nina held out her hand to Penny, who shyly offered hers in return. Nina pulled it to her lips and gummed Penny's knuckles, making her giggle the same giggle that hadn't changed since her accident when she was ten. "You think they have any Dora the Explorer coloring books? She's my total favorite, little dude. I like her backpack."

Penny smiled again—sweet—trusting. "Backpack, backpack," she chimed.

How Nina had known Dora was one of Penny's favorites might always be a mystery. Maybe she'd read her mind. Maybe she'd asked the staff when they'd checked her out for good this morning.

It didn't matter to Phoebe. It was the effort she made that did. The gentle tone that wasn't at all belittling her little sister's condition struck the place where Phoebe's heart once beat, clenching it.

As Nina pushed her wheelchair to the table, she poked her head over top of Penny's and said, "I'm sorry I haven't visited you before this, munchkin, but you know what our dad the truck driver used to say, Penny? Family is family together or away. Family is family . . ."

"Forever and a day," Phoebe whispered, finishing Nina's sentence, her throat tight.

Sam pulled her to his chest, nuzzling her neck. "I win this round."

She snuggled back against him, still in awe of this new set of emotions she was experiencing. "Which round is that? There've been so many."

He brushed his knuckles along the side of her face. "The Nina-nator-is-a-hard-shell-with-a-gooey-soft-center round. I never doubted for a minute she'd love Penny and Penny would love her back."

"She wants to bring Penny back to the castle to live—for good until we're safe, and I can take her full time. It was Greg who suggested it. On top of everything else, they're rich. They can afford to help me look after Penny." It was the biggest miracle in all of this.

Sam caressed her hand. "How do you feel about that?"

"I feel like it's right—and having family with her can only be good for Penny, right?"

"What about having *us* as a family. Would that be good for her?"

Phoebe turned and lifted her eyes to his, smiling. "What exactly is it you're asking me, Sam the Bug guy? We're kind of already hitched, if you know what I mean. Your *Hustler* days are all over but the cryin'."

"But you heard what Nina said. That just means we can't mate with anyone else. We could still go our separate ways and remain celibate forever."

"And miss out on all this fabulous? Surely you jest, Secret Agent Man," she teased. Phoebe knew where he was going—she was so ready to go with him.

"Here's what I propose. Let's let Penny get to know Nina and Lou. While they do that and we lay low until the coast is clear, let's take a chance on an eternity and get to know each other. So you can get to know Sam the FBI guy and I can learn how to help you take care of Penny properly. I meant what I said last night, Phoebe. That wasn't just me talking you up after awesome vampire sex. I'm not always easy to get along with. Switching personas to the affable, bug-loving Sam was always a way for me to hide from some pretty shitty stuff. It was my cover within a cover—I'm not sure you're going to like the Sam whose job demanded some hard choices."

"Did you make those job choices out of necessity, FBI Sam? Or did you make them because you're a total prick who likes to see people suffer?"

"I'd like to say they were mostly out of necessity, but there were one or two that were made simply because the bad guy deserved to suffer."

It saddened her to think Sam had seen things that left him with regret. But that he regretted anything at all was enough to convince her the circumstances had to have been grim. "Then I think I can live with that. Maybe someday you'll talk about some of that with me? I promise to tell you my most heinous ever personal styling job with a D-list celebrity. It's my favorite in-the-fashion-trenches tale," she teased.

Sam chuckled. "Deal. So we give this a go, then? Maybe do all the stuff I talked about before you knew who I was. Stuff I really meant, by the way."

She gave him a cocky grin. "Will there be cruel jokes about Tom Jones?"

"Only if you tear your panties off and throw them at the sound system."

There were so many things to sort through. So much more than what brand of shampoo to buy. "But where is home for you, Sam? It never occurred to me to ask."

"My family's in Wyoming still. But I haven't had a home-home in a long time. So it can be wherever you and Penny are, with lots of visits to my parents. They'll eat her up. Promise," he said on a lighthearted grin.

"I know this is going to sound crazy, but I'd like to be near Nina and the others. Mark, too."

Sam pulled her closer, fitting her to the tight ridges and planes of his body. "You fought hard to have them in your life. I don't see why you shouldn't reap the benefits of the battle."

"Really?"

Sam wisped his lips over hers. "Really-really."

And so it was.

Really-really.

EPILOGUE

Eight Months Later—Six and Counting Freaky-Deaky
Paranormal Accidents, Two Super Vampires, One
Doting Grandmother, Three Aunties Who Didn't
Understand the Words **Spoiled** *and* **Rotten,** *Four*
Uncles and a Demon Who Were Determined to Teach
Penny Football, and an Auntie Nina in a Pear Tree ...

Lou pushed Penny in her wheelchair outside in the sunshine of the backyard at Phoebe and Sam's new brownstone. Penny reached up to pat Lou on the face, and Lou's weathered hand gripped her granddaughter's. She planted a kiss on it and laughed, pulling Penny in for what must be her millionth hug since she'd met Lou. Mark blew bubbles for her in the late afternoon sun, smiling at her when she blew some back at him and they popped on his nose.

Phoebe pressed her forehead to the glass, pushing her sunglasses up on her nose. Lou and Nina made Penny so happy. Penny made them happy, too. She ate pot roast and watched the Game Show Network with her grandmother every Tuesday, and on Thursdays, Nina picked her up to take her for her favorite dinner at McDonald's and a movie of her choice—or sometimes they just colored in the multitude of coloring books Nina bought her. They painted, too, while they laughed out loud.

Penny went to a rec center Aunt Marty had found, where she was able to play with adults who had similar disabilities, and at least once a month, she never missed a shopping date with Marty and her toddler, Hollis. She also never missed coming home with more discount designer clothes than one closet and three dressers could handle. Auntie Marty's defense was simple—all the pretty girls were accessorizing with their wheelchairs these days because wheelchairs were tres chic.

Auntie Wanda taught her to knit and needlepoint, hanging her creations in frames all around her new bedroom while they read from Penny's favorite series they'd found together on Visit the Library Saturdays.

But Uncle Darnell was the bomb, if you asked Penny. He took her to their favorite amusement spot and taught her how to play miniature golf and ride the carousel, and how to not throw up after she'd eaten too much cotton candy. He'd also taught her to tell people who pointed at her to refer to the T-shirt he'd had made just for her. MY OTHER WHEELCHAIR'S A MASERATI.

In the last eight months since that night at O-Tech, both Phoebe and Penny's entire world had changed.

For the better. It was rich, full, more alive than it had ever been when she'd still had a beating heart.

It hadn't been easy. She and Sam had hit several rough patches as they'd struggled to get to know one another under their unusual circumstances. Phoebe had learned that this Sam wasn't exactly as communicative as Sam the Bug guy had led her to believe. His words didn't flow quite the way the charming entomologist's had, and in the beginning, she'd struggled to get through to the sullen, moody half of Sam. However, when the floodgates finally opened, they each learned how and when the best time was to approach each other.

FBI Sam was also a total slob.

In an all-out war of verbal assault Nina would have been proud of after she'd tripped over that straw that broke the camel's back pair of discarded cowboy boots, Phoebe'd threatened to burn his Stetson and dump the ashes on his pile of dirty man panties in the corner of their bedroom.

But Phoebe, if you listened to Sam, was no picnic, either. He complained that she had more jewelry than the store he'd shopped in when he was looking for accessories to his Halloween costume. "How many pairs of hooker earrings can a woman have?" he'd asked her just before she'd lobbed a bottle of her favorite massage oil at him.

But they'd learned, too. They'd learned they had a great deal in common. Like the love of a good board game and most especially a rousing game of Uno. They'd learned that marathons of *The Real Housewives of New Jersey* were best watched cuddled together on their bed.

They'd learned they both loved to sing badly in the shower—*together*. After they'd bought their brownstone, they'd learned that gardening at night by flashlight sucked, and if you trimmed your hedges at one in the morning, the neighbors weren't likely to invite you to their block party.

Sam learned that Phoebe loved flowers, and without fail, he brought a bouquet of them on their official date night. One day a week when they left Penny to bake cookies and watch DVDs with Archibald, who'd moved in with them to help Penny in the daylight hours, giving them time to just be a newly mated couple.

Phoebe learned that Sam really did love detective shows—even though they were mostly all just crap and as far from the real thing as you could get. She'd also learned that his passion for ice hockey superseded even her love of clothes and makeup. So she'd bought him a season pass to the Rangers games and sat faithfully with him through each game—even if, in her opinion, the only good part about chasing a black piece of plastic around the ice was when they got into fistfights.

The absolute seal on their forever thing was when Sam had finally revealed why he'd kept putting off picking out furniture for their soon-to-be-closed-on brownstone. He'd spent several weeks pooh-poohing her, and teasing her that she just wanted to shop while he, Greg, Heath, Clay, Keegan, and Darnell had built ramps and various wheelchair-accessible gadgets for Penny.

Yet, out of everything they'd learned, they'd learned they loved each other—deeply, madly—and neither would consider the idea that their differences couldn't be worked out.

Eventually.

Sam had decided to start up his own surveillance consulting business, and with the help of a good deal of the money he'd packed away doing FBI undercover work, the plan was set in motion. Mark continued to run his and Phoebe's business by day, doing the legwork so she wouldn't have to go out in the sunlight while she handled coordinating clothing and makeup from home. She only handled shoots or appointments that occurred at night, turning her into a bit of a celebrity with a rather Greta Garbo–esque reputation, and garnering them more clientele than they could handle.

She and Nina had also grown quite close through their love of Penny. Though they butted heads often, someone always ended up apologizing. Sometimes that someone was actually Nina. Okay, most times it was Phoebe, but every tenth fight or so, Nina gave in and called her to say, "Look, Wrong Almost All the Time Barbie, fighting isn't good for the kid. We're all she's got. So I'm fucking sorry we argued. I'm not sorry I told you your ass is fat. I'm just sorry you got so pissed about it."

In one particular shouting match, Nina had revealed to her that Sam and she weren't really mated because he hadn't bitten her in what vampires called bloodletting, leaving Phoebe appalled that she'd play that kind of cruel joke on them. Nina's defense was that if Sam had had the chance to run the fuck away from her, he would have, and because he made Phoebe so happy, she didn't want to hear her whine for an eternity.

But Sam thought it was the perfect excuse for them to have that ceremony Phoebe thought they'd missed out on. And on a warm July evening they'd consummated their union with Penny as their flower girl.

And it was good. There was so much good.

Sam came up behind her, pulling her to his chest with a grunt. "Hey, Vampire Barbie. What are you doing in here all alone? Everyone's in the living room watching the game. I got lonely without you," he whispered into her ear, making her shiver for the night to come when everyone went home and they could be alone.

Turning in his arms, she cuddled against the width of his chest with the sound of Nina and Greg playfully rooting for the Packers over the Dolphins while Darnell, Heath, Casey, Clay, Keegan, and Wanda teamed up against them. "I was just thinking about how lucky Penny is now. How lucky I am—*we* are."

"Is it squishy feelings time *again*?" he asked, using his mocking yet teasing tone. "I thought I met my quota this week and I was off the hook."

Phoebe lifted her head at their private joke. If Sam hid his feelings about anything that was bothering him, and she found out when he lashed out at her in irritation, he had to sing by way of apology. The first time he'd done it as a way to break the silence between them, dressed in an outrageous purple suit coat he'd borrowed from Mark, a brush for a microphone, and a pair of panties swinging around his index finger, Phoebe couldn't be angry anymore. She'd been too busy laughing. Since then, it was always Sam's way of apologizing—of offering of himself in a way that didn't cut him off at the knees.

American Idol the Vampire Edition had nothing to fear from Sam. But he sang less and less these days and smiled more and more. "Do you want to have to sing 'What's New Pussycat?' again for complaining? Remember how well that turned out the last time you had to pay up for clamming up? I think the neighbors offered to put you out of your misery," she teased, pressing a kiss to his jaw.

"You win," he said with his grinning dry sarcasm. "I'll give you whatever you want. *Whatever* you want."

Her lips lifted to his with a smile. "Oh, I know what I want and it has absolutely nothing to do with the shredding of a perfectly good Tom Jones song. Though, I'm happy to give you my panties . . ."

Sam scooped her up, wrapping her legs around him with a chuckle. "Think we could sneak in a quickie before we have to feed the werewolf-demon contingent?"

"No, you fucking cannot. Do the two of you do anything but crank each other?" Nina crowed from the doorway to their kitchen, grinning. "Jesus Christ and a miniskirt. This is family day, people! Get the hell out here and be part of the crazy family."

Sam and Phoebe laughed.

Yeah. It was *family* day.

Best day ever.